The Body
in the Gazebo

FAITH FAIRCHILD MYSTERIES
BY KATHERINE HALL PAGE

The Body in the Gazebo
The Body in the Sleigh
The Body in the Gallery
The Body in the Ivy
The Body in the Snowdrift
The Body in the Attic
The Body in the Lighthouse
The Body in the Bonfire
The Body in the Moonlight
The Body in the Big Apple
The Body in the Bookcase
The Body in the Fjord
The Body in the Bog
The Body in the Basement
The Body in the Cast
The Body in the Vestibule
The Body in the Bouillon
The Body in the Kelp
The Body in the Belfry

The Body in the Gazebo

A Faith Fairchild Mystery

Katherine Hall Page

An Imprint of HarperCollinsPublishers

THE BODY IN THE GAZEBO. Copyright © 2011 by Katherine Hall Page. All rights reserved. Printed in the United States of America. No part of this book may be used or reproduced in any manner whatsoever without written permission except in the case of brief quotations embodied in critical articles and reviews. For information address HarperCollins Publishers, 10 East 53rd Street, New York, NY 10022.

HarperCollins books may be purchased for educational, business, or sales promotional use. For information please write: Special Markets Department, HarperCollins Publishers, 10 East 53rd Street, New York, NY 10022.

FIRST HARPERLUXE EDITION

HarperLuxe™ is a trademark of HarperCollins Publishers

Library of Congress Cataloging-in-Publication Data is available upon request.

ISBN: 978-0-06-156206-8

11 12 13 14 ID/OPM 10 9 8 7 6 5 4 3 2 1

For my dear husband, Alan
Happy 35th Anniversary

Truth is stranger than Fiction,
but it is because Fiction is obliged
to stick to the possibilities; Truth isn't.

—MARK TWAIN, *Pudd'nhead Wilson*

Acknowledgments

My thanks to Dr. Robert DeMartino, Jean Fogelberg, Nicholas Hein, Amalie Kass, Kathy and Peter Winham, Valerie Wolzien, and the Poison Lady, Luci Zahray, for help from their various areas of expertise. Also many thanks to my agent, Faith Hamlin, and to my editor, Wendy Lee.

The idea for this book originated during a glorious week on Martha's Vineyard with my friends of over forty years, Kate Danforth, Mimi Garrett, Virginia Pick, and Margaret Stuart. Always, my thanks to them.

Chapter 1

The first letter arrived on a Tuesday. Ursula Rowe had no need to read the brittle, yellowed newspaper clippings that were enclosed. She knew what they said. But the few words on the single sheet of white stationery in the envelope were new. New and succinct:

Are you sure you were right?

She went upstairs to her bedroom—hers alone for too many years—and sat down on the antique four-poster bed they'd bought when, newly married, they'd moved into this house. The bed had pineapples carved on the finials—symbols of hospitality. She reached up and traced the intricately carved wood with her fingers. Pineapples. A great luxury for those early colonists—her long-ago ancestors. How had such exotic fruit made its way to New England? She'd never considered this before. Wouldn't they have rotted in the hold of a ship on the voyage from South America? Perhaps the pineapples came from the Southern colonies. That must have been it.

Her mind was wandering. No, her mind was trying to take her away from what was clutched in her other hand. The letter. She closed her eyes. Arnold had joked that the pineapples were fertility symbols. Certainly the bed had borne fruit—two children—and been the site of years of pleasure. He had been gone for such a long time, but she could still recall his touch, his whispered endearments, the passion. She'd never wanted anyone else.

Ursula read the words again—a single sentence written in a shaky hand. You couldn't duplicate it; it came only with age. So, the writer was old. She looked at her own hand. The raised blue veins were so close to the surface of her powdery, thin skin that it seemed they would burst through. Her fingers, once long and straight, were knobbed and for some years she'd removed all her rings except her wedding band, worn thin. An old woman's hands. The change had come so gradually—the brown spots first appearing as summer freckles to her mind—that even now she could scarcely

believe her age. She loosened her grip and put everything back in the envelope, tucking the flap in securely.

Where could she hide it? It wouldn't do to have her
daughter come across it. Not that Pix was nosy, but
she sometimes put Ursula's wash away, so the Sheraton chest of drawers was out. And the blanket chest at
the foot of the bed that had been her grandmother's
was out, too. Pix regularly aired the contents. There
wasn't much furniture in the room. Some years after
Arnold died, Ursula had removed his marble-topped
nightstand—the repository of books, eyeglasses, reading lamp, alarm clock, and eventually pill bottles—
replacing it with a chaise and small candlestick table,
angled into the room. It felt wrong to get into bed
during the day, but she'd wanted a place to stretch out
to read and, increasingly, to nap. Somehow the chaise
made her feel a bit more like a grande dame than an
old one. There was a nightstand on her side of the bed,
but her granddaughter, Samantha, often left little notes
in the drawer and might notice the envelope. Ursula
always saved the notes—bits of poetry Samantha liked
or just a few words, "Have sweet dreams, Granny."
Generally Ursula did. Her days had been good ones
and she felt blessed. Arnold, the two children, although
Arnold junior lived in Santa Fe and she only saw him
and his wife during the summer in Maine and on her

annual visit out there. Three grandchildren, all healthy and finding their ways without too much difficulty so far. But you never know what life will hand you. She stood up, chiding herself. The six words—"Are you sure you were right?"—had entered her system like a poison, seeping into the very marrow of her bones and replacing her normal optimism with dark thoughts.

The mail had come at noon when the bright sun was still high in the clear blue sky. She walked to the arched window that overlooked the backyard. It was why they had chosen this room for their own, although it was not as large as the master bedroom across the hall. Each morning this uncurtained window beckoned them to a new day. And it had a window seat. The window seat! She slid the envelope under the cushion. Done. She gazed out the window, feeling herself slowly relax. The yard sloped down to the Concord River, which occasionally overflowed, flooding the swing set that was still in place. Arnie and Pix had gleefully waded out to it as children, getting gloriously wet sliding down the slide into the shallow water. The family had always kept canoes there, too, under the majestic oak planted by design or perhaps a squirrel. It didn't matter. The tree was perfect for climbing, and a succession of tree houses. The grandchildren had added kayaks to the fleet and given her a fancy new one for her eightieth birthday, or had it been her eighty-fifth? Today the river flowed gently, its slightly rippled surface like the glass in the windows of Aleford's oldest houses. A good day to be on the water. However, she'd promised Pix never to go out for a paddle alone. Perhaps she'd do some gardening. Yes, that was the thing. Start to clear some of the dead leaves left by winter's ravages from the perennial border around the gazebo that Arnold had insisted they build near the riverbank. She'd been reluctant about it—no, not reluctant. That was the wrong word. Too mild. "Opposed." That was more like it.

Ursula had never wanted to see another gazebo again, not after that earlier summer. Not after the image that had still appeared unbidden and unwanted in nightmares—and her waking thoughts. Arnold had told her this one would replace that other gazebo. It would be a symbol of their new life and their future together, blotting out the horror forever. She could call it a pergola or a garden house instead if she liked. She'd given in. And he'd been right, of course. It had brought the family much pleasure—especially, screened in, as a refuge from the mosquitoes and other insects that living by the river brought. The grandchildren loved it, too.

Yet, Ursula had never loved it.

She left the room and went downstairs, heading for the back of the house and her gardening trug in the mudroom. She stopped outside the kitchen door. Suddenly she didn't feel like gardening or going outside at all. Suddenly she felt sick to death.

"My mother is never ill! I can't possibly leave now." Pix Miller was sitting in the kitchen of the house she'd grown up in; her friend and neighbor Faith Fairchild was across the table. They were both clutching mugs of coffee, the suburban panacea.

"I'll be here and you know Dr. Homans says the worst is over. That there's nothing to worry about. Never really was. A bad bout of the flu." Faith found herself imitating the doctor's very words and clipped Yankee tone.

"Dora will keep coming nights for as long as we want." Pix was thinking out loud. Dora McNeill was an institution in Aleford, Massachusetts, the small town west of Boston where Pix, Faith, and their families lived. Dora, a private-duty nurse, had cared for Aleford's populace for as long as anyone could remember. Her arrival at a bedside brought instant comfort, both for the patient and kin. "Dora's coming" was tantamount to a sickroom lottery win.

"I'll keep bringing food. I know she makes breakfast and what she thinks Ursula can tolerate for other meals, but Dora needs heartier fare." Faith was a caterer and her thoughts normally turned to sustenance before all else.

"Maybe I should skip Hilton Head and just go to Charleston. I could go down for the shower—it's in the afternoon—and come back the next day."

"Let's start with the fact that Ursula would be very upset if you didn't go for the whole time, which means both places. You wouldn't be able to tell her—she'd send you packing instantly—so the only way you could see her would be when she was asleep, or by sneaking a peek through the door. So, there's no point to staying on her account.

"Besides, she'll want a blow-by-blow description of everything. Sometimes I think she's more excited about the wedding than you are."

"I'm very excited about the wedding," Pix said defensively. "Our firstborn—and Rebecca is wonderful. I couldn't ask for a better daughter-in-law. Sam thinks so, too."

"Her parents will be wonderful, as well." Faith knew Pix was worried about meeting her prospective in-laws, even with her husband and offspring by her side. "They couldn't have produced such a lovely daughter if they weren't the same."

She then rushed on before Pix could come up with all the exceptions to this parent/child rule they both knew.

"You can't skip either week. Hilton Head is the whole bonding thing. They've even planned it so you're going during Dan's spring break from Clark. Samantha can work on her thesis anywhere, but Mark and Becca have been making all sorts of arrangements so they can take the time off."

Mark Miller worked on the Hill as a congressional aide; Becca, or rather Dr. Rebecca Cohen, was an environmental scientist with the EPA. A blind date had very quickly moved into a lifelong commitment with both sets of eyes wide open. Pix had thought the oldest of her three children would follow the pattern of so many of her friends' offspring and postpone marriage treacherously close to ticking clocks. Tying the knot at twenty-seven might mean grandchildren much sooner than she had imagined. It was one of those thoughts that was helping her to cope with the wedding.

"I'm sure we will enjoy spending time with Becca's parents and the rest of her family." If the sentence sounded as if she were reciting it by rote, it was because it was one Pix had repeated to herself many times.

"You're not still thinking about that picture, are you?" Faith said sternly. "Yes, her mother is younger than you are and, yes, she dresses well, but I'm sure she'd kill for your gorgeous long legs, and don't forget all the new clothes we bought. You'll look terrific, too."

Cynthia Cohen, "Cissy," was a petite brunette, and at first glance it was hard to tell the mother from her three daughters. The photo had been taken during Mark's first visit to the Cohens' in Charleston and he was in the center of the group beaming. Becca's father was presumably behind the camera. Mark had e-mailed it to his mother, who had promptly printed it out to show Faith what she was up against.

"Her makeup is perfect."

It had taken Faith a number of years to move her friend away from a dab of lipstick for formal occasions to mascara, eye shadow, blush, and gloss. Pix still favored nothing more than a swipe of Burt's Bees gloss on her lips for everyday.

"So is her hair."

"She'd probably just had it done—the picture was taken during the holidays—and besides, you have lovely hair," Faith said loyally. Pix *did* have good hair—chestnut colored and thick. She kept it short, and the only problem was its tendency to stand on end after she'd run her hand through it while engaged in contemplation, a habit hard to break.

"I still don't think I needed all those clothes. And you'll have to go over what goes with what again. At least I don't have to worry about where to get something to wear at the wedding. They want to use the same place for my mother-of-the-groom dress as the rest of the bridal party's attire, so that's settled. I have to make the final choice, though, and you know I hate to shop. Plus I'll be shopping with strangers."

"Samantha will be with you, remember."

"Thank God, I'd almost forgotten," Pix said, grasping at the lifeline her daughter's presence would afford. Samantha, her middle child, had always been the calmest, plus she was wise in the ways of the world of fashion, often to Pix's bemusement. The last time she'd had lunch with Samantha, Pix had offered to sew up the rips in her daughter's very short dress only to be told that they were on purpose. She was wearing it over a kind of leotard. Pix could not believe someone would pay money to buy what would be a dust cloth in her household.

Faith looked at her friend, drank some coffee, and wished she could grab Harry Potter's cloak of invisibility to accompany skittish Pix. Meeting new in-laws was nerve-racking, but it would be beautiful at Hilton Head this time of year and better to meet now than at the wedding, where there wouldn't be a chance to get to know one another with all the inevitable commotion. Faith should know—she'd catered enough of them. After the week at Hilton Head, everyone who had to get back to work was leaving, but Pix and

Samantha were continuing on to Charleston for fittings, wedding plans, and a bridal shower. It was late March and the wedding itself would be in early June—before the real heat set in. Pix had to check out the place Faith had helped her find for the rehearsal dinner—as well as make the final arrangements for all the out-of-town guests from Mark's side of the family. Considering this was a woman whose idea of a good time was birding at dawn in Aleford's Willards Woods and dressing up meant exchanging L.L.Bean khakis for a Vermont Country Store wraparound skirt, her nervousness over the nuptials and face time with belles from the South was understandable.

"You'll love Charleston, and I know the street their house is on—Hasell Street. It has to be one of the old houses, since Mark told you the family has been in Charleston for generations." Faith was grasping for any straw she could find. Charleston's fabled cuisine—the thought of chef Jeremiah Bacon's shrimp and grits with andouille gravy at Carolina's was making Faith salivate slightly—would cut no ice with Pix. Much as she adored her friend, there remained a huge gap in their respective food tastes. Pix's kitchen cabinets and freezer were filled with boxes that had "Helper" printed on them, while Faith's were jammed with everything but. Pix worked for Faith at her catering company, Have Faith, but kept the books. She'd accepted the job some years ago with the understanding that it would involve no food preparation of any kind except in dire emergencies such as pitching in to pack up cutlery, china, and napkins for an event.

Faith soldiered on. "You'll find out about the house when you get there. And don't forget the gardens. You know you love gardens. . . ."

Faith suddenly felt as if she were trying to convince a toddler to eat spinach.

"Anyway, everything will be fine," she concluded lamely.

"Except for my mother. She might not be fine."

She'd said it out loud, Pix thought. The dread that had been with her ever since she'd gotten the phone call from Dr. Homans that Ursula had suddenly spiked a high fever and was severely dehydrated. He was admitting her to Emerson Hospital for treatment, fearing pneumonia. It wasn't pneumonia, thank goodness. He'd discharged her as soon as possible—so she wouldn't pick anything else up—but she had been quite ill and still hadn't recovered. Pix knew her mother would die someday. It was all part of the plan and she didn't fear her own death. She just didn't want her mother to die.

Reading her friend's thoughts, Faith reached over and covered Pix's hand with her own, marveling as always at her soft skin treated with nothing more than Bag Balm. Faith felt a momentary pang of guilt at all the expensive creams of Araby that filled her medicine chest, but efficacious or no, Bag Balm was the cosmetic equivalent of a New England boiled dinner—lines she would not cross.

"I'm going to see if Mother's still sleeping," Pix said.

"If she isn't, I'll say a quick hello. I have to pick Amy up and take her to ballet." Amy Fairchild, a third grader, and her older brother, Ben, in his first year of middle school, both required a great deal of chauffeuring, and Faith had not taken kindly to this suburban mother's chore—although the fact that Ben would be driving himself in a little over two years filled her with dread.

"I'm sure she'll want to see you. She's been asking for you," Pix said.

"Tom told me the same thing when he came home last night."

Faith's husband, the Reverend Thomas Fairchild, was the minister at Aleford's First Parish Church. Ursula was a lifelong member, as were the Millers. Faith was a more recent arrival, born and raised in Manhattan. The daughter and granddaughter of men of the cloth, she and her younger sister, Hope, had sworn to avoid that particular fabric and the fishbowl existence that went along with it. Over the years they had observed congregations—composed of ordinarily reticent individuals—who felt perfectly free to comment on the way the minister's wife was treating her husband and raising her children. At First Parish there were a number of women Faith termed "Tom's Groupies" who were sure they would do a far better job than Faith at keeping him in clean collars and doing other wifely chores. They regularly dropped off dubious burnt offerings—casseroles featuring canned soups and tuna fish. Faith ceded the collar cleaning—amazing how hard it was to keep track—but stood her ground on the culinary front.

The fact that she succumbed to the Reverend in the first place was due to good old love at first sight. He was in New York to perform the nuptials for his college roommate and Faith was catering the reception. Shedding his ministerial garb, Tom had been in mufti by the time the poached salmon and beef tenderloin appeared on the buffet tables along with Faith bearing pâté en croûte. Whether it was the platter she was carrying or her big blue eyes that attracted him was soon moot. Later that evening in Central Park, during a ride in one of the touristy but undeniably romantic horse-drawn carriages, when she discovered his calling—he'd assumed she knew—it was too late. The heart knows no reason.

She left the Big Apple for the more bucolic orchards of New England and, like Lot's wife, looked back—often. Faith, however, did not become a pillar of salt, even the delicious French *fleur de sel* from the Camargue kind. What she did become was a frequent traveler back to the city for visits to the three Bs: Barneys, Bloomingdale's, and the late great Balducci's, as well as the lox counter at Zabar's.

"Maybe she wants me to cook her something special," Faith said, although, she thought, Ursula could have given the message to Tom, or Pix. More likely it was a request that Faith urge Pix not to change her trip plans. Pix was as easy to read as a billboard and Ursula had, no doubt, picked up on her daughter's reluctance to leave.

As they moved out of the kitchen to go upstairs, the doorbell rang.

"I wonder who that can be?" Pix said. "I'm not expecting anyone."

She opened the door and Millicent Revere McKinley stepped into the foyer. She was carrying a brown paper bag similar in size and shape to those sported by individuals in New York's Bowery before it became a fashionable address. Faith knew that Millicent's did not contain Thunderbird or a fifth of Old Grand-Dad. And it wasn't because Millicent had joined the Cold Water

Army around the time Carry Nation was smashing mirrors in saloons. No, Faith knew because Millicent's earlier offerings still filled the shelves in Ursula's refrigerator. The bag contained calf's foot jelly, the Congregationalist equivalent of Jewish penicillin, chicken soup.

Pix took it from her.

"How kind of you. I know Mother appreciates your thoughtfulness," she said. "Let me go up and see if she's awake."

"She doesn't need a roomful of company. That's not why I'm here, but you go check on her and I'll talk to Faith."

Pix handed Faith the bag. Millicent led the way back into the kitchen. She knew Ursula's house as well as her own, a white clapboard Cape perched strategically on one side of Aleford's Green with a view from the bay window straight down Main Street. Not much got past Millicent, who had been admitting to being seventy for many years now. Her hairstyle was as unvarying as her age. She'd adopted Mamie Eisenhower's bangs during Ike's first term and stuck to them. Millicent's stiff perm was slate gray when Faith met her and it now appeared as if she'd been caught in a heavy snowfall—yet a storm that left every hair in place.

Although not a member of First Parish, Millicent behaved like one, freely offering Faith advice she didn't want. Their relationship was further complicated by several incidents. The first occurred when Faith, early on in Aleford, had discovered a still-warm corpse in the Old Belfry atop Belfry Hill. With newborn Benjamin strapped to her chest in a Snugli, Faith did what she supposed any sensible person would do. She rang the bell. It produced immediate results, although not the capture of the murderer. That took Faith a while and came later. The most long lasting of these results came from Millicent, who was appalled that Faith had dared to ring the venerable icon—cast by Paul Revere himself, Millicent's many times removed cousin. It had sounded the alarm on that famous day and year. Subsequent peals were restricted to April 19, Patriot's Day, that curious Massachusetts and Maine holiday; the death of a President; and the death of a descendent of one of those stalwarts who faced the Redcoats on the green. None of these categories, Millicent was quick to point out, applied in Faith's case. Rapidly running down the hill screaming loudly would have sufficed.

The other incidents involved Millicent's saving Faith's life not once but twice. Since then, Faith had labored in vain to repay this debt, hoping to drag Millicent from the path of an oncoming train—the commuter rail passed through Aleford—or else surprise a desperate burglar intent on purloining Millicent's collection of Revere McKinley mourning wreaths, intricately woven from bygone tresses.

For the moment, all she could do was follow her savior into the kitchen if not meekly, then obediently, and put the Mason jar of jelly in the fridge.

"I'd like to give you the recipe, Faith, but it's a treasured family secret."

Faith could never understand why families that treasured their recipes wouldn't want to share them with the world, but in this case, she would not expect otherwise. Millicent hoarded information like the Collyer brothers hoarded newspapers—and everything else. Prying anything out of the woman was well nigh impossible. Faith had tried with varying success. As for calf's foot jelly, she had her own recipe. It called for a lot of boiling and straining, but when you added lemon juice, cinnamon, clove, and some sherry to the gelatin and put it in a nice mold, the result was quite pleasant. She'd recently come across the actor Zero Mostel's recipe, which was similar. An epicure, he never met a gelatin or—judging by his girth—a pudding, he didn't like.

Millicent got herself a cup and saucer from the china closet in the butler's pantry. Miss McKinley—not Ms., thank you very much—didn't do mugs, and poured herself a cup of coffee before sitting down. Faith had had enough caffeine for the day, but joined her at the table. She didn't have to pick Amy up for another half hour. In any case, it was a command performance.

"I hope Pix isn't upsetting her mother about this trip. The last thing Ursula needs is her daughter moaning about having to go away. Why these people want to spend all that time together with people they'll rarely see after the wedding is another story. In my day you got married and spent one holiday with one set of in-laws and another with the others. None of this bonding business."

Faith was interested in Millicent's remarks. The woman had never been married—"never cared to"—but brought her eagle eye to the institution. There was something to what she said, Faith thought. Tom's parents and her parents liked one another, but contact was limited to things like a grandchild's christening. They did live far apart, but Faith sensed it would be the same if the Fairchilds were a few blocks away down Madison in Manhattan or the Sibleys on the other side of Norwell, the South Shore town where Tom had grown up and his parents still lived. Their children had bonded to the point where they got married and that was enough for their elders.

"It's hard for Pix to go away now when her mother isn't completely recovered, but she's definitely going," Faith said.

"Problem is she won't admit Ursula is getting to the point where she may not be able to stay here. This flu business should be a wake-up call."

Faith had thought the same thing herself. Pix had a severe case of denial when it came to her mother. Pix's father had died suddenly in his early sixties, and for most of her adult life, Pix had had only Ursula. The idea that she wouldn't be in this house forever, frozen at some age between seventy and eighty, was anathema to Pix. Faith had never brought up the subject of Ursula's future. And Pix herself hadn't. It was obviously too painful. She was the exception to Faith's friends who were Pix's age—in their fifties. The subject of aging parents had replaced aging kids, although Faith had learned some years ago from these same friends that you're never going to be finished raising your children.

"She won't be able to do those stairs much longer." Millicent was complacently going down a list she had certainly reviewed before. "However, the staircase is straight, so they could get one of those chair-elevator things."

Faith pictured Ursula regally rising up past the newel post. Not a bad idea. Millicent was barreling on.

"The place is big enough for someone to live in, but she'd hate that. Could turn the library into a bedroom, but you'd have to put in a full bath."

"You seem to have thought this over pretty thoroughly," Faith couldn't help commenting.

"One does," Millicent replied, looking at Faith sternly. "*Semper paratus.*"

Millicent's bedroom was on the ground floor of her house. Faith doubted it was foresight. More likely just plain "sight," as in looking out the window past the muslin sheers.

"She has a lot of friends at Brookhaven. She could go there," Faith suggested, thinking two could play the preparedness game. Brookhaven was a life-care community in nearby Lexington.

"You know she'd never leave Aleford," Millicent said smugly.

Match to her.

This was true, Faith thought, and a problem for many of Aleford's older residents. A group had tried to interest Kendal, the retirement and assisted-living communities associated with the Quakers, in coming to Aleford. So far, nothing had happened, and if it did, it would be too late for Ursula. Faith almost gasped as she thought this. Not that Ursula would be gone soon. No! But a decision would have to have been made. She had to admit Millicent was right—an admission she generally tried to avoid. This last illness had shown that Ursula really couldn't continue as she had. Faith had been shocked to see the change in the woman after she'd come home from the hospital. It was dramatic, especially when Faith looked back at last summer. Ursula had climbed Blue Hill in Maine with them, setting a pace that left several gasping for a second wind.

Blue Hill was close to Sanpere Island in Penobscot Bay, where the Fairchilds had vacationed, at the Millers' urging, the summer after Ben was born—Pix was a third-generation rusticator. Eventually, enchanted with the island, the Fairchilds built a cottage of their own, an event that a younger Faith would never have predicted. "Vacation" meant the south of France, the Hamptons, Tuscany, and the Caribbean—balmy waters, not the rocky Maine coast's subzero briny deep.

And Ursula had seemed all right for most of the winter. As usual, she'd participated in the Christmas Audubon Bird Count, snowshoeing deep into the woods to do so. But when Faith saw her when she was discharged from the hospital, Ursula looked years older, her face an unhealthy pallor, her thick white hair limp and lifeless. What was the worst was the change in her eyes—those beautiful deep topaz orbs had acquired a milky film.

"When Pix gets back from gadding about, you're going to have to talk to her about all this."

"Why me?" Faith protested. Millicent was the one with all the ideas—and probably brochures.

"It's not my business," Millicent said firmly.

Faith didn't know whether to laugh or cry. Instead she got up.

"I have to pick Amy up at school."

Millicent nodded. "Yes, it's her day for ballet. You'd better get going."

The woman knew everything.

Pix came into the kitchen. She looked ill herself.

"She was awake, but she's drifted off again. She seems to be sleeping so much of the day now. But she said to thank you for the jelly, Millicent, and Faith, she wants you to come spend some time with her. 'A real visit,' she said. That's a good sign, don't you think?"

"Yes," Faith said. "And Dora can let me know when. She has my cell or she can leave a message at home."

"I'll tell her," Pix said. "But do you really think I ought . . ."

Faith nodded slightly toward Millicent.

"Don't tell me you still haven't decided whether to get those sandals we looked at for the trip."

Momentarily nonplussed, Pix picked up on the signal.

"They were expensive and I'd never wear them in Maine. I don't think I ought to get them."

Millicent looked suspicious. She said, "Shoes," sounding eerily like Margaret Hamilton as the Wicked Witch of the West saying "Slippers," before Faith cut her off with a "Good-bye" as she left to get her daughter.

The parsonage was quiet. Both children were asleep. Faith realized the nights when Ben went to bed before they did were numbered. Even now he'd still be awake except for soccer practice. Nothing like a coach who believed in laps and lengthy practice drills. Bless her.

"Hungry, darling?" she asked Tom, who was stretched out on the sofa next to her. They'd lit a fire in the fireplace, as they had for several nights, each time declaring it would be the last one until fall. Rather, Tom had made the pronouncements. There had been a blizzard on Easter Sunday her first spring in Aleford and Faith hadn't trusted New England weather ever since. The battle of the thermostat was ongoing and at times ugly—at least to Faith.

"Hmmm," Tom said. "I could go for a little something. What did you have in mind?" He got up and reached for his wife.

"Save that for later?" she said, settling into his arms. "For now how about some of that broccoli cheddar soup and a sandwich—pastrami on dark rye?"

After a scary bout of pancreatitis in November, Tom had been advised to eat small meals throughout the day and avoid alcohol. Faith had always teased him about being a cheap drunk—half a glass of pinot grigio and he was singing "O Sole Mio," so he didn't miss the sauce. It explained why she'd been sipping some Rémy Martin without him, though.

"Great."

"Stay put and I'll bring it in here."

"No, I'll come and keep you company."

Earlier they had been discussing Faith's conversation with Millicent and hadn't come to any conclusion other than gently trying to talk to Pix about future choices for her mother, with husband Sam there, too, once they returned from South Carolina. As Faith heated the soup and spread Tom's favorite horseradish mustard on the bread, she found herself returning to the subject.

"Ursula is determined to go to the wedding in June," she said.

"I know, and that means she'll do it." Ursula was one of the parishioners waiting to welcome the new minister at the parsonage upon Tom's arrival in Aleford a year before his marriage. She held the distinction of being the first female warden at First Parish and had served on the vestry several times.

"The drive is so long that the best thing would be for her to go down in stages, staying overnight or longer," Tom went on. "Or she could fly, but that's pretty taxing these days. She'd insist on standing in the security line—no wheelchair."

"Because of this," Faith said, "I wish they were getting married on Sanpere. But aside from the problem of where to house all the guests, Becca quite naturally wants to get married in her own temple."

Tom nodded. His mouth was full. He swallowed.

"And it's not just any temple," he said. "Her family have been members for generations. Kahal Kadosh Beth Elohim is the oldest synagogue building in the country after Touro in Newport, and the congregation is the fourth oldest. It's a place I've always wanted to visit and I'm honored that they want me to be a part of the ceremony."

Faith had been in Charleston several times before Tom appeared on the scene and since for the business. This was his first trip, and although the wedding was still many weeks away, Faith had already planned what they would see in the area when not involved with wedding events. It was a rare getaway for them. Ben and Amy were going down to Norwell, where they would be blissfully happy exploring their grandparents' attic and garage—the cars had never been parked in it. Why waste the space? In true New England fashion, the Fairchilds saved *everything*, carefully labeling containers, no doubt one with the proverbial contents "String Too Short to Be Saved." Weather permitting, there would be canoeing and fishing with Grandpa on the North River and perhaps a visit to nearby Plimoth Plantation with Grandma, who was a longtime volunteer.

Meanwhile Faith had booked their stay at one of Charleston's historic bed-and-breakfasts—from the picture, a delightfully furnished large room, kitchenette, and bath with a private garden below. She'd advised Pix on the venue for the rehearsal dinner—the Peninsula Grill in Charleston's fabled Planters Inn. It was romantic in that way only Southern places can be. While there might not be magnolias in bloom, somehow you smell them and, in your mind's eye, see women in low-cut gowns with powdered shoulders fending off beaux in the soft candlelight. Besides, the Grill made the best coconut layer cake in the universe—a towering confection that managed to be both decadently rich and still light.

Tom got up, rinsed his dishes, and put them in the dishwasher.

"Okay," he said to his wife, taking her in his arms. "I've had enough to eat, but I'm still hungry."

"Hmmm," she said. "Funny thing. Me, too."

Faith did not get a chance to go see Ursula until Friday. Dora went home for a few hours after lunch before returning for the night and Faith had arranged to come then. Ursula didn't need constant daytime care anymore—there was a Medi-Alert system next to her bed—but as it turned out she was seldom left completely alone. Pix was so uneasy about going away that she had enlisted her mother's friends to keep an eye on her, something they'd been doing as soon as Ursula had been up to receiving visitors. Faith had promised she'd be dropping in frequently. It was no chore. Over the years, both Faith and Tom had come to love Ursula dearly. She seemed—and acted—like a member of their family.

Dora had said her charge was awake, so as Faith ran up the stairs—ever so slightly worn in the center of each tread by years of use—she called out, "Ursula, it's Faith. Would you like a little company for a while?"

The answer came as Faith entered the sun-filled bedroom. "How lovely. And just the person I've been wanting."

Ursula was sitting up in bed. She looked better than the last time Faith had seen her, but still much too thin—the skin stretched over the high cheekbones her daughter and granddaughter had inherited looked translucent. She was wearing a quilted bed jacket; no doubt from Makanna's, that venerable, and now lamented, Boston ladies' lingerie emporium, Faith thought. It had served several generations, especially for their trousseaux. The peau de soie lacy slips and nightgowns may have left more to the imagination than Victoria's Secret garb, but perhaps they were even sexier. What was the line? "Putting all your goods in the shopwindow"? Keeping some of them behind the counter wasn't a bad idea.

"I'm at your disposal. Tom is picking up the kids and my dinner is all made. I just have to pop it in the oven." She pulled the slipper chair that was next to Ursula's bed up closer and took her hand. Ursula gave it a slight squeeze and let it drop.

"When I was young, we almost always had cooks. And when we didn't, Mother opened cans. She wasn't at home in the kitchen and I suppose that's the source of my lack of enthusiasm."

One passed down to *your* daughter, Faith finished mentally.

"But I didn't ask you to come to talk about recipes," Ursula said.

"I didn't think you had," Faith said, smiling. Ursula was looking so serious. She had to cheer the woman up. "Even though I *have* tasted your rum cake [see recipe,

p. 370] and it's fabulous." The rum cake gave off such a heady aroma that you felt you had imbibed even before a moist, buttery morsel crossed your lips.

Ursula didn't respond for a moment and Faith wondered if she was up to visitors, after all. Ursula's next words confirmed the thought.

"I'm a bit tired today."

Faith started to get to her feet.

"No!" Ursula said vehemently. "I need to talk to you!" She reached toward Faith and seemed agitated. "Don't leave."

Faith settled back into the chair. "Of course I won't. I just thought you might want to rest."

"I do. It's horrible. That's all I ever do, but I'd like you to come back in the morning. Pix will be gone by then—be sure to wait until the cab takes them to the airport—and besides, mornings are my best times."

"That's no problem. I can come tomorrow."

Ursula sank back against the pillows and closed her eyes briefly.

Opening them again, she said, "I have to tell you something. A story."

Faith nodded.

"It's about something that happened a long time ago."

"To you?"

Ursula ignored the question. "We'll need a lot of time. It's a long story and I must start at the beginning. When we get to the end, I will need your help."

"Anything," Faith said, softly stroking Ursula's hand.

"And Faith, you can't tell my family what I say."

"Not Pix?" Faith was surprised.

"Especially not Pix."

Chapter 2

"No, Pix, you will not need these." Faith plucked a pair of extremely worn sneakers from her friend's hands.

"They're in case I get a chance to go bird-watching in a marshy area. My other sneakers are too good."

Having packed the other sneakers herself, Faith would have employed another description. She'd gingerly wrapped them in tissue to keep them away from Pix's mostly new apparel and accessories.

"There are stores in South Carolina. If you go wading in any marshes"—Faith shuddered slightly at the thought—"you can make the ones already packed your 'marshy' sneaks and buy new ones to wear other places."

Pix looked at the two suitcases, filled to the brim, and ran her hand through her hair, a gesture she had been repeating frequently since Faith arrived to help her finish getting ready for the trip South. Her thick, short locks now resembled a pot scrubber.

"I really don't think I need to bring this much stuff. I'm sure I can get away with one suitcase. Sam is."

"Sam is staying less than a week and men can get away with less—nobody notices that they're wearing the same pants, and a navy sports jacket is all he needs for dinner so long as he brings a few different ties. Plus, he'll be on the golf course with Becca's father most of the time."

"It's very expensive to check bags these days." Pix's mouth curved down.

Faith repressed a sigh. "Samantha has checked all three of you in online, so you saved some money—and, in any case, it's nonrefundable."

That did it and Pix glanced about the room looking for something else to tuck in now that the money had been spent: her good bedside reading lamp? Some of the forest of framed family photos that covered every flat surface? An afghan?

Meanwhile, Faith was zipping the cases shut. Even though Pix was frugal—and generous—it wasn't the baggage fee that was upsetting her. It was leaving Ursula, hence Faith's inward sigh. She knew how Pix was feeling, how torn her friend was, and wished the timing for the trip had been earlier or later.

"As soon as the cab leaves, I'll head over to your mother's. I promised her I would wait to see you all off."

As Faith said that, she wondered why Ursula had been so emphatic that Faith witness Pix's departure. Did she think Pix would cancel at the last minute?

"And you've promised me that you'll call instantly if you think I should come home," Pix said. "Though she was looking better last night when I went to say good-bye."

"It's not going to happen; you're not going to have to come back, but you know I'd call you. And yes, when I saw her yesterday I thought she looked good and so did Tom. He stopped in at noon. He said he particularly noticed she wasn't as pale as when he'd last visited. She was quite cheerful—telling him that she planned to wear the same dress for Mark's wedding that she'd worn for yours."

Pix laughed. "We were married in December, so I'm not sure how appropriate garnet satin is for June. She can still fit into it is the point she's not so subtly making. My mother *does* have a streak of vanity."

"And with ample reason. She's beautiful still, but from the pictures, I can see she was a knockout when she was younger," Faith said. "Now, Ms. Mother-of-the Groom, you'd better get going. Look in that pocketbook of yours once more and be sure you don't have anything that airport security could mistake for a weapon—your Hiker Swiss Army knife, for example."

Sam had given it to Pix on their last anniversary and it had everything save the keg that a Saint Bernard carried. While Faith's notion of anniversary gifts ran more to things with carats, it had been exactly what Pix wanted and she toted it everywhere.

"It's in my suitcase."

Samantha came running into the room.

"The cab is here and Dad's already outside. Go to the bathroom and I'll tell them you're on the way!"

"I thought I was the mother," Pix said, heading for the toilet nevertheless.

Faith and Samantha exchanged glances and a hug.

"You'll have a wonderful time. And everything here will be fine," Faith said.

"I know. Becca's great. I've always wanted a sister and, even though she has two of her own, she's made me feel like one more already."

Pix emerged and grabbed her suitcases. She'd obviously glanced in the mirror and her hair was back to normal, but she'd forgotten lipstick. Faith decided now was not the time for makeup advice.

"Where are your bags?" Pix asked her daughter.

"In the cab, and let me take one of these. We have plenty of time, Mom, don't worry."

"Again, it's too early for role reversal. You've got a few more years to go." Pix had recently read an article about this female child/parent phenomenon and told Faith to be ready when Amy hit her twenties. The good news was that with such dutiful daughters, they would both have someone to do things like cut their toenails when they hit their twilight years.

"And I'm not worried, just being practical. There could be traffic on the Mass Pike." With that she squared her shoulders and set off down the hallway.

Soon Faith was standing in the driveway watching per Ursula's instruction. The cab turned out of sight onto Main Street and she ducked through the opening in the boxwood hedge shared by the Millers and the Fairchilds. Over the years, the space had been widened by numerous crossings between the two yards. She went straight to the garage. Tom was doing parent duty at the kids' soccer games, so Faith got in her car and drove the short distance to Ursula Rowe's.

A story. A long story, Ursula had said. She could hardly wait.

Ursula was out of bed and in her chaise, tucked under a duvet. Before she left, Dora had brought a glass of some sort of smoothie that she set on a small table, admonishing Ursula to finish "every last drop."

"It's my special protein shake," she'd told Faith. "She loves them."

Ursula had made a face, but as soon as the nurse was gone, she took a sip.

"If this is what it takes to get me up and around, I'd be a fool not to do it—however loathsome it tastes. I think Dora's secret ingredient is chalk."

Ursula took another swallow.

"I'm sure it will work Dora's magic," Faith said. "Let me get your water, so you can sip some after you finish. It might help."

Faith got the carafe and glass from the nightstand next to Ursula's bed. The preamble was continuing. Ursula was apparently waiting to start her story until after she'd finished the drink.

"Samantha wants me to get one of those cell phones. As if I needed one! There's a perfectly good phone in the hallway. She says she'd like to be able to talk to me when I'm in bed."

It was a good idea, Faith thought—and not just to talk to Samantha. Ursula had reluctantly given up her dial phones upstairs and down for touch-tones, but neither landline was a portable.

"I think the Millers have a family plan where they can add you as another number. It wouldn't be expensive,"

Faith commented, correctly guessing that Ursula was not only concerned with the newness of the technology, but the cost. While Faith knew Ursula was "comfortable," which in Aleford parlance meant many pennies both earned and saved, she also knew Ursula did not like to spend those pennies except on things like presents for her grandchildren and a number of charitable institutions. Some of Ursula's clothing, especially outerwear, had belonged to her mother: "Perfectly good tweed. It will last until I'm gone and then some." Frugal—and generous—just like her daughter.

Soon Ursula had drunk "every last drop" and taken several sips of water. She started in immediately.

"I was born in Boston, as you probably know. Not at home, but at the old Boston Lying-in Hospital. My Lyman grandmother was apparently shocked. She was a bit of a snob, perhaps more than a bit, and thought it rather common not to have the doctor come to you in the sanctity of one's own boudoir. Thank goodness my parents had more sense. Apparently I gave my mother a rather difficult time and there were no more babies after me.

"My father was in business and we lived on Mt. Vernon Street on the South Slope of Beacon Hill—the only side, again Grandmother Lyman's opinion. Sundays we walked up and over the Hill, past the State

House with its big golden dome, to church at King's Chapel. Boston has changed enormously since I was a girl, but not that walk, I fancy. The rest of the town is barely recognizable to me today. In my early years, there was no skyline. Just one skyscraper—the Customs House Tower. You can barely make it out now, so many buildings have risen up around it, and we certainly never imagined that anything as tall as the new John Hancock building could exist except in the imagination. Father's office was down the street from the Customs House. Peregrine falcons nested in the tower—and still do. I imagine they find it more aesthetic than some of the other buildings nearby. Father always grumbled about the clock on the tower—it never kept accurate time. This was the sort of thing that mattered to him, and his associates, I dare say. The area was, and is, Boston's financial district, convenient to the wharves, although the old buildings are expensive hotels and condominiums today, not a bit like the places where we'd go watch the ships dock. Father would sometimes take me with him when he went in on a Saturday and we'd go down to the harbor after he'd finished whatever it was he had to do.

"He used to joke that if the wind was right, we could smell molasses. I'm sure you've heard about the terrible Molasses Flood in 1919. The tank where it was stored exploded and killed more than twenty people. Over two million gallons spilled out in a wave that was over thirty-five feet high. Father always mentioned the statistics. Ten years later—the story I'll get to eventually starts in the summer of 1929—people would still claim some of the downtown alleys got sticky when it was hot, and perhaps it was the power of suggestion, but I *did* think I could smell it on those long-ago walks.

"Father was always so well turned out. Not dapper, never that. I could tell the change of season by his hats—homburgs turned into straw boaters with broad black bands in the late spring and summer. Top hats for evenings out. His shoes came from London. I believe a man actually came to the house to show him the styles and measure his feet. He had a gold watch that his father had given him for not drinking or smoking until he was eighteen, not that he did much of either afterward. One of my first memories is of listening to the watch tick at the end of its long, gold fob.

"Mother didn't work, of course. Women of her class didn't then. But she was very busy running the household. Unlike many of her peers, she had been an ardent suffragist, although I'm not sure my father was altogether happy about it. It's odd to think that I was born before women could vote. Although Mother could never have been described as a radical, she raised me to believe that men and women were equal and entitled to the same rights. She did a great deal of charity work and was an active member of the Fragment Society, the oldest continuous sewing circle in Boston. It was started during the War of 1812. Pix and I are members, too—although what we do is quite different from Mother's day. Mother might not have been able to do more than boil water for tea, but she did beautiful handwork, and I'm sure the indigent new mothers who received what she made for their layettes were thrilled.

"She had been a well-known beauty in her time and had a delicious sense of humor. She always smelled of lilies of the valley. It was the only scent she used. The only cosmetic. My father wouldn't have stood for rouge or even rice powder. I don't think she much cared. She was very interested in what she wore, though. Father had given her a pearl collar similar to Queen Mary's for a wedding gift and the pearls became Mother's signature jewelry, too."

Ursula paused before taking up the thread again.

"You're sitting here so patiently and I know you're wondering where I'm going with this, but I promise you, it's going somewhere. My story has a number of pieces, which will come together at the end. Just now with this piece, I'm trying to give you a sense of what it was like in Boston—for my parents and for me. They grew up in another century and the changes the twentieth brought were rapid and must have been bewildering to them at times. Especially the changes during the 1920s. I've often thought this was the beginning of the notion of a generation gap. Young people in the Jazz Age were so very different from the kinds of young people their parents had been in what was still the Victorian Age. Maybe it's a little like Samantha and her cell phone—all this new technology. We had 'talkies' and Lucky Lindy flying across the Atlantic. Pix thinks Samantha's frocks belong in the rag pile and the flappers' mothers must have thought the same way. Despite everything that was going on around me, though, as a little girl, my day-to-day life wasn't so far removed from that of my mother's growing up.

"We skated on the Frog Pond on the Boston Common in the winter, and the arrival of the swan boats in the Public Garden was the first sign of spring for us, along with snow drops in Louisburg Square. My brother and his friends sculled on the Charles River straight through until late autumn when the water started to freeze."

Ursula looked straight at Faith.

"Pix has never mentioned an uncle, has she?"

Faith shook her head. Ursula drank some water and leaned back again on the large down European square pillows Dora had arranged for her patient's comfort.

"My brother Theodore. He was always called 'Theo.'"

"Come on, Sis. All you have to do is slip downstairs once the mater and pater are asleep and unlock the side door. I'll lock it up again. Don't worry. I'm not about to risk the family plate."

Ursula Lyman cocked her head to one side and pretended to think. She knew—and Theo knew—that she'd do anything her adored big brother asked.

"Once the break is over and I'm back on campus, I won't have this kind of bother."

"Just the regular kind of bother—your studies." Ursula tried to look stern. Theo's first-semester grades at Harvard hadn't even been gentlemen's Cs. Their father had threatened to cut off his son's allowance if they didn't improve markedly. He'd stopped short of demanding that Theo move home. Leaving Westmorly Court, one of Harvard's "Gold Coast" houses on Mount Auburn Street, which Theo had opted for over the more plebian, and shabbier, freshman housing in the Yard, would make Theo's failings too public.

"I've been burning the midnight oil, don't you worry your pretty little head. A fellow has to have some fun, you know. So, what do you say—will you do it?"

Ursula nodded. Theo lifted his sister up and swung her around. She had been as much a surprise to him nine years ago as he imagined she must have been to their parents.

"But do be careful—and good, Theo, won't you?"

"I'm always good and careful," he said, laughing.

Theo set his sister down and looked in the tall pier glass mirror at the end of the broad front hallway where they'd been standing. Their reflection could have been a painting by Sargent—Master Theodore Speedwell Lyman and sister, Ursula Rose. Theo's hair was carefully parted in the middle and slicked down; he was wearing evening clothes. To please his parents, he was dining at their Cabot cousin's home on Beacon Street before making an appearance at one of the many debutante balls to which he and his very eligible friends were continually invited. But that dinner and the ball would merely mark the start of his evening. Later he and some of his chums were treating a few of the beauties from the Old Howard to a postshow supper at Locke-Ober—upstairs in a private dining room, the only part of the restaurant where women were allowed. He'd ordered Lobster Savannah, the house specialty, and they'd have to bring in their own magnums of champagne thanks to Prohibition—damn it all. Of course the ladies would be wearing considerably more than they would have been earlier. He hoped those dreary guardians of the public morality from the Watch and Ward Society wouldn't have stopped by to interrupt the show, which would push supper up later. The irony was that some of last season's debs, who were officially launched and therefore granted more leeway now, would be wearing outfits at the ball that were almost as revealing as the strippers'. He chuckled to himself and pulled a Butterfinger candy bar—her favorite—from his pocket for his sister.

Ursula was studying herself in the mirror. She was clad in the blue serge skirt, black lisle stockings, and long middy blouse she'd worn to school. Winsor had moved to the Longwood area of Boston some ten years ago and Mrs. Lyman regularly complained about the distance. "When I was a student, it was so convenient. Right here on the Hill. We could walk."

Ursula rather liked the commute. She wasn't allowed to explore Boston on her own yet, but she yearned for the day when she could go to the opposite side of the Hill to the West End and perhaps even down to Scollay Square. She was pretty sure that was where her brother would be for at least part of the evening. She'd seen the giant two-hundred-pound steaming teakettle that hung above the Oriental Tea Company not far from the Square down Tremont Street several blocks away from King's Chapel, but it was the limit permissible in that tantalizing direction. She wasn't interested in what her brother sought in Scollay Square. What she wanted to explore were the bookshops on nearby Corn Hill. But her world was carefully circumscribed by the Common and the Public Garden with occasional trips to the Boston Public Library in Copley Square, the Museum of Fine Arts in the Fenway, or Symphony Hall.

Each morning Mr. Lyman's chauffeur returned from dropping his employer off at his offices to drive his employer's daughter to school. While Ursula thought taking the subway would be great fun, she found plenty to entertain herself looking out the window of the big Packard.

"I wish Mother would let me bob my hair," she complained, turning away from the mirror and eagerly accepting her brother's proffered treat.

Theo yanked one of her braids. "Don't be in a hurry to grow up, squirt. It's not all that it's cracked up to be."

Although the evening promised to be great fun—Charlie Winthrop was picking him up after dinner in the Stutz Torpedo he'd just bought, plus Charlie always had the best hooch—Theo had a moment's longing for the days when he was a schoolboy at Milton, coming home on weekends with nothing much to worry about except beating Groton's football team. He hadn't made Harvard's team, but it would have been rare for a frosh. He missed playing, which was maybe why he was making up for it by all this other playing. Ursula was holding out the white silk scarf he'd dropped when he'd put on his overcoat. Her serious little face was crinkled in a smile. He promised himself he'd buckle down and give up the late nights at Sanborn's Billiards and Tobacco Parlor, hit the books, and make everyone proud—especially the girl standing in front of him.

"You're a brick," he told her, and with a wave, walked out into the dusk.

Faith drove slowly through the streets of Aleford to the outskirts of town where her catering kitchen was located. Her thoughts were so firmly fixed on the early twentieth century that she was startled when a Toyota Prius glided by. The car would have seemed like something from a science fiction novel in 1929. Nineteen twenty-nine. That's when Ursula had said her story started, although so far she'd been describing the years prior, her childhood, and Faith had been captivated by the picture of this bygone era drawn by someone who had lived it. Both Tom's and Faith's parents were younger than Ursula. And of those closer to her in age who would have remembered that significant year, only Faith's paternal grandmother was still alive—Olive Sibley. She lived in New Jersey with her daughter, Faith's aunt Chat, short for Charity. Sibley women had been named Faith, Hope, and Charity since Noah. Faith's parents had stopped with Hope. Whether this was due to an aversion to the third name on the part of Jane, Faith's mother, or the decision that two children were enough, Faith did not know. However, she did know that no one on the branches of the family tree had ever gone beyond Charity. What would it have been? Chastity, no doubt.

Listening to Ursula today, Faith regretted not having spent more time asking her grandmother about her childhood—or asking her mother and father about theirs. She resolved to take a recorder with her on her next trip to the city. And yes, Jersey—to Aunt Chat's. Charity Sibley had made a name for herself—and a great deal of money—in advertising. The firm she founded was a household name, as were the products in her account portfolio. Her colleagues and friends were astounded when she sold the business, retired early, and purchased a small estate in Mendham, on the wrong side of the Hudson. She had been contentedly raising miniature horses and prize dahlias ever since. The fabulous parties she'd hosted at her San Remo apartment in one of the towers overlooking Central Park continued in the new locale. New Yorkers, for whom the Garden State was a less likely destination than Mars, were soon happily crossing the George Washington Bridge.

The big question, Faith thought as she pulled up to work, was why Pix—who had revealed details of her life ranging from the name of her kindergarten class pet (Eleanor, a guinea pig) to where and when she and Sam first did "it"—had never mentioned having an uncle. *Theo.* It was a lovely, old-fashioned nickname. There were several possible answers to this question: He was the despised black sheep of the family, although Ursula's description of him so far had been very affectionate; he died well before Pix was born; or finally, Pix didn't know of his existence. Was this last what Ursula didn't want Faith to reveal? That Ursula had a brother? In the course of her story were other siblings going to emerge? Up until now, Faith had assumed Ursula was an only child. She'd indicated that there weren't any more babies after her birth, but what about older siblings besides Theo?

She'd reached the catering kitchen. Faith unlocked the door, hung up her coat, and took out some sweet butter from the refrigerator and flour from the walk-in pantry. Ursula clearly could not talk for long without tiring and Faith had left her dozing. It meant she now had time to prepare some much-needed puff pastry, *feuilletage,* for the freezer. *Feuilletage,* from the French for "leaf," was tricky and involved folding, rolling, and folding the buttery dough over itself again multiple times in order to get those ethereal, leaf-thin layers that would literally melt in your mouth. It was a task she had always loved—something about the repetitive motion was soothing. Not that anything particular was bothering her at the moment. She quickly knocked wood, tapping the counter with her wide rolling pin. Sure, Amy was dealing with a small group of mean girls in her grade, but she said she had only told her mother to show how well she and her friends were handling them. "We just laugh like crazy at everything they say and Sarah says stuff like, 'Aren't they hysterical,' and they get mad and go to the other side of the playground." It *was* a good strategy, but Faith, remembering some of the recent tragic outcomes of bullying, had called both the school principal and Amy's teacher, asking each to keep an eye on the situation.

After a very rough start in middle school, Ben had discovered that he loved English—although it might have something to do with the very young and very pretty student teacher who had recently arrived. He was currently turning out short stories about vegetarian vampires for his writing assignments. They were actually pretty funny, although that might not be Ben's intent. And Tom, thank goodness, was his hale and hearty self again. So, knock wood, no worries. Well, there was the economy and the fact that Faith's business was off by over half. In addition, clients for the events they were catering were substituting things on sticks and cheese plates for passed mini beef Wellington and lobster spring rolls; opting for wine and beer without the exotic cocktails that had formerly been all the rage.

Some of the puff pastry in front of her was for an event Have Faith was catering for a yacht club on the

North Shore. The Tiller Club had an annual game dinner in the fall and an old-fashioned clambake in the summer, both of which Faith had catered for years. The chairman had called Faith late last summer and told her there would be only one dinner this year and it would be a "Spring Fling" in late March. Faith thought he was being rather optimistic with the name—not the "Fling" part; the "Tillies," as the men called themselves, were nautical party animals, but March didn't suggest spring to her. However, just this week the plow guy had removed those long sticks he used to avoid running off the Fairchild's driveway during a heavy snowfall. This was a more accurate harbinger of the season than the poor crocuses that struggled to bloom, so the Tillies had been right.

Their first course would be a *champignon Napoléon*—delicious, but plain old button mushrooms sautéed in butter with a bit of cream and sherry added at the end, not the medley of wild (expensive) mushrooms she normally used. And the chairman had opted for chicken roulade, not prime rib, as Faith had first suggested, knowing from the game dinners the amount of red meat they gleefully scarfed down.

Two things wouldn't change on the menu. The dessert—boys at heart, they always wanted chocolate layer cake—and plenty of dinner rolls served throughout the meal, since tossing them, and rolled-up napkins, at one another made up much of the evening's entertainment. The club supplied the booze and, recession or no, Faith was sure it would flow as amply as it had in other years. One had to maintain standards, after all. The dinner was next Friday and she made a mental note to remind Scott and Tricia Phelan, who worked as bartender and server at most of her events. Scott's day job was at an auto body shop in nearby Byford, and Trish was working as an occasional apprentice for Faith, hoping to gain enough skill to find a job in a restaurant kitchen, bringing in some much-needed additional income. Their two kids were both in school full-time now and Faith wished she could put Trish on salary. Maybe in a few months.

Faith knew business would pick up. History repeated itself. There had been a big slump just before she left Manhattan for Aleford, marriage, and motherhood. There had been slumps here in Aleford. For now she could weather the storm without a bailout. Have Faith was still running the café at the Ganley, a local art museum, and it provided a nice, steady income. Before she took the job, Faith had checked out the fare offered by the previous purveyor. The lettuce in her salad was black and slimy; the canned tuna in the tuna salad reminiscent of the botulism-loaded cans from the

Spanish-American War. The brownies looked like cow chips. The café attracted more visitors to the museum, once word got out that food poisoning was no longer a risk.

Lost in thought and pastry, Faith was startled when the door opened. It was Niki Constantine, Faith's longtime assistant. A year and a half ago Niki had married Phillip Theodopoulos in an extravaganza that made *My Big Fat Greek Wedding* look like an elopement. Niki had grown up in nearby Watertown, during which time her mother had made her expectations clear to her only daughter. College, okay, but an engagement ring from a nice Greek boy by graduation; a June wedding; first grandchild a year later: "We don't want people counting on their fingers." Niki had rebelled, starting with culinary school instead of Mount Ida College, and then refusing to date any male remotely Greek in heritage, instead parading boyfriends who ranged from Lowell bikers to a Buddhist old enough to be her father, maybe grandfather. And then despite her best intentions, she had fallen hard for the man of her mother's dreams—Yale undergrad, Harvard MBA, handsome, family oriented (he had pictures of his parents, sibs, *and* their kids in his wallet), plus he was Greek. First generation. Throughout, Faith had watched from the sidelines, listening to Niki's descriptions and laughing. In addition to being the best assistant she could have wished for, especially when it came to desserts, Niki was also the funniest friend Faith had.

Niki wasn't smiling today.

"I thought you and Phil were driving down to see his parents in Hartford."

Just as Niki had found herself drawn inexorably into the vortex that was her mother's idea of a real wedding—Niki's gown had had so many crinolines she'd told Faith she felt like one of those dolls her aunt Dimitra crocheted skirts for to hide the toilet paper roll—she'd also been pulled into Phil's family, although she found that she enjoyed being an aunt to his numerous nephews and nieces. The fact that his mother made the best baklava in the world and always for Niki didn't hurt, either.

"Phil needed to go golfing—and I wasn't in the mood to read *If You Give a Mouse a Cookie* forty times in a row."

"Sit down, and as soon as I finish this, *I'll* give you a cookie. You look tired. Out late clubbing? Make some coffee. I wouldn't mind a cup."

Niki had refused to give up her lifestyle as a freewheeling twenty-seven-year-old and Phil was happy to go along.

When Niki didn't respond—unheard of—and instead slumped into a chair without removing her jacket, Faith hastily wrapped the packets of dough, crossed the room to the freezer, and set them inside. With all that butter, they had to go in immediately. She stood in front of her friend and said, "How about *I* make the coffee and *you* tell me what's going on."

Niki sat up a little straighter.

"No coffee."

Faith began to get very worried. Niki loved coffee, delightedly bringing ever more unusual blends to Faith's attention—the latest was Malabar Monsooned from India, its special taste indeed acquired from exposure to monsoons. Niki wasn't just a connoisseur. The stuff ran in her veins, and she joked that one of her ancestors' ships must have gone radically off course, ending up in Scandinavia instead of Macedonia.

Pulling a chair close to Niki's, Faith sat down and took Niki's hand.

"Tell me what's going on," she said quietly.

"Oh Faith," Niki said, bursting into tears. "I'm pregnant!"

"But that's wonderful!"

Niki had been regaling Faith and Pix for months with the various folk remedies her mother and aunts had advised to speed conception. Niki had told them she was sure plain old trying would eventually work, and meanwhile it wasn't "trying" at all, but more fun than should be legal—her words.

Faith added, "This is the news you've been waiting for . . ." before her voice trailed off. The woman sobbing in front of her wasn't shedding tears of joy. There must be something wrong with the baby. But it was so soon. She couldn't be far along. Faith would have noticed and Niki wouldn't have been able to keep it to herself, although she had told both Faith and Pix that no one was to tell Mrs. Constantine until Niki was at least eight months along. Niki didn't want to be wrapped in cotton wool and subjected to endless advice about what to eat, what not to look at—her mother had already advised against any movie scarier than *The Sound of Music* lest it affect her future grandchild's psyche.

"Is it the baby? Did they find something—"

Niki interrupted, rubbing her eyes with her hands in what looked like an angry gesture.

"No, I'm sure nothing's wrong. I haven't been to the doctor. Just did the test at home because I missed my period—and I'm never late. But you know me. Healthy as a horse. Phil, too, so the baby should be doing fine. That's not it."

She started to cry again. Faith got a box of tissues from under the counter. The only other time she could remember seeing Niki in tears was when the Constantines' dog died, a chocolate Lab they'd had all Niki's life. She swore that his coat was what inspired her to turn to truffles and the other sweets she loved to create.

Suddenly what Niki had said when she arrived came back to Faith, "Phil needed to go golfing." The ground was still hard and it was cold. Phil enjoyed the occasional round, but he wasn't a fanatic. Why did he "need" to golf today? In his corporate world, there was only one reason Faith could think of—networking. Big-time.

"Is something going on at work for Phil?"

Niki blew her nose.

"Just that he lost his job yesterday."

"Damn!"

There wasn't anything else to say. Faith put her arms around Niki. She was crying harder. This should have been one of the happiest days of her life. Phil had been steadily working his way up the ladder, but he'd only been with this firm for three years. There were a lot of occupied rungs above his.

Niki took another tissue and wiped her eyes.

"Yup. Handed him a carton and took back the key to the men's room. He started dialing as soon as he walked out into Post Office Square, and the only nibble he's gotten is this golf game with someone who knows someone who was at Yale with him."

The days when job hunting consisted of scanning the want ads in the *Boston Globe* and mailing out résumés were totally foreign to Phil and Niki's generation. Now it was all about networking, the golf kind, and the Internet kind.

"He's lined up interviews with some headhunters. The most immediate problem is his parachute. It wasn't golden. More like cheesecloth. A month's pay and three months' health insurance."

There it was. Health insurance, the policy had covered Niki, too, and now it was good for only three more months.

"But surely he'll find something before it runs out."

Niki shook her head. "He has friends who have been out of work for much longer than that. We have some savings and he can cash in his 401(k) . . ."

"Don't even think about it. I'll cover you and Phil, as an employee spouse, here," Faith said.

"You have no idea how much money that's going to cost you, especially with my preexisting condition."

"Expecting a baby isn't like cancer or heart disease. I'll talk to Ralph and we'll get it ready to go immediately in case you need it. And that's final." Faith could see that Niki was getting ready to argue some more. On Monday morning she'd call Ralph, her insurance agent, who handled Have Faith's business coverage, and tell him what was going on.

"Coffee now? I've got decaf beans," Faith offered, mindful of avoiding caffeine during pregnancy.

"I don't think so," Niki said, graphically gesturing—finger pointed down her throat. "That's how I first knew. About a week ago the smell started making me want to barf. I haven't actually been losing lunch, but feel like it a lot. Weird." Niki seemed to be considering the situation.

"Okay, how about a glass of milk and some cookies, then?"

Niki's responses—verbal and physical—meant she was edging back toward her normal self and Faith was relieved. Phil would find a job in due course and meanwhile Niki could enjoy her pregnancy, although there was an oxymoron in there someplace if Faith's experiences were anything to go by. Mostly she recalled having to pee constantly and panicking when she wasn't near a bathroom. Pix had told her it was one of the main reasons for joining a club in Boston. You could go downtown when pregnant without fear.

"And once little beanbag or whatever nauseatingly cute name you guys come up with for him or her in utero arrives, we're all set up here for you to bring the baby to work," Faith said.

When she had purchased Yankee Doodle Dandy Dining, the catering firm that had previously occupied the space, she had completely remodeled the facility. During the process, she created an area where her kids could safely play from the time they were toddlers well into elementary school. Amy still liked to come hang out when her busy schedule permitted it.

"I haven't thought that far ahead," Niki said, "but not having to pay for day care will save a lot. It also gives me an excuse to keep my mother from taking over."

Niki's mother indeed was a force of nature, but Faith liked and admired her, even while she understood how hard it was for Niki to have such a controlling individual hovering over her life. "Smother Love" might have been coined for Mrs. Constantine. Which was why Faith doubted Niki could keep her condition secret. However, Niki's brother was engaged and this could possibly deflect attention from Niki for a while, as his fiancée was only half Greek and her future mother-in-law was busy teaching her how to make all her future husband's favorite dishes. The situation had caused Niki to mention recently that there really were gods up there on Mount Olympus.

"Phil must be over the moon," Faith said, relaxing into their usual companionable mode.

Niki dipped her molasses sugar cookie into her milk and took a bite.

"I haven't told him yet," she mumbled.

The mode switched back.

"You haven't told him! Niki, eventually he's going to notice the patter of little feet."

"I know, I know. The stick only turned blue yesterday, and yes, I was really, really happy. Then he called with his news, and by the time he got home, I'd decided this was not the time to lay it on the guy that he'd better be out there hustling up some bread because there was going to be an extra place at the table for a bunch of years. Besides, I have a job, which brings me to the reason I came by. Oh hell, I came to tell you, you know that, but I also came to ask you a favor."

"Anything," Faith said.

"First, I don't want you to tell anyone I'm pregnant."

"Not even Pix?"

"Especially not Pix."

Ursula and now Niki. What was up with this? Poor Pix. Life was getting even stranger than usual.

"You know she can't keep a secret. The first time she saw Phil, she wouldn't be able to look him in the eye, would get all red, and he'd know something was going on."

"Sweetie! Pix is away for almost two more weeks. You can't keep this from him that long."

"I'll keep it from him as long as I want." Niki jutted her chin out, all traces of tears gone. "I don't want him to be distracted. He has enough on his plate without piling on a helping of fatherhood." Niki seemed to be favoring meal metaphors.

"Okay." Faith backed off. Niki didn't need Faith adding to her stress. "Anything else?"

"It's a biggie. And if you think it will affect the business at all, you *have* to say so straight-out."

Faith was mystified. Niki continued. "Could I use the kitchen here when we're not doing a job? I thought maybe I could set up a dessert-catering Web site to bring in more money. Get Mom to spread the word about my cheesecakes at her bingo nights."

Niki's cheesecakes *were* truly delectable. Poetry even. Besides the traditional New York and strawberry-covered cakes in a variety of sizes, Niki also did praline, Amaretto, chocolate macadamia, and a new to-die-for pomegranate with a raspberry liqueur glaze. She was working on one for spring featuring Madagascar vanilla beans and toasted coconut.

"You didn't even have to ask—and don't worry about hurting business. Our customers almost always want full-service catering for dessert buffets—servers and people to clean up. This will be fun. I'll help."

"No you won't. I'll get Tricia. She wants to learn more about desserts. And of course I'll use my own ingredients."

"Look, it will all work out. You know me. I'm not Little Mary Sunshine, but we'll get through this. And now, just for a little minute, can we shout for joy? You and Phil will be such wonderful parents."

"You're going to make me cry again. I'm doing that a lot lately. Better than throwing up, though."

Faith decided not to tell her that this would in all likelihood start soon. Hair-trigger emotions first, sore nipples, and then morning sickness, which often stretched into the afternoon in Faith's case. Plus, it seemed she had just recovered when the infant she'd produced started what the books termed with scientific precision "projectile vomiting."

"I *am* happy," Niki said. "Very, very happy."

"Me, too." Faith smiled. "How about we call your business 'Little Mary Cheesecake'?"

"Don't push it, boss," Niki said. "I'm more the Suzy Creamcheese type."

It was close to five o'clock by the time Faith got home and she was surprised to see that Tom's car was gone. Where could her family be? But there were lights on in the parsonage kitchen. It was a mystery.

Faith went in the back door and found her daughter making chocolate chip cookies.

"Don't worry, I wasn't going to turn on the oven until you came home, Mom," Amy said.

Faith gave her conscientious little girl a hug, praying that she stayed that way, especially during her teen years.

"Where is everybody else? Dad's car is gone."

"He had to go to some meeting. He left you a note, and Ben's doing homework in Dad's study."

After a series of incidents last fall, Ben's computer was now out of his room and in a more public part of the house. Faith and Tom had followed the suggestion of many educators that with this simple act, they could control their child's behavior without constantly looking over his or her shoulder. Just the presence of an adult helped kids think twice—or more—about their conversations in cyberspace, particularly ones about other kids. You might think you're chatting to one or two others, but in reality it could be one or two billion, a fact few kids absorbed fully.

What kind of meeting could be held on a Saturday night? Faith wondered. That time was sacrosanct for the clergy who were preparing for a Sunday service. Presumably they were getting in an even holier mood than usual, and perhaps adding a comma or two to the following day's sermon. In reality there might be ministers who wrote their sermons early in the week, but

Faith didn't know any and her husband was definitely not in that club. Most Saturday nights Tom Fairchild was frantically rewriting what he had decided before was just fine.

His note was written on the dry-erase family bulletin board.

"Sherman Munroe has called an emergency meeting of the vestry. No idea why. Back soon, I hope. Love, Tom."

Sherman—and don't ever call him "Sherm"—was one of Faith's least favorite parishioners. He was a relatively new arrival to Aleford. He'd lived in town for only five years, but as he was fond of saying, "My people started the place." There were some Munroes in the Old Burial Ground, so they *had* been around at the time of the town's incorporation, but as for starting anything, if they had, they hadn't stuck around to finish—the ones aboveground, that is. One and all had absented themselves until Sherman turned up after retiring from, according to him, a highly lucrative manufacturing business in Pennsylvania. Millicent Revere McKinley, whose frontal lobe was a veritable Rolodex of Alefordiana, conceded that he was descended from "those early Munroes," her tone suggesting that some other Munroes would have been preferable. She had followed it up with a few tart sentences expressing her opinion about locating businesses not simply out of state, but out of Aleford.

By taking on jobs no one else wanted to do, Sherman soon became a player at First Parish and a thorn in Tom's side. Everything that had occurred before Mr. Munroe's arrival had been done "bass ackward"—a phrase Faith particularly despised, along with "connect the dots." And now that he was on the vestry, things were even worse. Faith speculated about what emergency Sherman had dreamed up. Dissatisfaction with the brand of coffee being used for coffee hour? A reiteration of his ongoing objection to the haphazard way Sherman thought the sexton placed the prayer books and hymnals in the pews?

Faith had been looking forward to telling Tom about her conversation with Ursula and all of Niki's news. Like Ursula, Niki had recognized that the don't-tell rule excluded spouses and conceded that Faith would have to let Tom know she was pregnant.

Yet, most of all, Faith was annoyed about the stress this Munroe jerk was causing Tom. She was tempted to call his cell and tell him to come home for dinner. It was bad for him to skip meals. His postpancreatitis care had specifically included this warning. Someone occasionally brought cookies to the vestry meetings, but you couldn't count on it. And the meeting better not go late. Tom needed his sleep.

Faith was working herself into a very righteous snit when she heard the car pull in. Amy's cookies were in one oven, giving the house a delicious smell, and Faith had optimistically popped the country ham and potato au gratin made with a Gruyère-laden béchamel sauce in the other. She had broccoli crowns, the stems saved for soup, in a pot ready to steam at the last minute. Ben had set the table—it was his turn—and it looked as if the night would be salvaged.

The moment she saw her husband's face, she told Amy to go join Ben and read while he worked. Faith would watch the cookies, and dinner might be a while.

She didn't have to ask what was wrong. The words came rushing from Tom's mouth like an avalanche, each one pushing the next forward with deadly force.

"The independent audit we authorized has uncovered a shortfall. A large shortfall. Over ten thousand dollars is missing. Missing from the Minister's Discretionary Fund."

Faith was having trouble taking it in. She stood for a moment with the casserole she'd removed from the oven in her hands. "The Minister's Discretionary Fund?"

Tom sat down heavily, still in his coat.

"Yes, the Discretionary Fund."

Faith knew what it was. She'd just been repeating his words, hoping somehow she had heard him wrong. She hadn't.

The Minister's Discretionary Fund. Money that the Reverend Thomas Preston Fairchild alone had access to and for which he was solely accountable.

Chapter 3

Normally Faith liked the Sunday morning service, which was a good thing since she seemed to have been destined to sit through endless numbers of them starting in early childhood. Unlike First Parish, her father's church didn't have child care until relatively recently, so her mother had had to tote Faith and Hope with her, settling in the last pew on the right with books, puzzles, and boxes of animal crackers to keep her children occupied and quiet. It must have been nice for Jane Sibley when her daughters were finally old enough for Sunday school and she could enjoy the service without worrying about crumbs on the pew cushions. Faith's first Sunday after arriving in Aleford as a new bride, she had instinctively zeroed in on the same pew, only to be escorted to the front left by the

Senior Warden. "This is where the minister's wife *always* sits."

Today she was glad she couldn't see the faces behind her, although she imagined any number of eyes were boring holes in her back as she prayed for the hour to go quickly. What had happened at last night's meeting should be only from the vestry to God's ear, but more likely it was from the vestry to Aleford's.

She wanted to get Tom back home. He'd been up and out of the house before she'd had breakfast on the table, grabbing an apple cinnamon muffin she had just taken from the oven and resisting her plea to sit down and eat. She'd watched him striding over to the church, his unfastened dark robe billowing behind him. He reminded her of that cartoon character in *Li'l Abner* with a permanent rain cloud over his head.

She struggled to keep her mind on what was going on in the pulpit. The New Testament lesson. Sherman Munroe was the lector this morning. His ruddy, vulpine face shone with righteous well-being and he licked his lips before starting. She suppressed a shudder. It was like watching some sort of animal stalking its prey. Tom, in contrast, was pale and his face was drawn. He looked as if he needed to lie down.

"The Gospel lesson for today is from John, chapter six, verses four through fifteen."

Sherman read well. It was the familiar story of the loaves and the fishes. Tom was using this reading as the reference point for his sermon. Late last night he'd given it to her to read—something he rarely did. They had been pretending to watch television—a DVD of the British comedy series *The Vicar of Dibley*. When he hadn't laughed even once—it was the Easter Bunny episode—she'd suggested bed. He'd switched off the set and asked if she'd "look over" what he'd written for the morning. She'd poured herself a glass of merlot and made him a steaming mug of cocoa. She knew he'd wanted to make sure there was nothing in the sermon's references to the miracle—multiplying much from little—that could be misconstrued. Of course there wasn't and this reassurance seemed to be what he needed to finally fall asleep. She lay wide awake, shaken by what this accusation, not even made directly yet, was already doing to her husband.

The sermon touched upon the question of what it is that sustains us—those material and nonmaterial things that feed our lives. What goes into our individual loaves and fishes, and how we can use our faith to nourish not just ourselves but others—making those five barley loaves fill twelve, and even more, baskets. Tom was an able and often eloquent preacher. There were people in church every Sunday, not members either of First Parish or the denomination, who came solely for the sermons, which was fine with him. That his words could inspire, comfort, provoke thought, or simply interest someone was gratifying. It was one of the things he'd hoped his ministry might accomplish over the years. His own brand of loaves and fishes.

Today, though, Faith feared his words would be minimized by a delivery that was not up to his usual. He had stumbled during the Call to Worship and again when reading the General Thanksgiving. She only hoped he could get through the entire service.

Sherman was done and stepped down, resuming his seat across the aisle from Faith. Front row right. He glanced her way and lifted an eyebrow.

She hated him.

It had been his idea to hire an independent CPA who specialized in nonprofits to do the annual financial review. It had always been done in house prior to this year. She found herself wondering why he had not merely suggested it, but insisted on it. "Good business practice" was his oft-repeated rationale. But a church wasn't a business! During those discussions, Tom had come home from vestry meetings alternately furious and exhausted. "It's a total waste of money! What does the man think? That Mr. Brown has a Swiss bank account?" Mr. Brown was the sexton.

Sherman prevailed. It wasn't hard to see why he'd been such a successful CEO and now here were the results.

Faith directed her gaze to the early spring flowers—jonquils, tulips, and daffodils in pale yellows and ivories—that graced the altar in memory of Ursula's late husband, who had died at this time years before Faith had come to Aleford. She was sorry neither Ursula nor Pix could see them. Especially Pix, she thought, feeling a bit selfish. A terrible time to be away. Sam Miller, one of Boston's most esteemed lawyers, would make quick work of this mess. Well, he'd be back in less than a week and surely nothing would happen that fast. She thought about that raised eyebrow and the smug look on Sherman's face as he left the pulpit. Maybe Tom should call Sam. But it would spoil the family's happy time meeting the new in-laws. No, better to wait, unless things took a turn for the worse. The whole business was preposterous. Her emotions seesawed between extreme anger and extreme fear. In her anger mode, she wanted to leap across the aisle and smack that self-satisfied smile off Sherman's face. The fear mode was keeping her seated. She had no doubt the man was a formidable enemy. He'd be charging her with assault and battery as soon as her hand had left a mark.

Charges. Embezzlement was a crime. It all came down to that. Last night Tom had tried out a number of scenarios to account for the missing money and none of them worked. It all came down to him.

Sherman. Was it mere coincidence that the discrepancy turned up this year after his push for the independent audit? Could he possibly be involved in some way? A move on his part to discredit—and get rid of—the minister?

She began going over everything once more, her mind only partially on Prayers for the People.

Each year the church allocated a certain amount for the Discretionary Fund to be used as the minister saw fit. At the end of the fiscal year, the minister reported what had been dispersed and how much was left to be rolled over. The only other church record kept was a list in the minister's files of the amounts, but the list did not include to whom funds had been given or for what.

Faith had a pretty good idea of some of the recipients. A phone call would come; Tom would take off for a hospital, sometimes even a police station. Money for medicine and medical emergencies not covered by insurance, a family member who needed bail, a mortgage payment to avoid foreclosure, and money for the basics of life—fuel and even warm clothing during the bitterly cold months, food always. Some of the money came back; some didn't. All the transactions were completely confidential.

Besides the church's contribution, individuals made gifts to the fund in memory of a loved one or in celebration of an event. The Discretionary Fund account was separate from all other church accounts at the bank. Only Tom could sign the checks or use the PIN-protected ATM card.

He had no idea what could account for the huge gap between what he reported and what the bank reported as the total in the account for the last fiscal year. At the meeting, the vestry had asked him to go back over his lists of dispersements for five years. More if he was so inclined. They hoped he would be able to report to them in two weeks. It was Sherman who had suggested the deadline. "So this thing doesn't drag on too long."

She stood up for the hymn. *"O star of truth, down shining / Thro' clouds of doubt and fear."* The music filled the church valiantly, and tunefully—except for the inevitable warbling, off-key sopranos. *"Though angry foes may threaten"*—Faith's eyes shifted across the aisle. Sherman was adding his alto, that moist red mouth shaped in a perfect oval. Sundays meant three-piece suits from Brooks with a club tie. The few times she'd encountered him on a weekday, he hadn't strayed far from the fold—khaki pants with knifepoint creases, V-neck sweaters, and casual shirts all with the logo, a plump sheep dangling from a ribbon, the emblem of the Knights of the Golden Fleece, adopted for his store by the first Mr. Brooks in 1818. Sherman Munroe: a wolf in sheep's clothing?

"I must not faithless be." Behind her the organ music swelled as it brought the hymn to a close.

"Faithless." Not a problem. She sat down and turned her face up toward her husband's as he started his sermon.

She stopped thinking about the rumors that she had earlier imagined building up steam among those seated behind her, ready to envelop Faith and her family.

She stopped thinking about the odious man across the aisle.

She stopped thinking about Ursula and her story; about Niki and her problems; Pix and her insecurities.

She simply listened.

Pix was feeling loopy. She wasn't used to champagne at breakfast, but the resort was renowned for its champagne brunch, so champagne it was. Mimosas. And the food. She was a little drunk on that, too, starting with dinner last night—crab cakes the size of baseballs for starters followed by chateaubriand and ending with Turtle pie for dessert. The chocolate-pecan variety, not box or snapping ones.

Next to her, Sam was making quick work of eggs Benedict with smoked salmon instead of ham and Dan had asked for seconds on his brioche French toast with caramelized bananas, in addition to all sorts of other delicious things. He'd given his mother a bite and she could taste walnuts plus something else, a hint of rum? She'd opted for her favorite—two eggs over easy—but here served with Timms Mill cheese grits and a local hickory-smoked sausage. She loved breakfast food, but usually her meal consisted of hastily consumed yogurt, some fruit, and toast.

The men were all heading for the golf course and the women were due at the spa for a full day of manicures, pedicures, facials, and massages. Pix kept her nails short, and the last time they'd seen polish was for Sam's sister's big anniversary party last fall. They were clean, though. She'd never had a massage and wished she could ask Faith what to expect. She assumed she'd have to get fully or partially undressed and she'd hate to make a mistake. What if you were supposed to take only some things off and she was in the buff? At this thought she realized the champagne had definitely gone to her head. A massage mistake? She'd just do whatever Samantha did. Samantha would know. Her glass had been refilled by an unseen hand and she almost drained it before she remembered the alcoholic content of what she was starting to believe was the best orange juice she'd ever had. Fizzy.

The bride and groom—or was that the bride- and groom-to-be?—looked so happy. They'd both ordered huevos rancheros. Obviously they were meant for each other.

She looked at her watch. Twelve-thirty. Faith might be home from church if she'd cut her appearance at coffee hour short as she occasionally gave herself permission to do.

"Will you excuse me a moment? Please don't get up," she said.

Southern men had such beautiful manners and it had instantly rubbed off on her own husband and sons as soon as they'd arrived at the resort. Doors were opened, chairs pulled out, and when she or any of the other women rose, they all rose as one. A girl could get used to this stuff, Pix thought.

Heading for the ladies' room, she ducked instead into an unoccupied hallway leading away from the main dining room and pulled out her phone. Bless Samantha and her insistence on the family calling plan when she'd left for college. Pix couldn't imagine what she'd done before she had a cell phone. She'd already talked to Dora twice since arriving and was reassured that Mother was doing fine. Faith had called after her visit yesterday to report the same. And it was Faith she speed-dialed now.

But she didn't want to talk about Ursula. Or what one wears for a massage.

The parsonage answering machine picked up. Drat. Faith must still be at church.

"Hi, um, it's me. Or I, whichever." Pix hated leaving messages. She always felt self-conscious. "Anyway, give me a call when you get a chance. Everything's okay. Just, well, call me." She realized she'd been whispering. Very Deep Throat.

She returned to the table after going into the ladies' room and washing her hands. To do otherwise would have been dishonest, and there wasn't a deceitful bone in Pix's body. Although, as Faith had told her soon after they realized they were going to be best friends not just forever, but since they lived next door, for every day, "You couldn't tell a lie to save your face, just the rest of the world's."

The men stood up. Dan pulled out his mother's chair, first picking up the napkin the waiter had refolded and handing it to her.

Yes, a girl could get used to all this, but it could also get to be a little weird. "Weird" didn't even begin to cover it. She knew the champagne was muddling her thoughts. There were a lot to muddle.

Outside, the view looked as if the South Carolina Tourist Board had ordered it up. The sea and sky had been painted with one brush, a brush dipped in shimmering aquamarine. There wasn't a single cloud in the sky. Instead it seemed they'd all descended in a blinding white layer on the smooth curve of the beach at the foot of the lawn that stretched out from the resort's veranda, which was adorned with a long, beckoning row of rocking chairs. Pix thought about the dreary landscape she'd left, when? Just yesterday? Driving past palms and flowering shrubs from the airport, she had relaxed for the first time since the doctor had called with the news about her mother. The Harbour Town Lighthouse, striped like a fat candy cane, looked like a child's sweet. The Cohens had booked it for a sunset reception for the last night. Friends and family were driving from Charleston and other places to officially toast the betrothed couple. Pix was sure the view would be spectacular. The weather was cooperating and the forecast promised not a drop of rain. She sighed when she thought about all the preparations that were going into this wedding celebration. Maybe Samantha would elope.

The Millers had arrived before the Cohens, and Pix had stretched out on the chaise on their own private patio while everyone else had hit the beach. She wished Faith could see the room—a bed that must be larger than a king with a tentlike canopy and plenty of comfy, overstuffed armchairs piled with bright pillows. The bath was the size of one of her kid's bedrooms, complete with a rain forest shower and a whirlpool, both of which she intended to try as often as possible. But first she had closed her eyes just for a minute. . . .

There had been a scramble to get dressed and down to dinner. All her dread at meeting her future in-laws had returned and fortunately Samantha had stopped by, since Pix had completely forgotten to change her flats for heels.

Miles away from last night and at the brunch table, Pix absentmindedly drained the rest of her mimosa.

"Surely you aren't going to ignore the chef's famous sticky buns, Pix? You're in pecan country now," said Mrs. Cohen. No, it was "Cissy." They were all on a first-name basis as soon as they'd greeted each other. Apparently "Sister" was a common nickname in households like Mrs. Cohen's where she'd been the only girl growing up with two brothers. And her given name was Cynthia. It certainly wasn't any more unusual than "Pix." She had been tiny at birth, and Pix's father had referred to his new baby girl as his little pixie, a name promptly adopted by everyone and soon shortened to Pix. It no longer applied by the time she was two, and by the time she was fifteen and grazing the six-foot mark, it was ludicrous, but it had stuck. Given that Ursula had named her daughter Myrtle after both a favorite aunt and the ground cover with tiny purple blossoms, Pix had opted for the lesser of two evils, jealous of the Debbies and Margies in her class.

"Another mimosa to go with the bun?" asked Dr. Cohen, ever solicitous. His bedside manner was faultless. Pix put her hand firmly over her glass at the thought. At all her thoughts.

"No, thank you, Steve, I'll pass," she said, aware that she was speaking very distinctly. Loopy, yes, she was loopy and it was starting to give her the giggles.

Stephen Cohen, M.D. Her son's father-in-law-to-be. She glanced at her watch. She should have left the message on Faith's cell instead of the parsonage phone.

Stephen Cohen.

Steve. Her Steve.

Most Sundays, whether by prior invitation or as a result of an impulse on Tom's or Faith's part, the Fairchilds had guests at their Sunday dinner table. Happily, thought Faith, today was an exception. The other exception was staying at coffee hour until the bitter end. And if the coffee was anything to go by, the bitter dregs. She'd sent Amy home with Ben as soon as Sunday school had let out, ushering them through the side door and watching them cross the cemetery until they disappeared into the parsonage through the back door. Ignoring their disappointment at having to forgo the tomato juice and Ritz crackers offered up for First Parish's smaller fry (she had not managed to make even the slightest change in coffee hour from this to the choice of Triscuits and orange cheese or Vanilla Wafers for the grown-ups), she resolutely stood by her man and smiled until her mouth hurt.

At last, Tom and she walked out into the fresh air. She took his hand.

"For the moment, two choices. After some lunch, we can sit down and start trying to figure this all out. Or we can go off somewhere with the kids and try to forget it for a few hours. Which one?"

"Door number two," Tom said, pulling her closer to his side as they made their way between the rows of headstones with their lugubrious epitaphs. She always walked quickly by "As you pass by / And cast an eye / As you are now / So once was I" and slowed to consider what "She did what she could" might have meant to the survivor who commissioned it carved on the plain slate devoid of the angels or ghoulish figures so popular with those who practiced the art of gravestone rubbing. Faith did have a favorite epitaph, a more modern one. Her father had sent it to her after a parishioner had come across it on a trip: "Here lies an Atheist / All dressed up / And no place to go."

They'd reached the parsonage and stopped before going in.

"In any case," Tom said, "until I talk to the bank, all our speculation is just that. I need to compare my records to theirs."

"Okay, where to?" Faith was relieved that Tom had picked what she thought was the better course of action. She intended to get to the bottom of all this, but she needed more information. The first thought that had crossed her mind after Tom's announcement was that somehow the theft had occurred when Tom was ill. It was where she planned to start, anyway. She was already making a list in her mind. Who had taken over what?

"It's a good day for kites. Crane Beach?" he suggested. "Bring Frisbees, too?"

Crane Beach was a wonderful nature preserve up on the North Shore in Ipswich. The kites would soar with terns and other seabirds. As for the Frisbees, it would be a fun challenge tossing them in the wind and keeping them from the waves.

"Perfect. I'll pack snacks while you and the kids have some of the borscht I took out of the freezer last night. We just need to heat it up. There's still some of that dark rye to go with it."

Faith had made vats of borscht last August with the succulent beets from the garden of her Sanpere neighbor Edith Watts. Faith's secret was using red onions and adding a red bell pepper [see recipe, p. 365]. The color of the soup was glorious and she'd swirl some low-fat sour cream on top in the spiderweb pattern the kids loved. The Fairchilds had altered their diet somewhat since Tom's illness and Faith found there were things, like regular sour cream, that could be replaced with low fat or low sodium without a loss in flavor. Not butter, though. Real butter. She was with Julia on that one.

She noticed the light on the message machine was blinking and she was tempted to ignore it. Her clerical training was too strong, however, and she pushed the button. Being a man or woman of the cloth meant you were *always* on call.

It was Pix and she sounded as if she were phoning from the bottom of a well. Faith increased the volume and played the message again. It was typical Pix Miller. Much hemming and hawing and no information. This one was unusually cryptic, though. Faith knew Ursula was fine and Pix had made a point of saying that everything at Sea Pines was okay when she'd called after her arrival. Probably a sudden need for wardrobe advice. Except Samantha was there. Faith took out her cell and called.

"Hi, I just got your message. What's up?"

"Everything's great and this place is really lovely—the views, the room, and you would love the food. We just finished a fabulous brunch."

"You're with people, right?"

"Absolutely. And the guys are all about to hit the links, what ho, while we womenfolk get massages, the works."

Pix was sounding like a cross between P. G. Wodehouse and Zane Grey. "The links, what ho"? "Womenfolk"?

"Mimosas at brunch?" Faith asked.

Pix was an even cheaper date than Tom when it came to booze and had been known to get slightly tipsy on her mother's rum cake.

"Yes, several."

"Well, you certainly sound cheery. Now, maybe I can guess why you're calling. The massage? I don't think you've ever had one, have you?"

"That's right, and yes, Samantha is going with us."

"So that's not it."

"Nope."

"Is it bigger than a breadbox?"

Entertaining as the conversation was, Faith wanted to get going.

Pix lowered her voice. "Much, much bigger."

"Ah, a person. And he or she is there, so call me when you can talk. We're off to Crane Beach to fly kites."

"Keep an eye out for a snow owl. They might still be there."

"Of course," Faith assured her friend, although this had been most definitely the furthest thought from her mind. But it was the kind of thing Tom got excited about. Bird-watching. A New England trait inbred along with a love of Indian pudding and touch football. She made a mental note to tuck some binoculars and the Sibley bird guide in the canvas tote she'd packed.

"Coming," Pix called to her unseen companions. "I've got to go, but . . . well, I'll call later."

"Have fun, sweetie," Faith said, "and I hope they keep the champagne flowing. You deserve it."

Although the weather was fine and a pale sun shone, the sky and sea at Ipswich were a single shade of gray, almost indistinguishable from the color of the sand as the tide ebbed. The children's kites joined others, rising and falling in brilliant streaks. Tom and Faith walked along the tidemark toward a rocky outcropping in the direction of Castle Hill, a magnificent early-twentieth-century estate open in the warmer months for tours and concerts. Faith had catered events there and it was an exquisite setting, especially at night, the house sitting high on a bluff above the sea, with long views of the North Shore coastline.

Crane Beach was no Sanibel, but soon Faith's pockets were filled with tiny whelk shells and bits of beach glass.

There had been no sign of any snow owls, but plenty of the terns, gulls, and plovers. Tom had the binoculars around his neck.

After determinedly talking about everything except that which was uppermost in their minds, Tom finally said, "Okay. I've gone over and over the past year, all the money I've given out—it's not hard to recall things that are emergencies like this—and I keep coming up with the figure I gave them. No more, no less. Well, we won't discuss it now."

Faith stopped and faced him, forcing him to a standstill also. "It's like a sore in your mouth. You want to keep your tongue from touching it, but you always do. And it's always still there. I think we *should* be discussing this whenever we feel like it and especially as soon as you get back from the bank tomorrow morning."

"Someone there may be able to shed some light on the whole thing, I hope, but we'll have to wait to talk it over. It's one of my days at the VA hospital," Tom said. He took his wife's hand and they turned around, walking slowly back toward Ben and Amy, eyes still trained on the sand the way people do when they walk on a beach.

Faith had forgotten about the VA. Tom was one of the volunteer chaplains there.

"It could be someone at the bank. And he or she could be dipping into more accounts than just yours," Faith said.

Tom shook his head. "I suppose it's possible, but somehow I don't think that's it. Everyone's been there for ages and—well—they know their clients."

Hawthorne Bank and Trust did have branches in several localities, but was scarcely on a scale with Bank of America. There was a bowl of Tootsie Pops on the counter in front of the two teller windows and the bank sent you a birthday card each year signed by everyone at the branch. You were greeted by name. But Faith wasn't so sanguine. It didn't mean the individuals who worked there were immune to corporate greed, although there had been no signs of any bailouts, which seemed to be the signature of this sort of activity these days.

And as for knowing their clients, that might be why Tom's account had been selected. Tom, well respected in the community, a safe target. Or simply because of the nature of the account. This wasn't the first time that Faith had marveled at her husband's innate trust of his fellow man and woman. As for herself, she planned to stop by and start a conversation about vacation destinations. See who'd been on a cruise lately or planning one of those expensive tours of Egypt. The Boston Museum of Fine Arts had mounted a blockbuster Egyptian exhibit, "The Secrets of the Tomb," and suddenly half the population of Massachusetts seemed to be heading for the Nile and the rest were reading or rereading Alan Moorehead.

"The big question is whether the money was taken in cash from the ATM or in checks," Faith said.

"I've been thinking that, too. I get a copy of any checks cashed with my statements and they're all in a binder locked in one of the file cabinets in my office. When I need to distribute some cash, I go to the machine, but there's a record of that, of course, and I save the slips in the same binder attached to the appropriate statement."

"Tom, when is the last time you went over the statements?"

He looked up—and then down. "I've been meaning to . . ." His voice took on a defensive quality. "So much piled up when I was sick and there's never been a problem with the account. In the past I used to go over them for the end-of-the-year report and maybe a few times in between."

"And it wasn't something you could delegate to the parish assistant."

"No."

Soon after Tom's arrival, the parish secretary had been renamed the parish administrative assistant. For many years the post had been ably filled by Rhoda Dawson, who moonlighted on her days off as Madame Rhoda, Psychic Reader. Where was she now when they needed her? Faith wished ruefully. The last she'd heard Rhoda had moved to Sedona and had branched out into aura photography. The post was then filled by Pat Collins for several years. Last winter she'd joyously announced her engagement. She got married soon after and accompanied her military spouse to his new posting at Fort Drum in New York. This year's Christmas card had brought news of a baby due in July. Neither woman would have had access to the particulars of the fund, but somehow Faith's instinct told her that they'd know what had happened—or it wouldn't have happened in the first place. Maybe.

Most men are very bad with change and her husband was no exception. Tom grumbled even as he toasted

Pat at the party the Fairchilds threw for the couple. An ad was placed and the Aleford grapevine alerted. Tom hated all the candidates. They weren't Rhoda or Pat. Finally a friend at the Harvard Divinity School, where Tom had taught during a sabbatical several years ago, told him about Albert Trumbull.

Albert had been in one of Tom's classes and he'd liked the young man—bright and headed for a parish ministry. They'd kept in touch for a while after Tom left. The last Tom had heard Albert had decided to get a doctor of theology degree. And then, he'd abruptly applied for a leave. He'd been looking for a job other than at CVS while he tried to decide what his calling really was.

Tom had gotten in touch with him immediately. No better place to be while you decided whether you wanted to be in a parish than actually in a parish. Albert had arrived and stayed.

"Albert is going to be very upset about all this," Tom said.

"Should you call him when we get home? Give him a heads-up? He's bound to hear the moment he comes to work tomorrow." Faith didn't know the young man very well. He lived in Cambridge and had continued to attend Memorial Church in Cambridge with the minister the Reverend Peter Gomes, limiting his First Parish contact to workdays.

"You're right. I hate to do it by phone, though."

"Tell him what's going on briefly and have him come in early. You can head over to the Minuteman Café to drown your sorrows in coffee and buttermilk pancakes. You'll need plenty of sustenance before you go to the bank."

Tom slung his arm over his wife's shoulders. He was feeling better and he could tell from her suggestion that she was, too. When Faith's thoughts turned in their natural direction—food—he always knew she was okay. A mix-up of some sort. That's all this would turn out to be. He was beginning to think it was a good thing Sherman had brought in the outside CPA and this had come to the vestry's attention. Keep church business on the up and up. It would all get straightened out tomorrow.

They were both reluctant to end the day and sat watching the kids.

Faith had told Tom a little of what Ursula had related the day before and they talked some more about it, both agreeing that Faith should try to spend as much time as possible with her while Pix was away. Wherever the story was going, it was obviously of great importance to Ursula, and it could only help her recovery to have a sympathetic listener. Tom had been as surprised as Faith to hear that Ursula was not an only child. She had often mentioned her parents to Tom, as well as cousins she'd been close to, all of them gone now, but never a brother.

Their conversation turned to Niki.

"I'm worried about her," Tom said. "I wish she'd tell Phil right away. Okay, it's not the best time to break the news, but the longer she waits the worse he's going to feel when he does find out. If it were me, I'd be upset that my wife didn't think I could handle it all. And this isn't macho stuff. Partners, best friends, plus all those words that get said at the altar. You don't keep secrets from each other."

Faith had a very fleeting moment of remorse, remembering secrets she had kept from Tom, mostly having to do with dead bodies, but never secrets about things like a future visit from the stork.

"Absolutely, honey," she said.

The next morning Amy missed her bus again, and after dropping her off at school, Faith arrived at work feeling annoyed with her daughter. This was happening more and more frequently. Amy seemed to have no concept of time, and Faith hated playing the heavy, telling her to hurry up over and over again each morning.

The Ganley Museum Café was closed, like the museum, on Mondays, but Faith wanted to make up two soups—squash with apples and mulligatawny—for tomorrow. Other than the Ganley, the only obligation the catering firm had until the weekend was a dessert buffet for a library fund-raiser. Have Faith was doing it at cost. Libraries were a special passion of Faith's starting in childhood with her neighborhood branch in Manhattan and continuing to the present with Aleford's superlative library. Cutbacks both on the state and town level meant that the library had taken a hit, hence the pressing need for fund-raisers of all sorts. The tickets for the event Thursday night included desserts, beverages, and the opportunity to mingle with a number of local authors who would be signing their books— a portion of the sales would go to the library, too. Exposure for the writers, money for the library—win, win. And it wouldn't hurt Have Faith, either. They'd been prominently featured in the advertising. Niki was planning to feature several trays of rich butter cookies shaped like volumes and brightly iced with the titles of well-known books, including those by the attending authors. She was also doing several kinds of cakes that would look like fanned-out pages.

Niki was at the counter surrounded by springform pans. She greeted Faith with a grin.

"Never let it be said that my mother shirks from any opportunity to help her children. And said help has resulted in a multitude of orders for cheesecakes. Saturday night was Ladies' Night at bingo. I don't even want to think about how she got these orders, but I understand threat of the evil eye may have been involved."

Faith was relieved to hear the old Niki, and her light-hearted tone must also mean she'd told Phil the news.

"I'm sure Phil was overjoyed about being a dad. What did he say? And any nibbles from the networking golf? That's not the right word, but I don't know what else to use. Divots?"

"Turns out the guy is about to lose *his* job and he was hoping Phil had nibbles, divots, or whatever, for him."

"Oh dear," Faith said, hanging up her jacket.

"And I haven't told Phil yet," Niki mumbled.

"Oh dear," Faith said again. She pulled a stool over to the counter and sat down.

"You don't understand," Niki said. No mumbling now. She spoke defiantly. "A Greek man's whole identity is based on his work, his being able to take care of his family. At the moment, Phil only has a wife—an employed wife—so, not so much pressure. I'm not going to burden him with this until he at least has a viable offer."

"Not to be pessimistic, but you're the one who said how bad the job market in the Boston area is right now for MBAs. It could be a while. And what happens when he finds out that you've kept it from him all that time?" Faith recalled what Tom had said. "You're supposed to be partners—for better or worse. How will he feel when he discovers you've been going solo?"

"I don't know and I'm not thinking about it now! I'm just going to make and deliver these cakes!" Tears were streaming down Niki's cheeks. "Damn. Can you get me a Kleenex? I don't want salt dripping in the batter."

Faith pulled a carton from under the counter and moved the bowl away.

"I cry all the time when Phil isn't around," Niki admitted.

"Hormones," Faith said, stirring. It *was* hormones, but it was also Faith's words. She'd made her friend cry. "Look, you do what you think is best. I shouldn't be pressuring you. You know what's right for the two of you. Maybe it's a Greek thing, maybe not—"

Niki interrupted her. "Forget 'best.' I have no idea what I'm doing, boss. And don't shut up. Besides being creepily unnatural for you, I need to hear the other side. You could be right. You're probably right. Oh, I don't know."

"Go wash your face and I'll help you finish the cheesecakes and then we can get the Ganley stuff for tomorrow squared away. I'm spending the afternoon with Ursula."

"How is she doing?"

"Much better, and I'm hoping by the time Pix comes back, she'll be on her feet again."

"Pix at Hilton Head. It sounds like some kind of book. You know, like *The Bobbsey Twins at the Seashore.* My mother bought the whole series at some rummage sale when she first got here. She thought it was what American girls should read. I'm surprised I'm not named Nan or Flossie."

"I talked to Pix on the phone yesterday. She'd left one of her cryptic messages on the answering machine. I still don't know what it's all about. She couldn't talk and was going to call back, but so far no word from the South except that she'd been drinking mimosas, was going to have her first massage, and had encountered something larger than a breadbox, most likely a person, that she wanted to tell me about."

"Mimosas," Niki said wistfully. "No booze for the next eight or so months. You hear that, kid? Mommy's already sacrificing." She paused. "Omigod, I sound just like my mother."

It's a great* *deal to ask, Ursula Lyman Rowe said to herself as she waited for Faith Fairchild to arrive. She thought of the envelope tucked under the cushion of the window seat opposite her bed. She fancied she could see its shape outlined in the William Morris fabric slipcovering, and if she stared at it long enough she might make the paper rise, burning its way through the linen to the surface.

There's no turning back now, though. She knew Faith. She wouldn't let Ursula stop the story. She knew it was something important. Yet, what she didn't know was that at the end she'd have to make a decision herself.

Ursula sat up straighter. Tomorrow she'd insist that Dora let her sit up in her chair. The overstuffed armchair that Arnold had lugged home from an auction downtown. "A perfect reading chair," he'd said. And so it had been, by oneself or to a child curled comfortably on one's lap.

She was feeling better. Saturday night she had slept straight through until morning, not needing Dora to help her to the bathroom and especially not awakening unable to return to sleep—her mind filled with upsetting images.

She heard light steps in the hall. Faith had come.

"Hello, dear. It's so good of you to give up your time this way."

Faith bent over to kiss Ursula's cheek.

"It's a pleasure," she said, and meant it. She'd been looking forward to stepping back into Ursula's long-ago world all day, and not simply as a distraction from the preoccupations of this one. Tom had called to tell her briefly there wasn't much to tell. He'd go over it with her later.

"Open up my top dresser drawer," Ursula said. "At the bottom of my handkerchief box, there's a folder with a photograph. Would you bring it here, please?"

Faith did as she was asked. The box was square and covered in quilted satin that must have once been a brighter rose. A long narrow box that matched it was on the other side of the drawer. Gloves.

She lifted the lid and then carefully removed the stack of embroidered Irish linen handkerchiefs Ursula kept there, along with one of the sachets she and Pix made each summer from the lavender they grew in their herb garden at The Pines on Sanpere. Underneath was the flat cardboard folder with the name of a Boston photography studio in fancy script across the front. Faith took it out, replaced everything, closed the drawer, and walked back over to Ursula.

"Open it up," she said.

Inside was a sepia oval portrait of a man. Just his face. His hair was carefully parted in the middle and he was staring straight at the camera. Although he wasn't smiling—it looked to be a graduation shot or some other momentous occasion—the curve at the corners of his mouth and a glint in his eye suggested that the moment after the shutter snapped, he'd jump up laughing. There was a subtle energy in the face. He was very handsome—and very young.

"That's Theo," Ursula said.

Her next words took Faith completely by surprise.

"Have you ever been to Martha's Vineyard?"

Bewildered at Ursula's sudden change in topic, Faith answered, "Yes, I've been to Martha's Vineyard, but I don't know it well."

Fleeting images of freshly painted white clapboard, bright red geraniums in hanging baskets, wicker porch furniture, American flags, and a genuine Coney Island carousel where she once snatched the brass ring passed through her mind, as well as the Vineyard's "Hollywood East" reputation.

"That's where it happened. On Martha's Vineyard. In a gazebo."

Chapter 4

Ursula pulled her arms out from beneath the light throw Dora had spread over her and folded her hands together. She was stretched out on the chaise. The signal was clear. She was ready to pick up her tale.

"There was a catastrophic winter storm on Sanpere in 1929. Trees came down all over the island and it took many months to repair the damage, and even so just the worst of it. There were several large tamaracks near our house, and with their shallow roots, I imagine they must have been the first to go, stoving in the entire back roof. A big pine took care of much of the front. Father was able to arrange for a temporary fix to keep the weather out, but for the rest he had to wait his turn. As long as he was going to have to do such major repairs, he decided to enlarge the kitchen and add two more bedrooms over it plus a new bath that Mother had been wanting for ages. I was excited about the plans until I heard it meant we wouldn't be able to be there for the summer."

Faith nodded in commiseration. The idea of Sanpere in the summer without Ursula and her family was akin to the swallows giving Capistrano a miss in March.

"Father rented a very large house on Martha's Vineyard that one of his friends from the Somerset Club owned. The man and his wife were taking their daughter, who was just out, to England. No doubt her mama wanted to capture a title for the family. People did in those days."

"Consuelo Vanderbilt," Faith commented.

"Oh yes, the poor Duchess of Marlborough. Her life could have been written by Edith Wharton. In any case, the house on the Vineyard was much grander than either of our houses and I began to feel very guilty at how much I was enjoying the summer."

Ursula's family belonged to the Teddy Roosevelt school of rustication, Faith reflected. Plunges into the frigid deep at dawn, hearty hikes, plain food—as much simple living as money could buy.

"The cottage—that's what the owner called it—was in Oak Bluffs at the end of a long dirt road. It was set overlooking the water with open fields on one side and forest on the other. There were stairs down to the beach and the water was quite warm. I can still smell the beach roses, the same *Rosa rugosas* we have in Maine, but the scent was stronger, or perhaps that's a trick of memory. Along the front of the gray-shingled house, there were rows of hydrangeas with blooms the size of beach balls—quite impossible, but again that's how I see them in my mind's eye. Behind the house there was a massive garden with vegetables as well as flowers. The gardener told me it had been planted before construction was finished so it would look as if it had always been there. The house must have been about twenty years old and there were wide porches and verandas that went around it—we sat out there for tea and often in the evenings. I'm sure the whole thing would now be judged an architectural monstrosity with all sorts of conflicting styles—Arts and Crafts eyebrow windows, Gothic turrets, a Federalist widow's walk— but I adored it. My room was in one of those turrets and at night I could hear the sea and the faint rustle of eelgrass in the soft wind. The weather was perfect that summer. No storms. Blue skies and just the right amount of wind every day. The sailors were in heaven."

She reached for her water glass.

Faith said, "Let me get some fresh water for you, or would you like juice?"

"Water is fine."

"I'm not tiring you, am I?"

"Not at all, Faith dear. I haven't felt this well in weeks."

After she drank some water, Ursula continued. She was talking a bit more quickly now, as if she wanted to get to a certain point before stopping for the day. The almost dreamlike reminiscence gave way to narrative. Faith was pulled in once more. Ursula's description had been so vivid that Faith could clearly visualize the house and surrounding landscape.

"Mother liked it that Father was able to be with us more than he could when we spent the summer in Sanpere. He would often take a Monday to make a long weekend, spent a week in July and planned another in August. Despite the drive and the ferry, it was easier to get to the Vineyard than to The Pines. There was always someone coming or going. With so much space, Mother indulged her love of company. Her sister, my aunt Myrtle, visited a few times with my cousins, who were between Theo and me in age. The two sisters were very close. The flu epidemic in 1918 had taken their parents and their two younger brothers. We used to skip rope to 'I had a little bird / Its name was Enza / I opened the window / And in-flu-enza.' We had no idea what it meant and that millions had died, including our relatives. Mother never said anything. People didn't—at least in our family. Illness was never mentioned. I discovered what happened when I was older and living out in Aleford."

Faith was only too aware of this early-twentieth-century pandemic. The H1N1 swine flu had been the same strain as "the Spanish Flu" or "la Grippe" and there had been some tense weeks before the vaccine was available for the Fairchild children when a cough or slight fever was anxiously watched.

"Other friends of Mother's from the Fragment Society would arrive, and of course my parents knew many people from town who summered on the island."

"Town." Faith was amused at Ursula's Brahmin reference. "Town" always meant "Boston"—as if no other existed.

"Life on Martha's Vineyard was much more social than life on Sanpere. There were Theo's Harvard friends coming for the weekend or dropping in from their parents' places on the island. Father wasn't so keen on all of them. He didn't care for Charles Winthrop, who was older and in a rather fast set at the college, or a girl named Violet Hammond. She wasn't at Harvard, only men in those days. Father did like Schuyler Jessup, who was a great pal of Theo's. Scooter—he was always called that—was often around and usually brought a girl named Babs Dickson, whose parents were friends of Father and Mother's, with him. They later married. She was one of those athletic young women who always seemed to have a tennis racquet or a golf club in her hand. She wasn't in college, but some sort of finishing school. I have no idea what she could have been doing there in those days. Certainly not learning to embroider and curtsy. Her father thought college courses put too great a strain on a woman's mind. Such nonsense. What did he think? Her brain would suddenly explode? He didn't seem to mind her straining her body, and I remember thinking how beautifully she moved—very feline, and with all this pent-up energy.

"The weekends Father stayed in town, the group would always come down. At night they'd roll up the rugs in the living room and dance. Mother didn't mind. And all day long they kept the Victrola going. Rudy Vallee, Bix Beiderbecke, Louis Armstrong. There was a piano, too. Someone always seemed to be playing it. Scooter was the best. He had a very pleasant voice. Whenever I hear certain Cole Porter songs, they take me back to that summer."

Ursula gazed across the room at the large window. Faith had the feeling that it had become a kind of screen and Ursula was watching these figures from her childhood cavort across the sunlight.

"Theo had passed his English literature course on the condition that he write several papers over the summer. But he had failed mathematics, so would have to repeat it. Father hired a tutor, a serious young man who had just graduated and was entering the law school in the fall. He was from the Midwest, an only child, and neither parent was living, so he had to make his own way in the world—a scholarship student, which was rare in those days. He'd been the teaching assistant in Theo's medieval history class, and Father was convinced that their study sessions were the reason Theo had passed, and he was no doubt right. Theo called him 'the Professor' and soon everyone, even Father, did. I remember the first time I saw him. He had the most beautiful eyes I had ever seen—brown with tiny flecks of gold."

This brought a smile to Faith's face. A crush. Growing up, she'd had many herself.

"There weren't any children my age, and except for the people I've mentioned, no one was living at the house that summer besides the servants, although those who were local went home at night. I didn't mind. There was the whole outdoors to play in and my books to read indoors, and out. I also learned a new language—Martha's Vineyard Sign Language. I thought it was great fun. There was an extremely high percentage of hereditary deafness on the island dating back to the eighteenth century, peaking in the mid-nineteenth, but still quite prevalent, especially in Chilmark, well into the twentieth. The gardener was deaf, as were several of the kitchen help. One of them, who was very young and very pretty, made rather a pet of me. I learned to sign by watching the servants talk—all of the ones from the island used it, even the ones who weren't deaf. When I became adept, which was rather quickly—children pick up these things so much more easily than adults—I discovered that they liked my mother, feared my father, and thought Theo and his friends were very funny.

"I thought all the grown-ups were endlessly fascinating and I became very clever at finding places where I could observe them undetected. Under the piano in the living room was a good place. And then there was my own special place—not so much a place from which to watch people, but a kind of fort I'd made for myself underneath the rhododendrons next to a gazebo. It was quite an elaborate one that the owners had had constructed in the woods—more like a summerhouse or folly—a screened-in octagon with a wide bench around the sides. When I first happened upon it, I thought it belonged in something like Frances Hodgson Burnett's *The Secret Garden*, but upon reflection I decided it was more suited to Grimm. It was set away from the main house, deep in the woods down a dark, narrow path, nothing like a garden gazebo. It became my favorite spot. That hiding place by the gazebo . . ."

"You just don't trust me, Father! Dash it! The Professor's a good chap and I'm all for helping him out, but I don't need a tutor down at the Vineyard this summer. I'm more than capable of writing the papers myself, and as for the math, I would have passed the exam if I had felt better." Theo stopped short. He didn't want to go into the reason for the monstrous headache that had caused the numbers to swim before his eyes and the feeling that he might retch at any moment, which kept him from putting down what little he did know on the paper before him. It had been foolish to go off with Charles, but it was only going to be for a quick bite at Jim's Place in the Square, and then Violet had appeared with a friend. It would have been rude not to ask them to a show in town and supper afterward.

Violet. Theo tried to concentrate on what his father was saying. It should have been easy. The old man was shouting. But he kept seeing Violet's face—that impossibly alabaster skin, ruby lips, flashing sapphire eyes. He wished he were a poet. Maybe he'd give it a try. "Thine eyes like pools of melted sky." Not bad. Not bad at all.

"Theo! Have you heard one word of what I've been saying?"

"Of course, sir. You think I'm a 'wastrel' and need a watchdog. I give in. I'll let the Professor keep my nose to the grindstone."

Theo had absorbed enough from his English courses to know he had muddled any number of metaphors. He found himself trying hard not to smile. His father was right. He wasn't taking all this seriously. Slacker fellows than he was had graduated. It had been important to protest at the start, but Theo knew this was one he couldn't win so there was no need to drag the unpleasantness out.

Theodore Artemus Lyman—he'd given his son a different middle name, Speedwell, which seemed enormously ironic at the moment—sighed heavily and got up. "See that you do. I'll be getting weekly reports, and those papers must be submitted to the college by the end of July."

"Don't worry, Father. It's going to be a wonderful summer."

"That's what I'm afraid of," Mr. Lyman muttered as his feckless son escaped out the door.

Ursula crouched lower behind one of the tall blue and white Japanese porcelain jars that stood in the hallway on either side of the library door. Soon she wouldn't be able to fit into the space between the jar and the wall—it was getting to be a tight fit—and one of her favorite hiding places would be gone. You could hear everything that was said in the library, especially if the door hadn't been closed all the way as today. She loved the jars, with their misty scenes of landscapes that came straight from one of Andrew Lang's fairy-tale collections. She leaned her cheek against the jar's cool surface and closed her eyes, gently tapping the rim. She imagined that the soft, clear note was a temple gong and shadowy figures were moving in a rapid wave toward a shrine.

She leaned back against the wall and opened her eyes, in no hurry to move. School was over for the year and the house was in an uproar of cleaning and packing. Most of the rooms would be shut, the furniture draped like so many ghosts. Father would dine at his club and only use his library, one sitting room, and his bed and dressing rooms.

Poor Theo! It was a shame that he'd have to spend his summer studying, but Ursula was glad the Professor would be with them. When she had been introduced to him, she'd immediately asked him if he liked birds, and instead of answering "Only songbirds, kiddo," as Scooter had, the Professor had replied, "All birds or specifically shore, meadow, or woodlands?" He wouldn't be working with Theo every minute, and she'd already packed the Leitz binoculars she'd asked for and received for her birthday plus her little life-list notebook bound in bright red Moroccan leather, hoping he would join her when she searched for new sightings to add.

She was worried about what the storm on Sanpere had done to her things—her bedroom was in the back of the house, which had received the worst damage. Was her fern collection safe? She'd spent hours neatly pressing, labeling, and gluing them into a scrapbook. And what about the abandoned birds' nests she'd found and arranged on a shelf in her room? For all she knew they could be in a sodden heap in the middle of the floor. It was exciting to go to a new place, but she wished they could go to Sanpere for just a little while, even if they had to stay elsewhere. Her father had promised a full account of her things. He was going up in August to check on the work. She sighed. It was a long time to wait.

What was this summer going to be like? In her mind the two events—the damage to the Sanpere house and Theo's disastrous grades—had somehow merged together as the reason why they had to go to this new island. It might not make sense, but it was how she felt.

Why couldn't Theo just do his schoolwork and then go have fun afterward! That was why he kept failing. All that fun. He needed more serious friends, although Scooter was awfully nice. But a friend who would keep him from his weaknesses. A friend like the Professor.

Father had just said that Theo must get it through his head that he would have to make his own way in the world. Theo had laughed and said that was exactly what he intended to do—enter the business world like his father. He'd quoted former President Coolidge, "The business of America is business." Ursula knew this was one thing father and son agreed on—and on what a great man the new President, Herbert Hoover, was. Father had replied, "That's all very well, but you have to be a college man, son. You have to be a Harvard man, like all the Lyman men." Theo had answered that he knew that, although from the amount of money his barber on Dunster Street was making on the stock market, maybe college wasn't so important these days. In the next breath, he'd said he was kidding and his father had laughed. Told him to get some tips. "He shaves some pretty wealthy faces and my broker's is one of them, I'll have you know."

Ursula had hoped the talking-to would end on this cheerful note. Maybe Theo would have time to take her to the new Marx brothers movie, but Father got agitated about Theo's grades again and her brother rushed by her so fast she couldn't wiggle out in time to stop him.

She hoped he could wiggle out of the trouble he was in and make it a good summer. He just had to. Suddenly Ursula felt trapped by the big vase and struggled to slip out. Tossing her hair back over her shoulders and away from her flushed face, she decided she was too old for this kind of behavior and wished she could get back the talismans she'd placed in the jars that even now she could barely reach—a pearl button she'd found on the street, a British sixpence, the ticket from the first symphony concert she'd attended, and all those lines of poetry she'd written on tiny scraps of paper—offerings to oblivion. It would be impossible to retrieve them now without tipping the vases over.

The front door banged shut. Theo was gone.
Her eyes filled with tears.

Pix looked at her nails. She vaguely remembered that it was supposed to mean something if you looked at them with your fingers stretched out or curled into the palm—like wearing your circle pin on the correct side of your blouse collar. Somehow the manicurist had transformed them into perfect pink shells—and the same with her toes. She really should have them done more often.

And now she knew why people loved getting massages. She'd been so relaxed she'd dozed off. And that facial! Last night as she carefully applied her makeup—mouth and eyes—the glowing face in the mirror looked five, no ten, years younger. She felt positively sybaritic. And not at all like herself. Well, there was a reason for that . . .

She picked up her phone and, conscious of her nails, carefully dialed Faith.

"I was just going to call you! Your mother is doing so well. We had a nice, long visit this afternoon, and when I left Dora said she was going to get her up longer tomorrow and into her big chair after they do their constitutionals in the hallway. How was the massage? And the in-laws?"

"It's been wonderful. Cissy is the planner and she seems to have thought of everything. Yesterday was fun—and the massage was terrific. We'd all been together almost constantly since we arrived, and she was sensitive enough to tell everyone that for last night, we'd all go our own ways."

"Smart lady. This bodes well for the future, especially when it comes to sharing grandchildren. What did you and Sam do?"

"Absolutely nothing. Long walk on the beach and then a room service dinner on the patio we have right outside our room."

"This doesn't sound like the Sam and Pix Miller I know. Are you sure you didn't squeeze in something educational or strenuous?" Faith laughed. "Sounds romantic, however, so perhaps there was some exercise after all? I know you're blushing, Pix."

Pix was.

Faith continued. "But what was it you wanted to tell me? Your mysterious bigger-than-a-breadbox item."

"Oh Faith, you know that line from *Casablanca* when Bogart says, 'Of all the gin joints in all the towns in all the world, she walks into mine'?"

"Of course."

"Well, of all the weddings in all the towns in all the world, Dr. Stephen Cohen has walked into mine."

"What on earth are you talking about? Don't tell me you know him?"

"It was when we were in college, and yes, I know him."

"But isn't that a nice coincidence? A sign that this match was meant to be? One of those serendipitous cosmic coincidences? Unless he was and is a total jerk."

"No, the opposite, in fact. But Faith, I *knew* him."

"Are we talking about 'know' as in, say, the biblical usage?"

Pix raised her voice, "Oh honey, yes, I'm all ready to go. Just checking on Mother with Faith. Everything's fine."

"Sam came in?"

"Yes—and yes to your other question. Gotta run, talk to you later."

Faith closed her phone and looked out the window. Barring a blizzard, the daffodils would be in bloom for Easter, less than three weeks away. She found herself unable to alter her gaze, or move her body away from the spot where she'd been standing while she was on the phone. Cliché that it was, truly life was way stranger than fiction. No one could have made this up. Myrtle, aka Pix, Rowe Miller, her best friend and next-door neighbor and currently starring as the mother of the groom in a swanky resort in Hilton Head, South

Carolina, had, in her distant past, slept with the father of the bride.

Riveting as both Ursula's saga and Pix's still to be revealed were, Faith turned her thoughts to assembling a chicken dish, a variation of coq au vin, for dinner before picking up Ben from his clarinet lesson—thank heavens it wasn't something large like a tuba or loud like drums—and Amy from a friend's, where she was working on a science project. Faith sometimes thought all she'd ever remember about her children's school years were science projects. They seemed to pop up with alarming frequency and require an endless amount of time. Fortunately the papier-mâché model of the inner ear was being constructed at someone else's house this time. Faith was still finding Popsicle sticks from the scale model of a cyclotron that Ben made in fifth grade. Could that be right? Maybe she was confusing it with the scale model of the Alamo for history. She was in no hurry to see her children grow up and go off on their own, but she greeted each vacation from school and school-related tasks as a reprieve, with summer the best of all.

When Faith returned with kids, Tom was home ahead of them, and from the bleak smile he gave them as they came through the back door, she knew the news from the bank hadn't been good. She hustled the kids off to do homework and put the chicken in the oven. It was comfort food. The Fairchilds liked dark meat, so she had used the whole legs, adding carrots, onions, parsnips, and some garlic before dousing it with red wine and seasoning it with fresh sage and a small amount of salt and pepper. Covered, it baked in the oven for an hour before she took the foil off to brown it [see recipe, p. 366]. She was serving it tonight with potatoes she'd steamed, sautéed in oil and butter, before liberally sprinkling it with more sage [see recipe, p. 368].

"There's no question," Tom said. "The money was taken out of the account at intervals over about nine months or so using an ATM, and all from the one at the Aleford branch. Five hundred dollars is the limit that can be withdrawn in one day and that was the amount of each transaction. Twenty in all. The last one was made the night before we left for Maine in December."

"Merde!" She reverted to the strong French epithet she'd adopted when the kids were little, but old enough to understand, and mimic, the English ones. She had been hoping that the withdrawals would have occurred when Tom was verifiably somewhere else. "And the others? None when you were in the hospital?"

Tom shook his head. "Several when I was recuperating at home, but I was up and about. It's not a long walk to the bank."

Faith sighed. The parsonage, like the church, bordered the Aleford green, as did several old houses plus the historic tavern where the minutemen may have bolstered their courage by hoisting a few that April morning. Main Street snaked around the side and kept going straight through the town. With good binoculars, you could see the bank at, memorably enough, 1776 Main.

"When did the withdrawals start? That should tell us something."

"Just about a year ago. I have all the dates."

"Have there been any new employees at the bank during this time? It seems to me there was a new teller that winter."

"No new tellers, just several from other branches who filled in when someone was sick or had another reason for missing work. And they'd have no way of knowing my PIN. I'm the only one. No other changes in the additional employees, either."

"What about checking the tape from the surveillance camera?"

Again Tom shook his head.

"Mice chewed the wires. They didn't discover it until January. Nothing had recorded since the previous year."

This was a perennial hazard in rural Aleford. The Ganley Museum's cameras were always being attacked by rodents with a taste for what Faith imagined was a well-aged blend of plastic and metal—provocative with a hint of fruitiness.

Her husband looked exhausted and Faith decided the rest of this conversation could wait while he stretched out on the couch before dinner. He could watch the news. That would put things into perspective.

"Why don't you catch *The News Hour* while I finish dinner? We're not going to solve this now."

But we will, she added to herself.

Both kids somehow seemed to have developed their own versions of the Vulcan Mind Meld at too early an age, and during dinner Faith kept up a steady stream of conversation about Ursula's childhood reminiscences in order to keep Ben and Amy from figuring out that something was terribly wrong. It had been an effort at first, but soon they were all talking about what it must have been like in the predigital age. And then they got on to the Great Depression. Ben was filled with facts and figures.

"Thirteen million people lost their jobs. And they had these places called 'Hoovervilles,' after the President, where homeless people lived in cardboard cartons and slept under blankets made out of newspapers. They called them 'Hoover Blankets.' The day all the banks failed was called 'Black Tuesday,' but my history teacher said it isn't true that a lot of the rich guys who'd lost all their money jumped out their office windows. Maybe just a couple. She also said that even though a lot of those rich people did lose all their money, a lot held on to it and made even more."

Faith was impressed, both with her son and his teacher. Amy's mouth had dropped open.

"They only had newspapers for blankets! Why didn't the rich people buy them real ones?"

Tom and Faith looked at each other. One of those unanswerable questions, then as now.

"Well, sweetheart, they weren't thinking straight," Tom said.

"Or kindly," Amy added emphatically.

As Ursula, whom Faith had come to regard as a kind of Yankee Sheherazade, told her tale, the parallels between the summer of 1929 and the current economic situation were eerily similar—the ever-widening gap between rich and poor with the middle swallowed up in the process.

After dinner, Ben retreated to work on a story he was doing for extra credit in English. Bless the compelling practice teacher, Faith thought, and slightly uneasily added, and hormones. Amy was taking a shower at her mother's insistence. Eliminating her daughter's morning one might help her make the bus on time.

Tom had gone into his study only to emerge fifteen minutes later to make a cup of tea for himself.

"Want one?"

"No, thanks," Faith said. "But I'll keep you company with some milk and broken library books I brought home from work."

Understandably Tom looked puzzled.

"Cookies Niki's making for the fund-raiser," Faith explained.

Before the water molecules boiled, Tom's did. He was up and pacing around the room.

"I go back and forth. Resign—or not? Replace the missing funds . . ."

Faith gasped. Ten thousand dollars was a rather large chunk of change. And resign? This couldn't be happening . . .

"Except," Tom said, "both could be taken as an admission of guilt."

The little bird on the kettle was whistling. Faith made the tea.

"Tom, no one in the parish possibly believes you took the money. Maybe they think there was a careless error, but not malicious intent."

"Tell that to Sherman Munroe. The way he looked at me in church yesterday you'd think I was keeping a mistress in a fancy condo at the Ritz."

Tom's notions of what things cost were delightfully naïve. Faith had always paid for her own clothes and gifts for her husband from a separate account that she'd had since before her marriage, setting it up again when she moved to Aleford. Faith had curbed her youthful label fetish over the years, but still, if Tom had known what the deceptively simple little black dress Faith had worn to a recent party cost, he'd faint.

"The missing money might cover two nights. You and your mistress will have to scale down."

Tom reached for a cookie.

Faith reached for a pad of paper and a pencil.

"You're not going to get anything done tonight on your sermon, so let's make a start on finding out who's really responsible. Eventually this will lead to the money, and although I'm sure it's long gone, whoever it is will have to replace it—and then some." Faith was thinking jail time.

"You're right. I can't concentrate on anything else."

"Walk me through the whole thing. Where do you keep the Discretionary Fund records, the list of amounts? And where do you keep the checkbook and ATM card? Here or at the church?"

"They're all together in a file in my office at the church. Together with the bank statements, which are in a binder. The ATM card is slipped under the plastic thing that separates the checks from deposit slips in the checkbook wallet."

"And everything is sitting there in one of your file drawers, clearly labeled? Easy for anyone to access when you're not there?"

"Not so easy. It's one of the locked file cabinets and you'd have to know which one, plus have the key."

"Okay." Faith felt they were getting somewhere. "You keep the file cabinet keys on your ring with the keys to your office, the church, and the house?"

Tom looked down. "I'm afraid I keep those keys in one of my desk drawers."

"Unlocked?"

"Unlocked."

He looked guilty as sin. Faith got up and hugged him from behind, resting her chin on his head. He always smelled so good. A clean, slightly citrus soapy smell and something ineffable that was Tom.

"Obviously, this is a problem that goes with the turf. Trusting humankind." She wouldn't have him any other way, but it was going to hurt him now.

She began to think out loud. "Still, although this widens the field of suspects"—adding to herself, The entire congregation plus passersby—"we should focus on people who have been in and out of your office in the past year with some frequency. People who would know where you kept the checkbook and card, as well as the keys."

She sat back down and picked up the pencil.

Tom looked better. He reached for another cookie—the white lettering on the chocolate icing read, *The Hunch*. Faith took it as an omen.

"Albert, although I can't imagine—"

Faith interrupted him. "Yes you can. Think Dorothy Sayers, 'Suspect everyone.'" She wrote down, "Albert Trumbull, parish administrative assistant."

"All right. Next. James came on board as associate minister a year and a half ago when Walter retired."

For most of his career in the ministry, Walter Pratt had divided his time between First Parish and teaching at Andover Newton. He'd never wanted to assume the top job, telling Tom he was "content to watch from the sidelines." This was a false description of his active involvement. When Walter died suddenly of a massive coronary, Tom had taken it not only as a personal loss, but a loss of part of the parish's history. More than once since Saturday's meeting with the vestry, he'd wished Walter were by his side still.

Faith wrote down, "James Holden, associate minister."

Quickly Tom ticked off, "Lily Sinclair, our Div School intern—she arrived about a year ago, as I recall, and left in the beginning of this January for her last semester. Eloise Gardner, education director. I suppose we have to include the sexton, Eli Brown, he's in and out of my office. And the vestry. Some have a more visible presence than others."

"Sherman, for example."

"Sherman, for example," Tom agreed grimly.

It wasn't a long list, except for the vestry, which was composed of five individuals elected by the congregation plus the senior and junior wardens. Faith put those names on the bottom of the sheet. Meetings weren't held in Tom's office, so she'd ask him at another time to take a look and see if any of the names, other than Sherman's, popped up as people who'd been around more than the others.

She took his mug and made him another cup of tea.

Action was obviously the antidote for this poisonous situation. Yet, Tom couldn't be directly involved. Which left . . .

"Anyone working directly with you probably knows you keep keys in your desk drawers. Or if they don't, it would be the first place anyone would look. I think the next step is getting to know Albert, James, Lily, Eloise, and even Mr. Brown"—the sexton was pushing eighty and was usually called "Mr. Brown," as a sign of respect, Faith supposed—"a whole lot better. I'll start digging."

If it weren't for that fact that this was her beloved who was involved, she'd be greeting the prospect with pleasure. Incurably curious, she had already started to speculate on what might be under the rocks she turned over.

Pix knew she looked good even before her appreciative husband gave a low whistle when she came out to the patio where he was reading the morning paper. They'd had a leisurely breakfast before she went to get dressed. Faith had nixed Pix's dubious collection of jeans, many of them hand-me-downs from her boys once they shot up, all of them worn at the knees from gardening. The jeans she put on today were new and fit like a second skin, making her long, shapely legs look even more so. She was wearing a royal-blue tank top with a large, oversized broadly striped shirt in blue and white, the tails tied around her still slim waist. Kind of like Sandra Dee in one of those Tammy movies, Pix had thought when Faith demonstrated the way she believed the outfit worked best.

There was a wonderful place in Brooklin, Maine—Blossom Studio—that made glass beads, which were transformed into exquisite forms of jewelry. Sam had given her a simple gold neck wire with a large frosted Nile-green bead. She'd put that on at the last minute, and some makeup.

She'd only been away from Aleford for three days, but it felt like a month, a very pleasant month.

The Cohens had been coming to Hilton Head since Rebecca was born and Pix recognized kindred spirits in their desire to show off the place they loved. It was the way she felt taking guests around Sanpere for the first time. Today Stephen and Cissy had arranged an ecotour by boat with a captain knowledgeable not only about the Low Country's natural life but its history as well. The boat was large enough for all of them, but small enough to get close to the osprey, herons, ibis, egrets, and perhaps, away from the inlets and marshlands, dolphins. They'd be on the ocean heading for a picnic lunch on Daufuskie Island, one of South Carolina's Gullah Sea Islands.

Walking toward Sam, she'd flashed back to another time many, many years earlier when she'd emerged dressed and ready to go. She'd known she looked good that time, too, and the man—a young man, not long out of his teens—had whistled, too.

"Wow," he'd said. "I thought you were going to be a dog. Brian never said, I mean, excuse me, this is coming out all wrong, sugar. Let me start over." She'd been instantly charmed by his soft Southern accent, laughed, and taken his arm. His comment didn't sound all wrong to her, not at all.

When her roommate at Brown had first suggested Pix come with her for Green Key Weekend at

Dartmouth, Pix had refused. Mindy was from Savannah, and she'd met Brian when she'd gone home for the holidays. They'd been seeing each other since—or rather "keeping company."

"You can't sit and pine for that Sam Miller all weekend. It was time you two went your separate ways. I mean, you've known him your whole life, right? Isn't that kind of like incest? Besides, why should you be the one to mope around the dorm when he's the one who gave you that sad old line about needing some space? I swear, any man that says that to me is going to see some space—outer space."

Pix hadn't been able to contradict her. Everything she'd said was true.

"You need a real man, not one of these ice-cold Yankees. Brian's roommate, Steve, sounds perfect for you. Real outdoorsy. He said to bring your skis. He's premed. You'd never starve as a doctor's wife."

"Whoa," Pix had said. "If I do go, and I'm not saying I will, isn't it a little too soon to be planning a trip down the aisle?"

"It's never too soon for that, darlin.' "

Considering that Mindy was Phi Beta Kappa and applying to law schools, she wasn't just going for her MRS degree. But she had told Pix the beginning of their sophomore year when they'd started rooming together that although she planned to have a career, a successful one, there was nothing more important in life than being a good wife and mother.

From the Class Notes, Pix knew that Mindy had achieved all three of her goals, or so it seemed on paper. After graduation, they hadn't stayed in touch.

Several of the girls on her floor had raised an eyebrow when she mentioned she was going to Green Key at Dartmouth—one said something vague about testosterone and be prepared to run—but the more Pix had thought about it the more she'd decided Mindy was right. Sam Miller wasn't the only fish in the sea. And the more she'd gone over their last conversation when he'd said he wanted some space, wanted to see other people, the madder she got. Yes, they had known each other a long time—not their whole lives, just since middle school. But so what?

Walking toward her Dartmouth date, who was not short, as she'd feared, and very good-looking, she'd been glad she'd gone.

Just as this Hilton Head time was starting to pass in a rapid blur, that weekend had been a blur—except a blur of parties with lots of dancing. There was always plenty of some kind of delicious fruit punch at the fraternity houses, and she'd been amused by traditions like the raucous "chariot" races with fraternity members serving as the chariot horses, charging across the college green while onlookers pelted them with water balloons and eggs.

She never did go skiing, and by Sunday, she'd convinced herself that Steve, not Sam, was the real love of her life. She had a vague recollection of explaining this at length to Mindy Saturday night while sipping a lot of that yummy punch. She'd awakened with a start, and a headache, late Sunday morning in Steve's room, in Steve's bed.

They'd talked on the phone a few times and he was supposed to come down to Providence when Brian did. And then she was supposed to go to Hanover for some spring skiing. They never saw each other again and it was a pleasant memory of the kinds of things one does in youth and never again. Pix avoided all and any kinds of punch for many years.

The following summer she was home in Aleford running the tennis program at a local day camp. Early one evening—one of those perfect summer evenings when the light is so long it makes everything look like a stage set—Sam Miller knocked on her door, got down on one knee, held up a ring, and said, "I've been a complete idiot. First forgive me, and then marry me."

Which they did right after graduation the following June at First Parish with the reception at Longfellow's Wayside Inn.

When she'd seen Stephen Saturday she'd recognized him immediately, despite a receding, and gray, hairline. Mark had always referred to his future father-in-law as "Rebecca's father" or "Dr. Cohen." Steve had been premed when Pix knew him, but the country was filled with doctors with that last name. It had simply never occurred to her that the two were one and the same. Yes, her Steve—well, not really hers—was from the South, but in that insular way of her fellow Northeasterners, she tended to think of Dixie as one large cup.

She'd also been afraid she might have been mistaken. Context is everything, and she'd been finding as she grew older that more and more frequently people were looking familiar. She'd thought she saw her mother's dear Norwegian friend on the subway a month ago. It seemed an impossibility, but she was still about to greet her when she realized it wasn't Marit at all. Context. People greeted her and she knew she knew them, but from where? PTA days? Volunteering at Rosie's Place? Sanpere?

Yet, it had only taken a few seconds to be absolutely sure who Stephen Cohen was, and had been.

"I want to call Faith about Mother, since we'll be gone all day and I doubt our cell phones will work on the water. Would you go down in case they're already waiting? I won't be long."

Sam gave her a kiss, and then another.

"You want to blow this off? Just you and me today?"

Pix smiled. She supposed she was having what people called a "second honeymoon"—with at least one man.

"That would be terribly rude, but I'll take a rain check."

As soon as he was out the door, she called Faith, who was at work but said she had a moment to chat.

"Now, tell me everything, Ms. Miller. To think, you have a past I know nothing about! You sly little minx!"

Pix told her everything.

Faith reacted with enthusiasm. "I'm glad you kicked up your heels a little—that time and whenever else in your flaming youth. Clearly Sam was the one, but you needed to find out you could be the one for somebody else, too."

"It was all a long time ago," Pix said, "and I'm pretty sure those Dartmouth boys were pouring every known kind of alcohol into the punch bowl, but it happened and I'm not sorry. Not about that weekend."

"Then what?"

"Oh Faith," Pix cried. "He doesn't remember me!"

Chapter 5

Down East, Faith had occasionally heard someone described as being "sick with secrets," and while she didn't think she had reached that point, she definitely felt she was suffering from a surfeit of them as she sat next to Ursula in the early afternoon on Wednesday. There was the missing money at First Parish, which Faith hoped Ursula would not hear about, knowing how upset the former Senior Warden would be. And then there was Niki, whom Ursula knew. The older woman would most certainly think the news of a wife's pregnancy should be shared with her husband. However, these paled in comparison to the situation Ursula's daughter found herself in—a situation to be kept from her mother at all costs.

Faith had spoken to Pix the day before at greater length and had tried, in vain, to convince her that she had not aged beyond recognition since college. Yes, her hair was a bit shorter, but it showed no silver threads among the bronze. Nor had she gained weight, and if any cottage-cheese cellulite existed, it wasn't apparent, even in a bathing suit. A few crow's-feet at the eyes, but the rest of her face was smooth. Faith only hoped she would look as good as Pix did some years hence. Of course for Faith, there was always a Plan B involving a discreet "vacation." Pix had not and never would resort to cosmetic surgery. When the wrinkles appeared, as they would, she'd be one of those people who say they've earned them. Faith would be one of those people who say they've earned erasing them—the result not Joan Rivers or Nancy Reagan, but merely a slightly younger version of her own self.

"Okay, maybe he doesn't recognize me physically, but he should remember my name. It's not as if there could have been a lot of other people named Pix in his life, and especially not that weekend."

From what Faith had heard about the wild Green Key weekends of yore, there would have been a plethora of Muffys, Bunnys, and yes, Pixes from the Seven Sisters, Ivies, and other schools in attendance. But she was also sure this wasn't why Dr. Cohen didn't remember her friend's name. Faith had no doubt as to the reason.

"It's a guy thing. Think about it. Remembering names, especially female names, is not in their DNA. I've caught Tom stumbling over them more than once. Do admit, you've seen this with Sam—and your sons."

"Well . . . yes," Pix had said, "and my father could never keep people straight, female and male. Mother used to whisper in his ear at parties, she told me, so she wouldn't be embarrassed when he forgot that the next-door neighbors were Sally and Bob, not Susie and Bill."

"Okay, feel better now?"

There had been a long pause.

"So, I guess I was just a one-night stand?"

Faith had had to go through it all over again and at the end Pix had still sounded forlorn.

Before she'd hung up, Faith told Pix, "Don't you dare let this put a damper on everything. Tonight I want you in that strapless number we bought. I guarantee that Stephen Cohen and every other Y chromosome in the place will never forget you in that."

Pix had sworn her to secrecy and Faith would never violate the trust, but she wished she could tell someone, Niki in particular. Faith could discuss the situation with her, and yes, have a giggle. The person she had absolutely no desire to tell was the woman next to her now. Parents didn't need to know everything.

As she thought this she realized, however, she wasn't anywhere near this point with her kids.

This was going to be the third installment of Ursula's tale, and as each chapter was revealed, she seemed to gain strength and look better. "Sick with secrets." The phrase came back to Faith again. Was this what had been ailing Ursula?

"You are good to come and listen so patiently, Faith dear. I'm sure you have all sorts of better things to do," Ursula said.

"Please don't think this—and there's no rush. Things are very slow at work and I have plenty of time. Being with you is exactly where I want to be," Faith said, meaning every word and then some. Faith felt honored at having been chosen to hear whatever it was Ursula needed to reveal—and it transported her away from her other worries.

"Throughout life," Ursula began slowly, "there are times when you read about a terrible tragedy and want to turn time back for an instant. When you want to keep someone from getting on a plane or opening a door. Or you may even want to turn time back many years, granting someone a happier childhood instead of the one that led to misery and worse—that sort of thing. You say to yourself, 'What if?' Since that summer, my turning-back-time 'what if' has been,

'What if Father hadn't gone to Sanpere that August weekend?' "

Faith nodded. She knew the feeling well—and it worked in the other direction, as well. Times you didn't want to change. What if she hadn't accepted the catering job at the wedding reception where she'd met Tom? Their paths would never have crossed otherwise.

"As I mentioned, the house in Maine was undergoing major construction. In those days, getting to the island took much longer than five hours and involved train and steamboat travel. Father had hoped to get away from work at the end of July, but there were already rumblings of the crisis that would occur on Black Tuesday and he had to stay in town. He never discussed business with me and all I knew then was that Father was 'very occupied with work.' Again, if he had been able to go earlier, would it have changed what happened?"

Ursula looked steadily out the window for a few moments before continuing.

"I rather think not. Naturally Theo thought this would be the perfect time to have the house party he'd been talking about all summer and my mother agreed. He would have picked any time Father was gone for a long stretch. Unlike Father, who thought their music was an assault to the ears and their dress the same to the eyes, Mother liked having the young people around. She seemed very old to me, but she was only just forty. And, in any case, she never denied Theo anything. It was Father who didn't spare the rod—not literally, but definitely figuratively. I know the Professor didn't think the party was a very good idea. At the time I thought it was because Theo still had so much math to study if he was going to pass the course in the fall. Later I learned there were other reasons.

"Some of the guests were at their family houses on the island, but Scooter Jessup, Babs Dickson, Charles Winthrop, and Violet Hammond were all staying with us. I think those young women were the most beautiful creatures I've ever seen. I was completely captivated by them—the way they talked, and especially by the way they looked. Years later when I read Fitzgerald's *Gatsby*, there was a line that has stayed with me about Daisy Buchanan and Jordan Baker weighing down their white summer dresses 'like silver idols' against the breeze a fan was making. When I read it I was back in the living room of the house on the Vineyard watching from a corner as the music played and the breeze from an open window caused those sheer white linen dresses to ripple ever so slightly."

Ursula was back in the room now, too, and from her description Faith could clearly see the images of the women. Bobbed hair, Clara Bow mouths, and rolled stockings. Flappers. Those "silver idols."

"Violet Hammond was the most beautiful of all. She truly did have violet eyes. How could her parents have known the name they chose was going to be so apt? I've never heard of babies with such dramatic-colored eyes and I've never seen such eyes again, except in an Elizabeth Taylor movie. But not on a person I knew. The men were all mad for her. She had a very beautiful voice, too. Husky, not high-pitched, and she spoke softly. Years later I wondered whether this was so people, especially men, would have to lean in closer to hear her.

"And she wore a very distinctive perfume. She said she had it made up for her in Paris. It wasn't floral. Nothing as mundane as lilacs or roses. Sandalwood, or some other exotic Far Eastern scent."

"She *does* sound lovely," Faith murmured.

"Oh yes, exquisite. Her people were from Chicago. She'd been sent to Boston to live with a cousin of her mother's. I don't think I ever knew why, although I have an idea that she was taking a painting course at the Museum of Fine Arts. She was just out of school—I think it may have been Miss Porter's or Dobbs—and she'd been a famous beauty there, too, very popular with the boys at Yale. The cousin lived on Beacon Street across from the Common, and I don't think Violet received much supervision from her. Mother never said anything directly, but she made it clear that the Hammonds were not, well, people she'd care to know. I heard her talking to her sister, Myrtle, about them. The 'Chicago Hammonds' as opposed to 'our Hammonds.' It wasn't about money. Even though Violet had gone to an expensive private boarding school, it was my impression the family wasn't very wealthy. She never appeared in the same outfit twice, but I think that's why I have the idea she was doing something artistic—she was very clever with scarves and such. With Mother it wasn't about money—money wasn't important to her. Breeding was. This sounds terribly snobbish. It was terribly snobbish."

Ursula reached for the glass of water on the table next to her and drank.

"Are you hungry?" Faith asked. Ursula's hands were so thin. When she brought the glass to her lips, Faith fancied she could see the bones under her thin skin like an X-ray against the sunlight from the window. "I brought some of the currant scones you like, and the last of the strawberry preserves we put up in July." The strawberries in Ursula's garden at The Pines were the stuff of legend.

"Thank you, no. But could you stay a bit longer?"

"Until five. Tom is working at home today." Faith didn't offer any further explanation. After trying to write his sermon in the shadow of his file cabinets at the church yesterday, he had decided to give the parsonage study, neutral territory, a try today.

"As I said, everything hinged on Father's absence, and then Mother had to leave, too. The second 'What if?' but one that wouldn't have mattered if Father hadn't been so far away—and impossible to reach. No cell phones. Not even a landline at The Pines until many years later. She must have sent him a telegram. I wasn't told. She had received a telegram, though, early that morning. Aunt Myrtle had been rushed to the Massachusetts General Hospital for emergency surgery. Appendicitis. It was a much more perilous diagnosis in those days than now and Mother left for Boston at once, leaving the housekeeper in charge—and the Professor. Although he was only a year or two older than the others, he seemed like an adult. The others were still children, intent on having a good time above all else. Mother did suggest that perhaps the young people staying at the house might want to leave, but Theo said he thought 'Aunt Myrt' would be upset to know that her illness had caused anyone an inconvenience."

Selfish, foolish, or just very immature? Faith wondered to herself about Theo. Ursula obviously had adored him—and did still.

It was as if she had read Faith's mind, or perhaps her last words had triggered the defense.

"He wasn't a bad person, Faith. Not at all. Generous to a fault, especially with his friends. But I'm afraid he was weak, easily influenced, and not terribly interested in what Father and the Professor both had mapped out for him as a course of study. In the ordinary way of things, he would have squeaked through Harvard and done very well in business, perhaps with Father. People liked and trusted him. Although the years that followed weren't good for most of his generation."

"Those Depression years for young men in their twenties weren't much different from recent times," Faith said. "The highest unemployment is in that group."

Ursula nodded. She was glad her elder grandson was gainfully employed and concerned about Dan, the younger, soon to finish college.

"In any case, Mother left in a rush, reassured me that Aunt Myrtle would be fine, but said I should still add an extra prayer for her before I went to bed. Selfish child that I was—although at that age, sickness and death have little reality—I confess what was really worrying me was not my aunt, but whether I'd be able to go to Illumination Night. Do you know what this is, Faith?"

Faith did, having had the great good fortune to be on the Vineyard some years ago on the second Wednesday in August. She hadn't known about the Grand Illumination previously. For her, a grand illumination meant the lighting of the tree at Rockefeller Center at Christmastime.

"It was magical," she said. "I'll never forget the moment when all those strings of Japanese lanterns were lighted on the cottages, which are pretty colorful by themselves."

Faith had immediately coveted one of the little Victorian Carpenter Gothic–style houses. She'd learned the two rooms up and two rooms down with front porches trimmed with froths of lacy gingerbread scrollwork had replaced the tents pitched earlier in the nineteenth century by attendees at the Methodist camp meetings that became popular during the Revival.

The houses were painted in bright peach, rose, turquoise, and yellows with contrasting trim. When she'd expressed her desire, her friend had told her that the houses were passed down from one generation to the next, and even if one did go on sale, it was by word of mouth and gone moments later. This part of the Vineyard was also the setting for one of Faith's favorite books, *The Wedding* by Dorothy West, a member of the Harlem Renaissance. West had been coming to Oak Bluffs since childhood, her family part of the early African American summer colony who had made Oak

Bluffs with its famed Inkwell Beach an ongoing destination.

Illumination Night had obviously captured Ursula's imagination, too.

"By the summer I was there, Illumination Night was an old tradition and I'd been hearing about it for weeks, especially from the servants. By this time I'd become adept at the Vineyard sign language and considered Mary Smith, who worked in the kitchen, a new friend. She wasn't much older than I was and was walking out with the gardener. I think I mentioned this the other day."

Faith nodded. Ursula had mentioned the young woman, but not her name.

"The lanterns sounded like something out of a fairy tale—Mary told me that originally they were plain ones until a Japanese family opened a gift shop in Oak Bluffs in the 1870s when there was such a rage for Asian art. After that the lanterns had to be from Japan or China.

"And I thought the little houses were playhouses when I first saw them and used to beg to be taken to see them. Mother had a friend who owned one and I loved to sit on her tiny porch in a rocker that was small, too. There were always people strolling by and stopping to say hello. I'm afraid I wasn't missing Sanpere at those times, although at others I wanted intensely to be there.

"The huge tabernacle in the middle of the camp-ground looked like a rustic palace. I had never been inside and this was another reason why I had been counting the days until Illumination Night. As soon as we heard about it, Mother promised she would take me and I think she was excited to go, too."

Faith remembered the Tabernacle. It was interdenominational now, and Illumination Night, as well as the other summer events held there, was run by the Camp Ground Association. They should try to take the kids this year, although August meant Maine. Even Ben, who had recently adopted a world-weary air more reminiscent of Garbo than a seventh grader, would be impressed. The lanterns were what turned a summer band concert, albeit an extremely large one, into a unique experience. The lantern collection went with the houses—if they changed hands—and some were over a hundred years old, painted by artists or an owner's children and grandchildren. Many were still illuminated with candles. At dusk, someone who had been appointed, a terrific honor, lit the signal lantern at the Tabernacle and immediately hundreds of others festooned on the surrounding houses glowed. At eleven, they were extinguished, and church chimes filled the now quiet night, signaling the end of another Illumination Night.

Faith had even gotten into the old-time sing-along at the Tabernacle, especially when they sang "East Side, West Side, All Around the Town." The band concert that followed the sing-along had been heavy on Sousa. It had all suggested a simpler, carefree time, although as Faith listened to Ursula she doubted such a moment had ever existed even in "The Good Old Summertime."

"The weather that day was unseasonably warm, especially for Martha's Vineyard," Ursula said. "Perhaps that had something to do with it, too."

"You're all a bunch of slugs. Big fat oozing slugs!" Babs said. She was carrying her tennis racquet and dressed for the courts.

"Darling girl. It's too hot for tennis. Too hot for anything, except a dip in the ocean. What about it?" Theo looked around the living room at the group that had assumed a variety of languid poses, none more drooping, or aesthetic, than Violet's. She was stretched out on one of the cushioned wicker chaises. Her shapely legs and ankles, down to her bare feet—she'd kicked off her shoes—were nicely displayed.

"Too salty, and Babs, even your devoted Scooter isn't going to bake on that clay court. Run along and practice that divine backhand of yours." Violet's slightly sarcastic tone turned the compliment truly into a backhanded one.

Babs flushed, walked over to Scooter, who'd been idly playing the piano, and grabbed his hand.

"I suppose a walk on the beach won't kill you? You can borrow one of Violet's sunshades if you don't want to freckle."

"Hey, don't have a conniption, honeybun. Everything's jake. If you want to play tennis, I'll play. Violet isn't my mouthpiece."

"You're a doll." Babs planted a big kiss on the top of his head. "But it is hot. Let's walk now and play later."

"I thought it was 'Let's play now and pay later,'" Theo quipped.

"That's only you, Lyman," Charles Winthrop called out. He was looking at the ocean through a brass spyglass. "And speaking of paying, I believe you owe me several simoleons from last night. Damn, not a single sail. Nothing's moving. I'd hoped to get out today. Dickie Cabot said to come over if the wind was right and we'd head out. Nice little boat they have."

"If you call a yacht that sleeps eight with quarters for the crew little, then I'd agree. And Charlie, there are ladies present." Theo sounded peeved and seized on Winthrop's oath. He also considered it devilishly poor taste to mention the money he owed after several late nights of cards with a few fellows who'd dropped by. Charles wasn't the only one he'd lost to and it was partly the cause of a headache that was getting worse not better as the day wore on. The other cause was too much gin.

"Stop it, both of you," Violet said, swinging her legs to the floor and stretching like a cat. "Order some lemonade, Theo, and we can play mah-jongg in the shade on the porch. It must be cooler there."

Theo walked to the door and pressed a button to the left of it. Mrs. Miles, the housekeeper, soon appeared and he asked her if she could please bring some cold lemonade to the porch.

"Yes, Mr. Lyman," she said.

She was barely out the door when Violet gave a throaty laugh. "She has a beau, your Mrs. Miles."

"Really, Violet, the servants' affairs are of no concern to us. Leave the poor woman alone," Babs said.

"It's really very sweet," Violet continued, taking no notice. "He appears every night after dinner and lurks in the shrubbery until she's finished and then they disappear in the direction of the beach. A bit gritty for nooky, I'd say."

"And you should know," Babs said softly to Scooter.

"I heard that," Violet said, not in the least bothered. "Better to be the bees' knees than a Mrs. Grundy."

"Meow," Scooter said, and got up from the piano. "Are we taking that walk or not?"

"Taking it," Babs said. "See you in the funny papers."

Mrs. Miles returned with a tray. Ursula was at her heels. She'd been in the kitchen talking to Mary.

"Would you like the lemonade in here or on the porch, Mr. Lyman?"

"The porch will be fine. Let me get the door."

"The Professor would like you to meet him in the library, Theo," Ursula said. "I saw him in the hall and told him I'd tell you. And don't forget, you promised you'd take me tonight since Mother can't."

"What does he want now?" Theo ignored the rest of what Ursula had said.

"Go and swallow your medicine like a good boy. I don't want my Theo flunking out." Violet walked over and slipped her arm through his. "We'll be thinking of something fun for tonight's party. Charades?"

Theo brightened immediately. "Which reminds me, I've got to see a man about a dog in Edgartown as soon as I can get away from Herr Professor."

"Remember, Baby likes champagne, Daddy," Violet said as she squeezed his arm.

Ursula thought this sounded pretty stupid. Theo wasn't anywhere near old enough to be Violet's father. She knew it was slang—which her mother had forbidden her to use—but shouldn't even slang make some sense?

Violet dropped Theo's arm, and Ursula grabbed the other one, tugging on it slightly.

"You promised! And we don't have to stay too long. Just see the lanterns lighted and hear some of the music."

Theo shook her off and walked toward the door. "Later, squirt. I've got a date with an isosceles triangle."

She followed him out and down the hall into the library. It was smaller than the living and dining rooms, but bigger than its counterpart at the Lymans' Boston house. A large fireplace domi-nated one wall. The rest were lined with bookshelves that came halfway up the walls. Above and on top of them, the owner displayed his weaponry collection. There were elaborately etched swords, some in embossed silver scabbards that looked as if young Arthur had pulled them from the stone. In addition there were several very frightening-looking spiked maces and crossbows. Another wall was devoted to American weapons starting with the muskets the colonists used against the British, up through the Spencer carbines of the Civil War. The last wall was filled with African and South American spears. They were arranged like the spokes of a wheel with an enormous moose head as the hub. Ursula had spent hours in the library, reading and contemplating the décor. The moose looked slightly surprised to find himself surrounded by such foreign objects, she thought. There was a leopard skin spread out in front of the fireplace over the Oriental carpet that almost covered the entire floor, leaving only an edge of gleaming wood to show that the quality of what was beneath equaled what was on top. The leopard was headless. Doubtless, she imagined, if the house's owner had killed it, he would have displayed that head with the spears. He must have killed the moose and decided it would have to do.

A large library table was covered with richly illustrated books on the history of weaponry—and a number of guns ranging from a tiny pearl-handled revolver to the kind of gun Tom Mix carried in the movies. She'd learned many interesting new words from the books and it certainly was a very different kind of hobby from any of hers—the ferns and birds' nests in Maine, postcards in Boston. Her father collected stamps, which took up considerably less room.

"Sorry to drag you away from your friends, Theo, but we don't have a great deal of time left and there's still so much to get through." The Professor sounded tired, Ursula thought.

"Well, let's get to it, then," Theo said and then seemed to regret his tone. "You've been cooped up here all morning in this heat." When he wasn't tutoring Theo, the Professor was editing his senior thesis, which he hoped to publish. "How about some cold lemonade? Ursula, run out to the porch and get us both a glass."

"Thanks, I am feeling warm, so a glass of something cold would be very nice. Meanwhile, shall we start on page fifty in the text?"

Ursula was only too happy to fetch the drinks. As she left she thought, Page 50? That's all? The text was a thick one. Maybe they were reviewing. If not, Theo would never be through the book by the end of the summer.

When she returned the two men were in deep conversation, but it wasn't about mathematics. She knew it was wrong to eavesdrop, but could she help it if she had to slow down so she wouldn't spill on the carpet?

"Don't be sore, Theo. I'm your friend first and tutor second. You know that. Think of this as advice from one friend to another. It's just that with both your parents gone and word about this party all over the island, I'm afraid things are going to get out of hand. Can't you call it off and have dinner with the people staying in the house? Maybe ask one or two other couples? Roll up the rug afterward?" He was leaning forward, smiling persuasively, and Ursula wondered how her brother could possibly resist giving in.

Theo was on the opposite side of the desk, slouched in a leather chair. He was cleaning his nails with a sharply pointed stiletto—Ursula had asked her father what it was and he'd told her. He'd also told her not to touch it and would be appalled at the use to which Theo was putting it. The gold handle was elaborately enameled in emerald green.

The house's owner used it as a letter opener and it rested on a special little tray.

"Sorry, can't do it. I'd look like a chump. Vi, I mean the girls, would be very cut up. They're looking forward to putting on their glad rags. Not much chance here."

There was a brief silence.

"Best get to work, then."

Ursula almost burst into tears. How could Theo disappoint his friend—his wise tutor, wise counselor—this way?

She gulped and said, "Here are the drinks. I could get some cookies from the kitchen if you want. Cook baked this morning."

"That's very kind of you, Ursula, but I'm all set with this. Thank you." The Professor took the glass from her hand. Theo took the other glass.

"They light the lanterns at dusk, Theo. We could be back for your party in plenty of time."

Her brother was seldom cross with her, so Ursula was surprised at the vehemence of his next words.

"Can't you see we're working here? Now get going—and stop pestering me about a bunch of lanterns!"

Ursula started to answer back, but the look on his face stopped her. He was scowling. A rare sight.

"Illumination Night? It's tonight?" asked the Professor.

"Yes," Ursula said, her voice shaking slightly, "and with Mother gone there's no one to take me. Mrs. Miles was supposed to be off today, but said she'd stay since Mother had to leave. Mary is only working until just before dark, and I'd ask her, except I know she's going with . . . with someone else, and Theo said—"

"What I said was 'get going'!"

"I'll take you," the Professor said. "I've heard about Illumination Night for years."

"Don't you want to go to the party?" Ursula asked.

"No, I don't care to attend."

Daylight savings time had started earlier in the month, an event Faith always greeted with great joy. It might be freezing outside, and snow up to the windowsill, but there was light! Although it was close to five o'clock, sunshine was flooding Ursula's bedroom, giving the illusion of a balmy summer day.

"You must be getting tired," Faith said.

"No, happily I'm not." Ursula reached for Faith's hand. "Is there any way you could stay another hour? I hate to keep you from your family, but I really don't feel fatigued and I'd like to tell you some more of my story."

The tale was reaching its climax and perhaps its end, as well. Faith had sensed it all afternoon. She didn't want to leave.

"Let me give Tom a call. I'm sure it will be fine."

"I'll ring the bell for Dora. Some of Millicent's restorative calf's foot jelly for me, and tea for you instead, I think." Ursula smiled mischievously, knowing full well Faith's opinion of all things Millicent. She rang the little brass hand bell shaped like a lady with a wide hoop skirt, a gift from Samantha, who had found it in an antiques shop. It was always placed nearby.

Tom told her to stay as long as she wanted, and soon they were settled back with not only the tea and jelly but also some cucumber and cress sandwiches. Dora was well-known for her British-style cooking, particularly nursery comfort foods like jam roly-poly and rice pudding.

Ursula picked up where she had left off.

"Theo's guests were beginning to arrive as we left for the campground. Most of the women were quite dressed up for the Vineyard. Violet, who was acting as hostess, was wearing one of those long white satin backless dresses that movie stars like Carole Lombard and Jean Harlow had made so popular. She had a long rope of pearls, not real I'm sure, that she'd tied at her neck so they hung down her back. Her skin was almost as white as the necklace and as smooth. Babs was wearing a long gown, too. It struck me because I'd never seen her dressed up before and hadn't realized that she was quite lovely, too. It was sapphire blue and cut quite decorously compared to Violet's dress. The men who were staying at the house were all in dinner jackets, which must have been terribly uncomfortable. The heat hadn't broken."

Ursula slipped out from her hiding place beneath the piano and went into the dining room. Theo had had food delivered from some restaurant and the table was covered with platters of all sorts of delicious-looking things. She took a plate and started to reach for some lobster salad, stuffed back in the red shell, but realized that she was too excited to eat anything except some toast that had been placed next to a mound of caviar. She was momentarily tempted by the shiny black roe—she'd had it once and it tasted like the sea—but she decided to stick to the toast.

She heard the Professor's voice calling her name and then he was at her side.

"Time to get going?"

"Oh yes, please."

They left the crowded room and slipped into the kitchen, leaving through the back door into the still night. The last noise from the house that Ursula heard was a champagne cork popping and a woman starting to sing 'Yes Sir, That's My Baby.'

She had put on her best frock. Rose-colored silk. A dropped waist with a pleated skirt. Her mother would not have approved. Ursula had felt a twinge of guilt when she'd slipped it over her head—but only a twinge, and that soon disappeared.

If Mother wasn't back tomorrow, perhaps the Professor would take her to the carousel—the Flying Horses—in Oak Bluffs. Mother had heard that they were originally at Coney Island, a place Mother called 'a vulgar amusement park,' but she hadn't expressly forbidden Ursula from going.

She darted a glance at her companion. He was a grown-up, but not terribly old. Only twenty.

"Have you been enjoying your summer? I understand it's quite different from the place you normally go in Maine."

Ursula started talking and soon she felt as if she had never before talked to anyone so understanding. He wasn't at all condescending and she moved from a description of Sanpere Island to her desire to

explore Boston, and the whole world—her eager-
ness to grow up.

Blessedly, he didn't tell her not to be in a rush,
but spoke of his own hope to travel once he had
finished law school.

"Perhaps I'll be able to find a job that won't start
until the fall, allowing me a summer to roam. I've a
yen to go to the Lake District, Wordsworth country."

And Beatrix Potter's, Ursula almost said, before
deciding mentioning Peter Rabbit's creator might
seem childish.

A few minutes later she realized she could have
mentioned Peter, or anything else. The Professor
was interested in everything she was interested
in—his bird list was twice as long as hers!

He found seats for them near the front. The
Tabernacle did not disappoint. They sang lustily,
joining the others raising their voices, the notes reverberating into the twilight as the sun's last rays
struck the stained-glass panels below the wooden
tented ceiling. Through the open sides, Ursula
could just make out the unlit lanterns strung on
every porch, swaying slightly, waiting for the
signal. She thought the Tabernacle was indeed a
holy place, and very far removed from King's
Chapel.

The music was over too soon, but outside there were the lanterns, illuminated now—hundreds of them. They ate peppermint ice cream—"The color of your pretty dress," he said—and wandered about looking at the glowing orbs.

"I'm afraid we should be getting back," he said.

Ursula looked at her watch. Theo had given her a Gruen wristwatch for Christmas. Mother had told her not to take it to the Vineyard because she might get sand in it, but she'd packed it anyway, loath to leave one of her most precious possessions behind. Tonight she'd happily tightened the black grosgrain ribbon strap and thought she'd much rather have it than the pearls and other jewelry the women were wearing.

She'd only stayed up this late—it was just after ten o'clock—on New Year's Eve. The Professor was right, regrettably. It was time to go.

As they neared the house Ursula could see there were cars all over the drive and even some on the lawn. Father would be terribly upset, she thought. They had been hearing the music from quite far away and now, close to the house, it was very loud.

"Let's slip in the kitchen way again and I think you'd better go straight to bed. I'll be in the library if you should need me." He looked a bit anxious and Ursula knew he was concerned that the party showed no signs of winding down. Then he smiled at her. "It's been a lovely evening. Good night."

"Thank you for taking me. It was perfect."

Mary was helping the people who'd brought the food, but Ursula didn't see Mrs. Miles. Mary signed that she would be leaving soon for the Illumination and wasn't it wonderful? Ursula signed back that it was better than anything she had ever seen and, feeling a sudden shyness, raced up the back stairs, realizing when she got to the top that she hadn't said "good night" back to the Professor. She started to turn around, but he'd be gone. It didn't matter. She'd say "good night" to him twice tomorrow night to make up for it. Perhaps she'd tell him why.

As Ursula went into her room, she felt as if she were floating, like one of the lanterns. She changed, said her prayers, and got into bed. It was impossible to sleep. Her room in the turret was stifling even with the windows open. And the noise. Not just the music, but people were in the pool, directly below, splashing and shrieking. There seemed to be a constant stream of cars coming and going. Finally she decided to retreat to her place in the woods.

Her place by the gazebo.

She took a blanket with her and made a cozy nest beneath the rhododendrons. There wasn't anyone in the gazebo. She'd been afraid there might be some couples there, but it was empty, although someone had strung up some Japanese lanterns like the ones in the campground and lighted them. The noise from the house was muted.

She felt quite drowsy, but fought sleep to enjoy the novelty of sleeping outdoors. She could see the sky through the branches. It was a clear night and the stars were bright. For a time, Ursula amused herself by picking out the various constellations. Theodore Artemus Lyman was an avid amateur astronomer and had taught his children all the names.

I wonder whether the Professor is a stargazer, too . . . she thought fuzzily. The night air was cool at last. She slept.

Ursula hadn't been asleep long when she was awakened by the sound of loud voices nearby. Two men were arguing in the gazebo. She couldn't see them through the thick foliage, but she could hear them clearly. One was Theo; she wasn't sure who the other was. Theo was slurring his words. She'd let him into the house in Boston one night very late and he'd sounded the same. She'd had to help him up the stairs to his room. He was very unsteady. The next day he'd told her he'd never mix champagne and whiskey again, but it sounded as if he had tonight. *The other voice was similar.* How silly these men were to get drunk and quarrel, Ursula thought.

"I've got to have the money now. I told you they won't wait. They want the money tomorrow first thing! You said you'd have it tonight! I'm done for if my father finds out!"

"Can't do it, old chum. Jus' tell 'em."

"Snap out of it, Theo! I'm telling you I'm in a jam. They won't give me any more time. They've threatened to hurt me—and they will."

"No money here. Not on this little old island."

"Get it from somebody. What about your tutor?"

"Poor as a church mouse. Hey, that's funny."

Theo started to laugh and stopped abruptly.

"Whadya have to smack me for? Thought we were friends. Let's go back to the house. Need another drink. Want to see Violet. Violet with the violet eyes."

"Look here, I'll smack you again if it will bring you to your senses. You owe me the money fair and square. You knew we were playing for high stakes. Had to impress Violet, didn't you. Well, she wasn't. She thinks you're a sap."

"Watch what you're saying! I'm no sap. I'm gonna go ask her. Ask her what she thinks of you, too!"

Ursula ducked farther back into the bushes. She was starting to get frightened. Maybe she should run to the house and get the Professor. Theo, oh Theo, why did you have to get yourself in such messes! She had ten dollars left from her summer spending money. He was welcome to it and then this person would leave him alone.

"You're not going anywhere."

"Who's gonna stop me?"

"Me, that's who!"

"Come on, les go have a drink, buddy. Stop fighting. Make up. Friends. You're my friend, right?"

Theo's voice had lost its belligerent tone and Ursula was relieved. She heard a few thumping noises—they were crossing the wooden floor of the gazebo—followed by the sounds of running feet.

It was all right, then. They'd gone back to the house. She decided to stay where she was. It was so quiet and peaceful. A beautiful night.

It seemed as if she had barely fallen asleep again when she heard a woman's screams. She got up and ran out from under the bushes into the clearing. There were two people standing up in the gazebo. The lanterns were still lighted and the woman who was screaming was Violet. The other person was a man. His back was to Ursula and she assumed it was Theo. People were streaming out from the house—the path was visible from where she stood—and there was a great deal of commotion. She could hear cars starting up. A great many cars. Violet kept screaming and screaming. Ursula wanted her to stop. Why couldn't someone make her stop?

The gazebo looked bigger than it did in the daytime. She walked over toward the door. It was wide open. Someone tried to pull her away, but she kept going. The ground felt cold and hard beneath her bare feet and she started to shiver.

The other man wasn't Theo. Theo was lying on the floor. He was on his back and his eyes were closed. He's fallen asleep here, Ursula thought. Why is Violet screaming? And why hasn't he woken up with all the noise?

She went in and walked over to him, kneeling down to shake his shoulder. It was then that she saw the blood on his starched white shirtfront. It was so red. There wasn't much, but it was very red. Once he'd cut himself shaving and come to breakfast with a bit of tissue on his face; blood was still seeping through. Father made him leave. It was so very red, Theo's blood. Running through his body. So very alive that morning.

But she knew he wasn't alive now. He was dead. Knew the moment she'd knelt down. That's why Violet was screaming. But why was the Professor standing over him with the stiletto from the library in his hand? The blade was glistening red. The same color as Theo's blood. Nothing made sense.

The Professor's face looked very different from the way it had looked earlier that night. She put her hand on Theo's face, his lovely face. It was still warm. She took one of his hands in her other hand and held tight. And then Ursula laid her head down on his chest; she couldn't hear his heart beating at all. Violet had finally stopped screaming. Ursula had heard a slap, like in the movies. She didn't want to leave her brother surrounded by all these people, all these strangers, and she told the Professor to make everyone else leave. To leave the two of them alone with Theo. After she spoke, no one moved for a moment, or said anything, and then Charles Winthrop, Scooter Jessup, and some other men grabbed the Professor.

"Everyone heard your argument tonight," Charles said. "And now you've killed him, Arnold Rowe. Someone call the police."

Chapter 6

Arnold Rowe?

The Arnold Rowe that Ursula Lyman married?

The Arnold Rowe who was the father of Pix Rowe Miller?

As Faith walked home, she took little note of the soft spring dusk with its swelling branches silhouetted against the diminishing daylight. She arrived at her own door without remembering the steps that had taken her there. It seemed as though one minute she'd been sitting in shock next to Ursula and a minute later here she was taking her keys from her jacket pocket.

She did recall a scene in between. Dora had come into the room—almost as if Ursula's startling revelation had been a cue. She'd seemed to take in the situation with one swift glance and said in a firm nanny's-here-to-take-charge tone, "Now, we've had a lovely long visit with Mrs. Fairchild, but it's time for a bit of a rest."

Then she'd walked closer and seen the tears that had filled Ursula's eyes as she was describing the tragic scene she'd witnessed. She spoke even more sternly. "I'm sure it's all been very nice, but I think we'll take it easy tomorrow. I'm sure Mrs. Fairchild could come back Friday or Saturday."

Faith had felt chastened, although at the same time she thought *she* hadn't done anything. But who had? What had happened in the short time that young Ursula had been asleep? And an even more pressing question: What had happened in the days, months, and years following? It was absurd to think that somehow Ursula had met another man with the same name and married him.

She'd leaned over and kissed Ursula's soft cheek before leaving.

"I'm fine," Ursula had murmured. "Dora's a benevolent despot, thank goodness, and if you could come back later this week, I'll continue."

"I'm afraid this is too upsetting for you." Faith had been and still was concerned. Surely the tale had reached its climax and, hence, the end.

Ursula had shaken her head emphatically. "No, please. We have to finish. I need your help. . . ."

At that point Dora's efficient manner propelled Faith out of the room, down the stairs, and onto the sidewalk before Ursula could say another word.

There it was again. The mention of needing help. But for what? Faith was mystified. The crime had occurred some eighty-odd years ago when Ursula was in her early teens. Still considered a child in that era, even more so because of her privileged and protected upbringing. Things were so different now. The other day when Faith had picked Ben up at school, there had been a group of girls—total fashionistas—waiting in front for rides. Some had adopted the Japanese schoolgirl look, complete with eyeliner to make their eyes appear as large as the waifs in manga. Others were going for Miley Cyrus as Hannah Montana with skimpy tees and plenty of pink glitter. Their cell phones seemed welded to their hands like some sort of new life-form appendages, and their pocketbooks were the size of steamer trunks. They didn't carry knapsacks. What they did carry in common was an air of supreme self-confidence and independence. Faith wanted to believe that below the surface there was at least a little angst, but she wouldn't bet on it. No one would ever describe these girls as children, and the fact that their counterparts were gracing the pages of *Vogue* and other fashion magazines at this tender age reinforced the image. An image she hoped she could help Amy avoid while guiding her through the rocky shoals known as adolescence. Even the geek girls—in their own tight group as far away from the others as possible—had their iPhones attached and requisite suburban goth garb. Faith thought of Ursula curled up asleep next to the gazebo as the horrific events of that night progressed. Today's girl—wearing an oversized T-shirt instead of a long white cotton nightdress—would have called 911, tweeted, and posted on Facebook in a matter of seconds.

She looked at her watch. It was six-thirty, and stepping into the parsonage she was greeted with the scent of oregano. It signaled Tom's standby meal and one he was always happy to have an excuse to order: a large pizza with extra sauce, roasted peppers, Italian sausage, heavy on the oregano, from his friend Harry at Country Pizza, Aleford's one and only concession to fast food, and vastly superior.

"We're in the kitchen, Mom," Amy called out.

It was a happy scene. Faith got a plate and cutlery, and sat down, pleased to note that Tom, or one of the kids, had also made a big salad. What she wasn't pleased to note was the line on Tom's forehead that always surfaced when he was troubled.

"How's Ursula?" he asked.

"When I got there she was sitting up in that big chair by the window and dressed." Faith had been delighted to see Ursula in her habitual Liberty-print blouse and poplin skirt from Orvis. "Steady improvement these last days—by the time Pix comes home, she may even be out dividing her hostas or delving into some other planting chore." Faith was a little sketchy about gardening schedules. Tom was the one who got his hands dirty, and when he was pressed for time, Pix pitched in, saying there wasn't enough to do in her backyard, which was an out-and-out lie, since at the height of the season it resembled an outpost of White Flower Farm or Wayside Gardens. Faith's knowledge of seasonal blooms was strictly governed by what appeared in the beds in Central Park or on the wide median strip down Park Avenue.

"It's a busy week for me with the library fund-raiser tomorrow night and the Tillies on Friday," she said. "I'm not sure when I'm going to be able to visit her again. We'll see what Saturday looks like."

This was one of those times when Faith wished early on she'd adopted the European custom of feeding the children first and whisking them off to bed, or homework at this stage. The weight of what Ursula had just told her was palpable and she needed to share it with Tom. She also needed to know what was causing his telltale furrow. The phone rang and he jumped up. "I'll take it in my study." Not a good sign.

It could be one of Tom's groupies asking him to arbitrate on the crucial debate over the kind of flowers the Sunday school children should receive on Easter—pots of pansies or bulb plants?—or a parishioner complaining about last Sunday's choice of hymns. Faith was hoping it was this type of call, ordinarily ones that caused her to wish Tom had opted for a different line of work, used-car salesman, insurance agent, tap dancer, anything but the clergy. Tonight she'd take the interruptions as a sign that all was still right with the world at First Parish. They wouldn't be calling him if they thought he'd had his hand in the till, or rather collection plate. What she feared, however, was that it was one of the vestry, notably Sherman, with more bad news.

The kids were finished eating. "Put your dishes in the sink. I'll clean up, so you can get a start on your homework. And Amy, please put out what you plan to wear tomorrow—it's going to be a sunny day. No more missing the bus because you're busy trying on outfits."

"That's not fair, Mom. I don't do that. Much," Amy protested, and left the room in a huff, unusual for her. Faith feared it was a portent of things to come.

Ben was lingering at the sink. "She really doesn't do that. Did you ever think she might be missing the bus on purpose?"

Faith whirled around and looked her son straight in the eye.

"Benjamin Fairchild, what do you know about this? What's going on with Amy and the bus?"

Ben shrugged. "I think you should ask her. Much better for parents and kids to have direct communication."

Faith resisted the impulse to shake him. When had her son morphed into Dr. Phil?

"I intend to do that right away." She dried her hands and went upstairs. Tom was still on the phone.

She knocked on her daughter's door before going in.

Amy was sitting at her desk reading.

"What's up, Mom?"

Her little face looked calm and happy. Maybe Ben was wrong.

"Sweetheart, is there some reason you don't *want* to take the bus? Something going on during the ride?"

One look at her daughter's face told Faith there was. It crumpled and Amy didn't even try to stifle the sobs that erupted with the suddenness of a summer's afternoon thunderstorm.

"Is it those girls? The ones on the playground? Are they on your bus? Let's sit down over here." Faith awkwardly edged over to the bed, holding her daughter, feeling like a hermit crab. As they sat down, Amy buried her head in her mother's shoulder.

The sobs subsided; she hiccupped, raised her head, and nodded. Faith realized Ben was standing in the doorway.

"Josh's brother is on the same bus and he told Josh and Josh told me, but Amy didn't want you to know. I guess she thought you could just keep driving her in the morning, and you usually pick her up after school for dumb ballet or something."

"I told you not to tell, Ben!" Amy shouted at this convenient surrogate target.

"I didn't; she guessed. Kind of," he said, and started to walk away.

"Wait a minute," Faith said. "What else did Josh say?" She was pretty sure she wasn't going to get very coherent answers from Amy for a while.

"Just that they're these girls who think they're very hot. Like they date and stuff already."

"In third grade!" Faith was truly shocked.

"Well, not date date, but you know, go hang around where older guys are—sixth graders—and text stuff."

Faith had heard all too much about the craze for "sexting" among teens—sending suggestive photos, some pretty innocent, of girls at a slumber party egging each other on; others not innocent at all.

"Stuff like what?"

Ben gave her a look that told her he knew exactly what she was talking about. After the incidents last fall involving cyberbullying, her son's expertise in and knowledge of all things microchip was a given.

"Not that stuff. Stupid stuff like pictures of their dogs and cats wearing sunglasses and underwear. Supposed to be cool, but really lame."

Having dealt with the side issue—upsetting and weird as the image of pets in panties or what-have-you was—Faith got back to the matter at hand.

"Okay, so these girls who think they're so great, what are they doing to Amy?"

"Mom, I really have to do my homework. Amy will tell you. Just give her a moment." And he was gone. That avatar who had replaced her son—whom she'd previously thought was clueless about social interactions—was a guy after all. She was going to have to rearrange these thoughts from now on. Ben had quite suddenly become very savvy. Faith gave Amy a moment.

"These girls are teasing you. Only you?"

Amy nodded.

"Do you know why?"

Amy took a deep breath. "None of my friends are on my bus. It's just me. On the playground, there are more of us."

Simple math.

"And what are they saying?"

"I don't know. Well, like I smell bad and lately something else." Amy's voice dropped.

Faith waited.

"They keep saying that they watched me salute the flag in assembly and that I need a bra."

"Mean girls" didn't even begin to come close. Amy was as flat as a board, concave in fact, and here they were suggesting she was feeling herself up! Faith was ready to get names and get even. She tried to remember the yoga-breathing thing for calming down that her friend Patsy had taught her.

"A lot of girls in my class have bras, Mom."

"If you want, we can go to Macy's tomorrow after school."

Amy brightened considerably.

"But," Faith continued, "I'm not sure this will solve the bus problem."

"I could let them see a strap," Amy suggested.

Faith knew these girls even if her sweet daughter didn't. "They'll find something else, I'm afraid. How about tomorrow morning sit in the front seat right behind the driver?"

"I can try, but usually Stacy Schwartz is there and I don't really know her. She's in fourth grade."

"Sit with her," Faith said. Stacy was probably seeking protection, too. "And I'll think about this some more." Plus she'd call the school again.

"But we can still go to Macy's?"

"We can still go to Macy's."

Leaving her children to their labors and thankful, as always, that she had left this sort of thing far behind, Faith went downstairs to finish cleaning up in the kitchen. The door to the study was closed. She put her ear to it and Tom was still on the phone. She hadn't heard the phone ring, so it was the same call. While she hoped it was not a serious matter—death, disease—she also hoped for a minor crisis, one that had absolutely nothing to do with the Minister's Discretionary Fund.

As she wiped the counter, she heard the study door open. Tom came into the kitchen.

"That was Sam. I left a message for him earlier to give me a call, asking him to call as soon he got back to Aleford."

Faith was relieved. Sam must have had to come back early for some reason and now he could help deal with all this. The Hilton Head group had been due to split up tomorrow morning, with the ladies heading to Charleston for the bridal shower; the rest returning to jobs and school.

Faith's respite from worry was short-lived.

"Sam isn't going to be back in Aleford until the middle of next week at the earliest," Tom said. "He has to go to California to depose a number of people involved in the class action suit the firm has been working on since last fall. He's the only one not in court right now."

"So this means . . . ?"

"This means I told him everything that's been going on, and as soon as he's back—unless by one of God's miracles it's all been cleared up—he'll go over everything. I've retained him as my lawyer, Faith. He advised I do so and I thought it was a good idea."

Ever since Tom had broken the news, Faith had been avoiding the harsh reality of the situation he was in. The word "lawyer" brought it into sharp focus. She moved closer to her husband and put her arms around him.

"Sam will take care of it," she said. "This is what he does. He'll see something everyone, even the bank, has missed. What else did he say?"

"He pretty much asked me the same questions you did—who had access to the file, the keys. He also wondered if I'd been aware of anyone standing behind me when I used the ATM. Apparently there's this thing called 'shoulder surfing'—stealing someone's PIN by looking over his or her shoulder when they enter it. There are other ways, too, but he didn't go into them. I'm trying to think back, but it's hard. That ATM area at the bank is pretty small and sometimes people are filling out deposit slips while you're using the machine or just waiting their turns. I've done it myself."

She should have thought of this! Someone hacking into Tom's account! Several years ago when Faith had taught a cooking for dummies course during the project week at Mansfield Academy, a local prep school, she'd met Zach Cummings, a computer whiz—although there must be some other techie term that was more precise, and colorful. Since then they'd stayed in touch. While she'd been at Mansfield she became involved in a murder investigation. Zach, innocent of any wrongdoing, had been pulled into the chaos. He was at MIT now and she'd e-mail him tonight. She felt hopeful again, and also a bit as if she were riding one of those Martha's Vineyard carousel horses—up, down, up, down, all in the space of a few seconds. Yes, a hacker. This had to be it. The unknown stranger. The equivalent of a tramp passing through town—or rather in or near town since all the withdrawals were from the same ATM. Tom was merely unlucky. Very unlucky. It was like having your credit card number stolen by a server in a restaurant or someone who identified the card's numbers from the touch-tones when you used it in a public place like an airport. The ATM didn't make any noise, or did it?

Tom mentioned "God's miracles." Well, sometimes God needed a little help.

"Let's go sit in the living room," Tom said. "Kids doing homework?"

"Yes, presumably reading English assignments, although Ben is so eager to make a good impression on the practice teacher, he's probably composing a sonnet for extra credit."

Throughout the evening, despite all the other distractions, Ursula had been very much in Faith's thoughts. She told Tom about Theo's death and Arnold Rowe's presence.

"I never met him," Tom said. "He'd passed away before I came to First Parish, but everything I've heard about Arnold Rowe has always made me sorry I didn't know him. Not just from Ursula and Pix, but others here and on Sanpere."

"I wish I had, too. But Tom, if there had been any hint of scandal, don't you think we'd have heard?"

This had been puzzling Faith.

"Not necessarily. It was so long ago and didn't happen in town. I knew Ursula was born in Boston and had roots there, but it was always my impression that she'd grown up here. Arnold, too. I had no idea she was in her teens, or maybe it was even later, when she moved to Aleford. And we don't know about her husband. As for Sanpere, there are no secrets on the island, that's for sure, but once you cross the bridge—or in those days got on the steamer—well, what happens in Vegas stays in Vegas."

Faith nodded in agreement. "I've thought of all this, but how and why did their parents keep Theo's death—his whole life, in fact—and Arnold Rowe's possible involvement, from Pix and her brother, Arnold junior? You hear a lot of family secrets, but isn't this a little extreme?" Faith often lamented the fact that Tom's calling necessitated the keeping of such secrets. Secrets she'd love to know.

"You'd be surprised," Tom said. "Without going into specifics"—Oh, do just this once, please do! Faith said to herself—"I've had people tell me that they've just discovered a parent was married before, and with issue, that they had a sibling who died, and yes, an aunt or uncle they never knew existed. One parishioner answered a knock on the door to face her father's duplicate. Her father had been dead for some years, so you can imagine the shock it gave her. It wasn't a twin, but a brother two years younger who had been estranged from the rest of the family since he had run off as a teenager. He was never mentioned. There was no way his niece would have known of his existence. What was even stranger was that without ever having any contact with his older brother all those years, he'd adopted the same mannerisms, haircut, style of dress, even the frames of his glasses were identical. For some reason this struck her the most. She kept saying, 'He was wearing my father's glasses!'"

Family secrets. Tom was right. She could think of some examples, too. And something else could have played a part.

"In this case, don't you think it's generational, as well? Parents didn't tell their children everything the way they tend to now."

"I imagine when Ursula relates the rest of her story, this may be clearer. Certainly I didn't know much about the lives of my parents and the rest of the family—or their friends—when I was growing up. The two spheres—adulthood and childhood—touched at mealtimes and a few other points, not the continuous hovering that goes on now."

"Helicopter parents," Faith said.

"Exactly, and I hope we're somewhere in between. Too many secrets isn't a good thing."

Faith knew Tom was thinking about last fall. No, too many secrets wasn't a good thing at all.

She thought of Niki, about Pix, Ursula of course, and someone out there who knew where the missing money was.

Sick with secrets.

Across town Ursula Lyman Rowe was in bed, but not asleep. It wasn't the moonlight streaming through the window that was disturbing her slumber. It was what was below, under the cushion.

There had been a second letter in today's mail. Dora had brought it in after Faith left. The long white envelope was mixed in with get well cards and several bills. Ursula opened it first.

There weren't any clippings this time. Just a single sheet of the same paper with a single sentence in the same hand.

You saw the knife in his hand.

Faith loved the Aleford library. She loved all libraries, starting with the earliest she could remember, the Sixty-seventh Street branch of the New York Public Library. It was one of those endowed by Andrew Carnegie. While the Aleford library had not had Babb, Cook, and Willard, Beaux Arts architects, as the Sixty-seventh Street library had, it was still a gem.

Constructed in the early 1920s, the original fieldstone building had been expanded and renovated several times, most recently the children's room. An anonymous donor had provided the funds for much-needed new furniture, fresh paint, and a wondrous entryway from the main library that transformed a previous small dark corridor into a bright, exotic jungle. The two walls had been mirrored, creating the illusion that the flat rows of lush green plywood foliage placed in front extended for acres. The librarians had fun periodically changing the cutouts of parrots and other creatures that peeped from behind the leaves.

Tonight's fund-raiser was taking advantage of most of the library's square footage. Have Faith had set up enough dessert stations so people would be able to nibble at will and not have to stand in line, or jostle each other. Coffee was in reference and there were flutes of prosecco at the circulation desk. Aleford was a dry town and likely to remain so—a package store, a "packy," in *our* Aleford!—but dispensation was granted for special events at venues like the library and the Ganley Museum. The Minuteman Café, the café at the Ganley, Country Pizza, and the deli counter at the Shop 'n Save were the only places for food not prepared by individual Alefordians. If you wanted booze with your meal, you had to drive to Concord or Waltham.

Lincoln, Aleford's other abutter, was dry, too, although Faith had heard rumblings about a new restaurant with a liquor license. She'd like to have been a fly on the wall at *that* town meeting. Whenever the matter came up in Aleford, the picture of inebriated diners careening through the streets of town—diners from "away"—was painted with such broad strokes that those in favor of lifting the ban never stood a chance. The fact that the glass-recycling container at the Transfer Station, the dump, was the size of a boxcar and filled with a far greater number of empty wine and whiskey bottles than jelly jars did not enter into the discussion. Faith would have loved a nice little bistro in town where one could meet friends, have steak frites, and a glass of *vin.* Not in her lifetime, or rather Millicent's.

She spied Millicent coming in the front door. She was on the board of the Friends of the Library and involved in tonight's arrangements. She was carrying a large punch bowl.

"Some of my grandmother Revere's gunpowder punch—minus the pinch of gunpowder, of course. I'll put the bowl where you tell me and perhaps one of your helpers can get the punch cups and the containers of punch from my car? I know there's coffee, but people might like something with a little kick. There's ginger beer in it."

She looked at Faith with such patently false disingenuousness that Faith couldn't help laughing. They both knew the punch was intended not simply to compete with the prosecco, but obliterate it. Gunpowder, indeed.

"All right, Millicent. We'll put it out alongside the wine and you can dispense it. I'll send Scott Phelan out to your car. Where is it?"

"In the back, but I'll need to mingle. I'll line up some of the Friends to help ladle."

There was no need to describe Millicent's car to Scott. It was famous. He worked in a garage and body shop in nearby Byford. Every time he saw Millicent at a function while working for Faith he said the same thing: If there were more people like Millicent, he'd be out of a job. He also said he'd give anything for the car. She had purchased the Rambler in 1963 and drove it so rarely—she could walk most places—that it still looked as if it just came off the showroom floor. Not a scratch, not a dent—nothing to fix. Mint.

As Faith helped Millicent set up, she seized the opportunity to pump her in what she hoped would be a subtle way first about Arnold Rowe and then about Tom.

"It's a shame Ursula can't be here tonight. She's such a fan of David Hackett Fischer's." The noted historian would be giving a brief talk and introducing the other invited authors.

"We *all* are," Millicent corrected her. His book *Paul Revere's Ride*, signed to her, took pride of place next to Millicent's family Bible.

"I understand Ursula's husband was quite the history buff also." Faith felt fairly safe in her assertion. If you lived in Aleford, willingly or not, you were a history buff.

"Oh yes, Arnold was quite a scholar."

"I'm sorry I never got the chance to meet him. From what I've heard he was very interesting."

Millicent snorted. She was the only person Faith knew, other than certain teenage boys, who made this sound in public. Millicent could get away with it; the boys not.

"If by interesting you mean endlessly gazing at stars, collecting rocks, counting birds, and reading Plato in the original Greek, then yes, Arnold Rowe was interesting. Other than that a rather dull man; Ursula was the one with sparkle. Arnold was nice, but the kind of person nothing much ever happened to. Good in a husband, I suppose. Steady."

Faith felt as if Millicent had handed her Arnold gift-wrapped. If Millicent had an inkling that there was anything dark in his past, she would not have told

Faith about it, but she *would* have dangled a multitude of tantalizing hints in front of her. Millicent's Arnold Rowe sounded very respectable, and maybe not too much fun at parties. Faith decided to continue to press her luck.

"Hard for Ursula to have been widowed so long and I don't believe she has brothers and sisters."

Millicent didn't like it when people knew things she knew. "Yes, she was an only child—as was Arnold." So there.

"I didn't know that," Faith said. It was important to keep Millicent happy.

Scott brought the cups and libations and for a while she was busy helping Millicent transfer the contents of several plastic liter bottles into the bowl and floating on top the orange and lemon slices Millicent had brought in an ancient Tupperware container.

"You must try a little." Millicent beamed.

Faith had sampled the brew on other occasions and it wasn't bad. While not revealing all of grandmother's secret ingredients, Millicent had given Faith the basic recipe some years ago. Roughly two-to-one ginger beer to orange juice with grated nutmeg, cinnamon sticks, lemon zest, and possibly the secret ingredient was a dash of clove since Faith could definitely taste it and Millicent never mentioned it. In an earlier day, a pinch of gunpowder *was* added, which would have imparted an odd flavor—and could not have been good for you. Faith had the idea that the whole thing had originated in England to celebrate Guy Fawkes's failed attempt to blow up Parliament. In which case, the British—used to vegetables boiled into mush and other treats—would no doubt have welcomed the gunpowder's kick.

"Delicious. Very refreshing. We should serve this for the parents at church at our end-of-the-year Sunday school picnic. It's been quite a year at First Parish."

Faith cast her rod.

And got back a very rusted, very dented tin can.

Millicent looked her in the eye. "I suppose that's what some people would call an understatement. I hope the Reverend will be here tonight. The important thing is to keep going."

It was ludicrous to think that Millicent—all Aleford, and even most of Middlesex County—hadn't heard about Thomas Fairchild, embezzler.

Many miles south, but in the same time zone, Pix Miller was standing outside at the top of the Harbour Town lighthouse looking at the sunset. She was holding a glass of champagne. When she thought back on this stay at Hilton Head, glasses of champagne would figure prominently.

It was their last night and she was sorry. Each day had been a perfect blend of time together and time alone, time alone with Sam. She'd seen dolphins, birds of all sorts, and spectacular sunsets. The one that was stretched out in fiery golds and pinks sinking into the sea in front of her now was the most gorgeous. Or it could be the champagne. A girl could get used to this. She'd been running that phrase through her mind a lot this week, too.

Mother was fine. Better than fine judging from Faith's and Dora's daily reports. During the first enthusiastic description of how much Ursula had improved virtually the moment she left town, Pix had been slightly miffed. More than slightly. Why hadn't Mother shown this kind of progress when her daughter was there? But then Hilton Head, her hosts, having Sam and her children around, and maybe the whole Southern charm thing began to smooth away the rough edges. She had been dreading being in Charleston, shopping, and being on her own without Sam. It was one thing to be on familiar turf like Sanpere and quite another to be someplace completely new. Now she was looking forward to it. And anyway, Samantha would be there.

And Stephen.

The fly in the ointment.

He had not indicated by even the merest flicker of an eye that he recalled Miss Rowe. Maybe Faith was right. Maybe it was a guy thing. She hadn't told Faith that Sam never forgot a name or face, but he was a lawyer. Different wiring?

The music from the party drifted out. The Cohens had hired a DJ and he was playing everything from the Beatles to Black Eyed Peas.

"Having a good time, Mom?"

It was the groom. She gave him a hug.

"Heavenly, darling. You picked a wonderful girl and a wonderful family."

"Don't I know it—and she thinks the same about us."

Pix grabbed the moment. "Dr. Cohen, I mean Stephen, looks so familiar. Could we have met him before, do you think? Has he said anything?"

Pix blushed. This was not prodding. This was stepping in it.

"Met you and Dad before? I think he would have said something, and I don't know where. They go to New York City once or twice a year for the museums and opera, but unless you sat next to them at a performance, I wouldn't think your paths have crossed."

There it was.

"Your father doesn't like opera."

"You don't, either, you just think you should," Mark teased her.

She decided to change the subject.

"I'll be making all the final arrangements for the rehearsal dinner when I get to Charleston. I know the groom doesn't have much to do, but are you all set?"

"Done and done. Picking up the rings next week, and I've ordered silver penknives engraved with each of their initials for the ushers. I got Dan a Swiss Army watch that does a ton of things, including the ability to set multiple alarms—wish I'd had that in college. I'm having something engraved on the back of that, too."

Much to Pix's delight, Mark had selected his young brother as his best man.

"He'll love it."

"Let's see what else? I set up spreadsheets so the Cohens could keep track of the RSVPs and separate ones for Becca and me for thank-you notes. My bride says electronic ones are out and is writing them by hand. Plus you've seen the Web site, right?"

It was all a little much—spreadsheets? Were the vows going to be in the form of a PowerPoint presentation? Pix was glad Rebecca was old-fashioned enough to nix e-thank-yous.

"You haven't, have you? Oh Mom, you are such a Luddite! Anyway, it's not too cutesy. Just one picture of us and the rest info."

Sam came up on Pix's other side. He was chewing.

"You have got to go inside and have some of this food. I thought nothing could top last night, but this is something else again!"

The night before, acting on Faith's advice and with the resort's help, the Millers had hosted a Low Country boil on the beach for their soon-to-be in-laws. Pix had been dubious—a pot full of what sounded like wildly disparate ingredients: shrimp in their shells, smoked sausage, new potatoes, small rounds of corn on the cob, whole onions, and Old Bay seasoning plus water—but it had been fantastic. Faith had told her it was also called "Frogmore stew," a South Carolina staple named after the place where it originated, no frogs involved.

"I'm supposed to make notes for Faith about what's being served. She wants to add a Southern station to her catering offerings."

"Take my iPhone, Mom. You can snap some pictures and text her the descriptions," Mark said.

The twenty-first century. Not too shabby. She realized she was echoing her kids' highest words of praise.

"Give me that thing and show me what to push."

Mark laughed. "Love you, Mom."

"Love you, too, sweetie."

Soon Pix had captured, and sampled, the buffet: a bountiful raw bar; Charleston crab cakes; shrimp with cheese grits—Boursin, the server told her and she dutifully noted it for Faith—slices of roast pork with apples and dates; wild rice; biscuits with shavings of country ham; salad dressed with Vidalia onion vinaigrette; and the desserts! Pecan pie and Key lime pie, red velvet cupcakes, flourless chocolate cake with praline sauce, pineapple upside-down cake with rum sauce—Pix had resolutely stuck with champagne, but rum seemed to be flowing not just in the food, but in the mojitos—and an ambrosial layer cake new to Pix, hummingbird cake. Cissy Cohen urged a piece on her as she was taking the photo. "Nobody knows who invented it or where the name came from. It just appeared in the late nineteen sixties, and since then, you can't have a dessert table without it. My mother says it's called 'hummingbird cake' because it's as sweet as the nectar the birds like to drink, but I've also heard that it's called this since it makes you 'hum with delight.' Take a bite."

Pix did, and the combination of crushed pineapple, chopped ripe bananas, and chopped pecans—were they the official nut of South Carolina?—in the rich cake topped and layered with cream cheese frosting didn't make her want to hum. It made her want to sing out loud. Dessert was Pix's favorite form of food. She had the LIFE IS SHORT; EAT DESSERT FIRST pillow to prove it.

"You need some more champagne." Stephen Cohen was carrying a bottle of Mumm's.

" 'Need' may not be the correct word, but it is lovely. Thank you so much for tonight—and the whole time here. It's been perfect."

"Well, we plan on having many more of these good times," he said, looking into her eyes.

Recklessly Pix grabbed a fork and tapped the side of her glass. People had been making toasts all evening. She raised her glass as the room grew quiet.

"Many thanks to Stephen and Cissy, our hosts, and"—she faced Mark and Rebecca—"to you especially, but to everyone, 'May the best day of your past be the worst day of your future.' "

Past? What had she said? Had she gotten the quote right? She knew it was something about the past and future. She'd left out the middle about the present, though. Or maybe there wasn't a middle part. Stephen poured her some more champagne and kissed her cheek. Cissy patted her arm and said they were going to have so much fun in Charleston.

"Hear, hear!" someone cried out, and everyone clapped.

Sam appeared at her side.

"Very nice, dear."

Samantha appeared on her other side with a plate.

"I think you need to eat something, Mom," she said, laughing.

Faith brought the last of Niki's book cookies out and refilled the platters. They had been a big hit. Tom had arrived just after the talk and now he was speaking with the library director, making his apologies for being late. Faith could tell what he was saying by the look on his face. His face was an open book, appropriately enough for the evening's venue. Always had been and she hoped always would be. It was impossible for him to dissemble. Tonight, however, she wished he looked less like he'd lost his best friend and more like a man without a care in the world. No, maybe a little care, as befits a man of the cloth, but definitely a man without anything on his conscience—or money stashed in an offshore account.

He came over to her and picked up a cookie, *Crime and Punishment.* She snatched it back. "Try this one with the chocolate frosting," she said, handing him *The Hound of the Baskervilles* after skipping over *Gone with the Wind.* "Everything okay?" It wasn't like Tom to be late. Yankee that he was, if they were invited for seven o'clock, he'd stand on the doorstep a minute before and push the doorbell on the dot. New Yorker that Faith was, she'd first of all never invite guests that early, and next, plan on the earliest arriving thirty minutes late.

"Sam called. He was on his way to a big do the Cohens are throwing, but he wanted to caution me not to talk to anyone, not the vestry, no one, about any of this until he's back and can be present."

"That sounds like a very sensible idea," Faith said, knowing full well that her husband didn't view it that way at all. To him, it was an admission that he had something to hide that he could speak only with a lawyer present.

"I suppose."

"Anyway, you can talk to me. A wife can't testify against her husband, or for," she added hastily, as a look of alarm crossed Tom's so very expressive face. "I'm sure it won't come to any sort of court action," she bumbled on, cursing her runaway mouth.

"I'd better find out when we're supposed to make the pitch. Soon, I'd imagine, before people start to leave," Tom said, ashen- faced after his wife's remark.

The library board of trustees was composed of some town elected members plus all the "standing clergy." For Faith the phrase always conjured up images of some people sitting surrounded by others in robes standing over them. Weeks ago, the library director had asked Tom and Father Hayes to speak about the current, and omnipresent, fiscal crisis and hopefully coax a few checkbooks from pockets.

Court action, wives immune from testimony—what was she thinking of! Tom disappeared into the crowd and Faith saw Sherman Munroe give him one of his smarmy looks. She was sure this was a man whose face never betrayed him, just assumed whatever nasty pose he wished. It was all she could do to keep herself from seizing the bowl and dumping gunpowder punch over his head.

"Another success, boss. Looks like there won't be a single crumb left. Tricia will be disappointed." Scott began to clear away the serving platters that were empty.

"I made up a plate of goodies for you to take home."

"Thanks—and hey, I hope Niki gets one. Now that she's eating for two."

"Did she tell you she was pregnant?" Faith was surprised.

"Nah, but I've been through it twice, and remember, I'm one of five; Trish is one of seven, so somebody's always got a bun in the oven. I guess by now I've got some kind of babydar."

"Well, she isn't telling anyone, not even Phil—he lost his job, in case you didn't hear—so whatever you do, *don't* let her know that you know."

Scott shook his head. "Might not be a good time, but secrets from your old man? A big no-no. Trish pulled that, I'd be madder than hell."

Niki picked that moment to appear.

"Could you empty the coffee urn, Scott? I, well, I—"

Faith broke in. "I need you to help me scout the library for anything left around. I wouldn't want the librarians to find a dirty coffee cup shelved with New Books."

She wanted to help Niki out. She also didn't want the smell of the coffee to provoke sudden, uncontrolled evening sickness—much worse to discover on the shelves than a cup.

Scott winked at her.

Secrets. Too many secrets.

Have Faith's next event was less than twenty-four hours later, but the scene was markedly different. Occupants of the White House came and went. Hemlines rose and fell. Tides ebbed and flowed. Moons waxed and waned. But the Tiller Club remained unchanged. The Tillies, as they always referred to themselves, had first seen the light of day as a group of sixteen sailing buddies who'd grown up in places like Pride's Crossing, Hamilton, and Manchester-by-the-Sea on the Massachusetts North Shore. Despite boarding school and later college, they always managed to be home during the summer and spend every waking moment on the water. At age sixteen, they'd decided to formalize the bond with the club, adopting a crest with crossed tillers rampant on an azure shield topped by the prow of a ship emblazoned with "Carpe Tela"—"Seize the Tiller"—their boyish motto. The first of the club's bylaws defined the process for adding new members. One carefully vetted Tillie of their same age would be added each year. Niki, then Ms. Constantine, had been with Faith at the first Tillie dinner, and throughout the evening it was this bit of Tillie trivia Niki kept coming back to in astonishment. "So," she'd kept saying, "when they're all ninety-nine—and these WASP sailing types live forever—they're going to have to beat the bushes, or rather troll the briny deep, for someone named Chandler or Phelps who's still capable of steering straight at that age?" It had boggled Faith's mind, as well. So far—the Tillies were now forty—there had been no problem finding suitable candidates.

The Tillies took their social gatherings almost as seriously as their sailing. Most, in fact, combined the two, with cruises up the Maine coast to Northeast Harbor in the summer and to the Bahamas in the winter, during which there was much traveling between yachts for a "gam," which mimicked earlier whaling-ship visits back and forth solely in the amount of alcohol consumed by the captains. Ahab would not have had the Wheat

Thins with WisPride and Goldfish crackers thoughtfully provided by the wives, although there may have been hardtack to go with the grog.

Tonight's Spring Fling, the Tillies' concession to the club's slightly diminished funds, was a mere blip, the chairman assured Faith. A year hence, at most two, would find the traditional fall game dinners and summer clambakes firmly reinstated.

Faith was familiar with the yacht club in Marblehead. It was where the fall dinner had been held each year. The club didn't provide meals in the off-season, which was why the Tillies had needed a caterer, but it was possible to hire the club's waitstaff and Faith had always done so. Tonight she had pared that down, bringing both Scott and Tricia, whom she could depend on. Besides, the Phelans needed all the extra hours they could get with business at the body shop off. Scott was already busy tending bar—the Tillies may have opted for chicken instead of beef, but they weren't about to stint on alcohol. No silly drinks like Cosmos or Blue Martinis were bringing a more pronounced flush to cheeks ruddy from days squinting at the sun. It was strictly a scotch, bourbon, and possibly gin and tonic crowd with good clarets at dinner.

Servers were passing hors d'oeuvres: tiny duck beggar's purses, blood-orange-glazed shrimp on bamboo skewers, mini Cuban sandwiches, goat cheese gougères, and tuna tartare on potato crisps. No lobster, no smoked oysters or caviar, but she'd also set out platters with an assortment of roasted peppers, sausage slices, stuffed grape leaves, cubes of smoked gouda and jalapeño jack cheese, with plenty of bread sticks and crackers. She'd learned early on that the Tillies might have obediently eaten their veggies in the nursery, hence all those strong bones and good teeth, yet they didn't want to see anything resembling a crudité now. She'd mentioned Brussels sprouts sautéed in walnut oil and topped with toasted walnuts as an accompaniment for one of the game dinners, and the then chairman had looked as horrified as if she'd worn high heels on the teak deck of his Herreshoff.

The room was filling up and it was warm enough for some of the guests to sit out on the porch that stretched across the back of the club, facing the water. Each Tillie was allowed to bring one guest, and from the increasing volume of conversation, it appeared tonight was full muster—another happy Tillie dinner. As she crossed the large living room, Faith realized that the "cottage" on Martha's Vineyard that Ursula had been describing must have resembled the club, a late-Victorian wood-shingled structure with a decorous amount of trim. The floors were covered by good, and appropriately worn, Orientals. The fireplace that dominated one end of the room was massive. Genre seascapes in dire need of cleaning and photos of notable yachts and crews hung in between the trophy cases that lined the walls. The furniture tended toward comfortable leather sofas and oversized wing chairs.

The next two hours passed quickly as Faith and Niki hustled to get the food out. As Tricia and the waitstaff from the club served the traditional chocolate cake and coffee, Scott helped pack up the food and used dinnerware. He and Tricia were having babysitter problems and had to be home sooner than usual. They'd take the van. Faith and Niki could manage the rest, loading Faith's car.

"Sit down," Faith told Niki. "They're going to move on to their cigars and brandy. Things are starting to wind down, but they haven't inducted this year's member, which always takes a while."

Tillie events were rigorously choreographed. At the height of the evening, ribald toasts were made and they threw their napkins, tied into knots, at one another, dislodging their wives' headbands and causing their bow ties to run downhill. By the end of the evening they'd calmed down and took the swearing in of the newest Tillie seriously.

"I'm not tired," Niki said. "And you're the last person I expected to treat me as if I were made of glass. Another reason not to tell Mom—or Phil."

"You've been on your feet all night, missy. And I believe I have, in the past when you were not enceinte, told you to sit down when I thought you were tired."

"Okay, okay, maybe I'm a little sensitive."

Faith started to tell her it was hormones and then thought better of it. She also decided not to bring up the conversation they'd had in this very kitchen several years ago about communicating with one's spouse. Faith had hit a rocky patch in her marriage where she and Tom, especially Tom, were deliberately passing like ships in the night—the image appropriate to tonight's venue jumped back into her head. Each tentative start to discussing their problems that Faith placed in Tom's path had been ignored. It was Niki who'd set her straight, saying in essence that if Faith had wanted meaningful communication she was looking to the wrong gender. The phrase "we need to talk" was viewed completely differently by men and women, sending each in a diametrically opposed direction. Women to a side-by-side conversational exchange; men out the door for parts unknown.

It had been a big help, that talk. Niki and she had laughed—and cried a bit. Not long after, Faith and Tom weathered the storm. Tonight Faith wished she could remind Niki about the way Faith's taking the initiative, albeit obliquely, had solved the Fairchilds' problems.

"I know what you're thinking," Niki said.

"No you don't."

"Oh yes I do. This kitchen always brings it back and don't you dare throw my words in my face."

"I think you're doing it for me," Faith said.

For a moment she thought Niki was going to explode—she had inherited her mother's famous temper—and then she started laughing.

"I guess I am, but Faith, I'm not telling him. Not yet."

The sound of a utensil on a glass calling for quiet came from the next room.

"Come on, let's peek," Niki said, going to the door.

There was no need. The chairman was coming through it.

"Please join us as we wrap up the evening. As usual you've given us a splendid time and we all want to thank you before it ends."

Faith took off her apron, Niki followed suit, and they went into the dining room. The lights had been turned up.

"The membership committee head is going to introduce our new member and then I'd like to publicly thank you," the chairman whispered.

Faith smiled back at him, as she did at whoever was chairman each time the thank-you was proposed. If the script ever changed, she'd know that hell had frozen over.

"No surprises," Niki said softly into Faith's other ear as the newest Tillie stood up. "This isn't going to be the year they induct an African American, Jewish, Native American woman apparently."

But it *was* a surprise. When the newest Tillie stood up, Faith knew the name before it was announced.

The Reverend James Holden, First Parish's associate minister.

"I know James," she said to the chairman, so startled that she forgot to lower her voice.

"Good man, Holden. Great sailor. And damn lucky. Just bought the prettiest little Bristol thirty-three I've seen in a dog's age. Stole it from some poor guy declaring bankruptcy for only ten thou."

Ten thou, Faith thought. Ten thousand dollars.

James Holden was making a pretty little acceptance speech—and Faith could hardly wait to ask him where he'd come across all the pretty little pennies he'd used to buy the pretty little boat.

She wished she could jump up and corner him right now. After all, "Time and tide wait for no man"—or woman.

Chapter 7

"Afterward I was very ill for a long time," Ursula said, her words in concert with the steady downpour outside the window. The rain had started as Faith drove home from Marblehead the night before, building to a window-rattling thunderstorm in the early hours of the morning. Soccer practice had been canceled and both kids had quickly filled the unexpectedly free day with various activities with friends. Tom was rewriting his sermon yet again, and after checking with Dora, Faith had come to see Ursula, who was sitting up, looked well, and picked up the threads of her tale almost as soon as Faith entered the room.

"Scientists say you can't contract illnesses from shock, although a shock can make you feel ill, but I developed a serious case of scarlet fever. I had, most probably, contracted it days earlier on the Vineyard, but the symptoms were overlooked. I freckled in the sun and my high color had also been ascribed to too much exposure—and excitement. Before she left for Boston, Mother cautioned me to wear my broad-brimmed straw hat and stay in the cool shade.

"I don't remember leaving the island or even what happened immediately after I found Theo in the gazebo. Mother had a school friend who'd married an English-man and was living in Bermuda, where he had been posted as an adjunct of some sort to the governor. After I was out of danger, she and I went to stay with them in Hamilton for the rest of the fall and on into the winter.

"When I returned, my entire world had changed."

Faith was very close to her sister, Hope, one year younger. The thought of losing her was unbearable. Theo had been older, but the siblings appeared to have had a similar bond, especially on Ursula's part.

"It must have been terrible to return to the house, knowing he was gone from it forever," Faith said.

"The thing was that it wasn't my house."

Faith nodded. "It must have seemed like a totally different place without him."

"No, it really wasn't my house. While we were gone, Father sold the Beacon Hill house and moved us to Aleford."

Seeing Faith's astonishment, she added hastily, "Mother knew all about it, and on the steamship back, she told me we'd moved, but I hadn't fully taken it in until Father picked us up at the pier and we drove past the Boston Common without slowing down.

"He'd managed to hold on to the firm without declaring bankruptcy on Black Tuesday, but barely. Uncharacteristically he'd been investing heavily in the market and lost everything. And then there were Theo's debts. I learned all this later. At the time, I was protected as much as possible from the grim financial reality my parents were facing in the midst of their intense grief. And guilt. Mother blamed herself for leaving, although I don't see how she could not have gone. How could she have known? And her sister did have a close call. I believe, though, that to the end of her life, she wished she had insisted that the guests leave. Mother thought Mrs. Miles, the housekeeper they'd hired for the summer, would watch over things—she was quite a martinet—but she'd slipped out. Probably to meet someone to go to Illumination Night. Mother rued hiring her. And Father blamed himself for just about everything from renting the Vineyard house to not being strict enough with his son, although he may also have privately reproached himself for being too strict.

"During those times creditors did not expect to be paid—no one had money—but Father felt honor bound to settle Theo's accounts and his own even if it meant selling everything. The building with his offices and the house both went. The Pines in Sanpere didn't, but that was just because no one wanted to buy a big place like that on an unfashionable island. I believe for a while he thought that Mother and I might live there and he'd rent a room near where he'd rented office space. He let the servants go. When I think back, it must have been a terrifying time for him. Many of his wealthy friends were weathering the crisis, but an equal number were going under."

Then as now, Faith almost blurted out.

"He was too proud to ask anyone for a loan. Fortunately he had many loyal clients who stuck with him, although their reduced incomes meant a reduced income for him. Years later, after his death, Mother told me that he had worried all that summer about a fiscal crisis, but he was in the market too deep to pull out. He thought he'd suffer losses, and then he lost it all.

"Mother had inherited a house in Aleford from a maiden aunt and it had always been rented. Now it was to be our new home. I'll never forget arriving from Bermuda in the late afternoon—it was quite dark—driving down Main Street, which looked very pokey to me after Commonwealth Avenue. The house was on Adams Street, up the hill from the green. It's changed hands many times since we lived there and I barely recognize it. The current owners gutted it and added another story and all sorts of enormous windows."

And, Faith thought, probably a home gym, media room, spa, great room, and heaven knows what else—retromedieval banquet hall?

"It was a fair-sized early-nineteenth-century Colonial, but the ceilings were low and Father looked even taller coming through the doorways, which the top of his head just grazed. A local woman, Mrs. Hansen, helped Mother with the housework and the cooking—you've heard me talk about my Norwegian friend, Marit. That's how we met. Mrs. Hansen was her mother and Marit was my age. Mr. Hansen was a builder, and there was no work during the Depression, so they went back to Norway a few years after we moved to Aleford."

"I thought you'd been born here and grew up in this house," Faith said.

"After so much time, it seems like it, but my parents were both still alive and living in the Adams Street house when I got married and moved into this one . . ." Ursula paused. "You must be wondering about that."

"Arnold Rowe, the tutor. Your husband? Yes?"

Faith had hoped that Ursula would start with an explanation after her dramatic revelation the previous time, and it had been all she could do to keep from asking her about the Professor. Ursula, however, was telling her tale in her own way.

"It's the rest of the story and it's quite complicated," Ursula said.

"That's all right. Complicated is fine. The kids are with friends; Tom is with . . . well, himself and his maker, and I have as much time as you want."

"Good—but Dora will be cross if I don't eat. I've started going down to the kitchen for some meals. She left something in the fridge. If you'll take my arm, we can go see."

Dora had left what amounted to a ploughwoman's lunch—a more delicate version of the ploughman's wedges of cheddar cheese, relish, butter, and crusty bread. There was cheese, but thinly sliced, some chutney, the bread and butter plus salad, and with a nod to the Hanoverians, a modicum of Ursula's favorite— liverwurst.

After settling Ursula with a full plate and putting the kettle on for tea, Faith excused herself to make several phone calls with her cell.

"It's terribly rude, I'm sorry, but I wasn't able to reach two of the people I'm hoping can come for Sunday dinner after the service tomorrow."

"Don't be silly. I just may make Samantha happy and get one of those things myself. They're awfully convenient," Ursula said.

Seeing James Holden, the newest Tillie, had caused Faith a restless night until suddenly in the wee hours of the morning she'd had an idea, a plan to "catch the conscience of a king." She wasn't going to stage a play, but she was going to set a trap, and if it did not snare a mouse, it would at least have been baited.

She was going to give a dinner party, or rather a Sunday dinner party. She often invited people for post-church luncheon, so it would not seem out of the ordinary, and she was going to seed the guest list with her friends the Averys. Will and Patsy Avery were not members of First Parish, so had no idea of the current situation—otherwise Patsy would have been on the phone to Faith immediately. They had adopted siblings Kianna, age five, and her brother, Devon, age three, last fall after a prescient doctor asked them whether they wanted to reproduce themselves or raise a family together. For Patsy and Will, the answer was family, and they had found one in these harder-to-place older children, who were now also an extension of the Fairchild family. Ben didn't mind it one bit that Devon worshiped him—and Faith suspected he liked the opportunity to play with LEGOs again. Amy and Kianna were equally inseparable and the four children would consider it a treat to have their lunch in the kitchen, away from the grown-ups, before going out to play on the swing set. Tom and his brothers had constructed it shortly after

Ben was born, much to Faith's amusement. It would be some years before the infant could climb the tower or go down the slide, but the Fairchild boys had worked in a frenzy to get it ready—and it did seem in retrospect that Ben was on it in a very short time.

The other grown-ups she was inviting were the Reverend James Holden—Faith intended to steer the conversation to boat purchases—and Eloise Gardner, the education director, who was also on the list Tom and Faith had drawn up. Eloise was a clotheshorse. A few pairs of Manolos, a Prada bag, plus trips to Sonia Rykiel, Ralph Lauren, and Burberry would eat up the missing money in a flash.

She hadn't left messages on their machines when she'd called earlier, wanting a definite reply, and she was in luck. She reached them both and they would be happy to come. James had been previously, but Eloise hadn't and expressed particular delight at the opportunity to sample some "real food," confessing that her own "cuisine" was limited to the boxes in the freezer with "Lean" in front of the word. If Eloise turned out not to be the guilty party, Faith resolved to invite her for meals often. No one should be subjected to that kind of life.

Albert Trumbull, the parish administrative assistant, and Lily Sinclair, the former divinity school intern, as well as the vestry members on the list, would have to wait their turns for scrutiny.

She noticed she had a text and, after opening it, was pleased to find a response to the e-mail she'd sent to Zach Cummings Wednesday night. He apologized for not getting back to her sooner—and told her to call. He'd be around all weekend. He'd written, "Another mystery?" and added a winking smiley emoticon.

Things were looking up.

"Pour the tea and let's sit here awhile. I love to look at the river, no matter what the weather," Ursula said.

It was still pouring steadily and a pool had appeared at the bottom of Ursula's yard that hadn't been there earlier in the day. Faith hoped Tom had remembered to turn on the sump pump, so the parsonage basement wouldn't flood. For a brief moment she thought longingly to the time in her life when she'd had no idea what a "sump pump" was.

"Here's where I say, 'Reader, I married him,' although not for many years. It was, in fact, quite a while before I thought of Arnold Rowe at all. It never occurred to me that he hadn't gone on to law school, completed his studies, and joined the ranks of desperate job seekers. I didn't know about the trial and had blocked the image of him in the gazebo from my conscious mind. My unconscious was not so cooperative.

That first year I was plagued by nightmares, waking with feelings of terror; but not wanting to disturb my parents, I would turn on the light and read until sleep, uninterrupted, returned.

"The same aunt who'd owned our house was an alumna of the Cabot School here in town and had left a substantial endowment for scholarships. Mother approached the headmistress, and upon returning from Bermuda, I was enrolled there as a day student. Life took on a semblance of normalcy with new routines. Father took the train into town; I walked to school; and Mother managed the house, although her heart was in the garden. In the spring, that's where I'd find her, sometimes with tears in her eyes and I knew she'd been thinking of Theo. I missed him dreadfully and I didn't have anyone to talk to about him. Mother and Father never mentioned him, or what had happened. There were no visible pictures of him in the house, nothing to indicate he had ever existed."

"Why do you think this was?" Faith asked. It seemed so extreme. Theo hadn't committed a crime. He was the victim of one.

"Mostly because it was too painful—and people didn't 'let it all hang out' in those days, remember— but also because Aleford represented a new beginning for the family. The trial started in late October. Any reports would have been eclipsed by the day's more dramatic accounts of bank and business failures. In addition, although Aleford was the same number of miles from town then as it is now, much more distance separated the two when it came to communication at that time. It was truly a backwater.

"Earlier, in August, there had been a quiet funeral at King's Chapel and afterward he was buried in the Lyman family plot at Mount Auburn cemetery. I was too ill to be present."

Ursula sounded as bereft now as she was then. Faith's heart ached for her. Barely out of childhood, she had had the initial loss repeated over and over again with no one to talk to about her brother, no one with whom she could remember the happy days, years that had preceded his untimely death.

"He always kept Butterfinger candy bars in his pocket for me. They were my favorite. I haven't been able to eat one since . . ."

Ursula hated Aleford. She kicked a stone on the sidewalk. It felt so good, she kicked another. Cabot wasn't anything like Winsor, her old school. The day students, especially the ones on scholarships, were second-class citizens so far as the boarders were concerned. And how did they know—these girls who brought their own horses and talked of summers in the Adirondacks? Horses. Cabot was a very horsey school. Ursula had never ridden. The only horses she ever saw had been the ones the mounted police rode on the Boston Common.

She missed her friends. In the first months after the move, her mother had said not to worry, that they'd keep in touch and that Ursula could visit them often. And there had been a few letters back and forth, no one saying what they must all have been thinking, but these had petered out. The visits never materialized, and the only time she went to town was to go to church and see her cousins afterward. Even that wasn't every Sunday. Her parents had started attending First Parish out here. It was nothing like King's Chapel. A boring white church with a steeple just like every other one you saw on the greens of New England. King's Chapel was made of stone, soaring pillars in front and inside vaulting that took your eye to the beautiful sky-blue ceiling above. It was the oldest church in Boston and didn't have a steeple. So there. She kicked another stone.

It was wicked to feel this way. She knew that, and in a flash she thought that Theo would have understood. He would have said, "Don't worry about it, squirt. Everything's going to be hunky-dory." But it wasn't and hadn't been.

She'd shot up the first spring here. Not surprising given how tall her parents were, but she felt like Alice after she'd nibbled the cake labeled "Eat Me." The Cabot girls her age were petite and dainty. She hated them. If it wasn't for Marit she didn't know what she'd do. And even with Marit, she wasn't able to talk about Theo.

Theo. She missed him all the time, and it seemed each day brought a fresh reminder, fresh pain. Last week she had been looking in the living room bookshelves for something about King Arthur and came across one of Theo's books from his course on medieval history with his name and address printed in his sprawling handwriting on the title page. The Professor ran the study sessions for the course, which helped Theo pass, and that's why Father had hired him to tutor Theo over the summer. Ursula had dropped the book, but picked it up immediately and rearranged the others to fill the space it had occupied. She took it to her room, searching in vain for any notes or underlinings Theo might have made, and slipped it behind her Little Colonel books in her own bookcase. Theo had given her a copy of his formal freshman portrait. The photo and now the book were all she had of him. His gift, her treasured wristwatch, had disappeared, lost that night or during the days that followed. She didn't want another one, and in any case, they were too expensive for the Lymans now.

She turned on Adams Street. It was the beginning of their third fall in Aleford. Nineteen thirty-one. Soon it would be 1932. Father had been able to let Sanpere for the last two summers at what Mother said was a "giveaway price," but it was something. Ursula hated the thought of strangers at The Pines. Maybe next summer . . .

Would things ever get better? She'd heard Father tell Mother that so many shoe and textile factories, the mainstays of Massachusetts manufacturing, had closed that former workers' children were barefoot and in tatters. People were going hungry, too. Several Sundays ago they had passed a long line of people on Tremont Street, and when she asked what it was her mother told her they were waiting to get served at a soup kitchen. One man facing the street had a placard around his neck saying he would work for food. That his children were starving.

She was wicked. She had food and a very pleasant roof over her head. A school to go to when so many others had none of these things. She pinched her arm and vowed to stop being so self-centered.

She was almost home. Adams Street was lined with tall maples and oaks. The leaves were brilliant reds and golds and would start falling soon. Falling, too, on Theo's grave. A grave she'd never seen. She blinked back her tears, wiped her eyes, and stood up straighter. She didn't want to upset her mother.

Aleford. What a stupid name. She hated this place and was counting the days until she'd be old enough to leave and never come back.

"**Well, your** two lovebirds are certainly discreet," Patsy Avery said to Faith as she came in through the kitchen door. Will and the children went straight through to the living room.

"Lovebirds?" Faith was startled, but not so startled that she failed to take the sweet potato pie from Patsy's outstretched hands.

"Didn't you say you'd asked the Reverend Holden to come? I recognized him, but not the woman. They were holding hands as they walked down the church driveway toward the cemetery, but dropped them as soon as they got to where you might see them from your back window. There they are now coming around to the front door."

"The woman is Eloise Gardner, our education director. Are you sure their hands didn't just touch in a sort of friendly accidental way?"

226 · KATHERINE HALL PAGE

"Nope. This was fingers entwined. Nothing accidental about it, unless you call love an accident, which it certainly can be."

The front doorbell rang.

"Tom," Faith called. "Could you get that? It's our other guests."

Eloise and James. This was definitely a new twist, Faith thought. Tom hadn't mentioned anything about a budding romance between the two, but then, it wasn't the sort of thing he'd notice, not until he was invited to the wedding. And Faith rarely saw the two together. Eloise was around after Sunday school, but she generally didn't attend coffee hour—too many parents wanting to grab her attention, Faith assumed.

Did Patsy's observation make Faith suspect either individual or both more, or less?

She turned her attention to the roast. Faith was a firm believer in traditional Sunday dinners. Today it was a leg of lamb with new potatoes and asparagus. The first asparagus was coming in from California and Faith was roasting it at the last minute in the oven with olive oil and garlic, a drizzle of lemon when she took it out. The tips would be slightly crunchy, the stems tender. The potatoes had been steamed and were in the pan with the fragrant lamb to brown. She'd seasoned the roast with more garlic and rosemary. If James and

Eloise were an item perhaps she should leave some breath mints on the table at the end of the meal.

"What's this?" Patsy asked, pointing toward a small dish filled with some sort of red jelly.

"I refuse to spoil lamb with mint jelly, no matter what my husband got used to as a child. But he still wants something like it, so that's red pepper jelly."

"Will has to have Heinz catsup with his scrambled eggs and the eggs have to be almost burned because that's how his mother made them. What will our children be laying on their poor spouses, I wonder?"

"Given what you put on your table, they're going to have a hard act to follow," Faith said.

"Ditto, but I plan on teaching both of mine to cook—a gift to whomever. And you've already taught Ben and Amy to do more than push a button on the microwave."

This was true, although there was plenty of button pushing, but both kids had always enjoyed messing around in the kitchen with mom, something Faith had never experienced.

Things were going well. There was nothing like good food and a glass or two of wine—a nice, full-bodied 2008 Porcupine Ridge Syrah from South Africa—to make people feel relaxed. Will was talking about how growing up in New Orleans, he and his friends would sneak into Preservation Hall and other jazz joints when they were young teens.

"The music never left and the rest of the city is definitely coming back," he said. "That Super Bowl win didn't hurt."

"Didn't hurt," Patsy cried. "Folks are still hanging their Saints banners all over the place and don't even think of wearing a cap or T-shirt anywhere in Louisiana with another team's name."

Faith decided it was time to try to steer the conversation in the direction she'd intended.

"Are you a sports fan, James? I know you must follow things like the America's Cup." She addressed the whole table. "I learned last night that James is an accomplished sailor when he was inducted into the Tiller Club. Have Faith catered the dinner."

"Congratulations," Will said. "My time on the water has been strictly limited to trying to get crawfish in the bayous, but I've always wanted to sail."

The Reverend had flushed at Faith's words. Yes, she'd been pretty obvious and now she was going to push it even more.

"James just bought a new boat, the club chairman told me. I don't remember exactly how big it is, though."

"Not that big," he said quickly. "I was able to get it for a very low price. The owner was forced to declare bankruptcy."

"So I heard. A great bargain. What was it? Ten—"

Before Faith could finish the sentence, everyone's attention turned to Eloise Gardner, who'd spilled what was left in her wineglass down the front of the light beige blazer she was wearing with a black pleated skirt.

"Club soda," Patsy said, getting up.

"I'm so sorry, but I don't think any went on your tablecloth or the rug," Eloise said.

"Don't worry. Patsy's right about the club soda and I have plenty in the kitchen," Faith said. The three women left the table, and as Faith went through the door, she heard James say, "So what kind of law do you specialize in, Will?"

Captain Holden had seized the tiller and was steering in another direction.

Club soda worked its magic and the wine had not spilled on Eloise's ivory-colored silk blouse or the scarf she was wearing draped across her shoulders.

"Your jacket should be dry enough to wear by the time you leave," Faith said.

"Even if it isn't, I won't need it. It's so warm today. Winter may truly be behind us."

Patsy straightened Eloise's scarf. "There, you look fine. And I love the nautical pattern."

Faith loved it, too. The scarf was from Hermès—the Christopher Columbus model to commemorate his supposed discovery of America. Hermès scarves like this one cost about $400.

"It was a gift from—a gift from a friend." Eloise stumbled over the words.

Patsy gave Faith a knowing look.

"Well, that must be a very thoughtful friend—and a good thing the wine missed it. As long as we're out here, why don't we give these starving children some dessert and put the pie in to warm?"

There were cheers from the round table by the window where the kids had been watching the cleanup. Nobody had spilled anything at their table, they seemed to be saying.

Eloise, Patsy, and Faith returned to the dining room. Clearing plates, Faith thought to herself, as Sigmund had said, There are no accidents. . . .

The party broke up after dessert. Will took the children home—Devon needed his nap—but Patsy insisted on staying to help Faith and headed for the kitchen. Eloise expressed her appreciation for the "gourmet meal," retrieved her damp jacket, and left. As Tom was seeing her out, Faith was left alone in the dining room with James.

"A delicious meal, as always. Thank you," he said.

His stern expression was at odds with the appreciative words.

"I'm glad you were able to make it," Faith said.

"I come from a family of sailors," he said abruptly. "Holdens have always owned boats. Airing First Parish's dirty laundry in public is not my style and I wasn't about to respond to your innuendos, but I can assure you that I am not involved in any way with Tom's problem."

Faith felt as if he had slapped her. He might as well have. And "Tom's problem"? The good Reverend was firmly distancing himself.

"I'm not sure I know what you're getting at, James."

"Oh, I think you do and I'm telling you to stay out of my business. Boat buying or anything else I do on my own time has nothing to do with my commitment at First Parish."

Faith knew he was speaking of "commitment" as in "calling," but it certainly suggested "confinement." She realized that she didn't know much about James. Although he'd been at the church almost two years, she still thought of him as newly arrived. He wasn't particularly outgoing, but both Tom and the vestry seemed happy with him, and she hadn't heard any complaints from the congregation. She hadn't heard much praise, either.

Tom came in. "Care to sit in the living room for a while, James? Another cup of coffee?"

"Thank you, no. I have to be in Cambridge soon."

I'll bet you do, Faith thought. Eloise lived near Inman Square.

He left and Tom went out to join the kids in the backyard. When Faith went into the kitchen, where Patsy had already filled the dishwasher, she could see her husband, rake in hand, heading for the thick winter leaf cover on the perennial beds.

There wasn't much food left, but Faith put it away and was starting on the roasting pan when Patsy said, "Leave it to soak and pour me another cup of coffee. One for you, too. I want to know what's going on."

Faith had been waiting for this. Like her husband, Patsy was a lawyer, a juvenile public defender. Faith and she had been involved in two investigations over the years and Faith had learned that nothing much got past Ms. Avery. She couldn't tell Patsy what was going on at First Parish, but if Patsy guessed . . . Faith laughed to herself as she admitted this was one of the things she'd hoped would happen today.

"Tom barely said two words all through lunch and he's attacking those poor flower beds as if the leaves were hiding Satan himself," Patsy said. "You start telling us about some boat and Reverend Holden looks like he's been caught with his hand in the Poor Box." Faith tried to suppress her gasp at Patsy's apt description.

"So that's it," Patsy said slowly. "Money. Of course. A financial irregularity at First Parish. You don't have to say anything. I know you can't. You suspect James Holden and maybe the Sunday school director, too."

Faith lowered her head toward her coffee to take a sip. It could also have been seen as a nod.

"But somehow Tom is being blamed, judging from the way he's behaving—and the look on his face. One of those 'My dog is lost; can you help me find him?' kinds."

Faith took another sip.

"Does he need a lawyer?"

"He has one," Faith blurted out. "Sam. He's away for the rest of the week, though."

"Okay, I didn't hear anything. Sam Miller is a good choice, especially as he knows the cast of characters. But before I leave, answer me one question: Why did Ms. Eloise pour her wine down her jacket so carefully? I saw it and she did a fine job of dribbling it so it missed her very expensive scarf and white blouse. Hmmm?"

"Hmmm," was all Faith could think of in reply.

Dora had come in Ursula's kitchen door the day before, closing her wet Mary Poppins umbrella behind her. She'd smiled broadly at the scene. Ursula's plate was almost clean. She was popping a last bit of liverwurst in her mouth. Faith had been afraid Dora would chase her away, but instead she had suggested she make a fire in the living room fireplace. "You can stretch out on the couch, Mrs. Rowe, and Mrs. Fairchild can keep you company a bit longer. Her visit today looks like it's done you a world of good."

Faith was conscious of a gold star about to be pasted next to her name in the Book of Dora.

Once Ursula was ensconced in front of the fire with an afghan that Faith recognized as Pix's handiwork, she began to talk.

"As I said, I hadn't given any thought to Arnold Rowe. I tried not to think about that night at all, although it was always with me, not far from the surface. I was very restless in Aleford and had never settled into the Cabot School. I thought of myself as a city girl.

"Time went by, I turned sixteen and shortly afterward two things happened that changed my life forever. The first was finding a box of clippings about the murder and the trial. The Adams Street house had a large attic and things from our Boston house that Mother wanted to save, but didn't have room for downstairs, were stored there. She never liked to go up in the attic—mice and spiders—but I loved it. There were two small round windows at either end, so it wasn't dark. I'd often take a book and curl up on a chair that I'd dragged closer to the light at the end overlooking the garden. The trunks and boxes didn't interest me, but one day Mother asked me to go through them for some curtains when I went up to read. She thought she could have Mrs. Hansen cut them down for the kitchen. The Hansens were going back to Norway, much to my dismay—I was already missing Marit—and Mother wanted to get as much sewing as possible done before they left.

"I found the curtains after much searching and was about to close that trunk when I saw there was a letter file in the bottom. These were large hinged boxes covered with marbleized paper where people used to file correspondence. My father had rows of them on the shelves in his office and I wondered what this one was doing here. I opened it and saw that the folders were filled with newspaper clippings and letters from a Boston law firm.

"I knew what it contained even before reading a single word—and why it had been tucked so far away. Perhaps that wasn't a bad idea, and I considered leaving it where it was, unread. I was torn between not wanting to be reminded of that summer and wanting to know what had been happening during the time I had been ill. And then one of the headlines caught my eye: 'Sentenced to Life: Tutor Convicted of Murdering Pupil.'

"I felt sick. All the time that I'd been going about my little life, Arnold Rowe had been in prison for his life—the Charles Street Jail, to be precise."

Faith wondered whether Ursula knew that the jail, closed in 1973 because overcrowding violated the constitutional rights of the inmates, had reopened in 2007, after extensive remodeling, as a high-end luxury hotel ironically named the Liberty Hotel. Faith wasn't sure whether such features as the Alibi Bar in the old drunk tank, the Clink restaurant with its vestiges of the original jail cells, and even the phone number (JAIL) represented a witty or totally inappropriate sense of humor. In its day, just before the Civil War, it had been hailed as a step forward in prison architecture with four wings to segregate prisoners by gender and offense extending from a ninety-foot-tall atrium. The multitude of arched windows set into the granite structure let in light and air, but didn't let anyone out, of course.

"I started to read straight through. The first clippings described the murder itself and I immediately knew something was wrong with the reports. First of all, the party was described as a 'small gathering of friends,' and then there was a reference to an eyewitness who saw Theo go toward the gazebo at midnight followed by Arnold Rowe. I felt terribly confused. Certain parts of the night were as clear in my memory as they had been when they happened and I knew that Theo had been in the gazebo arguing with someone, a man, well before midnight. I'd been asleep and they'd awakened me. My watch had a luminous dial, quite a new thing, and it was eleven-thirty. I wasn't able to identify the man's voice, just Theo's, but I did know it wasn't Arnold's. So who was there earlier with Theo? I read through the rest of the articles on the murder, including the news of Arnold's arrest. There were far fewer about the trial, which was held in Edgartown at the Dukes County Courthouse. By that time, the country was caught up in the aftermath of the stock market crash. People were more concerned about their next meal and a roof over their heads than what was characterized as a fight turned deadly between two Harvard students. The trial was short and the guilty verdict swift. A court-appointed lawyer represented Arnold. I couldn't find any indications of his line of defense. Without the proper facility on the island, Arnold had been immediately transferred to the prison in Boston."

Ursula had been only sixteen! Faith pictured herself at that age. Her sister, a year younger, had mapped out her entire future—Pelham College undergrad,

Harvard for an MBA, summer internships at the appropriate firms, and finally partner with a corner office on a top floor with multiple-figure bonuses. And it had all come true. Faith meanwhile had been busy thinking up ever new excuses to get out of gym and ways to get Emilio, the very cool Italian exchange student, to notice her. Ursula at that age was dealing with issues an adult would have had difficulty with—complicated by grief over an irreplaceable loss.

"Finding the box was both liberating—I now knew more about what happened—and depressing—there were still so many unanswered questions. Had there been a thorough investigation? And what about the reporters' mistakes? It was not a small party, but a very large one. There was a single sentence mentioning a 'fierce' argument earlier in the evening between my brother and Arnold Rowe. Yet, at the time when it supposedly occurred we were at Illumination Night. The word 'fierce' surprised me, too. Theo could get annoyed, but even when he'd overly imbibed—in fact especially then—he was always very easygoing, and I'd never heard the Professor raise his voice.

"I returned often in the following weeks to reread the contents of the box until I had it virtually memorized, and then there was the second stroke of luck. Or divine intervention, if you will. I firmly believe in both.

"Mother and I had taken the train into town to see Aunt Myrtle. My cousins, whom I had thought would be there, weren't at home. Seeing that I was at loose ends, my aunt sent me to Stearn's to buy gloves on her account. I'm sure she noticed the ones I was wearing were outgrown. In those days you didn't go into town without a hat and gloves. The department store was on Tremont Street across from the Common. I wish you could have seen it—it closed in the late 1970s. Such elegance."

"My mother and I still miss B. Altman in New York—it sounds like the same kind of place."

"I had selected a lovely pair of gray kid gloves when I heard a couple talking behind me. The man was urging the woman to buy a coat she had just tried on. He was tired of shopping and didn't want to go to another store. She was resisting. I recognized both their voices immediately and told the saleswoman I wanted to try the gloves on in brown so I could remain at the counter. The woman was Violet Hammond and the man was Charles Winthrop. They hadn't changed much, especially Violet. She was still turning heads.

"When the saleswoman brought the gloves for me to try on, my hands were shaking. Violet and Charles were continuing their discussion directly behind me. He was growing increasingly angry and I didn't simply recognize the voice of the man who had been a guest at the Vineyard, but I recognized it as the man who had been arguing with Theo in the gazebo. Charles Winthrop was there well before Arnold. Charles Winthrop was the one who was desperate for money. Charles Winthrop had killed Theo."

"Are you all right, miss?"

"Yes, just a bit faint. I'll be fine in a minute."

Ursula desperately needed to sit down. She was leaning against the counter, the neat rows of gloves arrayed on the shelves beneath the glass. So many kinds of gloves. Long, short, even the arm-length kind debutantes and brides wore. They began to swirl together in front of her eyes. She closed them to keep from passing out.

Charles Winthrop. The voice. The other noises. He'd hit Theo. In her mind she heard her brother again, "Whadya have to smack me for? Thought we were friends." The thumping noise. Charles must have hit Theo again, hit him too hard. The sound she'd assumed was both of them running back to the party had been Charles alone. Charles running away to do what? Involve Arnold Rowe. Find someone else to blame. Maybe it was an accident. It had to have been. People didn't go around killing people like that. He'd hit Theo too hard. It had to be that.

No! It wasn't supposed to be at all. Theo was dead and Charles was guilty. Not the young man in a cell a short walk away.

"I'll be a good little wife, Charlie. Calm down. People are starting to look at us. It's a perfectly adorable coat."

The couple moved off. Ursula told the saleswoman she'd take the gray gloves. By the time they were signed for and wrapped, she had regained her composure.

"The couple behind me just now. Do you know who they are?"

The girl answered readily, "Oh yes, miss. That's Mr. and Mrs. Charles Winthrop. Very good customers."

Ursula had had to be sure. And she was also sure of her next stop. Her mother and her aunt would talk for hours more. She tucked her parcel in her purse and turned her steps toward the Charles Street Jail.

The fire was burning low, but Faith didn't want to interrupt Ursula by putting another log on. Outside the rain had tapered off, but the sky was still dark.

"I've never told anyone about all this, except Arnold of course. A few days ago you and I were talking about coincidence. Cosmic coincidences, a dear friend used to call them. If Aunt Myrtle hadn't sent me to Stearn's it's unlikely that I would ever have seen the Winthrops. I was seldom in town, and in any case, we didn't travel in the same circles.

"Unlike today, that day was beautiful. Early spring, like now. As I walked down Tremont Street past King's Chapel and, yes, continuing on through Scollay Square into the West End, where the jail was located, I felt a warm presence. It was as though Theo were near. It gave me courage and strengthened my resolve. I thought I knew now who had killed him, but even so I realized I had known all along that Arnold hadn't."

Ursula paused, staring into the embers in the fireplace.

"That being so, I was just going to have to unmask the real murderer myself."

Chapter 8

It took Faith about twelve seconds to decide Lily Sinclair was a total bitch.

Hoping that face-to-face contact would give her an advantage in discovering any involvement on Lily's part, Faith didn't call the young divinity school student, but took a chance at finding her home early on a Monday morning. Lily lived in Somerville off Davis Square. Faith was meeting Zach Cummings at a nearby Starbucks at ten. Zach lived in Somerville, too. Somerville was a very happening place, much more affordable than Cambridge. New restaurants, bars, cafés, and shops had sprung up like mushrooms, fortunately not displacing old favorites like Redbones barbecue.

The face-to-face was not going well. Yes, Lily was home, but for a while it seemed Faith's interaction with her would begin and end quickly on the front porch of the double-decker's first-floor apartment. Lily's name, plus two others, was listed by the buzzer. Lily had answered the door, but didn't take the chain off. The opening was wide enough to reveal that her visitor was someone known to her and not an assailant, but she still didn't make a move. Her face was impassive.

"Hi, Lily. It's Faith, Faith Fairchild."

"Yes, I know. What do you want?"

That's when Faith rapidly jumped to her conclusion. At the same time, she realized that she really didn't know the people with whom Tom worked anymore. When they were first married—and continuing on to when the kids were younger before she had started the business again—she had had much more contact with everyone working in the church offices. Walter, James Holden's predecessor, had been a dear family friend.

Lily had been one in a string of interns that were little more than names to Faith, but she thought she had parted on good, if not close, terms with the young woman. She'd brought Lily a going-away gift her last Sunday in church back in January and had received a smiling thank-you. What had happened since then?

"May I come in?" Faith was beginning to feel like someone selling encyclopedias.

The door closed, and then opened wide. Lily, who was wearing Hello Kitty pajamas, led the way down a short hall into the kitchen at the rear of the apartment. It was obviously shared. Dishes were piled in the sink and a pot of what might have been chili was on the stove, its burners encrusted with many other offerings. Lily sat down and picked up the spoon sticking out from a bowl of cereal. She didn't offer Faith anything—neither a seat nor food. Faith was happy at this particular rudeness as it meant she wouldn't have to say no. It wasn't that the place was a health hazard, well maybe, but it certainly was unappetizing.

"I know why you're here," Lily said, crunching her granola.

"You do?" For a moment Faith herself had lost the thread. She was distracted by a makeshift clothesline strung from a knob on a cabinet to a catch on one of the windows. It was adorned with rather gray BVDs and decidedly not gray thongs.

"Look, I didn't take the money. I never even knew about the fund. And if you must know, my time in Aleford, or should I say Stepford, convinced me a parish ministry is the last thing I want. I've taken a leave from the Div School." She put her spoon down and drank the milk from the bowl.

Faith concentrated on the first words.

"How do you know about the missing money?"

Lily shrugged. "I guess it's no big secret. Al told me."

Albert Trumbull, the parish secretary, or rather administrative assistant. Faith didn't really know him all that well, either. Certainly she wasn't on an "Al" basis with him. She longed for the good old days with Madame Rhoda and her psychic powers, a mystery at first when the woman appeared to be living a double life, but oh so much more explainable than all this young weltschmerz. Albert was on leave from the Div School and finding himself, too. *O tempora, O mores.*

Faith thought she should express concern over the second half of Lily's remarks. The missing money could wait a bit.

"It sounds as if you weren't happy at First Parish and I hope your time with us didn't contribute to your decision. You know Tom is always available to talk with you."

Lily flushed and pushed her bowl away. "Oh, he's a talker, all right, and let's just say my time with you didn't 'contribute,' it *caused* my decision."

Before Faith could say anything more, Lily got up and moved toward the door to the hall. The interview was clearly over. Faith had no choice but to follow.

As Lily virtually pushed her out, Faith managed to ask, "Do you have any idea who might have taken the money?"

Lily smiled wickedly. "I'd suggest you ask your husband. The talker."

Walking back toward Elm Street and Starbucks, Faith's mind was filled with questions for her husband, but they didn't have to do with the missing funds. They concerned Ms. Lily Sinclair.

Faith was on her second latte—she'd indulged in whole milk for the first one to soothe her troubled soul and was now nursing a skinny one—when Zach Cummings walked in. She'd scored two comfy armchairs, placing her jacket on the unoccupied one and ignoring an occasional angry look. Let them displace some of the other customers who seemed to have moved in with their laptops permanently—and nary a cup of joe in sight.

She waved Zach over and handed him her Rewards Card.

"Go nuts. Get whatever you want," she said. Zach was taller than he'd been when she'd met him at Mansfield Academy years ago, but still as thin, and still dressed in black. His legs looked like pipe stems and he was wearing a T-shirt with a screwdriver pictured in white that read I VOID WARRANTIES.

He reached into a pocket and waved his own card. "I've got it. You good?"

She nodded. It was hard to remember he was an adult now. Or almost.

He returned with what appeared to be a Venti of black coffee.

"So, what's up?" he said.

"I need to know how someone could get access to someone else's bank account through an ATM, withdrawing a significant amount of cash over the course of a year."

"Same machine?"

"Yes—and twenty transactions."

"For the limit each time?"

Faith nodded.

"And this is all theoretical, right? You're helping someone write a book or something so everything you say is off the record and vice versa?"

"Completely theoretical, hypothetical, even rhetorical. I'm a little muddled—it's been a bad morning."

Zach shook his head. "I'm sorry, Faith." His expression indicated he was talking about more than her morning. He set his coffee down.

"Well, to start, have you heard of shoulder surfing?"

"Yes, but I don't know that much about it except it's a way to get a PIN by peeking over a shoulder somehow."

"It's the simplest way, especially for a nonhacker. All you have to do is act casual and watch someone enter their PIN at an ATM or a place like this—a cybercafé that has WiFi, even a library. At crowded airports, they sometimes use miniature binoculars to look at people using bank terminals. Shoulder surfing would be the first thing I'd consider, especially as it's the same location for each transaction. Try to recall who was close by before the first withdrawal. Was it a stranger or someone our theoretical person knew?"

"Okay, what next?"

"It gets a little more complicated, but not by much for anyone with a modicum of computer smarts. These are all phishing scams, spelled with a 'ph,' and are what they sound like—throwing out some 'bait' to see what gets caught in the net, on the Net. They try to trick you into revealing things like your Social Security number, passwords, credit card numbers—you get the picture. You'll get an e-mail or IM that seems to be an authentic one from your bank or the IRS. It purports to be alerting you to a serious problem. In order to correct it before it gets even worse, you must respond immediately with your information. It may even take you to a Web site that looks exactly like your bank's. A recent scam claimed to be from UPS and had you enter your credit card number to track a recent attempted delivery. Most people are getting stuff all the time, or if not, might assume someone had sent a gift, so this was very effective until it was flagged."

Faith was stunned. "I had no idea that there were all these risks. It's a wonder anything online is safe."

"This is just the tip of the iceberg. I'm assuming your, sorry, your friend's account was a random attack—caught in that big net. But it may have been targeted—'spear phishing.' Again, there would have been an e-mail message or IM, but addressed specifically to the account's user. There's also 'spoofing,' which is forging data, particularly an address, so that it seems as if it's secure. Misspelling one word, for example, which most people miss."

"Spoofing, phishing—who thinks these things up?"

"Oh, hackers are fun guys. Look at me," Zach said.

Faith did—hard.

"Whoa, I'm a White Hat. One of the good guys. I get paid to try to hack into systems and find out where they're vulnerable. It's a nice gig."

"What else?"

"Ask the person if they've received a message to call the bank, or a phone call purporting to be from the bank or your credit card company giving you a number to call. Again there's an urgent problem. The phone number you punch in takes you to the phisher's, or in this case visher's—voice phising—VOIP account, where you are asked to enter your bank account number and so forth."

"VOIP?"

"Voice over Internet Protocol—basically what it comes down to is making 'phone calls' over the Internet. You have no idea that it isn't originating from a regular phone number."

"I don't think there have been any calls like this, but I'll check."

"If you could arrange it, the best thing would be for me to take a look at the person's computer. What is it, by the way?"

"There are two—an old MacBook and a newer Dell." The Dell was in Tom's office and had replaced his previous PC a year or so ago. She gave a start.

"What's wrong?" Zach asked.

"The PC. I'm pretty sure the withdrawals started at the same time it arrived."

"Interesting." Zach got up and stretched. "I need more coffee. Want anything?"

Faith shook her head, but asked him what he was drinking. Black coffee seemed pretty boring and Zach was not a boring guy.

"They have something I like called the 'Gazebo Blend.' That with two shots."

Skimming over the thought of all that caffeine, Faith focused on the name, and the coincidence. "Gazebo." There are no accidents, she said to herself. It was getting to be a mantra.

When Zach returned he said, "Of course, the easiest way to get into someone's ATM account if you have stolen the card is to guess their password. That provides access into anything password-protected on their computer, too."

"With all the possibilities, I'd have thought this would be the most difficult."

"People are innately trusting—or lazy. They go for the simplest to remember and they use one password for all their accounts. 'One, two, three, four, five, six'—occasionally with more numbers in sequence—is the number one password, followed by 'QWERTY,' an individual's birthday, phone number, pet name. You get the idea. Your password should have at least six letters—longer makes it more difficult for a hacker, as does mixing letters and numbers. And you should change your passwords with some frequency, but people don't. They're afraid they'll forget a new one— and they're . . ."

"Lazy," Faith finished for him. A whole world of possibilities had opened up. Tom wasn't lazy, but he was trusting. Very trusting. It went with the territory.

"If this is someone you know, I'll bet you can guess his or her password." He drained his cup. "Gotta run, but I can come out next weekend and have a look at all your computers. Check them out. Make sure you have the proper spam filters."

Ben would be in heaven. Zach was a god so far as her son was concerned, and the highlight of his year to date had been a trip to MIT's new Media Lab with Zach.

"You've been an enormous help. I wish there was something I could do in return."

"You kept me out of jail, remember? I'd say that should do it for anything you want for the rest of your life," Zach said, smiling.

Faith's phone was vibrating. It was Tom.

"I need to take this," she said.

"Go ahead. I have to get to class, so I'll say good-bye."

Faith answered the call, giving Zach a swift hug as he left.

"Hi, honey. I was about to call you. I'm still in Somerville."

She had told Tom about meeting with Zach, but not about trying to see Lily. After both encounters, she was now itching to get home and talk to her spouse.

"What did he have to say?"

"Too much to go over on the phone. I'll be home in half an hour. Can you get away?"

"Shouldn't be a problem. I'll make lunch."

Faith hung up. She had certainly married the right man. He had his priorities straight.

Tom had made toasted cheese sandwiches, or toasted "cheesers," as he called them. It was his comfort food, together with Campbell's cream of tomato soup. While Faith maintained that "food snob" was a compliment, especially in her case, she had relaxed somewhat as the years passed, realizing that one person's caviar with the appropriate accompaniments (her ultimate comfort food) might be another's processed soup. The Fairchild pantry always had some cans of tomato and cream of mushroom soup, Tom's other mainstay, for times like this.

Before she told him about Lily, she gave him a summary of what Zach had said—she'd taken notes on her phone—and recommended they accept his offer to go over all their computers.

"According to Zach, because I know you so well, I should be able to guess your password. First we eliminate your birthday, or the birthday of anyone close to you."

Tom nodded.

"And it's not our phone number or a series of numbers in order starting with one."

"Nope." Tom seemed proud of himself. He'd avoided the usual traps.

"Then it's 'FAITH,' and you use it for everything."

His face fell. "How did you guess?"

"I know you, honey."

And so did a whole lot of other people. She pictured what now seemed the most probable scenario. Take the keys from his desk, unlock the file, remove the bank card, stroll over to the ATM, enter the PIN, and voilà, a wad of cash in your pocket. Reverse steps. It wouldn't have taken more than fifteen minutes total, a bit more if you had to walk around the block until the ATM was empty. Wouldn't want any witnesses. Of course, it could be someone local who had an account at the bank, too, in which case it would seem completely normal to be waiting to use the cash machine.

She went over it with Tom. "Next time you talk to Sam, sketch this out for him."

"I feel like an idiot," Tom said.

"Why should you feel anything except ripped off and furious? You haven't done anything that millions of Americans don't do every day. Pick a PIN they can recall easily. You are not a crook."

Bypassing the Nixonian echo in her head, Faith went on to reassure Tom that she was positive they were on the right track.

"I'm certain we know how and where it happened. We just have to find out who. And now, please tell me why Lily Sinclair hates us, and Aleford, so much."

"You went to see her, too." It was a statement.

"Before Zach. She referred to Aleford as Stepford, said her time at First Parish caused her to abandon the idea of a parish ministry, ,and has currently dropped out of the Div School. She knew about the missing money. Albert told her. Oh, and she thinks you took it. Plus, I'd say she is not your greatest fan. Many references to you as a 'talker.'"

Tom rubbed his hand across his forehead. Faith thought she saw a new line. At this rate, the furrows were beginning to resemble a south forty.

"She had some difficulty around this time last year running the youth group and I had to speak with her. Several times. I guess she thought of them as talking-tos. I would have called them pastoral counseling, something she might emulate even. That sounds a little stuffy, I know, but my other interns never seemed to mind. In retrospect her silence during them might have been hostility rather than what I took as embarrassment over her behavior. Even though she'd been through four years of college and a year at Harvard, she seemed very young to me. When problems surfaced, I put them down to her immaturity."

"What kinds of problems? I don't remember that you mentioned having any issues with her."

"I didn't think they were major. She had trouble establishing boundaries with the kids, and the first talk I had with her, aside from our regular meetings about the internship, was after one of the mothers called me to tell me that Lily had been telling what the mother thought were inappropriate jokes and using inappropriate language."

"Sexual?"

"No, just thoughtless remarks about how stupid adults could be, parents in particular. How they didn't understand their own children. When I mentioned it, Lily told me that she wanted the kids to open up about problems at home, but someone was getting it all twisted around. I made some suggestions about other ways to create trust and she seemed to be listening, but she did demand to know who the mother was pretty emphatically. I'd used 'she,' so it was clearly a female parent. I didn't tell her, of course."

Hence the Stepford reference, Faith thought. And although she knew Tom wouldn't tell her, either, she had some candidates—as Lily must have also.

"When another mother called a few weeks later with virtually the same complaint, I may have been a little more forceful in my criticism. That was the time she said almost nothing.

"And then there was that business at the end-of-the-year Sunday school picnic," Tom said.

This Faith did remember. As people were leaving, two boys in the seventh grade class began to pelt their friends with water balloons from a stockpile they'd stashed in the cemetery. They bombarded Lily, too, who thought it was great fun. Her sopping wet T-shirt made it clear that she wasn't wearing a bra. It wasn't a case of *Girls Gone Wild*—flat-chested Lily was not a candidate—but one of the mothers had hastily run up to her and thrown a tablecloth around her shoulders. Lily started to shrug it off and then, seeing Tom's approach, apparently had second thoughts, wrapping it tight before heading into the church. Faith could still see the defiant "F-You" look Lily had flung over her shoulder at the crowd as she stomped off. "Immature" didn't even begin to describe it. She'd made her youth group seem like a gathering of elders.

And there were the Hello Kitty pajamas the other day, although that didn't necessarily mean anything. Faith knew any number of adult women with this unaccountable taste in clothing and accessories. Hope had given Amy a darling Hello Kitty pocketbook last summer. A note of whimsy, wit for Faith's own spring wardrobe? She gave herself a mental slap.

"Plus," Tom said, "I heard later that she really lost it running the Christmas pageant. I was still laid up, but Eloise filled me in when I was writing Lily's evaluation in January and asked everyone for input."

This was a hard one. The Christmas pageant. Taken by itself, she would have been solidly on Lily's side. Faith had considered adding "but not running the Christmas pageant" after "in sickness and in health" to their wedding vows. She'd seen what it had done to her mother the very few times she'd caved and become involved. Parents got crazy—"What do you mean, my child is going to be an ox!"—and as the big day drew near, the kids got crazy—"What if I have to pee when I'm watching my flocks!"

"What happened?"

"Not a mother this time, but a father. Apparently he'd set his sights on Mary for his darling daughter, and when he arrived at a rehearsal and saw she was Angel Number Three, he told Lily to make the cast change. She told him to stuff it and banned parents from coming to rehearsals. He organized a protest, pulling his child from the pageant and getting several other parents to do the same. Eloise had to smooth a lot of ruffled feathers."

"Thank goodness we were away!" The Fairchilds had been on Sanpere for the holidays while Tom recuperated and it had been heavenly.

"Eloise knew Lily would be leaving soon and she only told me so I could make some subtle suggestions in the evaluation about controlling one's temper when interacting with parishioners."

Tom reached for another toasted-cheese sandwich. He'd made a stack of them. "I'm not surprised Albert told her what's happened," he said. "They became close friends, brought together, now that I think of it, over doubts about their calling. Maybe she came to First Parish with them; maybe her time with us created them—or Albert did. He certainly stoked the fire. I guess I haven't talked about her much with you because I feel as though I failed her. When she finished the internship, I knew she wasn't happy. Maybe I should go see her."

"No! Bad idea. Very bad idea. Nothing you could say will make Ms. Sinclair change her opinion of you, or the town. Or even about the ministry. Stay away from her. I'm sure Sam would tell you the same thing."

"I wasn't going to mention anything about the Discretionary Fund," Tom said. "Just see if she wanted to talk about leaving school."

"Fine, but that decision isn't going anywhere for a while. See if you think it's still a good idea when this is all over."

When we find out whether Lily's to blame for more than bad taste and stupid remarks, Faith added to herself.

"Tom, how do you suppose Albert found out about this? I'm assuming you told James."

"Actually I didn't. I planned to, but he already knew and the conversation ended before it started."

"Again, how did these people find out? I thought vestry meetings were executive sessions—confidential?"

"They are," Tom said slowly. "We know Albert told Lily and I think we can assume James told Eloise."

Faith had filled him in on yesterday's display of affection. Handholding might seem tame to the layperson, but it was the equivalent of second base for the clergy.

"Eloise and Albert are pretty tight. A lot of what she's in charge of for the Sunday school and youth group involves the calendar and Albert oversees scheduling. They live near each other in Cambridge. I heard him tell her about a new restaurant in their neighborhood and she said they should try it out."

So her husband wasn't as oblivious as Faith thought. She might not be the only eavesdropper in the family.

She was sure, though, that he hadn't reached her skill level.

"That leaves James," she said. "Is there anyone on the vestry who might have leaked this to him?"

"Dear God. There is. Sherman Munroe. They have some sort of connection."

"A connection?"

"Yes. Sherman was the one who brought James to the attention of the search committee."

"Hello, Mother."

"Pix dear, how lovely to hear your voice."

"And yours sounds much stronger than it did on Saturday morning when we talked. How do you feel?"

"Much more like my old self, which is a very old self, of course."

"Mother!" Pix hated to hear Ursula talk this way.

"Tell me about the shower. I wish I could have been there."

"I wish you could have, too. It was wonderful. Our hostess lives in a beautiful home across from the Battery, the promenade overlooking the river. From the house's portico we could see Fort Sumter. Oh, and Mother—her garden! She kept apologizing because it wasn't at its peak yet and looked 'scrawny,' but it was gorgeous. Carpets of daffodils and tiny anemones, and then huge camellias, azaleas, and of course magnolias. Everywhere in Charleston you can smell jasmine, and redbud trees thrive here—all the ones I've tried to grow have died. The shower was in the garden with the food set out under a pergola covered with wisteria. Each guest received one of Charleston's famous sweet grass baskets, small ones filled with sugared almonds. I took a lot of pictures."

"I'm sure Rebecca was thrilled. She's a lovely girl. Mark is a lucky man."

"We're all lucky. I know it's a cliché, but I do feel as if I've gained another daughter. It was a nice old-fashioned shower. Samantha made the bridal 'bouquet' from all the ribbons, and the gifts showed that they had been chosen with care by everyone."

Care—not poor taste. Pix had attended a shower for the daughter of a friend a few months ago, and it turned out to be a lingerie shower with the offerings so raunchy that Pix, who did not consider herself a prude, was mortified. Flavored panties that dissolved at the crotch! She hadn't read the invitation carefully, just noted the time and date. When the bride opened Pix's set of pots and pans, the room grew quiet and then burst into laughter. Apparently the young woman, who was in law school, used her oven as an annex to her overflowing closet and the flat cooktop as a place to pile textbooks. No one said "dinosaur," but Pix had felt her skin beginning to look scaly.

"It sounds like you and Samantha are having a fine time," Ursula said.

"We are. The Cohens have been the perfect hosts, both at Hilton Head and here. And Cissy has included me in everything. Saturday we went to Becca's final fitting. She looks like a princess in her gown. It's ivory satin, strapless—very simple—but they've had a little jacket made from some antique lace Cissy found, which makes it unique. But I don't want to tire you out talking. I'll call again tomorrow."

"Give my love to everyone—and I want to hear all about your dress, too, darling."

Ursula's interest in fashion hovered between zilch and nada, so Pix took the comment for what it was—a nice thing for a mother to say to her daughter. She closed her phone and resumed her walk. She was strolling down King Street, basking in the sun—and the anonymity. She loved Aleford, but it was rather nice to be in a place where everybody didn't know your name—or the names of your children, husband, pets, and so forth. Plus any number of other details about your life. She snapped another picture of a palm tree. She wasn't in a rush. Life had slowed down almost to a crawl. The Cohens had arranged for Pix and Samantha to stay in Cissy's brother's guesthouse, a short walk away from their home. The kitchenette had been stocked for breakfast and it meant that Pix didn't feel they were outwearing their welcome by staying with the Cohens.

Tomorrow Cissy and she were meeting with someone at the Planter's Inn to finalize the menu and other arrangements for the rehearsal dinner. The following day Cissy had declared to be a day off from wedding plans and the ladies were going to head out to Sullivan's Island to a beach house that belonged to someone in Cissy's family. Pix was beginning to think that between the two of them, Cissy and Stephen were related to almost the entire population of South Carolina. Every time a name came up, one or the other would explain to Pix that it was a cousin twice removed or the sister-in-law of a brother-in-law. Mark had said the wedding would be a big one. That could be a major understatement.

She paused to look in the window of an art gallery featuring the work of a number of Gullah artists and caught sight of her reflection. Maybe Faith was wrong. Maybe she bore so little resemblance to the college girl she'd been so many years ago that there was no way Stephen could have recognized her. Okay, it was still bothering her. Every time she'd found herself alone with him for a few minutes—like last night on the brick patio behind their house drinking a glass of wine while Samantha helped Cissy and Rebecca's sisters in the kitchen—Pix had been tempted to say something. But what? "That Yankee in your bed Green Key Weekend was me"?

She turned away and continued her walk. No, that would be tacky in the extreme. She had to let it go and be content with who she was in the present—the mother of the groom. The past was past.

Wasn't it?

One of the things Tom and Faith had discussed in between everything else they seemed to be discussing was why Ursula seemed so driven to tell her story now. Tom thought it was because she'd been ill. He'd often had individuals confide long-held secrets to him as they approached death, and although Ursula was on the mend, the intimations of mortality had been strong during the winter months.

"But she keeps alluding to something she wants me to do when she's finished talking," Faith had pointed out. "That sounds like something specific has happened that's caused her to tell me all this now."

"Possibly, although what she wants you to do could be as simple as helping her tell her children about their father. With Pix out of town she has the time to be alone with you to work it out."

The next day back with Ursula, Faith thought Tom might be right about Ursula's wanting her help, not in telling Pix and Arnie, but in deciding whether to tell them at all. Yet the thought that this wasn't the whole impetus for revealing her secret nagged at Faith nevertheless.

"Pix is having a wonderful time in Charleston. She called yesterday."

"I talked to her, too," Faith said. "The Cohens are going to be wonderful in-laws."

"I'm looking forward to meeting them at the wedding."

"Me, too." Nothing was going to keep Ursula away from the wedding of her first grandchild, and Faith hoped she would be at all of them.

Ursula abruptly changed the subject, plunging back into the past.

"I never thought the guards wouldn't let me see Arnold. That's how naïve I was. Or that he wouldn't want to see me. I walked into the jail, told them that I wanted to visit Arnold Rowe, that I was a relative—a fib, but I thought, given the circumstances, justifiable—and one of the men at the desk told me to wait. I'm sure they thought I was a great deal older than sixteen. I was wearing a suit, hat, and gloves plus I was quite tall for my age. He brought a chair for me to sit on. I assumed it would be a while and I began to worry about what I would tell my mother. Fortunately he returned soon and escorted me to a nice little room. I later learned it was the warden's sitting room. A guard came in with Arnold and then left us alone. I scarcely recognized him. He was so pale and thin."

"Miss Lyman, what on earth are you doing here?"

Arnold Rowe had been curious to find out who his "cousin" might be since both his late parents had been only children. Possibly last on the list he'd considered as he made his way through the series of barred doors was Theo's sister.

Ursula had planned various openings, but as soon as she saw Arnold the words that were uppermost in her mind came spilling out.

"I know you didn't have anything to do with my brother's death and I think I know who did."

"I think we should sit down," Arnold said. "I know I need to."

He indicated the horsehair settee next to the fireplace. It was slippery and slightly scratchy; Ursula sat on its edge as Arnold started to speak.

"First of all—and the most important thing—is to say how sorry I am about Theo's death. There are no words that can convey the depth of my sorrow. He was not just my student, but also my friend, and the guilt that I feel will be with me every day for the rest of my life. I should never have left the house that night."

Ursula started to speak, but Arnold held up a hand.

"No, there isn't any excuse. I should have demanded he end the party when we returned from Illumination Night. It was getting quite wild. At the very least I should have stayed with Theo. I've never been able to say these things to your parents. I asked the lawyer the court appointed for me to deliver a letter with these sentiments, but he, for reasons of his own, would not. At some time you might deem appropriate I hope you will convey what I've said."

Ursula shook her head. "They never speak of him—or that night. I only learned recently that you had been convicted of . . . convicted of his murder."

"I am guilty of it in my negligence, but please believe me, I had nothing to do with the act itself."

"I do believe you." Ursula looked straight into his eyes. "As soon as I read the newspaper accounts of the trial, I knew the wrong person had been arrested. That the wrong person was in prison. Today by mere coincidence I got final proof of it."

Arnold looked astounded. "Proof?"

She quickly told him first about the time discrepancy and then about the conversation she'd overheard just before the murder took place.

"I've often wondered how you came to be there. The sight of you, so young, beside Theo's body, is one I can never—and should never—erase from my mind." He had tears in his eyes and Ursula felt her own fill.

"It was definitely Charles Winthrop speaking. I'm positive."

She described being at Stearn's and hearing the voice again, the voice that had been reverberating consciously and unconsciously over the years.

"I don't think he planned to harm Theo, but he was not in control of himself." She shuddered slightly as she recalled the vehemence of his words: "You're not going anywhere."

She told Arnold what she believed had happened. A night that had begun in innocent, albeit self-indulgent pleasure, gone terribly wrong as an argument over money turned deadly.

"But what doesn't make sense to me is how there was enough evidence to try you. Let alone convict you."

"The first year I was here I thought of nothing else. I was innocent. How could it have happened? My lawyer was young and very impressed by the names of those involved in the prosecution—wealthy Bostonians, prominent old families. The owner of the house you rented pushed for a speedy trial. He made it clear to my lawyer that he was out for blood, my blood, on behalf of your family. I had a hard time even getting my lawyer to listen to my account of that night. And I had two eyewitnesses who saw me, me alone, going down the path toward the gazebo after midnight. He finally interviewed them, but said afterward he wouldn't call them to testify."

"Who were they?"

"Mary Smith, who worked in the kitchen, and the gardener, Elias Norton."

"I know, or rather knew, Mary. She was deaf and I learned to sign from her."

"Elias is deaf, too. I thought that was why the lawyer wouldn't put them on the stand, but that wasn't it—there were plenty of interpreters available on the island. He said they weren't friendly witnesses. I wanted to talk to them myself. I'd learned to sign, too—the whole phenomenon of the Vineyard deafness and subsequent sign language had interested me—but there was no way I could contact them except through him. And the most damning testimony of all came from Violet Hammond."

"She's Violet Winthrop now, remember."

Arnold nodded. "I'm not surprised. She was after him all that summer and poor Theo was like a lovesick calf. I tried to talk to him—Violet was costing him a lot of money, and had been during the school year what with champagne suppers at Locke-Ober and the like. He wouldn't listen. I thought she'd find someone else and leave him alone, but she enjoyed stringing him along, even though Charles was the one she wanted. I wish I had been more persistent."

Ursula interrupted. "He wouldn't have listened. I saw the way he looked at her, too, and she is very beautiful. What was her testimony?"

She had a feeling she knew. . . .

"She testified that she overheard a violent quarrel between the two of us and that I threatened Theo to the point where he ran out of the house, apparently in fear of his life. She said she saw me follow him and immediately got Charles Winthrop to go after us both. She said we'd been drinking heavily. Winthrop corroborated her story. He described going after us as soon as she alerted him, coming upon us in the gazebo when it was too late.

"But they lied!" Ursula flushed angrily. "Didn't your lawyer challenge them? And what about your testimony?"

"He didn't question them at all and he'd told me early on that he wouldn't put me on the stand. That the prosecutor would, as he said, 'eat me for breakfast.'"

It was getting late. Ursula knew she should leave, but not yet. She needed to hear more.

"What made you go out to the gazebo? How did you know Theo was there?"

"As I said earlier, the party had become wild. Word of it had spread all over the island and cars filled with crashers kept arriving. Most of the servants, including the housekeeper, had disappeared, no doubt to the Illumination, but also to avoid any involvement. I saw a young lady tuck a small silver cigarette box into her bag, which I promptly retrieved, much to her fury. The house was filled with valuables. I knew we might need to call the police, but I didn't want to do it without telling

Theo first. I thought I could get him to announce the party was over and tell people to leave himself— a face-saving gesture. No one had seen him. I went out to the pool. It was filled with partygoers, some had shed their clothes. I was at my wit's end and then someone, a man, told me he'd seen Theo heading in the direction of the gazebo quite a while ago. I thought he must have arranged to meet Violet there as I hadn't seen her, either."

"So this man saw you, too? Who was it?"

"I didn't know him, had never seen him before, and even though I begged the lawyer to put an announcement in all the papers seeking his help, nothing ever came of it.

"And then several people began shouting at me that Theo was in the gazebo and wanted me there. They seemed to think it was some kind of joke."

"And they were never questioned, either?"

"No."

"So you went after Theo—and found him." *Ursula's voice trembled.*

"Yes." *Arnold put his hand briefly over hers.* "Would that I had gone sooner."

"What can I do?"

"Nothing. You've been kind enough to listen." *Arnold's expression was resigned.* "It's not as horrid here for me as most. I've been teaching classes in all sorts of things from basic reading and arithmetic—many of the inmates never learned—to history. Civic groups donate books. We never know what we will get. As time has passed I've been granted certain privileges like seeing visitors without a guard, although you are my first."

"What about your classmates at Harvard? The professors? Surely they would take up your cause!"

"That's not how things work, Ursula. Again, it was wonderful of you to come, but I think you'd best not visit another time. This is no place for a young lady."

Ursula stood up. She'd tell her mother she'd taken a long walk, which was partially true, but even a lengthy promenade about the parts of town where she was permitted wouldn't have taken up this much time.

"I intend to return, Mr. Rowe—and I intend to get you out of here. The best way is for me to find out as much as possible about what really happened and present the facts to my father. He is a fair man and he would never want an innocent person to be unjustly confined. If need be, a judge will have to order a new trial."

Arnold Rowe shook his head slowly. "You make it all sound so easy. I'm afraid you are going to be terribly disappointed—and hurt."

"Perhaps—but I have to try. We know that Charles Winthrop was desperate for money and that Violet Hammond was, if not his fiancée at the time, about to be. They had every reason to lie. I'll say good-bye for now."

Arnold opened the door and the guard showed her out.

"Good afternoon, miss," he said.

Ursula walked down West Cedar Street toward her aunt's house on Louisburg Square. She felt as if she had passed from one world to another and was struck by how normal things looked in this one. The people she passed nodded and smiled slightly. The old, wavy amethyst glass in the windows of the Beacon Hill houses were unchanged, the brass door knockers and handles as bright as the day they were installed. The brick sidewalks uneven from years of use. Cars passed slowly. It was all as it had been before she'd rung the bell at the Charles Street Jail, but it would never be the same for her again.

Arnold Rowe had been framed. She was certain of it.

Her mother barely noted her tardiness and rushed her off to catch the train back to Aleford. On the way

Ursula showed her the gloves and the purchase was met with approval. The motion of the train, the sound of the tracks, was soothing and for a moment Ursula allowed herself to feel happy. Arnold had looked a shadow of his former self—emaciated and deathly pale, but there was no pallor in his warm brown eyes or the smile that crossed his lips several times. She had found him; she was going to help him. And she would start now.

Charles Winthrop had needed money right away. Theo hadn't had any to give him, nor was there any money in the house. As she'd walked back to her aunt's, Ursula had thought of something. She needed to ask her mother a question and the sooner the better.

"I know it's very hard to talk about Theo, Mother, but I've been thinking of him so much today. Perhaps, in part, it was being near the old house. I would like to have something of his as a keepsake. Would you and Father let me have the pocket watch Father gave him when he turned eighteen?"

It had been gold, and was a reward for not smoking or drinking.

Her mother looked very tired.

"In all the confusion of that night, some of his things were lost. We don't have the watch."

"Or his signet ring?"

All the Lyman men were given these rings with the family seal when they were confirmed.

"That was lost, too."

Ursula had her answer. It was as she thought.

The train was slowing down for the Arlington station. She watched the landscape come to a halt, but she wasn't seeing the town center, she was back in the gazebo caressing her brother's hands. His fingers were bare.

The ring was already missing.

Chapter 9

"My greatest problem was figuring out how to go off to Martha's Vineyard for an entire day. I couldn't tell my parents. Finally the simplest solution was the most obvious one. I cut school."

Faith had been reeling from Ursula's account of her sixteen-year-old self marching up to the Charles Street Jail, gaining admittance, and embarking on an investigation to free a convicted murderer. And now this? Cutting school? This was the kind of thing people like Ursula, and her daughter, never, never did without at the least a gun to their heads.

"I told Mother that I was involved in a project that required my presence both before and after school. I would have to leave early and might be quite late. Mother was not particularly interested in academics, although she was a reader—she was quite fond of Mazo de la Roche's novels, and all she ever wanted as gifts were the newest Jalna and a box of Fannie Farmer chocolates. I knew she wouldn't ask me any particulars, so I told myself I wasn't really lying. I did have a project. A large one.

"We'd been in Aleford for some time, but I didn't know many people in town. Since I attended Cabot, not the public school, I knew I wouldn't run into any fathers on the train who might recognize me. In any case, I took a very early one before rush hour. I changed to the train for Woods Hole and the ferry in town. Before I boarded I called school. Mother and I had very similar voices and people often mistook us for each other on the phone. I simply told the secretary, Miss Mountjoy—you can imagine what fun the girls had about that name, especially since she always looked as though she'd received dire news and perhaps she had."

Ursula got back on track. "I said that Ursula would not be at school today, but would return tomorrow. She said, 'Thank you for calling, Mrs. Lyman,' and I hopped on the train."

At this point Faith was no longer reeling—nothing further would surprise her, she was sure—but had a strong sense that the nation had lost a valuable resource. FBI agent? Spy? G-woman?

"I had time to think on the ferry over. It was a beautiful spring day, so warm it could have been July. . . ."

Ursula stood on the deck watching the gulls circle overhead and wished she could be a little girl again on Sanpere sailing with Theo in his beloved catboat. It had been built on the island and he'd helped, a little boy himself at the time. Friends had much larger boats and Theo never turned down a chance to go "yachting," but she knew he was never happier than when he was in his own boat sailing down Eggemoggin Reach up into Jericho Bay.

The trip was taking longer than she'd remembered and her time on the Vineyard would be shorter than she hoped. She knew that neither Mary Smith nor Elias Norton had been live-in employees. Mary lived in Oak Bluffs with her family, happily not far from the ferry landing. She'd pointed the house out to her once when Ursula had received permission to walk into town with Mary, who was doing various errands for Mrs. Lyman. Ursula didn't know where Elias lived.

The salt air had dried her throat out and she walked quickly to the Smiths' house. Mary would give her a glass of water and they'd talk. Everything was going to be all right. Ursula closed her eyes for a moment. All morning she had steadfastly pushed any thoughts about the enormity of what she was doing from her mind, as well as any thoughts of failure.

Outside the tidy Cape, a young woman was weeding the front garden. Ursula started to speak, then, seeing her resemblance to Mary, signed instead. Her effort was returned with an appreciative smile. She was relieved to know that her signing skills were still intact. Mary and Elias had married and were living only a short walk away. There wasn't a cloud in the sky as she set off.

Even if it had been possible—if they had been able to hear and speak—Ursula would not have wanted to talk with them on the phone. Nor had she wanted to write to them. She had wanted to appear unannounced, wanted to present Arnold's case, her case, and gauge their reactions without their prior knowledge.

Mary opened the door, and the first thing Ursula noticed was that the woman's obvious surprise seemed more like fear. Elias stood behind his wife in the doorway. Neither of them moved or responded to Ursula's signed greeting. Ursula hadn't thought beyond finding them and getting them to tell her what they'd seen that night. That the couple might not want to cooperate, not agree to see her, simply hadn't occurred to her. She congratulated them on their nuptials. The well-wishes triggered a polite response. Mary invited her in and Elias stepped back, both still visibly ill at ease.

"Would you like tea, miss? Or something cold?" Mary signed.

"I'd love a glass of water, thank you," Ursula replied.

They both disappeared to what Ursula assumed was the kitchen in the back of the house. The parlor was small, spotless with a few cherished possessions on the mantel—a framed wedding portrait, a pair of brass candlesticks, and an iridescent glass vase filled with blue hyacinths.

When they returned, Ursula's heart sank at the look on Mary's face. The woman was blinking back tears and her hand shook slightly as she handed Ursula the glass of water. In contrast, Elias's face was blank, his mouth set in one firm line.

The only thing to do was start from the beginning and tell them everything—finding the newspaper articles, encountering the Winthrops in the department store, and finally her visit to Arnold in jail. Mary gave a gasp at this last piece of information and started to lift her hand, but dropped it back in her lap. Elias had sat impassively throughout Ursula's account. When she stopped signing and drank some water he stood up, firmly taking charge.

"We're very sorry about young Mr. Rowe, but we don't know what we can do to help him." He tapped Mary on the arm and she jumped up. No other kind of sign was necessary. The visit was over.

"Please," Ursula implored. "Please sit down again and just tell me what you saw that night in the woods. Arnold saw you both. You must have seen him, too."

"It was a long time ago. We talked to the lawyer fellows when it happened and it's all over now."

Mary's hands were clasped behind her back. Ursula stood up and signed her thanks. Despair slipped over her, threatening to engulf her completely, but she had to leave the house, get back to the ferry, and make her way home. At the door, she signed one last question.

"Is Mrs. Miles, the housekeeper, still on the island?"

A look of disgust crossed Mary's face, the expressive face Ursula remembered so well from their times together. Mary's emotions were always close to the surface.

"That one! A she-devil to work for and she took off that night for good. I haven't laid eyes on her since she went out the back door in her Sunday best before it was even dark, neither has anybody else."

Elias took Mary's hand and held it.

What did he want her to keep from saying, or was it a gesture of affection? Ursula wondered. She thought the former, and after wishing them well—she could tell Mary was expecting and, from the lack of any children's toys or things in the room, assumed it was their first—she went out the front door.

As soon as she heard the door close, Ursula darted around the side of the house. She was sure they would be discussing her visit and thought she might be able to see into the room from a side window, but Elias's green thumb had produced forsythia bushes and spirea in such abundance that it was impossible. She was about to give up and head for the landing when she heard steps on the back porch of the cottage. She had a clear view of the yard from where she stood and stepped farther into the cascading blooms, blessing them now for their protective cover.

Mary was carrying a basket of wash to hang on the line and Elias was following her, signing away like mad even though her back was turned. He reached out to stop her; she dropped the basket and began to sob. It was all Ursula could do to keep from running out to comfort Mary herself.

"Run after her, Elias. The ferry won't be leaving for a while. What we did was wrong!" she signed frantically.

"We didn't tell any lies."

"We didn't tell the truth, either." Mary wiped her eyes with her apron. "We saw that boy lying in the summerhouse as plain as day. You thought he'd passed out from drink. And we never checked! Somebody else was nearby in the woods, but we couldn't see. It wasn't Mr. Rowe, because we did see him close to where the path started at the house. He was running toward us and it was after we'd gone by Mr. Theo."

She stopped signing when she saw Ursula emerge. Elias seemed to be battling two warring instincts; his expression was tormented.

"I guess I know when the Almighty is trying to tell me something," he signed to Ursula. "All you told us, and your coming here today, was meant to be. We did see Mr. Rowe, but we don't know how your poor brother came to die and that's the truth. Let's go inside and sit down again. We'll tell you everything. If you miss the ferry, I'll run you over to the mainland in my skiff."

Tea appeared rapidly—and a plate of oatmeal cookies. As they sat in the parlor, Ursula remembered that Arnold's lawyer had said Mary and Elias would not be friendly witnesses. A better description would have been "terrified" ones.

Elias signed that the prosecutor had warned them that he would bring up what he imagined they had been doing off in the woods if they took the stand.

"It was a lie. I respected my Mary, but people want to believe the worst! He told us he'd make sure it got out and no one would hire servants with such low morals. It didn't matter how good we were at our jobs."

Ursula was shocked. She felt as if she had left the few remaining remnants of her childhood behind over the course of the afternoon, a childhood where, before Theo's death, she'd believed that all adults told the truth and nothing bad could happen to anyone she knew.

Mary looked tired, and Ursula told them she would be in touch. In fact, she didn't know what her next step would be, other than toward the ferry, which hadn't left. She hugged her old friend, now restored to her, and Elias went with her. As the ferry pulled away, he waved once.

She waved back and went to the prow of the Naushon. As she faced Woods Hole, crossing Vineyard Sound, the world seemed newly made and she imagined herself as a kind of figurehead—a sort of Winged Victory.

It was after dinnertime when Ursula walked into the house. She had planned to phone, but had just made both trains. Her mother rushed over to her.

"Ursula! Where have you been? We were just about to start calling around!"

"I've been to Oak Bluffs and I need to tell you why."

Her earlier exhilaration had left her and now she was exhausted.

Her father got up from his chair.

"Sit down. Have you eaten today? And I think a drop of brandy might be a good idea."

Mr. Lyman had thought the whole notion of the Thirty-second Amendment was misguided, making criminals out of otherwise law-abiding citizens. He wasn't much of a drinker himself, but saw no harm in keeping decanters of port and sherry as well as a bottle of brandy.

Ursula was not used to spirits and choked at the first swallow, but soon the alcohol's warmth suffused her body and she realized she was hungry. She made short work of the sandwich her mother brought.

It took a long time to tell her parents what had transpired and her mother had not wanted to hear any of it at first.

"It won't bring Theo back. Why stir things up again?"

"I'm sorry to disagree, Dorothea," Mr. Lyman said. "If what Ursula has been telling us proves to be true, we must do everything in our power to clear Arnold Rowe."

At midnight, Ursula knew she couldn't talk any more. Her mother had gone to bed with her usual Ovaltine and her father told her to go, too. He wanted to make some notes. While he believed her, he wasn't totally encouraging.

"I'm not sure how to proceed," he said. "The only evidence against Charles Winthrop is a young girl's recall of an extremely traumatic night. Lawyers for Winthrop would be able to easily discredit your testimony, questioning why you hadn't mentioned it at the time to anyone—the fact that you were ill and didn't know any of the particulars of the charges, or even the outcome of the case against Arnold, will not make a difference, I'm afraid. They'd also bring up the notion of false memory after so many years. They will also"—Theodore Lyman hesitated—"put your motivation down to a schoolgirl's crush."

Ursula started to protest.

"No, daughter. I believe you, but the Winthrops are a very powerful—and proper—family. They are not about to have it come out that their son was in debt to the worst sort of bootleggers and involved if not actually in committing the crime of murder, then in covering it up. Young Charles knew his actions, had they come out, would have resulted in his estrangement from the family—emotionally and financially."

On this note, he kissed her good night and told her not to set her alarm. He'd call the school to tell them she'd be late.

She thought she would have trouble falling asleep, but Ursula sank almost immediately into oblivion—sleep, the sweet escape.

"Ursula," Faith said, "this has been an amazing story. I know it has a happy ending"—she assumed they had reached it—"otherwise there wouldn't be a

Pix or an Arnold junior. I wouldn't be sitting here, either."

"This part *did* have a happy ending, but it's not over. I'll explain shortly. To finish up about Arnold's imprisonment—Father consulted his own lawyer, William Lloyd, taking me with him. The next day both men went to the jail and spent a long time talking to Arnold. After that everything happened quickly. A judge in Dukes County ordered a new trial, but before they got to jury selection, Mr. Lloyd asked that the charge be dismissed in light of new evidence that exonerated his client beyond the shadow of a doubt. Of course it had all been worked out beforehand. Mary and Elias had been deposed, as was I. Arnold's full account was presented to the judge also. The charge was dropped and the case was left open: 'Murder by person or persons unknown.' It was hard on Mother. Not that she wanted Arnold in jail, but she had hoped that justice would be done. That Charles Winthrop would be punished— she'd come to believe he'd been responsible. But there wasn't enough evidence to arrest him. Both he and his wife stuck to their accounts of that night."

"And Arnold was freed right away?" Faith said.

"That very day. Father eventually found him a position as private secretary to a business acquaintance who was very open-minded—difficult to find any sort of job in those times and there was Arnold's incarceration, however mistaken."

"And what about you? It must have been hard to go back to Cabot after all these dramatic events."

"It was. I'd never felt very comfortable there. I missed my old school. By the time I graduated it was understood that Arnold and I would marry. It was merely a question of when. He came out to Aleford often at my parents' invitation. No one could ever take Theo's place, but they began to rely on Arnold for advice and I think he brought them a measure of comfort—he'd been so close to Theo. I know it did me.

"Things had improved somewhat for Father, but I knew that going to college would stretch their finances considerably. I went to Katie Gibbs instead and got a job as a secretary in a large law firm—lawyers seem to figure prominently in this tale. Arnold wanted me to go to college—Wellesley, in fact, where dear Samantha went. I told him he could be my college and he took the job seriously. He would have made a wonderful professor, but his life went in another direction. We were married quietly at The Pines on Sanpere on my nineteenth birthday. Arnold had risen in the firm and eventually became a partner, but that was much later. We wanted to be near my parents and bought this house. You know the rest—or most of it.

"The day Arnold was freed, he came to the house for dinner. At the beginning of the meal, Father gave thanks. We all said 'amen' and Father added that from then on, we would never talk about what had happened again. And we didn't."

"Not even with your husband?" Faith found this almost beyond belief. She knew New Englanders were tight-lipped, but this was taking things to a whole new level.

"I imagine it's hard for you to understand. You were raised in such a different time. It wasn't a guilty secret, but it wasn't something we wanted to trumpet from the rooftops. We needed to have a normal life again. When the children were born, we did discuss whether to tell them or not. We certainly wouldn't tell them when they were young, and by the time they were older, there didn't seem to be much point."

Yet they had arrived at a point now. The point where the story ended and its purpose began.

"What do you want me to do, Ursula?" Faith asked. "Be with you when you tell Pix? Or tell her myself? Perhaps with Tom, as well?"

Ursula shook her head. "Not yet. I can't think of that now. Go over to the window seat. There are two envelopes tucked underneath the cushion. The first arrived some weeks ago, just before I went to the hospital. The second more recently. Bring them here, if you would."

Faith removed the envelopes and gave them to Ursula, who handed one back.

"Please open it and look at what's inside."

Faith read the contents, glancing quickly at the newspaper clippings, focusing longer on the words on the single sheet of paper:

Are you sure you were right?

"And now this one." Ursula handed her the other envelope. It contained only the sheet of paper, apparently the same kind as the other. Again a single sentence:

You saw the knife in his hand.

"Do you know who's sending these? Why would—"

"Wait, dear." Ursula slipped a third envelope from her pocket, removed the letter, and handed it to Faith. Two lines this time:

Time will tell.
I'm waiting, but not for long.

"It came yesterday," Ursula said. "I've been expecting it."

Normally the Uppity Women's Luncheon Club was Niki's favorite gig. Years ago Sandra Katz, who lived in Aleford, decided that she had women friends she enjoyed being with who should get to know each other. What started out as a December holiday luncheon, which Have Faith catered, became an informal club meeting at various members' houses several times a year. The only rule was no cooking—no pressure to match or surpass a fellow Uppity's prior menu. For such a small gathering, only Faith or Niki needed to be there. After a while, it became clear that the women were getting a kick not just from Niki's great food, but her sense of humor, and it became her assignment.

The women were married, divorced, or never married. They ranged from stay-at-home moms to a college dean, and were all now somewhere in their forties. Sandra, who worked raising funds for nonprofits, was the unofficial president and the person who got in touch with the catering company. Thinking spring, Niki thought of eggs—hard-boiled on the seder plate, hard-boiled and colored in an Easter basket. That took her to the idea of breakfast for lunch. Before she was married, exhausted after working all day, she'd often had breakfast for dinner—crispy bacon, maybe a sausage, scrambled or poached eggs with toast. Faith and she had been experimenting with an eggy breakfast puff. The batter was poured over a peach or pear half placed in a ramekin, and when it looked like a golden-brown popover it was ready [see recipe, p. 369].

Sandra loved the idea of the puff, and Niki thought she'd add mini BLTs using turkey bacon with tiny grape tomatoes. She'd also put out a large bowl of fresh strawberries—they were coming in from Watsonville, California, now and delicious. She'd toss them with a little bit of sugar to release their juice and set separate small bowls of several flavors of yogurt—the Greek kind, of course—alongside. The Uppities wanted a salad, so she'd do a simple one of fresh spring greens with a lemon–poppy seed dressing—also on the side. Some of the Uppities were always doing Atkins, Pritikin, or the grapefuit or cabbage soup diet. Before they sat down to eat, she'd serve Kir Royales—crème de cassis and champagne—both alcoholic and non, with cheese straws. A mild cheese so as not to interfere with the taste of the drink.

There would be more cheese for dessert. Sandra had said they were celebrating their tenth anniversary to-gether and she wanted a cake—a chocolate cheesecake. What she'd actually said was, "Screw carbs. This is a celebration and we all look pretty damn good. Besides, isn't chocolate supposed to be healthy now?"

Niki was with her on that one, and there *was* evidence that dark chocolate lowers both blood pressure and cholesterol, and it has eight times the number of antioxidants of some fruits, to protect the body from aging. The Uppities would appreciate this last tidbit of knowledge.

The food was packed and she was ready to leave. Should have left. Faith was at Pix's mother's house and Tricia was over at the Ganley café making sure everything was going smoothly there. Niki slumped into one of the beanbag chairs Faith had placed in the play area for her kids. It felt great. Maybe she could just sit here, letting the chair cushion her, for the rest of her pregnancy. It was appropriate. She'd resemble a beanbag herself by the end of it.

She got up, locked the door, and set out for the job. She hoped the women wouldn't expect her usual "wit and charm"—a compliment passed on through Faith. She felt funny today, but not funny ha-ha.

Today's hostess lived in a beautifully restored Arts and Crafts house with a decidedly nonperiod kitchen. It didn't take Niki long to set up and another Uppity luncheon was launched. Going in and out of the dining room, she heard snippets of their conversation, which ranged from spouses to kids and a lot about politics in between—"My skipped period was early onset menopause! I was so relieved! The only diapers I want to change in the upcoming years are my grandchildren's!" and, "It's so nice when he's away. The bed's a snap to make and I can have a glass of wine and soup for dinner. But then if it's too long, I don't like it." And, "Honestly, if I talked to my mother the way she talks to me, I wouldn't have seen twenty." The dean had addressed the whole table at one point. " 'Underachiever'! The boy's drag-ass lazy, but if I told his parents that, I'd lose my job in a heartbeat—plus we could kiss those all-important future donations good-bye. These days my job is ninety-nine percent fund-raising and one percent education."

The rhythm of their conversation, their lives, was ordinarily very comforting, but today Niki found herself feeling more and more depressed. What were she and Phil going to do? With a blatant view to the future offspring, both sets of parents had given the newlyweds the money for a down payment on a small house in Belmont. "Good schools," her mother had assured her. She'd memorized *Boston* magazine's annual ranking list. "And good property values." She'd bought that issue, too. But now they couldn't keep up the mortgage payments with what Niki alone made. In the past, various restaurant owners and chefs had offered her jobs that paid more money. She'd turned them down, cherishing not just the relationship she had with her boss, but the freedom she had to experiment with new things in the kitchen and her flexible work schedule. Three years ago, she'd taken several months off to travel, ending up in Australia and almost settling there. She knew that with the current economy the jobs she'd been offered before—and many of the restaurants—no longer existed. Even if she could tear herself away, it wasn't an option.

True, the cheesecakes were selling well, but woman cannot live by cake alone. At that thought, she lighted the numeral ten candle she'd stuck on the top of the cake and opened the door, singing "Happy Anniversary to You."

Sandra blew out the candle and Niki started to cut slices.

"I'll do that. Why don't you get the coffee, and Lisa, please get a chair so Niki can join us?"

Niki had been dreading this moment. Not joining them—she always did at the end—but the coffee.

"How about I serve and maybe someone else can bring in the pot?"

She'd plugged in the coffeemaker earlier and so far so good in the olfactory department. Pouring it out would be another matter.

Sandra raised an eyebrow. She'd never heard Niki say anything but "Sure" to a request.

"No problem, I'll get it. Why don't you sit here?"

Niki flushed and sat down at the head of the table, right in the limelight where she absolutely did not want to be.

"Great lunch as usual, Niki. I love that puff thing. Is it hard to make?" Pamela was tall and slender with the kind of short haircut that only the best stylist could deliver. She was a Wharton graduate. She and her husband had moved into town now that their children were out of the house. They lived in a condo at the Four Seasons and Niki was pretty sure Pamela's cooking nowadays was room service.

"It's very easy. I'll e-mail the recipe to anyone who would like it."

Sandra returned with the coffee and started pouring.

"I know you want some, Niki. And you take just milk, right?"

"I'll pass today, thanks."

"On the milk?"

"No, the coffee."

"Okay." Sandra pulled the chair Lisa had brought in up to the table. "You've been looking like you lost your best friend since you got here. What's going on?"

"Nothing," Niki said, and started to add a further denial, but one of the other Uppities interrupted.

"Come on, sweetie. You know all our secrets and then some."

It was true. Over the years Niki had heard them unburden themselves to one another in sorrow and in joy. She burst into tears.

"You're pregnant!" Sandra happily clapped her hands together. "The smell of coffee and hair-trigger hormones, oh Niki!"

"We'll make the next luncheon a shower," Pamela said. "I love to buy baby things, and given my daughter's track record with men, I'll be a grandmother at eighty."

"Is that biologically possible?" the woman next to her teased. "Isn't your daughter twenty-eight?"

"So, she'll adopt. I should only be so lucky."

It was inevitable. Niki found herself spilling her guts to the roomful of sympathetic women. "Spilling her guts" was an apt phrase, she thought, as a torrent of words spewed forth. She told them about Phil's losing his job and not wanting to burden him further with her news. And described how depressed she was feeling most of the time. During the rest, she was feeling nauseous.

She'd hardly finished when the Uppities whipped out their BlackBerries and iPhones, looking up contacts; making notes for themselves about Phil's qualifications; and entering how to reach him.

"You may have heard about the old boys' and old girls' networks," one said. "But they're nothing compared to the Uppity Women's."

This was the woman, Niki recalled, who had a bumper sticker on her Lexus that read, WOMEN WHO SEEK TO BE EQUAL TO MEN LACK AMBITION.

"Now you go home and tell Phil everything," she said. "It's time for you to start enjoying being pregnant. Not the morning-sickness part, but the rest—and believe me, there will be plenty of joy."

"Tell me about it," Pamela said. "I never got so much action. I was horny; he was horny. That's why pregnant women have such a glow."

"It was the big boobs that did it for my husband," Sandra said. "He went nuts."

This led to a few more comments on sex and a discussion about getting picked up at Trader Joe's, especially on Saturdays at the Sample Station.

"Forget Costco, it's all families, although there is stuff to try that you'd normally never eat—deep-fried pizza last time I was there. The Roche Brothers cheese counter is good, too. I love the come-ons, 'Do you think this Brie is ready—subtext, I am.' Even you married gals should give it a whirl; it's great for the ego."

Niki began to laugh so hard she had to make a mad dash for the bathroom to pee. This was beginning to

happen a lot lately and she'd seriously considered getting those nonsenior Depends-type things that Whoopi
Goldberg was advertising to keep from "spritzing."

They helped her clean up and sent her on her way.
She decided to go directly home and bring the van
back to work later. The Uppities should be cloned, she
thought, and then changed her mind. She wanted to
keep them all to herself.

"**Who do** you think is sending these?" Faith repeated
her earlier question. She'd moved back to the window
seat and had spread the letters out on the cushion.

It was still raining heavily, as it had been on and
off for days. Every night the news showed footage of
people near the swollen rivers being evacuated from
their homes by Zodiacs and even canoes. Faith had
received two reverse 911 calls from the Aleford police
announcing road closures, and this morning she'd seen
ducks swimming on her front lawn.

But it could have been brilliant sunshine and eighty
degrees. Her mind was on the papers beside her.

"Who?" she repeated. "It has to be someone who
saw your husband in the gazebo—and knows that you
were there, too."

"Which most likely means it's one of the people who
was staying in the house, although I suppose it could

be any of the partygoers—the few still alive." Ursula shook her head. "Very unlikely. It just had to be said. No, it's one of the four, and easy to eliminate two of them. Charles Winthrop was older than the rest and I'm sure he's been gone awhile. I know that Schuyler—Scooter—Jessup died just after Arnold. His wife, Babs, is alive, however. We used to run into each other in town at the Chilton Club from time to time over the years, but of course we never mentioned that night."

Of course, Faith thought. Not the thing to do.

"Which leaves Violet Hammond, Violet Winthrop. The envelope has a New York City postmark and the Winthrops left Boston before the war so Charles could run the family's Manhattan office."

"How did you know? They wouldn't have kept in touch, would they?"

Ursula shook her head. "No—thank goodness. I didn't want anything to do with either of them, but I did want to know where they were, especially early on. I suppose I was nurturing notions of, well, revenge. I used to think I'd uncover some kind of evidence that would bring Charles to trial. As time passed, there were other things to think about, especially during the war years and after the children were born."

During the last few minutes, everything had become clear to Faith. The cause of Ursula's illness, the need to tell someone what she believed to be the truth, and now the kind of help Ursula wanted from Faith.

She was asking Faith to prove her husband's innocence—a task she thought she had accomplished almost seventy years ago. A closed book—until the letters arrived sowing their insidious seeds of doubt.

Yes, Ursula wanted Faith to solve Theo's murder, irrefutably.

"Tell me what you want me to do first."

"We don't have much time. I'd like to get this settled before Pix gets back, or near enough. And then, there's the implied threat in the third letter. I think I know what it means."

Faith did, too. "That the writer intends to use information about the crime to hurt you in some way? Knows, perhaps, that it was kept secret and plans a tell-all story, but where? I can't imagine the media would be interested in such old news."

"Nor can I, although it might make a splash for a while in the Aleford and Boston papers. And I wouldn't want to see my family's private affairs in the headlines." Ursula pursed her lips.

Faith knew that Ursula belonged to the school that believed a lady was only mentioned in the press three times: when she was born, got married, and at her death. No, she wouldn't like the notoriety at all.

"The writer means to go public in some way and I have to find out how. And find out what it is she believes happened that night. Yes, she. It has to be Violet because of the postmarks—and I think she was a rather unscrupulous woman. She's a very old lady now and I suppose this is her idea of fun. She used to enjoy stirring things up—she was quite sarcastic, but that voice of hers tended to make even the meanest remark sound melodic. I don't know why she's waited so long to go after me—and my family. Perhaps something reminded her of that summer recently."

"All will be clear." Faith wished she felt as confident as she sounded. Ursula was asking the impossible—that Faith trace this old crime and unmask the culprit. Yet truth dealt with the possible, not the reverse, and Faith intended to do everything she could to reveal it.

"So," she said, "I'll find out where the old witch lives and go talk to her. Tell her to stop bothering you or we'll get some kind of restraining order. She *is* making threats."

Ursula nodded in agreement.

"She lives on East Seventy-second Street. I have the phone number."

"How did you get this? I thought four-one-one wouldn't give out an address."

"I didn't call information. I called that nice reference librarian Jeanne Bracken, and she got it for me. She said something about 'Googling' the name, but I think we had a bad connection because of all this rain. The wires must be soaked."

Faith decided there were more important things to discuss, but she made a mental note to explain to Ursula sometime that "Google" was not a form of baby talk.

"I could go Thursday, or maybe even tomorrow," Faith said. She could take the shuttle and if there was time swing by Zabar's on the West Side for deli.

"Thursday would be fine. And tomorrow, do you have time to pay a call on Babs Jessup? I have her address and phone number, too. If you agree, we could call now."

Faith was a little mystified.

"I thought you were sure that it was Violet Winthrop who is responsible for the letters."

"I am, but forewarned is forearmed. I have a feeling that Babs might tell you what Violet has been up to all these years. I don't think she liked Violet. In fact, I'm sure of it, but the Jessups and Winthrops were related."

"So she'd know?"

"Yes. Should we make the call now? Probably sometime in the morning would be best for her. She's an old lady, too. We all are—and that's generally when we feel the best."

Faith hated to hear Ursula refer to herself as an old lady.

"Anytime in the morning would be fine." She'd been mentally rearranging the next two days, who might pick Amy up for ballet, what to take out of the freezer for dinners.

The call was made and a woman who identified herself as Mrs. Jessup's companion told Ursula eleven o'clock would be a good time. After she hung up, Ursula reported the companion had said that Mrs. Jessup enjoyed visits and would be delighted to meet Mrs. Rowe's friend. Faith was all set.

Phillip Theodopoulos was sitting in the little room off their bedroom, which they'd made into an office. He was hunched over his computer at the desk and didn't hear Niki come in. She put her arms around his neck from behind his chair and he started in surprise.

"Hi, honey. How'd it go? Fun with the Uppities?"

He always enjoyed hearing her accounts of these luncheons, even though at times he felt like a target, along with the rest of the male sex.

"Not just fun. I have three things to tell you. First, I saved you a big slice of cheesecake—chocolate hazelnut. Second, the Uppity Women's network is on the job, or rather going to find you a job. I'm a little surprised your phone hasn't rung yet."

She hugged him tighter.

"And the third?"

"You're going to be a dad."

Chapter 10

S tanding at the front window, Faith pulled the drape farther to one side so she could watch Amy get on the bus. Mothers with younger children were gathered at the stop. Faith wished she could join them, but that would only make Amy more of a target—"Kindergarten Baby Amy has to have her mommy walk her to the bus" or some other taunt. The bra had offered an enormous amount of support—psychological, not physical. Amy marched out each morning, chest—what little there was—forward, a smile on her face. If she'd known the song, Faith imagined her daughter would have been belting out "I Am Woman." Time to teach it to her.

The bus stopped, the children got on, and Faith turned away. Amy had moved and was now sitting in the front seat. She said the teasing had stopped. Faith wasn't complacent. Mean girls were devious and sometimes smart. They'd find something new, or someone. The school was implementing a more current antibullying curriculum. That would help. And meanwhile, she would continue to ask her daughter how her day had been much more thoroughly.

Amy looked like a child—long, straight fine hair the color of good butter; eyes the color and sheen of wild blueberries. She was growing fast and it was a pleasure to watch her move on the sports field and off. She loved to dance. Yet Amy wasn't going to stay a child for long, especially not in twenty-first-century America where the media was constantly bombarding kids with messages to grow up fast, inventing a whole new market: "tweens."

Her appointment with Babs Jessup—Mrs. Schuyler Jessup, she corrected herself, picturing a Beacon Hill grande dame—was not until eleven. She'd drive to the Alewife T, where she could park the car and take the Red Line to the Charles Street stop near Beacon Hill— an impossible place to park.

It was too early to leave, so she put in a wash and changed sheets. At nine the phone rang. It was Tom.

"Albert just called. He's picked up some sort of bug and won't be in today. He said it's not bad. He just needs a day or two. The thing is, I know he meant to take a folder home with him yesterday that has articles he's collected on how to make the church greener. He's preparing a report for the congregation's consideration."

"I assume by 'greener,' you mean a paperless newsletter and toilet paper recycled from grocery bags or what-have-you."

Tom laughed. It was good to hear.

"Yes. No plans to repaint our pristine white clapboard. Anyway, could you drop it off at his place on your way? I'm sure he'd be very grateful and you know how conscientious he is. He'd hate to waste time even while recuperating. This would give him something to read in bed."

Faith quickly rearranged her plans. She'd have to leave a little sooner and park in the garage under Boston Common after she dropped off the folder in Cambridge.

"I'll come and get the folder in a few minutes."

"Meet you halfway in the cemetery?"

"Oh Reverend Fairchild, you do say the most romantic things!"

It all seemed to be coming to a close. Tomorrow Faith would fly to New York and confront Violet Winthrop. Given the woman's age, it would have to be done gently, but given the woman's actions, firmly. Faith had called her sister, Hope, and made a tentative arrangement to meet for coffee in the late afternoon before returning north. This was still Ursula's story, not hers, so she'd alluded vaguely to having to meet with someone on the Upper East Side. Hope was born with a client-confidentiality gene and never pried—not overtly anyway.

Sam Miller would be back tonight and was coming straight to the parsonage from the airport. Pix was leaving Charleston—reluctantly from the sound of recent conversations—on Friday morning.

The rain had finally stopped.

She was driving down Route 2 toward Cambridge. Magic 106.7 FM was playing Dan Fogelberg's "To the Morning." What kind of a day was it going to be? Faith wondered, listening to the words of the lyrics. She felt more optimistic than she had since Tom had come home from the emergency meeting of the vestry called by Sherman Munroe. The man himself, or his name, had been popping up ever since. Was he the "shoulder surfer" or other kind of hacker? Was it all a setup to get rid of a minister he didn't like? Church politics were never pretty. Yet, why not confront Tom directly if he was dissatisfied? Of course, Faith imagined Sherman was always dissatisfied and probably always devious. She realized that he was a man who enjoyed manipulating others, and reveled in his own power. This may all have been a game to him; one he thought he couldn't lose. Everything remained unresolved. And Tom would always have the implicit accusation hanging over his head. The vestry had wanted to avoid police involvement from the first—dirty linen and all that. Thank goodness Sam would arrive soon. He might insist the authorities be informed and a proper investigation conducted.

The song was ending. *There is really nothing left to say but / Come on morning.* A beautiful voice. A beautiful song. Faith hummed the tune and thought, Okay, come on, morning.

Albert had lived off Kirkland Street near Harvard Square since moving to the Boston area. Miraculously Faith found a place to park. She'd never been to his apartment, and when she went up the front steps, she realized that there was no way to leave the folder in an entryway or tucked behind a storm door. Both substantial outer and inner doors were locked. She pushed the buzzer next to his name and waited by the intercom. It was a nice brick building, and obviously secure. She'd never given much thought to where he lived, but was a little surprised at how nice the building was. The rent would have been high for a student, although he was making a decent salary now. Maybe he had roommates, although his was the only name listed. She rang again. He must be asleep. She hated to get him out of bed when he wasn't feeling well, but Tom had seemed to think Albert wanted the material. She gave it one more try and called Tom.

"Albert's not answering the bell. Did you call him?"

"I did, but he wasn't answering the phone, either, so I left a message on his machine. I figured he was asleep, or maybe in the bathroom."

Faith didn't want to dwell on the possibility of stomach flu.

"Give me his number and I'll try."

"Okay, and if he still doesn't answer, look and see if his car is there, although I can't imagine he'd go out. He has a parking place next to his apartment and you know the car."

Faith did, as did her kids. They wanted a Mini Cooper just like Albert's, complete with the Union Jack roof.

"All right."

The phone rang four times before the machine kicked in. Faith told him she was leaving the packet for him propped up against the door. It wouldn't be seen from the street, and didn't contain anything of value. Rain wasn't predicted, and if it did shower, the porch had a roof. She hung up and went around to the side of the building. The only car there was a Honda Civic of a certain age. From the look of the tire pressure, it had been there awhile.

There was a small yard enclosed by wire fencing and the other side of the building was separated from the next by an alleyway. No room for cars. She walked up the street to Broadway. No sign of the Mini Cooper. She walked the other way to Kirkland. Nothing there, either. She called Tom again.

"Are you sure he said he was home?"

"Absolutely. This is very odd. Do you think he had to go to the doctor's, or even the hospital?"

"I wouldn't start to worry yet," Faith said. "He told you it wasn't serious. Do you have his cell?"

"No," Tom said slowly. "I've asked him several times—in case I need to get him in an emergency—but he's been kind of funny about it. I've had the feeling he didn't want me to know."

It was a little past ten o'clock. She had an hour to get to Beacon Hill.

"I'll talk to you later, sweetheart. Stay by the phone, okay?"

"Faith, what's going on? Where—"

She switched her phone off and got in her car. Albert was definitely not home and Faith had an idea where he might be instead.

Albert Trumbull's Mini Cooper was parked on Cameron Street in front of Lily Sinclair's apartment. Faith didn't know whether to feel glad that she'd been right or sad that she'd been right. She pulled up next to it and called Tom.

"Honey, I think you should come and have a chat with Albert. I'm at Lily's apartment in Somerville and his car is parked in front."

She could hear Tom's sigh over the phone.

"Maybe he loaned it to her while he was sick?"

A person could drown clutching at straws, Faith thought. She also thought it was time for her too-nice husband to get tough.

"I doubt it and I doubt he's making some kind of pastoral call. If you want me to check it out, I'll go see. But Tom, get going now. You need to talk to him. To them. Call it a hunch."

"But Albert?"

"Tom!"

"Okay. I'm leaving."

Faith double-parked, deciding to take her chances on getting a ticket. She might get lucky even if the Somerville police did cruise by. The Mini was so small that her Subaru wagon looked like someone had inexpertly parked too far from the curb. She sat for a moment.

Faith trusted her hunches, but she realized she might be able to get some confirmation if Zach was available. She dialed his number.

"Hey, what's up? We're still on for Saturday, right?"

Zach was coming out to go over the security programs on their computers.

"Saturday is still fine. I was wondering if you could take a quick look at a Facebook page for me? Her name is Lily Sinclair."

"Sounds like someone working in a gentlemen's club. It's real?"

"Oh yes."

Lily had been enrolled at the Div School. Despite what Zach thought, "Lily Sinclair" couldn't be an alias.

"Here she is. Not bad. And her face isn't, either."

"Zach!"

"Just kidding. Actually she looks very nice. Cool taste in music."

"Just tell me if there are any photos or comments about a boyfriend."

"Would his name be Al? And would he be an Anglophile— his Mini Cooper has a British flag painted on the roof?"

"Yes, and yes. You're a doll. Thank you so much! See you Saturday."

"I take it you don't want me to friend her?"

"Absolutely not."

A hunch had just become a fact. She got out of the car.

Before she rang the bell, she took a look around. The double-decker backed onto another the next street over. It was attached to its neighbor on one side and separated from a single-family dwelling by a narrow driveway on the other. She'd blocked Albert's car in, but he could still leave from the back door and get to the street down the drive. She pictured herself chasing him into Davis Square and hoped it wouldn't come to that. Not only would she feel ridiculous, but she didn't have the time.

She rang the bell and heard steps in the hall.

"I'm coming, hon. Silly girl, you left your keys on the table."

The door opened wide, and while Mr. Trumbull, sometime divinity school student and administrator at the First Parish church in Aleford, was registering extreme surprise at seeing his boss's wife on the doorstep, said wife stepped across the lintel and closed the door behind her.

"Tom's on his way. We need to talk. Lily out for coffee? Or something else to cure what ails you? By the way, glad you're feeling better."

Albert was wearing pajamas—pale blue cotton ones like the kind Brooks Brothers sold. Faith didn't think young men wore these, opting instead for more casual nightwear or nothing specific. Albert had frozen in place. The only thing moving was his mouth and this was opening and closing like a fish out of water desperately gasping for air.

"Why don't we sit down over here while we wait for Tom—and Lily?" Faith wasn't worried anymore that Albert might try to take off. She was, in fact, wondering if she could get him to move into the living room and sit on what she recognized as an Ikea couch and one of their Poang chairs. She gave him a little nudge and he shuffled into the room, collapsing on the couch.

"I . . ." He stopped and didn't start again, just rubbed his hand over his eyes and bowed his head. Faith hoped he was praying. He needed to.

She got up, went into the hall, and opened the front door, leaving it ajar. She wasn't counting on Lily to be as docile as her boyfriend. This way, having forgotten her keys, Lily would think Albert had left the door open for her while he was getting dressed. If Faith answered when Lily rang, she would most likely make a run for it.

Faith returned to the living room and looked at Albert closely. Definitely bed hair. They sat in silence for what seemed like a very long time. Faith didn't want to start without Tom—or Albert's significant other.

"Where is Lily?"

"Starbucks," he whispered.

"What is she getting?"

"Iced mochas and apple fritters."

Faith nodded. The mocha might be a little sweet, but she'd suffer. No way was Albert getting it. He could have the fritter, though. Unless Tom was peckish. Faith had pretty high standards for fritters.

"Where are you? Why is the door open?"

Lily was home.

"In here," Albert said hoarsely. Maybe he did have a sore throat. Faith resolved not to get any closer. "Mrs.—" Once more Albert clammed up, but this time it was because Lily interrupted him. For a moment Faith thought the young woman was going to toss the cardboard tray holding the drinks and pastry at her.

"I knew you'd figure it out. Your sanctimonious prig of a husband couldn't in a month of Sundays! And, you." She whirled around and took several steps toward Albert. Faith was hoping she'd get close enough for Faith to snatch a coffee. She needed it. "You probably told her everything."

Albert cowered. Faith had never actually seen anyone do this, but that's what it was. He put his arms above his head and folded himself into a sitting fetal position.

His behavior had an immediate effect on Lily. She put the tray down on the floor, sat next to Albert, and threw her arms around him.

"My poor baby! Has she been horrible?"

The bell rang and Faith sprinted to the door. She didn't trust Lily not to disappear with her "baby" into the kitchen or elsewhere, barricading them both in. The woman was in tigress mode. The look she'd shot at Faith bore the promise of much harm, bodily harm.

Tom had his hand raised to ring again. She didn't want to think how fast he must have been driving, although Aleford wasn't that far from Somerville, a straight shot out Route 2.

"It's been Lily and Albert all the time," Faith said, "and I've only got five minutes before I have to leave for my appointment with Mrs. Jessup. Come on." She pulled him into the living room, skirting the Starbucks tray. The ice in the coffee was no doubt melting, but Faith had changed her mind. She didn't like mochas that much anyway.

"Why don't you tell me what's going on, or rather what's been going on." Tom addressed the two of them. He looked very tired and very stern.

Lily released Albert and he sat up straighter.

"It was all my idea. Albert has nothing to do with it." She looked a lot like Sydney Carton approaching the guillotine.

"I'm assuming you're talking about taking the money from the church's account."

Albert's face was ashen. He croaked out, "It wasn't just Lily. I'm equally to blame. More so." He cleared his throat; his next words came out louder and stronger.

"You shouldn't have treated Lily the way you did, Tom. Talked to her the way you did. It wasn't fair. She was just trying to do her job, and in my opinion, she was doing a damn fine one!"

"Wait a minute." Faith hated to leave, but she had to get going. Before she did, she needed to inject a little reality into the situation.

"The two of you stole ten thousand dollars from the church, cast the blame on an innocent person, and somehow it's my husband's fault?"

It was Lily's turn.

"You bet it is! We wanted to turn the tables on him. See how he felt being treated like a criminal. And aside from what he did to me—I was committed to my calling before he sowed all those seeds of doubt—the parish needed to see that their emperor had no clothes. He's fooled parents into thinking he's so in touch with their kids, but he has no idea what's going on with them and the issues they have. I heard that his own kid was in trouble at school, too. The way Tom is alienating the younger generation, his sainted First Parish is going to find itself without a congregation when all his suck-ups die off. And he had no right to rake *me* over the coals. I have a father who does that!"

Seeing the look that passed between Tom and Faith, Lily added, "And don't start with any psychobabble. This has nothing to do with what's happened between my father and me. It's all Tom's fault. Period."

During Lily's diatribe, the Reverend Thomas Preston Fairchild had turned beet red. Faith had seen him lose his temper a few times. It was scary. When Lily had mentioned Ben's trouble at school, Faith thought Tom was going to explode, but he'd waited. Steam rising from the center of Vesuvius, but not the main event. That was coming now. He was going to lose it. And he did. For the next few minutes the "sanctimonious prig" let Albert, still cowering, and Lily, suddenly sobbing, have it. About the laws of man, and yes, God, that they had broken. About their self-centeredness. About the betrayal of their calling, and on and on.

"We didn't spend the money," Lily interrupted at one point.

Faith had been wondering about this. Starbucks was pricey, but Albert had had the car before the thefts and Lily wasn't shopping on Newbury Street, except maybe at the Second Time Around. What had they done with the loot?

Albert brightened. "Yes, it's all here. In an envelope with the withdrawal slips under Lily's mattress. We'd always intended to give it back."

Tom blew up again. The lava flow wasn't quite as monumental as before, but still very impressive, fed by the force of the anguish he and Faith had suffered over the last twelve days. The idea that they had been toying with his life—with the life of his church—was intolerable. Under the mattress, indeed!

Reluctantly Faith took her leave as Tom was calling Sam. It was like skipping out before the last act of a play, a play like *The Mousetrap*. Tom would tell her about it later. She couldn't keep Mrs. Jessup waiting. She couldn't let Ursula down. Not at this point.

Mrs. Schuyler Jessup was wearing a daffodil-yellow nubby wool suit over a delphinium-blue and white striped silk blouse. Faith was immediately reminded of the flowers she'd seen as she walked from the Common to the Mt. Vernon Street address. Everything bloomed earlier in Boston and it had been a nice reminder of what was to come in Aleford.

Introductions were made and Mrs. Jessup instructed Faith to call her "Babs."

"My family called me 'Babby' for many years, but I put a stop to that when I married Scooter. It was bad enough being Babs and Scooter. Will you have coffee or tea?"

Faith hesitated. From the look of the room—the export porcelain, Chippendale and Sheraton furniture, damask upholstery, walls crammed with artwork collected by many generations—she was sure the tray would be loaded down with the appropriate sterling vessels. If she chose coffee and Babs normally had tea, the companion, a pleasant-looking, slight middle-aged woman hovering at the door, would never be able to carry it all.

"If you're wondering what I take, it's coffee. I know 'elevenses' is a British custom, but I've never been a tea drinker. Besides, there's all that fuss with strainers, lemon slices, and extra hot water pots."

"Coffee is fine—it's what I prefer, too."

Entering the room, Faith had been struck by the thought that ninety really is the new seventy when it came to Ursula and now the woman before her. She recalled that Babs had been described as athletic in her youth and she looked as if she were still scoring below par. Her spine was ramrod straight and the only softness evident were her skin and snowy white curls, kept away from her face by a headband that picked up the blue in her blouse. She was wearing pearls the size of pigeon eggs.

Coffee and a plate of tasty-looking macaroons arrived. The companion poured out and then discreetly disappeared.

"I'm sorry to hear that Ursula has been ill. Our families knew each other, but I'm afraid we lost touch when the Lymans moved out west."

If Faith hadn't known Babs was referring to Aleford, a twenty-minute drive, she would have assumed the woman meant the Territories.

"She's on the mend and I'm sure will make a full recovery."

"There. We've taken care of all the niceties, so why don't you tell me what she's sent you to see me about?"

Faith had been afraid she'd have trouble changing gears from larceny to murder. The present to the past. Driving over, she'd been euphoric—and furious. She'd called Tom as she was walking down Charles Street. Sam was sending one of the firm's associates over. No crime had been reported, so Tom couldn't call the police in at this point, nor did he want to—however, a crime had been committed. He didn't know how to proceed. Sam was trying to get on an earlier flight and meanwhile had told Tom to stay put. Lily and Albert were definite flight risks. The associate would be reinforcement, and a witness. Tom told her that Albert had stopped cowering and started crying. He was continuing to break into tears at regular intervals. Lily, however, had regained her composure and had refused to say anything further except to call Tom several names that were not going to help with Saint Peter, should she get that far. The scene was pretty much what Faith had thought it would be.

At the Jessup house, the turmoil of the morning receded the moment she'd stepped into the downstairs hall and walked up the curved stairs, the mahogany banister soft and gleaming after centuries of use. By the time she was ushered into the sun-dappled living room, Faith was imagining herself stepping into a Henry James novel or Marquand's *The Late George Apley*.

"It has to do with the death of Ursula's brother, Theo."

Babs put her cup down. "We loved Theo. He was my husband's best friend. Scooter never got over his death. We were so young and this sort of thing had never happened to us—I mean, a tragic accident, a death, illnesses. Those were supposed to come later in life, and at that point we didn't think past the next week."

"You do know what happened afterward? About the way Arnold Rowe was cleared?"

"Oh yes. I must confess that I didn't really notice Ursula much at the Vineyard. She was just Theo's little sister, although now the age difference scarcely matters.

At the time, there was a great deal of talk about the way she marched into the jail and some people were rather scandalized. It all died down quickly. There was other, bigger news during those Depression years and then the war."

Faith went on to tell her about the letters and handed over the copies she'd made for Babs to read herself. She handed them back, holding the papers in her fingertips as if they were contaminated with something.

"I'm afraid I still don't understand why you're here. Pleasant as it is. What does Ursula want?"

"Any information you might have about Violet Winthrop. That's who she thinks is sending these. She doesn't know anything about her, or her husband, except that he was transferred to New York some time in the thirties. I'm going to New York tomorrow to speak with her."

Babs gave a wry smile. "And since, unfortunately, we are related by marriage, I'm the one to fill you in."

"Yes. We're trying to figure out why she might be doing this. Ursula thinks it could be boredom. I'm not so sure."

"And you would be right, knowing Violet. I doubt it's that simple. Let's get some hot coffee. I need another cup and it's time for some sandwiches." She pressed a spot in the design on the Oriental rug and the companion appeared so quickly she must have been sitting near the door. She said she'd brew some fresh coffee and bring another tray, whisking away the one on the table in front of Babs.

The old lady settled back in her chair. Faith noticed a malacca cane next to it, the only indication that Mrs. Jessup needed help getting around.

"Tell me about yourself while we're waiting. I know your husband is a minister. I'm afraid I would have been quite inadequate as a clerical spouse. For one thing, I have a tendency to laugh in church."

Babs was a kindred spirit and Faith soon had her laughing with stories of Faith's life.

The sandwiches were egg salad, freshly made, with a little chive, on sourdough—not the usual WASP equivalent of Wonder bread with the crusts removed. More coffee was poured and Babs started talking about Violet Winthrop, née Hammond.

"She was quite a piece of work. I disliked her intensely and we were thrown together quite a bit because Theo was madly in love with her, as was Charlie Winthrop. Neither of them would have married her. She was a fling, and common sense, plus family pressure, would have prevailed. I still don't know how she managed to get Charlie to propose, but he did, very shortly after Theo was killed. Perhaps he was feeling his own mortality. And Violet was extremely beautiful. It was something to walk down the street with her. People, men and women both, would stop to stare at her. And oh, how she loved the attention.

"She had been considered fast at school. I think it was Miss Porter's, maybe Rosemary Hall. My mother wasn't happy about my going around with her, but I told her I couldn't very well not, since Scooter was such good friends with the men she dated. Mother needn't have worried and I told her so. Violet liked men. Period. She didn't have, or want, girlfriends. She certainly wouldn't have had any influence over me. We were both females, yes, but chalk and cheese—you can decide which was which. This doesn't help you, though. Ancient history.

"They moved to New York soon after they were married. It was a small wedding at her people's out in Chicago. Charlie wasn't terribly bright and he was in the way in the office here, according to one of our Winthrop cousins. The New York office had a spot for him where he couldn't cause much damage. Essentially it was a place to go every day—the family taking care of one of its own. The Winthrops did make rather a lot of money during the war years and he came in for a great deal of it just by being one. There's a daughter, Marguerite. Charlie wanted Scooter to be her godfather, but I told him absolutely not. I think he said he was an agnostic or something and wouldn't do a good job. It wouldn't have fooled anybody else, but probably fooled Charlie, who wouldn't have paused to consider that at the time Scooter was a junior warden at church. There were no other children and Marguerite never married to my knowledge. Charlie died many years ago and the last I heard mother and daughter were still living in the same town house they'd been living in at his death. On the East Side somewhere. You have to understand, I didn't just dislike Violet because she was always quite awful to me—made me feel like a kind of freak because I enjoyed sports, terrible catty remarks about my muscular calves. Those things hurt when you're young and insecure. No, I also disliked her because I thought she was completely amoral. No heart. However you want to put it. She used people. The only person she cared about was herself. Poor Charlie."

And poor Theo, Faith thought, and said, "This helps a great deal." They hadn't known about Marguerite Winthrop. Could she be responsible for the letters?

"Although," she said, "I still don't know why she, or perhaps her daughter, would decide to torment Ursula at this point. Malicious mischief? She wants some kind of last thrill?"

"Dear Faith, don't kid yourself. Violet did a lot of things for thrills, but I doubt this is her object now."

"Then what?"

"Money, of course."

"Ursula and I talked about the possibility that it was blackmail of some sort, that the letters were veiled threats to bring the whole thing up again. But she's a wealthy woman. Why would she need money?"

"Not 'need,' 'want.' When you go to see her, how about a little wager that she has one of those needle-point pillows with YOU CAN NEVER BE TOO RICH OR TOO THIN on it."

It was a sucker bet. Faith politely declined and, after a heartfelt promise to visit again, took her leave. She had a great deal to think about.

There was a time when flying had been fun. That time was long past. First there had been a long wait in the security line, then a further wait when some-one's laptop case strap got caught in the conveyer belt, bringing everything to a halt, and finally a wait by the gate while the plane—late arriving—was serviced. The wad of gum below the window and crumpled napkins at her feet were evidence to the contrary, but Faith didn't care. She just wanted to get to the city.

With only her handbag, she was out of the terminal quickly and grabbed a cab. Despite her errand, her spirits lifted as soon as she saw the familiar skyline. She was home.

It was odd to drive past her family's apartment ten blocks north of her destination. Her parents were in Spain, a rare vacation that presaged more, longer ones. For some time now, her father had been urging the congregation to form a search committee and engage an interim. "I may have to actually quit in order to make them realize I can't keep being their minister forever." Jane Sibley, a real estate lawyer, had gone part-time some years ago. She was urging her husband to retire, as were his daughters. Faith was happy they were away. The last time she'd seen them her mother looked wonderful, as always, but her father looked extremely tired. He'd never bounced back after a serious heart attack several years ago. While she understood how hard it would be for the church to let go of their longtime leader, she was entertaining thoughts of standing outside a Sunday service leafleting the congregation with a letter begging them to let him leave.

She'd called Hope when the plane had landed and they were meeting at the Viand coffee shop on Madison, not far from the Winthrops' town house. Faith was in need of an egg cream, that quintessential New York delicacy consisting of U-Bet (and only this brand will do) chocolate syrup, very cold milk, and very fizzy seltzer. No eggs involved. It went very well with Viand's pastrami sandwich—not to be compared with Katz's, but that was too far downtown.

As soon as she was finished with Mrs. Winthrop, and perhaps Miss W. would also be there, Faith was to call Hope. She put her number on the screen and activated her iPhone's GPS tracker, InstaMapper, which Hope had insisted she install and was now insisting she use. It would allow the mistress of time management to schedule her arrival at the coffee shop to coincide with her sister's arrival there, thus not wasting a minute of Hope's billable hours.

Faith had called the Winthrop house from Ursula's on Wednesday and left word on an answering machine that Mrs. Rowe was not able to come herself, but someone else representing her would arrive on Friday morning and to please call back if it was not convenient. There had been no call.

Faith paid the cabdriver and approached the house with some trepidation. Compared to the others on the block, the place looked shabby. The evergreens in the large urns on either side of the front door were dry and most of the needles brown. The brass knocker and door handle needed polishing. The door itself could use a fresh coat of paint.

Noting that she seemed to be arriving unannounced often lately, Faith pushed the bell. She hadn't given her name when she'd called; she wasn't sure why, but the whole enterprise seemed to call for anonymity—and even stealth.

She could hear a chime sound faintly within. She waited and pushed again. Nothing. She stepped back and looked at the façade. All the drapes were drawn. Perhaps they were away. Perhaps she should have called from the airport. The house certainly looked unoccupied. As she was considering whether or not to stay, she saw one of the drapes twitch. Someone was peering out a second-floor window. She stepped back and rang again.

The intercom crackled.

"Yes? Who is it?" The voice was firm and clear.

"My name is Faith Fairchild. I'm here on behalf of Ursula Rowe."

"Her daughter?"

"No, but like one."

Faith wanted to establish her bona fides.

The door buzzed and she opened it, stepping into a large foyer tiled in black and white marble. It was hard to see the pattern, however, because of all the mail, junk and otherwise, strewn about.

"Well, don't just stand there. We've been expecting you."

The voice came from the back of the house. Faith walked toward it through a dining room, the furniture covered with dust so thick it would have provided hours of scribbling pleasure for a child. Several botanical prints hung on the wall, which also showed the outlines of other artwork that had been removed. The room smelled musty.

"We're in here. Come on." The voice was impatient.

"Here" turned out to be the kitchen and the disorder continued. Empty cans of cat food were piled in one corner and the sink was filled with dirty dishes. There was a small patio beyond a pair of French doors and the only light in the room was coming through the grimy glass. Faith, endowed with the native New Yorker real estate instinct, immediately began to see the place scrubbed clean, staged, and up for sale, calculating the price as she looked about for the house's owner. It took a moment to distinguish the human occupants from the cats, as both looked gray with tangled coats. In the case of the nonfelines, the coats were layers of sweaters and hair that badly needed cutting—and washing. One of them stood.

"I'm Marguerite Winthrop and this is my mother, Mrs. Charles Winthrop," she said regally. Faith wasn't sure whether to extend her hand or curtsy. In the end she did neither, but took the chair Marguerite had indicated.

Apparently, however, it was Violet's show.

"I knew Ursula would have to respond." It was the same voice Faith had heard over the intercom. Faith tried to hold her temper. She thought of what the letters had done to Ursula. The crone in front of her suddenly reminded her of Sherman Munroe. Both their voices were filled with smug entitlement. That whatever they did would always have been justified merely by who they were.

"Mrs. Rowe was literally made ill by your letters. If you don't stop sending them, we intend to seek legal action."

Violet laughed. It was a deep, throaty laugh and Faith thought if she closed her eyes, she might see the beautiful young woman Violet had been. The woman whose voice sounded like money, like Fitzgerald's Daisy Buchanan. There were also traces of a younger Violet beneath her rather grotesque makeup—a slash of red lipstick, purple eye shadow, powdery white foundation, and dark brows that had been penciled on in thin, surprised half-moons.

"Did you hear that, Marguerite? Little Ursula is threatening me with legal action. I suppose I should be quite terrified."

Faith stood up. "This is obviously a waste of time. Mine, that is. I don't know why you sent those hateful letters, but this is not a threat. If you send more, or attempt to contact Mrs. Rowe in any way, we will get a restraining order."

"I believe the only one being restrained will be you. Now, Marguerite!"

Marguerite grabbed Faith and shoved some kind of cloth over her face. The woman was surprisingly agile and all those sweaters were concealing a strong body. Warm sweaters. Faith was feeling very warm herself. Very, very warm. Her body was on fire. She tried to pull off whatever it was Marguerite was holding over her nose and mouth. It had a sickeningly sweet smell. I have to breathe! I have to get away from these women! From this house! were Faith's last thoughts for some time.

When she slowly became conscious again, she was indeed restrained—tied securely to the chair with ropes and bungee cords. Her vision cleared. The two women were drinking something from mugs advertising a local blood bank. She hoped the liquid was tea or coffee.

"Ah, you're back," Violet said.

After trying to move, Faith discovered her ankles were tied to the front chair legs and her arms, extended straight down, were pinned to the back ones. Her hands were free and she could move her fingers. Not that this did her any good. She had no idea how long she'd been out and she had a foul taste in her mouth. Her head ached.

"As soon as you feel you've recovered—it shouldn't be long, we practiced with the chloroform on each other—you're going to call Ursula and suggest a trade. What was the amount, Marguerite?"

"We thought a hundred thousand dollars was a nice round number."

"Of course," Violet said. "We want it transferred directly into our bank account here. Ursula was so thoughtful sending you on a weekday when all this business can be taken care of quickly. We were afraid it would be a weekend, which would drag things out."

"Wait a minute. You must be insane! You're holding me hostage until Ursula pays you?"

"That's been our plan from the start, although we thought she'd send her actual daughter, or her son."

They *were* insane. Faith felt as if she'd been transported to a remake of the film *Grey Gardens*.

"I'm not calling her," she said. "And in any case, she doesn't have that kind of money."

"Oh, but she does, or she can get it easily. And I think you'll find it increasingly unpleasant here if you don't call."

Faith willed herself not to let the terror she was starting to feel show. This couldn't be happening. She was in the middle of New York City—on the Upper East Side, for goodness' sake!

"It's nothing personal. We've been driven to this by that crook Bernie Madoff. We should be tying him up—or that wife of his—but that would have been more complicated, and Bernie, at least, is not reachable. He ruined us! At this point we can't even pay the electric bill."

"Wait a minute. You may have lost your money through Madoff, along with a huge number of others"— Faith was tempted to add, Who are not tying people up, yet thought it wise not to dwell on the situation— "but your house is worth many millions."

Violet looked aghast. "Sell our home! I'd starve to death first. I'll have you know my husband, Charles Wendell Winthrop, bought this house for me when we first moved to New York City and he intended that I should live here for my entire life, as did he. When I do die, it will of course go to my daughter."

Faith had the feeling Violet was now regarding her as some sort of malevolent real estate broker who had happened by to try to swindle her further.

"I won't call Ursula. That's final."

Violet's smile was nasty.

"Marguerite, dear, it's time for you to practice your piano." She added, "My daughter is an accomplished pianist who could have had a brilliant career were it not for the petty jealousies and dirty politics of the concert world. 'Marguerite' is French for daisy, a name that would have been too common. From birth I had intended her for great things. My husband used to call us his two flowers."

The younger flower left, disappearing into the gloom of the dining room and thereafter to parts unknown.

"She's a sensitive girl and I didn't want her to overhear us."

Faith could feel sweat start to trickle down various parts of her body.

"I've killed once and I will kill again, Mrs. Fairchild," Violet said matter-of-factly. "If Ursula doesn't wire the funds within twenty-four hours, you'll be dead."

It was the first part of what she said that struck Faith.

"It was *you*, not your husband—and certainly not Arnold Rowe. *You* killed Theo."

Violet nodded. "Such a long time ago that it doesn't really matter anymore. Not then, either. Theo Lyman was getting to be quite a bore. Every time I'd turn around, there he would be, acting like an idiot, trying to impress me. Oh, they had money, the Lymans, I'll grant you that, but it was gone soon enough. Thank goodness I had the sense to stick with Charlie. And he with me. But then, he rather had to." Violet smiled in reminiscence. "He was grateful. Oh yes, very grateful—starting that night—and I made sure he stayed that way. Yes, starting all those years ago on a warm summer night on Martha's Vineyard . . ."

"What's happened? You look terrible. Have you been in some kind of fight?"

"Violet, my God! You've got to help me. I don't know what to do. It wasn't my fault. He wouldn't give me the money!"

"What are you talking about? Calm down! Here, come into the library. Nobody's there."

She stood with her back against the door so they wouldn't be disturbed. Charles sat down on one of the couches and put his head in his hands. After a moment he looked up; his face was streaked with tears.

"I killed him. Theo's dead. I swear it was an accident. He was laughing and wouldn't listen. I pushed him. Maybe I hit him. I don't remember. He fell against a bench." Charles jumped to his feet and came toward her speaking rapidly.

"*I never meant to hurt him. Just wanted to scare him a little. Oh God! What am I going to do? I'll go to prison. No one will believe me!*"

"*I believe you, Charles. Start at the beginning. Where were you?*"

"*I need a drink. There must be something to drink in this place. What does he need with all these things?*" *Charles gestured wildly at the weapons displayed throughout the room.*

"*I'll get you a drink in a minute. Tell me what happened from the start.*" *Violet kept her voice steady and calm.* "*Sit down again.*"

Charles sat on an ottoman closer to Violet and looked up at her.

"*I owe some men some money. A lot of money. If I don't pay them first thing tomorrow morning they'll go to my father—and they'll hurt me. Said I wouldn't be playing tennis for a long time. I kept telling Theo. Out in the gazebo in the woods. I didn't want anyone to hear us. He was pretty loaded. Just laughed and wanted to go back to the party. Kept saying he didn't have any money. Everything's a blur. I got mad. You've got to believe me. I never meant to hurt him. He was so still. Didn't move. I ran back here to find you.*"

Violet nodded. "We don't have much time. First, you were never in the gazebo tonight. Nobody saw you leave, did they?"

Charles shook his head.

"Next, I want you to give me ten minutes and then find a couple of people, people you don't know—that won't be hard in this crowd; I have no idea who these crashers are. Tell them Theo wants the Professor out in the gazebo right away. It won't make sense to them, but they'll think it's a game and start shouting for him. Then find Rowe yourself. Keep an eye on him, but don't let him see you. As soon as you see him leave the house, follow a little ways behind. Get Scooter and some others to go with you. Tell them something's happened; you don't know what. Now repeat it all back to me— and don't have anything more to drink until later. When you leave now, go wash up and pull yourself together."

Charles repeated what Violet had told him to do and left the room. She walked slowly about. It was her favorite place in the house and she'd often thought she'd like to meet the man who collected all these weapons, bagged the game. A real man. Not like Charles, or Theo. But Charles was going to do just fine. Charles with all that Winthrop money and position. Nobody was going to snigger at Violet Hammond behind her back again. She knew what people said about her. It was coming to a happy ending a bit sooner than she planned—so long as Charles did exactly as he was told. And he would. Tonight, tomorrow, and in the future. After all, a wife couldn't testify against her husband, could she?

She picked up the stiletto letter opener on the desk with her handkerchief and climbed out the window. It didn't take long to get to the gazebo.

Theo was unconscious. There was almost no pulse, such a slight flutter that she almost missed it. She shuddered in repulsion—his face already re-sembled a death mask—but quickly pulled herself together and took his gold watch and his signet ring. They would have to keep the bootleggers—she knew what Charles had been up to—happy for now. If Charles's father got even a whiff of scandal regarding his son, he'd cut him off for good. And that wouldn't do at all.

Someone was coming—walking rapidly down the path. She heard Rowe call Theo's name.

Theo wouldn't be answering.

She plunged the stiletto into Theo's chest and slipped out the door into the woods to wait.

It was perfect. She heard the Professor's anguished cry and Charles's arrival with the others. When she went back into the gazebo, slipping in with several others, she saw that Arnold had pulled the knife from Theo's chest and was standing over him. She screamed—and kept on screaming.

Everything was going to be fine.

"My family has always been devoted to music, particularly the piano," Faith said. "I'd love to hear your daughter play. What kind of piano do you have?"

Violet rose to the bait.

"We have two, of course. A Steinway grand in the living room and a Baldwin in her music room. When she began to show her talents, we converted one of the bedrooms into a studio for her. It's soundproof, otherwise you could hear the music from here."

"What a shame I can't. It would be such a treat."

Would overweening pride overwhelm Violet's judgment? It was the only way Faith could think of to get the woman to untie her.

"Oh no you don't, Miss Smarty-pants. When I get word that the money has been transferred, perhaps Marguerite will give us a brief concert. For now, you'll be staying right where you are."

Pride did not go before a fall. They sat in silence for a while and then Violet burst out, "Now are you going to make that call or aren't you? My patience is wearing thin."

Faith was about to say no again when she realized that each time Violet had voiced the demand, she'd insisted Faith make the call. Why couldn't Violet make it herself, or even darling daughter Marguerite? Surely they had the number and they could hold the phone up to Faith so she could speak to prove she was actually here—and in extremis. Maybe, no probably, the phones were landlines and not portable. Violet would have to untie her and she wouldn't want to risk it.

So, Faith had to make the call using her cell. Violet was isolated from the world, but not completely. She'd assumed whoever came would have one.

It was a glimmer.

"All right. Bring me your phone," Faith said, feigning defeat.

"Don't you have your own? It's a long distance call. I don't see why I should have to pay for it."

The illogic was breathtaking—and breath giving.

"My phone is in my purse, which must be somewhere on the floor." They must have taken it from Faith's shoulder when she was knocked out. She hated to think of what it rested on. "The phone is in the outside pocket." She'd placed it there so she could call Hope easily.

Violet got up. She may not have been as athletic in her youth as Babs Jessup, but she still had excellent posture and didn't seem to require a cane or walker to get about.

"Is this it?" Violet asked dubiously. She held up the iPhone. Clearly cells in all their incarnations were a novelty.

"Yes. I have Ursula on something called 'speed dial' so I could get in touch with her once I made contact with you. Just run your finger across the screen and the number will ring. Hold it to my face and I'll tell her what's going on."

Please, Hope, catch on. Please . . .

"Are you there yet?" As always, her sister got right to the point.

Faith interrupted quickly. She couldn't have asked for a better opening.

"Yes, I'm here with Violet, Mrs. Winthrop, that is. And Ursula, I'm afraid things haven't gone well. For us, I mean. Mrs. Winthrop and her daughter, Marguerite, had the misfortune to lose a great deal of money with Bernard Madoff. They are demanding a trade. In return for my safety, they want you to immediately transfer a hundred thousand dollars into their bank account."

Faith could almost see the stunned look on Hope's face as she rapidly processed the bizarre call.

"I see. Have they harmed you in any way?"

"No, Ursula, but they will if the money isn't in their account within twenty-four hours. At the moment I'm tied up in their kitchen. Actually, a lovely room with French doors leading to a back patio. The house itself is quite grand, although being on the ground floor, I can't say what the upstairs is like."

"Give me that thing." Violet was almost snarling. "You'd think you were going to move in! Now listen to me, Ursula Rowe, I have nothing to lose and everything to gain, so you'd better start getting the money together if you want to see your precious friend alive."

There was a pause. "She wants to talk to you again." Violet held the phone up.

"Keep the phone on. I'm setting all the wheels in motion. Good-bye."

Hope must have assumed she was on speakerphone. Bless her. She could be counted on to think of everything.

"She's getting everything started. Just leave the phone on the table and she'll call back for your account information."

"All written down in this." She waved a large ledger—the kind Faith associated with Melville's

Bartleby. "That wasn't so hard, was it? We'll have you out of here in no time."

Faith was sure that's exactly what Hope was planning, too.

Her sister had friends in high places, so when New York's finest shortly arrived, some at the front door, which Violet refused to open, but more over the wall and into the back patio, Faith was not surprised. She was, however, understandably enormously relieved. When the police shattered one of the glass doors to get in, Violet threw herself at Faith, knocking the chair to the floor, all the while screaming something about an unholy alliance on the part of Ursula, the Madoffs, and poor Faith herself. Marguerite was discovered deep in Beethoven's "Moonlight" sonata and the two women were bundled off to the precinct charged with an entire laundry list of felonies, and thence, Faith assumed, soon to Bellevue, where their tattered apparel would be exchanged for more appropriate—and restrained—white jackets. Hope arrived on the heels of the police and accompanied her to the precinct.

"It isn't that I think you need a lawyer; it's that you need a sister," she said. "Aside from wanting to see you safe and sound with my own eyes, I'm aware that the police don't know you the way I do. I haven't heard *this* story yet, but based on the past, I do know it will be a hard one to swallow."

Faith never did get her egg cream and pastrami on rye, but took a rain check. She spent the night at Hope's and left early in the morning. She wanted to go home. That home.

Aleford.

Chapter 11

No matter what form the wedding ceremony takes—in a church, a temple, or a field of daisies—the receptions all follow the same patterns. The toasts to the new couple, the first dance, breaking bread, more toasts, more dancing, neckties loosened, high heels slipped off, and late in the day or night, a feeling of great ease. Two families have become one— for the moment or forever. Degrees of separation disappear. Discoveries are made—"My sister Sally must have been in your class!" and "I was born in Orange Memorial Hospital, too!" The dancing becomes freer—and closer during the slow numbers. Time is suspended. Lights are lowered.

The reception had arrived at this point and Faith was sitting with Tom at the Millers' table. She was breathless from the hora that one of Rebecca's aunts had initiated, sweeping the women in the room into the circle, including Ursula, who knew all the words to "Hava Nagila," most others chiming in only at the chorus, but with gusto. Earlier the bride and groom had been hoisted on chairs for that hora, the dancers snaking about in a joyous procession as the song continued on and on. Joy. So much joy.

Tom, sans collar, had acquitted himself so well in Hebrew during his part of the ceremony at Kahal Kadosh Beth Elohim that the Cohens' relatives and friends were asking who the new rabbi was. The chuppah—the canopy under which the couple stood, which symbolized the home they would make together, a home open on all sides for anyone to enter—was composed of a blanket of flowers. Faith had never seen one quite like it, nor the flowers that were everywhere at the reception—roses, orchids, and other varieties in ivory, the palest of greens, and as many kinds of pink as Chanel's lipsticks. The bridesmaids wore midcalf pastel strapless sheaths and carried calla lilies. They looked like lilies themselves.

Their parents escorted the wedding couple to the chuppah. Cissy and Pix wore deceptively simple, flattering cocktail dresses, cut exquisitely in two slightly different shades of lavender; Sam and Stephen sported elegant pale gray vests under their tuxedos. Grandchildren escorted grandparents to their seats and Ursula in her garnet satin looked like royalty.

"Happy, darling?" Tom placed his hand over his wife's.

"Very," she said. "And we have two more days here all to ourselves. Well, there's the brunch tomorrow, which will be fun—but after that, it's just you and me, kid."

"Sounds perfect."

Faith moved her chair closer to Tom's and leaned back against his shoulder. She was content to sit and watch the dancers whirl by for now.

When Rebecca and Mark had stamped on the wineglass wrapped in the napkin at the close of the ceremony, Faith was reminded of the act's additional meaning, apart from being a historic reminder of the destruction of the temple in Jerusalem. That the breaking of the glass symbolized our imperfect world, and the act carried a message for all present—to work hard each day to mend it.

There had been much mending of various sorts since April's dramatic beginning. After countless vestry meetings preceded by consultations with Sam, Tom—and First Parish—had decided not to prosecute Albert and Lily. In fact, Tom decided to keep Albert on for a number of reasons: he'd been doing an excellent job; was clearly not cut out for the ministry, yet very much wanted to be a church administrator; and perhaps most pressing—Tom wanted to keep an eye on him. At first Faith had been vehemently opposed to this "turning of the other cheek," but Tom had explained that although he didn't feel that he had brought the whole thing on himself as Lily had described, he cared deeply about the young man and setting him adrift just didn't make sense.

Lily was a different story, and while they were still struggling to sort out what to do, Lily herself came up with the solution, asking to meet with Tom and then the vestry accompanied by her mother. Her father was refusing to have anything to do with her at the moment.

She had confessed everything, describing the deep depression she'd fallen into at divinity school that had taken a manic turn during the internship. She was seeing a therapist and was feeling clear about what she really wanted to be doing—nursing. To start, she hoped to be able to work in Haiti with a view to returning to the Boston area in a year to enter an RN program, gaining the skills she needed to go back or go to another part of the world.

If Faith thought it was all a little too pat and the ends a little too neatly tied up, she kept her mouth shut. Sherman Munroe and others in the church were falling all over themselves trying to atone for their suspicions and she was unabashedly enjoying it. The Minister's Discretionary Fund, and everything else requiring passwords, PINs, and so forth, had been protected as only Zach could. He boasted that First Parish was now on a level with the Pentagon, although he had added that neither place should be complacent. Hackers weren't.

And there was further mending. Pix had arrived at Logan Airport late that Friday morning to find not only her own husband waiting for her, but Tom, in great agitation, waiting for his wife. "I seem to have missed something," Pix had said, never dreaming how much. Over the next few days she'd found out—mostly from her mother.

In the weeks that followed they learned that the Winthrop women were indeed destitute. When Charles Winthrop died, the family told Violet that she could expect nothing from them save a spot next to him in the family plot at Mount Auburn Cemetery and they did not wish to see her until she was ready to use it. Violet was thin, but she wasn't too rich since she refused to sell the town house. Faith strongly suspected the cat food tins had not been enjoyed solely by the Winthrop pets.

They also learned that Marguerite was adapting well to life in prison—three squares, clean clothes, and fresh bed linens. She had changed her name to Daisy and was entertaining the other women in the upstate prison with medleys of show tunes on an old upright whenever she got the chance. Her mother was in a secure psychiatric facility.

"They're playing your song. Shall we dance?" Tom said. The music had stopped, and was starting up again.

Faith stood up and began to sing along, "Start spreading the news . . ." as Tom led her onto the floor.

She'd been very careful about champagne, but Pix was still feeling very rosy. Aside from her own wedding, it was the happiest one she had ever attended. She only wished her father could have lived to see his beloved grandson as an adult, a fine young man with a lovely bride.

After Ursula had told Pix the whole story, Arnie flew in and Pix heard it again. When she and her brother talked later, they admitted that they had always suspected that there was something major their parents hadn't shared with them, but thought it might be that their father, older than their mother, had been married before.

Pix drained the glass she'd been nursing. It was hard to believe all that had happened while she had been enjoying the Cohens' hospitality, blissfully unaware, in South Carolina. Cissy and Steve were coming to Maine in August for a week of sailing, kayaking, and, in Cissy's case, painting. She was a talented artist and confessed she'd always wanted to do watercolors of rockier shores.

"Don't tell me it's Pix!" The man standing in front of her looked very familiar and it took only a few seconds for Pix to gasp, "Brian?"

Brian had been Stephen Cohen's Dartmouth roommate and Pix's Brown roommate's boyfriend. She knew Mindy hadn't married him, but obviously he had stayed in touch with Steve. He was laughing.

"Mind if I sit down?"

"Please do." Now what? Pix wondered. Would it all come out? Was he the type to grab the mic and make a joke about Green Key Weekend for the amusement of all?

"Just about missed the whole darn wedding. Car trouble and finally we just ditched it and rented one."

"You were from Savannah, as I recall." Pix tried to sound nonchalant. It wasn't working.

"Talk about coincidences! The mother of the groom and the father of the bride—"

"Please," Pix interrupted, and then was interrupted herself by Dr. Stephen Cohen, who had suddenly appeared at their side.

"Brian! You made it!"

"I wouldn't miss Becca's wedding for the world, old buddy. And the first person I run into is Pix . . . wait a minute, I've got it—Rowe. Mindy's roommate. She's still in Savannah, too. Hotshot lawyer and there's talk of a run for the statehouse. Married a cousin of my wife's and we're all family."

Pix was feeling dizzy and wondered whether it would be rude to excuse herself.

"Speaking of family. You two are family now!" His grin couldn't possibly get any broader, Pix thought dismally. Any minute now, he'd start spreading the news. No, wait, that was the song. Oh, she couldn't think straight at all.

"Yes, it's great," Steve said. "Pix and I have had fun talking over old times and the only fly in the ointment is that her husband can beat me at golf. I think Mark can, too, but he's smart enough to let me have a few strokes. Maybe now that they're married, it will change."

Pix knew they were talking about golf scores, but she'd stop paying attention after the part about catching up on old times.

"Well, I need to congratulate the bride and groom and dance with my wife. She had us taking lessons last winter, said we were getting stodgy. Y'all take care now."

"It was good to see you again," Pix managed.

Stephen gave his friend a hug and said, "Now, about that weekend. You understand it's Pix and my little secret."

"Not to worry." Brian zipped his lips and walked off.

"You knew it was me! All the time?" Pix didn't know whether to be indignant or jubilant. "I thought you'd forgotten."

"Wait a minute. I'd thought *you'd* forgotten. And yes, this is starting to sound like a bad sitcom," he said, laughing.

Pix was speechless. It was the one thing that hadn't occurred to her—or Faith. That Stephen would think Pix didn't remember *him*. It really was very funny and she started to laugh, too.

Sam and Cissy came dancing over, finishing with a flourish, both singing "New York, New York." It was that kind of song.

"Hey, you two, what's so funny?" Sam asked.

"Nothing," Stephen said, taking Pix's hand for the next number.

"Absolutely nothing," she said, stepping into his arms and matching her steps to his.

Ursula sat listening to a long story Rebecca's aunt was telling about someone. It wasn't clear whether this person was in the present or past, but it didn't seem to matter. Ursula had discovered that people in Charleston tended to regard the living and the dead much the same when it came to storytelling, even as to tense.

She watched the couples on the dance floor, her eyes picking out her own children and grandchildren with pride.

The living and the dead. Oh Arnold, I wish you were by my side—or whirling me about the way you used to when we would go dancing at the ballroom in Newton at Norumbega Park. So elegant—and you were, too, my darling.

The living and the dead. She saw Theo's face in Dan, her youngest grandchild, who was the same age Theo had been when he died. Arnold was buried on Sanpere, but Theo was nearby in Cambridge at Mount Auburn. Faith had taken her the week after her return from New York and the two of them had laid a spray of white lilacs on the grave. Ursula knew Faith was keeping the details of her trip from her and Ursula didn't mind. Being shielded was a blessing at this point in life. She suspected Violet may have told Faith that she alone was responsible for the murder. It didn't matter. Her brother was gone.

"It's a slow song, Granny. Would you like to dance?"

Dan had shed his jacket and tie. Like his mother, he had a habit of running his hand through his thick brown curly hair and it was no longer slicked down as it had been during the ceremony.

"I'd love to. Will you excuse me?" Ursula addressed the table and, taking her grandson's hand, walked onto the dance floor. They were playing Cole Porter. "Easy to Love." She hummed along as they danced and through half-closed eyes saw their faces.

Good night, Theo.

Good night, Arnold.

Excerpts From
Have Faith In Your Kitchen

By Faith Sibley Fairchild

with Katherine Hall Page

Borscht

1 small red bell pepper, diced	2 ½ quarts stock or water
3 tablespoons olive oil	2 bay leaves
1 large red onion, sliced	½ teaspoon thyme
3 cups peeled and cubed beets	Salt
(approx. 3 large beets)	Freshly ground pepper
Juice from ½ lemon	Sour cream

Heat the olive oil in a large soup pot. Add the onion slices and diced pepper. Sauté, stirring over medium heat, just until the onions start to give off some liquid. Add the rest of the ingredients except the sour cream. Bring to a boil and then turn to a simmer. Cook until the beets are tender.

Place in a blender or food processor, or use an immersion blender to process until the soup is smooth, but still has some heft to it.

Serves 4–6.

This is an easy summer or winter soup recipe. It is best made a day ahead. Serve it cold in the summer and hot in the winter topped with sour cream. To make the spiderweb garnish, pipe concentric circles of sour cream on the top of each portion. Drag the tip of a sharply pointed knife through the circles to create the effect.

Baked Chicken with Red Wine, Sage, and Root Vegetables

2 ½ pounds chicken	2 tablespoons fresh sage
1 tablespoon olive oil	½ teaspoon salt
½ pound parsnips	½ teaspoon freshly ground pepper
½ pound carrots	1 cup dry red wine
1 large yellow onion	

Faith's family likes dark meat, so she uses four whole chicken legs.

Preheat the oven to 350°.

Rinse the chicken and pat it dry with a paper towel.

Drizzle the oil in a casserole large enough to hold the chicken and vegetables. Faith prefers the oval ones from France, but Pyrex is just fine, too.

Place the chicken pieces in the casserole.

Peel the parsnips, scrub (or peel) the carrots, and cut both into chunks, about an inch long.

Peel the onion and cut it into eighths.

Arrange the assorted vegetables around the chicken.

Strip the leaves off the sage stems. Roll them into a small cigar shape and slice into thin strips (a chiffonade). Sprinkle on top of the chicken and vegetables along with the salt and pepper.

Pour the wine evenly over the casserole.

Cover tightly with aluminum foil and bake for 1 hour.

Uncover, baste with a bulb baster or a spoon, and bake for another 45 minutes, basting occasionally. The chicken should be nicely browned. Let the dish rest for 5 minutes.

Serves 4 amply. Be sure to spoon some of the liquid on top of the chicken and vegetables when serving.

What is nice about this dish is that it omits browning the chicken, which you would do in a more traditional coq au vin. It takes less time to prepare and Faith created it as a heart-wise version for her husband. She uses a salt substitute and takes the skin off the chicken unless she's making it for company. You can vary the vegetables—turnips are good also. She serves it with the following:

Sautéed New Potatoes with Sage

Small red potatoes	2 tablespoons fresh sage
1 tablespoon unsalted butter	Salt
1 tablespoon olive oil	Freshly ground pepper

While the chicken is baking, start the potatoes.

Faith figures 3 potatoes per person.

Wash the potatoes, cut them in half, and steam them until you can pierce them with a sharp fork.

Set aside.

About 15 minutes before the chicken is ready, sauté the potatoes in the butter and oil. Unfortunately, a butter substitute does not work with this dish. Once the potatoes start to brown sprinkle them with the sage and add salt and pepper to taste.

The potatoes will be done at the same time as the chicken and should be slightly crispy.

Faith makes this basic recipe often to accompany meat, poultry, or fish, varying the seasoning. Rosemary is one of her favorites.

Fruit Breakfast Puffs

4–5 tablespoons unsalted butter, melted

4 peach halves, fresh or canned, or pears,
strawberries, or other fruit

4 large eggs

¾ cup flour

¼ cup white sugar

¾ cup milk
(whole, 2%, or 1%)

3 tablespoons
fresh orange juice

Preheat the oven to 400°.

Cover the bottom of 4 large (approximately 4 inches in diameter) ovenproof ramekins with 3–4 tablespoons of the melted butter.

Place the peach, or other fruit, on top and set aside.

Whisk the eggs in a mixing bowl and add the flour, sugar, milk, and orange juice, blending well.

Add the reserved tablespoon of melted butter and mix well again.

Divide the batter evenly among the ramekins and bake on a baking sheet for about 20 minutes or until puffed and golden. Serve immediately.

This is a very pretty presentation. The batter puffs up nicely, almost like a popover.

Faith adapted this recipe from a breakfast puff she had at the very charming Englishman's Bed and Breakfast in Cherryfield, Maine. Many thanks to the hosts, Kathy and Peter Winham.

Ursula's Rum Cake

2 ½ cups sifted all-purpose flour

2 teaspoons baking powder

1 teaspoon baking soda

½ teaspoon salt

2 sticks unsalted butter, room temperature

1 cup sugar

2 large eggs

1 cup buttermilk

Finely grated zest of 1 lemon

Finely grated zest of 2 oranges

1 cup chopped walnuts

Glaze ingredients:

3 tablespoons fresh lemon juice (from lemon grated for zest)

½ cup fresh orange juice (from oranges grated for zest)

1 cup sugar

5 tablespoons dark rum

Preheat the oven to 350°. Grease and flour an 8-cup kugelhopf or bundt pan.

Sift together the flour, baking powder, baking soda, and salt, and set aside.

Beat the butter in an electric mixer until soft. Add the sugar and beat to mix. Add the eggs one at a time, beating after each addition. On low speed, add the sifted dry ingredients in three additions, alternating with buttermilk, scraping bowl as necessary.

Remove from the mixer and stir in the zest and nuts.

Pour into the prepared pan, smooth top, and place in the hot oven. Bake for 55–60 minutes, until top springs back when pressed lightly.

Remove from the oven and set on a rack.

Immediately prepare the glaze.

Place the juices and sugar in a saucepan over moderate heat and stir with a wooden spoon until the sugar is dissolved and the mixture comes to a boil. Remove from heat, add the rum, and stir.

Pierce the top of the cake with a cake tester. Spoon the hot glaze over the hot cake (still in the pan), spooning a little at a time. When you notice glaze oozing around the edge of the cake pan, use a metal spatula or knife to ease the edge of the cake away from the pan, allowing the glaze to run down the sides. Continue this until all the glaze is absorbed. It will be absorbed, believe me.

Let the cake stand for 10 to 15 minutes, until the bottom of the pan is cool enough to touch. Then cover the cake with a plate, hold the plate tightly in place against the cake pan, and flip over the cake and pan. Remove the cake pan from the cake. Let stand for at least two hours until cool and cover with plastic wrap. Can stand overnight before serving.

Truth be told, this extraordinary recipe is not Ursula Lyman Rowe's, but Valerie Wolzien's—the author of many of Faith and my favorite books: the Susan Henshaw mystery series and the one featuring Josie Pigeon. Slice a large piece of cake and settle down with, say, *Murder at the PTA Luncheon* or *This Old Murder* or *Death in Duplicate,* or . . .

Author's Note

*"Life, within doors, has few pleasanter
prospects than a neatly arranged and
well-provisioned breakfast table."*

I came across this quotation from Nathaniel Hawthorne's *The House of the Seven Gables* during the
dead of last winter, a very cold, long one. Visions not of
sugarplums but of eggs Benedict, sour cream waffles,
bagels and lox, streaky bacon, beignets, and café au lait
immediately danced in my head. Breakfast is my favorite meal.

The word "breakfast," from the Middle English,
means just that—breaking the fast engendered by
a night's sleep. However, our ancestors all over the
globe ate a much heartier breakfast than we normally
do, as a necessity for the hard day's physical labor that
followed.

In the present day, those of us who eat at home do so lightly, and well over sixty percent of us grab 'n' go—a doughnut and coffee or some other combination from a drive-thru before physically, but not psychologically, less strenuous work.

Even before Kellogg's, grains have always played a prominent role in breakfast composition and remnants have been found at Neolithic sites. In the United States, the Pilgrims started the day with maize—another one of those life-saving gifts from the Native Americans—grinding the kernels and mixing them with water to form "mush." It was not what the early colonists had been used to—wheat breads, coffee or tea with milk—but when they added maple syrup (tapping the trees was another skill they picked up), the concoction was quite palatable. They drank hard cider or ale to wash it down. This did not mean they went about their labors pie-eyed—although I'm sure there were exceptions passed out under the haystacks. These fermented beverages were safer to drink than many water supplies throughout this period and earlier world history.

The Victorians' mid- to late-nineteenth-century menus were a breakfast lover's dream. Excessive in all things comestible, they did not stint at the morning meal, and although Nellie Grant's 1874 wedding repast marked a special occasion, it was typical of upper-class breakfast fare: Soft-Shelled Crabs on Toast, Chicken Croquettes with Green Peas, Lamb Cutlets with Tartare Sauce, Aspic of Beef Tongue, Woodcock and Snipe on Toast, Salad with Mayonnaise, Strawberries with Cream, Orange Baskets Garnished with Strawberries, Charlotte Russe, Nesselrode Pudding, Blancmange, Ice Cream Garnished with Preserved Fruits, Water Ices, Wedding Cake, Small Fancy Cakes, Roman Punch (a rum concoction), Chocolate, and Coffee.

In the South and some Mid-Atlantic states, Hunt Breakfasts, which originated in Britain, were sumptuous affairs with staples similar to what was still found some years later at the Edwardian breakfast sideboard, resplendent with silver chafing dishes: Scrambled Eggs in Cream, Country Sausage with Fried Apple Rings, Creamed Sweetbreads and Oysters, Capitolade of Chicken (a kind of hash), Kidney Stew, Bacon and Fried Tomato Slices, Waffles, Hominy Pudding, Broiled Salt Roe Herring, Baked Country Ham, Spoon Bread, Beaten Biscuits, Buttermilk Biscuits, Jellies, Apple Butter, Honey, Damson Plum Preserves, and Coffee plus Bourbon and Branch, no doubt in stirrup cups. Reading over this list transports me to breakfasts I've had in the South—nothing better in the morning than grits and eggs, a real biscuit, and a thick slice of country ham with redeye gravy.

These two menus are from the pages of *The American Heritage Cookbook and Illustrated History of American Eating & Drinking* (1964). If one turns up in a book sale, grab it. Not just fascinating reading, and some very interesting recipes, but a feast for the eyes, as well.

Hawthorne's quotation prompted me to think about my favorite breakfasts, starting in childhood. My father came from the generation of men who quite literally could not boil water. Somewhere along the way he learned to make pancakes, although I believe Aunt Jemima may have helped him out. He made them in shapes, some of which required a bit of imagination to define, but we loved them. My mother sent us off to school each weekday morning with a good breakfast under our belts—Cream of Wheat, Wheatina (not a general favorite), Quaker oatmeal, sometimes eggs and bacon, but always freshly squeezed orange juice. Frozen OJ had become available after World War II, but Mom didn't believe in it (or Tang or Pop-Tarts, introduced in the 1960s, which of course made them immediately desirable and exotic).

I grew up in the trading-stamp era and after a certain amount accumulated, we would each get a turn to select something from the S&H Green Stamps catalog, that Book of Wonders. My brother picked a waffle iron, and waffles with fruit and other toppings began to appear at weekend breakfasts. He later chose an ice-cream maker, the kind that used rock salt. It was wooden and you had to turn a crank, producing the best ice cream I've ever had, thereby showing not only an early appreciation for good food on his part, but also the recognition that if you wanted tasty things to eat, the best way was to learn how to do it yourself. I've always been grateful to him for this nugget of culinary wisdom. Meanwhile I was trying to amass a set of matching luggage. I got as far as a Black Watch plaid overnight bag and a cosmetics case.

My mother came from a Norwegian-American family. Breakfast in Norwegian is *frokost,* "early meal," and a meal it is. A number of years ago I was with my mother and my aunt in a hotel on the West Coast of Norway at breakfast time. A tour leader was looking for someone who spoke French to help explain the offerings to two sisters from Brittany. I was happy to oblige (they hadn't thought it necessary to know English, the language of the tour, as they would just be looking at scenery). I walked them past the vast array— herring in a number of sauces; *leverpostei,* a kind of liver pâté, I explained; smoked salmon; smoked eel; *gravlaks,* fresh cured salmon; shrimp in cream sauce; cold sliced venison; lingonberry sauce; sliced tomatoes;

cucumber salad; a medley of cold and hot cereals; fresh fruit; *wienerbrød* (Danish pastries); a variety of breads; Ry-Krisp and other crackers; cheeses: Jarlsberg, *gjetost* (a sweet brown goat cheese, an acquired taste), my personal favorite, *nøkkelost;* and mounds of boiled eggs, to name some of the offerings. The women were aghast, searching in vain for a croissant or even a small toasted piece of a baguette. "*Le petit déjeuner norvégien, c'est bizarre,*" one said. Fortunately there was plenty of good strong coffee, the national drink after aquavit.

I long for these Norwegian breakfasts, but Kviknes Hotel in Balestrand is far away. We duplicate the spread on Christmas morning, but there's no fjord out the window.

I'm also extremely fond of a traditional British fry-up as served in Bloomsbury's Gower Street House Bed and Breakfasts in London. I also recently had the pleasure of a number of proper English breakfasts in Bristol at Crimefest, the annual international crime fiction convention "Where the Pen Is Bloodier than the Sword." The incomparable Colin Dexter was the guest of honor. Bristol is noted for its sausages, a delicious bonus to a wonderful four days. My French ladies would look just as askance at the British breakfasts— plates filled with fried tomatoes, fried mushrooms, fried eggs with fried bread swimming in baked beans, accompanied by streaky bacon, sausages, maybe a kipper, toast, lashings of butter, jam, and strong tea. Mueseli made an appearance at roughly the same time as crunchy granola in the U.S. and appears to be here to stay. I skip it, not only because I don't have room to eat it, but also because it puts a damper on all that joyful artery clogging.

This is not an activity I espouse on a regular basis, but sometimes the craving for a certain kind of breakfast is irresistible. In Maine, I head for the Harbor Café in Stonington and order two eggs over easy with hash browns, wheat toast (more a concession to taste than health), sausage links, and a bottomless mug of coffee. At the end of the meal, I always save a toast triangle, which I spread with one of those Kraft marmalade packets as a kind of dessert. My favorite marmalades have been produced by Keiller in Dundee, Scotland, since the 1790s. Legend has it that the spread was invented by Mary, Queen of Scots', French cook. I'm particularly partial to Keiller's Three Fruits variety.

Diner breakfasts are wonderful and cannot be replaced by Egg McMuffins. You are never going to hear "Adam and Eve on a raft with some joe" in a fast food chain.

So many of the breakfast foods we love were brought to this country by immigrants. Doughnuts came with the Dutch, "Oily Cakes," which are also ancestors of fried dough, that staple of amusement parks and fairs. Doughnuts became a national favorite with the invention of the doughnut machine in the 1930s, a fact that makes me think of the beloved classic children's book by Robert McCloskey, *Homer Price*. Homer's uncle has a diner and a doughnut machine that under Homer's hands becomes unstoppable, spewing out the toothsome confections much to the townspeople's delight and later consternation

German immigrants brought us sticky buns; the French, *pain perdu*—French toast—and croissants. Eastern European Jews gave us bagels and blintzes, congee and dim sum are from Asia, and huevos rancheros from Mexico. All now are breakfast staples.

My breakfast musings also took me back to A. A. Milne's poem "The King's Breakfast." Frederic G. Melcher, co-editor of *Publishers Weekly* and originator of the Newbery and Caldecott medals for children's literature, was a member of my church in Montclair, New Jersey. He used to come and read poetry to the Sunday school classes and this was one of his favorites. I can still hear his voice as the poor king, " 'Nobody,' / He whimpered, / 'Could call me / A fussy man; / I only want / A little bit / Of butter for / My bread!' " And isn't this just what we all want?

Breakfast in the twenty-first century is very much a social ritual. Retirees meet for breakfast, as do young mothers with strollers in tow; job seekers network at breakfast; the Scouts, fire and police departments, and all sorts of organizations, raise funds at pancake breakfasts. Brunch provides a special occasion to visit with friends and family. And brunch's basic eggs Benedict has been transformed into a multitude of versions, replacing the ham or bacon with smoked salmon, various kinds of sausage patties, duck, and even avocado slices. Eggs Sardou, created at the legendary New Orleans restaurant Antoine's, tops the English muffin with an artichoke bottom and anchovy fillets, and covers the poached egg with a hollandaise that includes bits of chopped ham and slices of truffle. Variations on this recipe omit the anchovies, ham, and truffles, substituting creamed or steamed spinach. There are several widely differing accounts of the origin of eggs Benedict, but my favorite credits a Mrs. LeGrand Benedict of New York City, who, during the 1860s, asked Chef Charles Ranhofer at Delmonico's to devise something new for her to eat at lunch. Obviously a woman after my own heart.

Breakfast for lunch, breakfast for dinner, and above all breakfast in the morning.

THE NEW LUXURY IN READING

We hope you enjoyed reading
our new, comfortable print size and found it
an experience you would like to repeat.

Well – you're in luck!

HarperLuxe offers the finest in fiction and
nonfiction books in this same larger print size and
paperback format. Light and easy to read, HarperLuxe
paperbacks are for book lovers who want to see
what they are reading without the strain.

For a full listing of titles and
new releases to come, please visit our website:
www.HarperLuxe.com

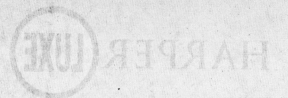

P9-CRI-872

THE "LIBERATORS"
My Life in the Soviet Army

"Recommended to all . . . Suvorov's black humor sparkles on practically every page. It's potently cynical, bitter, and funny. But it is also deadly serious."

—Best Sellers

"His chronicle, told with gallows humor, piles detail upon personal detail to create a canvas of startling conflicts."

—Philadelphia Inquirer

"Effective . . . entertaining."

—Kirkus

"Suvorov's account of life in the Soviet army is one of total, brutal discipline, one of clumsiness, waste, fraud, and rigid rules."

—Parameters, Journal of the
US Army War College

"Bitterly satirical and devastatingly frank . . . highly recommended!"

—North County News (NY)

"VIKTOR SUVOROV" is the pseudonym of a former captain in the Soviet Special Forces who also served as a top agent in the GRU. Since his defection to Great Britain, he has been under sentence of death by the Supreme Court of the Soviet Union. His identity and whereabouts are a closely guarded secret.

Berkley Books by Viktor Suvorov

INSIDE THE SOVIET ARMY
INSIDE SOVIET MILITARY INTELLIGENCE
INSIDE THE AQUARIUM
THE "LIBERATORS": MY LIFE IN THE SOVIET ARMY

My Life in the Soviet Army
The "Liberators"

Viktor Suvorov

There is on earth no sadder ditty
Than the tale of the Central Committee!
—Russian Folk Song

BERKLEY BOOKS, NEW YORK

This Berkley book contains the complete
text of the original hardcover edition.
It has been completely reset in a typeface
designed for easy reading and was printed
from new film.

THE "LIBERATORS": My Life in the Soviet Army

A Berkley Book/published by arrangement with
W.W. Norton & Company

PRINTING HISTORY
Norton edition/September 1983
Berkley edition/May 1988

ISBN: 0-425-10631-4

A BERKLEY BOOK® TM 757,375
Berkley Books are published by The Berkley Publishing Group,
200 Madison Avenue, New York, NY 10016.
The name "BERKLEY" and the "B" logo
are trademarks belonging to Berkley Publishing Corporation.

PRINTED IN THE UNITED STATES OF AMERICA

10 9 8 7 6 5 4 3 2 1

CONTENTS

Preface

How I Became a Liberator

The Party is our helmsman—Popular song

The General Secretary of the Party set a task: there must be a sharp rise in agricultural output. So the whole country reflected on how best to achieve this magnificent aim. The Secretary of our Regional Party Committee thought about it, as did all his advisers, consultants and researchers.

To tell the truth, it was a ridiculously easy task: the climate of our Region is similar to that of France—there is plenty of sun and warmth and water. And our soil is splendid. The black earth is nearly a metre thick and rich enough to spread on a slice of bread. There are also plenty of technicians and specialists. The only misfortune is that the people themselves have no interest in work because, however much a peasant works, the reward for him, personally, will be just the same, since to pay for a peasant's labour according to results is, of course, quite impossible. Just imagine what would happen! Your hard-working peasant would soon be rich while layabouts would remain beggars. A rift would appear and then inequality would creep in. And all this would be contrary to the ideals of socialism.

So the First Secretary of the Regional Party Committee and all his advisers gave much thought as to how to increase agricultural output without infringing the principle of common material equality. And at last it dawned on them what to do. They could achieve the desired increase by using fertilizers.

A vast meeting, thousands strong, complete with brass bands, speeches, placards and banners, was urgently called at the local Chemical Combine. To a man, they shouted slogans, applauded, chanted patriotic songs. After that meeting, a competitive economy drive was launched at the Chemical Combine to harvest raw materials and energy resources. It lasted throughout the winter and, in the spring, on Lenin's birthday, all the workers reported at the Combine and laboured all day, without wages, using up the raw materials which had been saved. During the course of this day, they produced several thousand tons of liquid nitrogen fertilizer and, in accordance with the meeting's resolution, they decided to hand over all this fertilizer, free of charge, to the Region's collective farms.

It was a real red letter day for labour, and not only the newspaper correspondents of the local and republican press but also those of the central newspapers came in person to the Combine. In the evening, both the All-Union radio and the Central Television programmes reported this remarkable feat. The Central Committee of the Party officially commended the initiative of our chemical workers and appealed to all Chemical Combines, throughout the country, to launch competitions aimed at economising on raw materials which would later be used to produce additional amounts of fertilizer, to be handed over, in turn, free of charge, to neighbouring collective farms. Let our country bloom! Let it blossom forth like a vernal garden!

When the labour fête-day ended, the labour daily grind began.

The next morning, the Director of the Chemical Combine telephoned to the Regional Committee and said that, if the collective farms did not, during the next twenty-four hours, collect the free fertilizer presented to them, the Chemical Combine would come to a standstill: all its tanks were full to overflowing with excess fertilizer production and there was nowhere to put current production.

There followed a series of insistent calls from the Regional Committee to all the small District Committees, and from them to all collective farms. Each of the fifty regional collectives had immediately to take away the 150 tons of the fertilizer presented by the Combine. The news that our own collective had been given such an amount of fertilizer free of charge did not please our Chairman. Our collective farm owned seventeen lorries, but only three of these had tanks. One was used for milk, another for water, the third for petrol. Those used for milk and water could not possibly be used for liquid fertilizer. There remained only the one used for petrol. The lorry was old and battered beyond recall. The capacity of its tank was one and a half tons of liquid.

The distance from our collective farm to town was seventy-three kilometres; taking into consideration the state of our road, that meant five hours there and five hours back. I was the driver of this lorry.

'Now look here,' said the Chairman, 'if you do not sleep for twenty-four hours, if your battery does not pack up, if your radiator does not melt with the heat, if your gear-box does not jam, if your lorry does not get stuck in the mud, you can do two trips in twenty-four hours, and bring back three tons of this bloody fertilizer. But you have to do, not two, but a hundred trips!'

'Right,' I said.

'That is not all,' he said. 'We are short of petrol. Of course I will give you petrol for three trips but, for the remaining ninety-seven, do the best you can. Push your lorry with your arse if you have to!'

'Right,' I said.

'You are our only hope. If you cannot do a hundred trips, you know only too well I will be dismissed from the chairmanship.'

I knew it. I knew also that, although our chairman was not to everyone's liking, nevertheless his replacement was a bloody sight worse.

'Any questions?'

'Yes. Even if I do a hundred trips—without petrol—where shall I put all this fertilizer?'

The Chairman glanced anxiously round the broad farmyard and scratched the back of his head. Where indeed? 150 tons of liquid, poisonous, stinking matter? Lenin's birthday is in April, worse luck, but the fertilizer only goes on the soil in June. So where to keep the fertilizer until June?

'Look here,' he said. 'Don't start nattering on about it. Get yourself to town as soon as possible. All the region's farms are busy with the same problem. Somebody may have some bright idea. You just watch what the others do and then you do the same. Get a move on! And don't return unless you've succeeded.'

I sighed, spat on my palms like a boxer before a fight, then got into my wretched lorry and set off to town over the bumps, pot-holes and huge puddles, which the spring sun had not yet dried up.

There was a long queue of trucks of different makes, dimensions and colours standing outside the Chemical Combine. But the queue was moving fast. I soon discovered that lorries, which had only a moment before been loaded, were already returning and taking up new places in the queue. Every one of these lorries ostensibly needed many hours to deliver its valuable load to its destination and then to return. But they rejoined the queue in a matter of minutes. Then came my turn. My tanks were rapidly filled with the foul-smelling liquid and the man in charge marked down on his list that my native kolkhoz had just received the first one and a half tons of fertilizer. I drove my lorry out through the Combine's gates and followed the group of lorries which had loaded up before mine. All of them, as if at a word of command, turned off the road and descended a steep slope towards the bank of the river Dnieper. I did the same. In no time at all, they had emptied their tanks. I did the same. Over the smooth surface of the great river, the cradle of the Russian civilisation, slowly spread a huge poisonous, yellow, stinking stain.

Having emptied my tank, I headed again for the Combine and another one and a half tons of fertilizer were marked off for our kolkhoz. And so it went on. The work proceeded vigorously and noisily. Tens of lorries, hundreds of trips, thousands of tons! Never in my life have I seen so many fish. And I would never have believed that there were so many fish in the Dnieper. The whole surface of the river, from one side to the other, was crammed with the dead bodies of pike, bream and other fish. And still the lorries came, in a never-ending stream. And every driver knew that, if we did not succeed in emptying the gigantic reservoirs of that huge Combine, it would grind to a halt—and this would be a crime for which our unfortunate Chairman would have to bear responsibility.

The militia appeared suddenly at noon. The whole region was cordoned off: we were all detained. The representatives from the Combine also appeared, and then a young adviser from the Regional Committee turned up in a black Volga car. With an expression of disgust, he examined the place of work. He put a small white handkerchief to his little nose: the stench was unbearable. After a short chat with the Combine's representatives and with one of the detailed drivers, he got back into his car and drove off. After him disappeared both the militia and the Combine's representatives. We were ordered to proceed. Clearly, having acquainted himself with the situation on the ground and understanding all the implications, the adviser found our solution the best one.

And what other kind of solution could possibly be found?

Donate all this excess production to the State? But where would the State find the reservoirs to store such a huge amount of liquid? The kolkhozes had nowhere to store it and nothing to transport it in. Should it be recorded as the work quota? But, in that case, what to do with the still unprocessed raw material arriving at the Combine in an endless stream? If this production was taken as part of the work quota, the inspectors would of course sense that something was wrong and ask where so much excess production had come from. There would be investigations etcetera. So it was better to let things go on as they were.

Towards evening, we finished the job. Everyone took delivery of his final load of liquid, but this time no one carried it off to the river, but instead to his own kolkhoz. It was then relayed to Moscow that everything was going well and that this year's harvest would be a record, thanks to the Regional Committee's First Secretary. Moscow promptly replied with a congratulatory telegram to the First Secretary and to all workers of the Region. And that was that.

Late that night, I delivered one and a half tons of the fertilizer to the kolkhoz and reported to the Chairman that I had fulfilled the task ahead of time. He thanked me but did not go into detail. Everything had been clear to him from the very beginning. He had long been accustomed to the fact that, whenever the Communist Party issues instructions, these invariably end in a way no one wishes to remember.

'Where shall I put this one and a half tons?' I asked.

'Keep them yourself! If necessary, I could produce record harvests without fertilizers. But what's the point?'

And that was that. I poured the liquid over my own tiny private plot. It proved an unpardonable mistake. Apparently, there was too much fertilizer for my tiny area of ground and I applied it at the wrong time. In May, when all the neighbouring kitchen gardens were producing strong shoots mine was barren. I was horrified. What would I eat during the winter? I was not going to become a soldier until the following spring: so how was I to live until then? The money I would receive for my work at the kolkhoz would be hardly enough for two months of very frugal existence. The peasant's only hope is his private plot which is not much bigger than the palm of his hand. And if nothing grows on that—what then?

I had to make some urgent decisions. But what? I could not run away from the kolkhoz: under socialism a peasant has no right to a passport, although everybody else has an internal passport. As a result of this simple restriction, a peasant cannot live in a town, cannot marry a town girl or stay in a hotel. Travelling on a plane is also forbidden. Who will let you board an aircraft without a passport? Maybe you are a criminal?

Don't think it is just a Soviet communist caprice, either. It is a vital necessity. If you are trying to establish material equality among the inhabitants of any country, you must introduce similar measures against the peasants. If you make all people equal, there will be mass migration of peasants into towns, where the working day is limited, where one need not work on rest days and holidays, and where one can have a holiday in summer. But, if all the peasants go to live in towns, your state of universal equality will perish from hunger. And, in order to prevent that state of affairs, you will be obliged to revert to the free market system, that is to capitalism, or else keep the peasants in their villages by force, by barbed wire, guard-dogs, threats and the introduction of special anti-peasant legislation.

I was a convinced supporter of the material equality of all mankind and therefore was prepared to spend all my life without an internal passport, which means never flying in an aircraft, never staying at an hotel and never marrying a town girl. But, in compensation, we would have equality. There would be no exploitation of man by man and we would have no rich and no poor!

That bloody fertilizer which ruined my harvest also ruined all my plans and forced me to look for some new way of life. The choice was not great: I could land up in jail, where the food is free, or I could become an officer, where the food is also free. Taking into consideration the fact that it is not difficult to land in jail, I decided to exploit this possibility only if I did not succeed in becoming an officer. And that didn't turn out to be particularly simple!

In order to become an officer, I had to become a citizen of my country, in other words somehow or other obtain a passport. They say that, in the USSR, the acquisition of a passport for going abroad is so difficult that it sometimes takes a man's whole life to achieve. But, for anyone not entitled to receive one, to obtain an internal passport is an altogether more difficult task. If you have an internal passport and are trying to obtain one allowing you to go abroad, theoretically the law is on your side. You can protest, go on hunger-strike or write letters to Brezhnev. In the end, if you persist, you may well be successful. But how to obtain an internal passport if you are not entitled to one by law? If you are just a Soviet peasant and if the law is against you and if you live in a country but are not considered a citizen of that country but only its peasant? If you have no right to any form of defence? If you are born simply to work, simply as an integral part of the agricultural work force, then what do you do? What can one do if one does not represent a legal entity, just like for instance, a horse or a pig, which also has no right to an internal passport (let alone one for going abroad) and which is similarly forbidden to stay in hotels or to travel by air?

To all intents I, like any other Soviet peasant, was an outlaw. And yet, in spite of everything, I managed to get a passport. It is a very long story indeed which I take no pleasure in recalling. I had to blackmail the kolkhoz Chairman, deceive the Chairman of the village Soviet, bribe a village Soviet Secretary as well as an employee of the Military Commissariat: there was no other way.

And, after all that, my passport was still not quite legal. At any moment, it could have been proved that, even though I had been born in the USSR of Soviet parents, whose ancestors down several hundred years had never crossed any frontier or had any contact whatsoever with foreigners, I had illegally appropriated the name of a USSR citizen. So, as a matter of urgency, I had to change my half-legal passport for another officially-issued document in my name. And, to achieve that, I entered the Kharkov Guards Tank Command School. They took my passport and I was given a new red 'military Card' in its place. Now nobody on earth could send me back to the kolkhoz. There is no way back from the Soviet Army.

While still a trainee, I participated in some of the biggest ever training exercises by Soviet troops on Soviet Army training grounds, each of which could accommodate on its territory several completely sovereign states. So, I had the opportunity of seeing from the inside the life of the most famous Soviet divisions, such as the 120th Guards Rogachevsky Motor-Rifle Division, the 2nd Guards Taman and the 41st Guards Berlin Division. Even at that time, I was staggered by the fact that each one of them was living a double life: one for show to the outside world, while the other inner reality was something quite apart and completely different.

In 1967 I was to become an officer. I served in the 287th

Novograd-Volynsk Training Motor-Rifle Division of the Kiev Military District. At the time of the events in Czechoslovakia, I commanded a motor-rifle company of the 24th Samaro-Ulyanovsk Iron Motor-Rifle Division. Later I served on the Staff of the Leningrad Military District, and in diversionary troops, and after graduating from the Military Academy I served on the 10th Chief Directorate of the General Staff.

During my Staff service, I took part in many important training exercises like, for instance, that of the 3rd Shock Army of the Group of Soviet Troops in Germany.

The story related in this book starts from the moment when, while still a trainee at the Kharkov Guards School, I arrived in Kiev together with a group of my comrades to hand over battle equipment to the Kiev Tank Technical School. The hand-over dragged on for several days and, in order to save us from boredom, they entertained us with various studies and with service at the control check-points and other control points.

After a sleepless night, each member of a control check-point team was allowed to sleep, without undressing, in the small room beside the control point. When the story starts, I was asleep.

PART ONE

PART ONE

Kiev Tank-Technology School Check Point. 25 March, 1966.

The Glasshouse

'SOLDIER! BOY!'

'Well?'

'What do you mean, well? Fucking well get up, I tell you, we're all on a charge!'

Shielding myself from the blinding sun with my arm, I tried to postpone the moment of awakening.

'I was on guard duty all night so even under regulations I am entitled to sleep three hours . . .'

'All you're entitled to is your cock in your pocket! Get up, I tell you, we're all on a charge.'

The news of our arrest made no impression on me at all. The only thing I realised clearly was that a good one and a half hours' compensation for a sleepless night was lost beyond recall. I sat up on the hard bench and rubbed my forehead and eyes with my fist. My head was cracking from lack of sleep. I yawned, stretched until my joints creaked, then sighed deeply to disperse any remaining sleep, and twisted my head about a bit in order to relieve a stiff neck.

'How much did we get?'

'Five for you—you were lucky, Viktor. But Sashka and I've

been clobbered with ten days each while Vitya, the sergeant, got all of fifteen!'

What a bloody life our poor old sergeants have at Military School! You are paid five roubles extra for the job but they take twenty-five roubles' worth away from you.

'Where's my automatic?' I exclaimed.

'Everything's back at Company HQ—automatics, cartridge belts and bayonets. The Sergeant-Major will bring the equipment and food vouchers in a few moments, and then a bath, a haircut and off we go.'

In the main room of the Pass Check Point, the officer cadets of the first course, who had been precipitately removed from their usual occupations, were being handed documents and were counting the instruction files. Their sergeant was a very understanding fellow and was listening to us in a businesslike way, and nodding his head concernedly.

'I never took my eyes off him, and shouted the command as loudly as I could, and my lads opened the gate at once and, like lions, they devoured him with their eyes. And there you are: I didn't do a bloody thing and he clobbered me with fifteen, and my lads got ten each.'

'Okay, Kolya, never mind, get on with it!'

The other lads from the guard came in after us and, under their escorts, we all went for a haircut and a cold bath.

The cleanliness in the 'Reception Room' of the Kiev Garrison glasshouse was blinding.

'Comrade First Lieutenant, Guards Officer Cadet Suvorov presents himself at the Garrison Prison to serve his sentence.'

'How many?'

'Five days' arrest.'

'What for?'

'Bugger it,' flashed through my mind, 'What was it really for anyway? Why *was* I on a charge?'

The First Lieutenant, who had an unusually broad face and tiny feet, drilled into me with his small leaden eyes.

'What for?' he asked again.

'I don't know.'

'Who arrested you?'

'I don't know.'

'You'll soon find out here,' the First Lieutenant promised. 'Next.'

In came my sergeant.

'Comrade First Lieutenant, Guards Sergeant Makeyev for . . .'

'How many?' ugly mug cut in.

'Fifteen days.'

'Who sentenced you?'

'The Deputy Commander of the Military District, Colonel General Chizh.'

'What for?'

'We are guarding the School Check Point.'

'Ah-hah,' the First Lieutenant smiled understandingly.

He, of course, knew—indeed all three armies of the district knew—this habit of Colonel General Chizh, invariably to arrest the guard on duty at the Pass Check Point. It was an established fact that he arrested only those guarding the Check Point, but he did it without fail, on every visit to any school, regiment, battalion, division, at any training ground, firing range or depot. He did it anywhere and everywhere. Whenever he was passing through the Check Point, he arrested all those on duty and he meted out standard punishments. Fifteen days to the head of the party, ten days to those actually on duty, and five days to those resting and awaiting their turn on duty. It had been going on for many years. All three armies and many separate units, sub-units, military establishments and other organisations, all suspected that the Deputy Commander was striving to establish for himself some special kind of reception ceremony, not provided for under regulations, but what exactly he really wanted no one could actually guess throughout all the years that he held this high office.

Two savage-looking lance-corporals appeared on the threshold of the 'Reception Room' and the reception had officially begun.

'Ten seconds . . . UNDRESS!'

Boots, belts, caps, coats, everything was instantly thrown on to the floor. Now, stark naked, we all stood in front of ugly mug.

'About turn! Bend forward! Open up!'

At this point a First Lieutenant of the Soviet Army examined our arses. Smoking in the glasshouse is forbidden, so sometimes heavy smokers try to smuggle in little pieces of cigarettes, by wrapping them in paper and pushing them into their anal passages. This trick is well known to the glasshouse authorities and is dealt with mercilessly.

Meanwhile, the savage-looking lance-corporals had been carrying out a brief but thorough examination of our clothes and boots which were lying on the floor.

'Fifteen seconds . . . GET DRESSED!'

If you are arrested not in town, but in a unit or while at a military school, and if you are well prepared and have your food vouchers ready and have had a bath, try to find an extra five minutes to change your boots for larger ones. Anyone who knows what is in store for you will willingly give you his. Wearing your smaller size, he will suffer no less than you, but he will wait patiently for your return. Large-size boots spell salvation in the glasshouse. If your boots are difficult to put on, then the few seconds given you for 'Get Dressed' or 'Undress', would not be long enough and five days on a charge could easily become ten or even fifteen.

'Documents on the table!'

'Lance-Corporal, collect all the belts!'

While in the glasshouse, no inmate is allowed a belt, in case he tries to commit suicide. The history of the Kiev glasshouse does, however, know of one enterprising and inventive chap who, while in solitary confinement, with nothing but a stool screwed to the floor, still managed, by tearing away the lower hem of his shirt, to make for himself a short, thin, but very strong rope. All this was achieved with the utmost caution, under the almost constant supervision of the escort sentries who, day and night, patrol corridors. After having made a small loop, the end of which he tied to the stool's leg, he rolled on the floor, tightening the loop, for about ten long minutes. In the end, and in spite of every obstacle, he just managed to strangle himself.

'Money . . . watches?'

'No.'

One never takes such valuables to the glasshouse, as they will be taken away and old and broken ones will be returned in their place. And there is nowhere to go to protest!

'Flashes and badges?'

'And what are you bloody well doing with Guards badges? Do you think you're going to a carnival?'

'Comrade First Lieutenant, we are officer cadets of the Kharkov Guards Tank High Command School.'

'But what the hell are you doing lolling about in Kiev?'

'We brought over some equipment for the Kiev Tank School. The hand-over of the equipment was delayed and, so that we shouldn't be idle, we were given different duties—some in the kitchens, others at the Control Point, and our lot were sent to the Pass Check Point.'

'Lance-Corporal Alekseyev?'

'Here.'

'First of all, send all these guardsmen on firewood duties.'

'Right, Comrade First Lieutenant!'

Across the asphalted, incredibly clean courtyard, we were taken to another small inner courtyard surrounded by a very high brick wall. The first thing which surprised me was the glaring orderliness of it all. All the sawn logs were arranged in such an accurate pile that their ends formed a polished wall. Every log had to be cut to a standard size of exactly twenty-eight centimetres and an error of one or two centimetres was severely punished. All these logs were destined for the stove, and such exactness in sawing them was completely pointless, but order is order.

The logs, which we were to cut with the same exactness, had been brought in one to two days earlier, and they were not just thrown down in a heap, but arranged with indescribable love and even, one would say, artistry. First of all, they were sorted according to thickness, with the thickest underneath and the thinnest ones on the very top. But whoever had built up this stack of logs apparently possessed an even finer artistic taste, as they had also taken the colour of the logs into consideration. Those at the right-hand end were darkest in colour, while to the left they gradually changed in colour, ending with completely white blocks. It fell to us to demolish this artistic creation and to cut the wood to the standard size and then build it up again into a pile.

Here too, in the same yard, lay the stump and roots of an entire tree of absolutely unimaginable form, resembling anything you wished, except a tree. It was a fantastic intertwining of immense cables and ropes, or maybe of something else, but in any case the image was very flexible. The intertwined sections were of such a complicated form that it was hard to believe that nature could manage to create such a wonder. But in spite of the complexity of these knots, looking for all the world like a coiled snake, this immense block nevertheless retained very great solidity in all its elements, and had been lying there most probably for more than a decade, judging by the thousands of old and new notches made in it by a saw.

All those who did not realise fully where they had landed and who still manifested any obstinacy were given the task of 'cutting some wood', that is to say of sawing this particular block. After one hour, somebody from the glasshouse authorities would come to see how things were going and he always feigned surprise that nothing had yet been accomplished; punishment inevitably followed. This particular task was always allotted to only one man at a time and never to two. And this one man was always supplied with a long, supple but absolutely blunt saw, which could be operated only by two men.

When we entered the yard, a dark-haired soldier was trying vainly to succeed in making at least a single cut. After twenty minutes, he was taken off and accused of shirking. And then, depending on the mood of the management at the time, the behaviour of the unlucky wood-cutter would be appraised as they saw fit, from shirking and insubordination (if he tried to prove that the task was impossible) to economic sabotage and refusal to obey orders. And, after such an accusation, the Chief of the glasshouse or his deputy could do just as he wished with the poor wretch. That wooden block is destined to have a long life. I, for one, am quite sure that it still lies there to this day in the very same place and that some unfortunate is still trying vainly to saw it up. He bites his lip, there are tears in his eyes, and his face registers total desperation . . . but time runs out . . .

Once we had started to saw the logs to the standard twenty-eight-centimetre size, we learned another very interesting fact. We intended first to saw them and then to arrange them according to their thickness and colour, and, only after that, to sweep up the sawdust.

'Oh, no, that won't do, it isn't done like that here. Here, there must always be order!'

So then, after having sawn only one log, we started to gather up all the sawdust by hand, down to the smallest speck. There was no broom and, after the second log and been sawn, the same process began again, and so on . . .

In the meantime, the glasshouse escort was wheeling in one poor wretch after another to saw up that unique block.

'What about sawing some wood, brother?'

Towards seven o'clock, the glasshouse yard became increasingly noisy. Lorries started to arrive, bringing back those on charges who had spent the whole frosty day working on countless different projects. Some had been moving tank tracks at a tank-repair works. Others had been unloading batches of artillery shells. They were all frozen, wet, starving and tired to death.

And still they were all ordered to form up upon arrival, because after work, without any break, a three-hour training exercise was the order of the day. We also were ordered to form up, and that was exactly the moment when the count of time served by each inmate officially started—the whole working day up to this moment had just been loosening up.

Kiev glasshouse knows only two sorts of training—drill and tactics. I make no mention here of political training because this does not take place every day, but only twice a week for two hours each time, and not in the evening but in the morning, before work. I will tell of this later but for the moment I will concentrate on drill and tactics. One and a half hours are spent on drill and it is a pulverising business. Approximately a hundred inmates, in single file, move along the perimeter of the yard. They don't walk but they just slash along, marching to attention, lifting their legs to an unthinkable height. There is no one in the yard except the inmates—no superiors, no escort—but the yard shudders from their mighty tread. Only sometimes, one of the savage lance-corporals emerges from the porch:

'Hey, you! . . . with the big ears. No, no, not you—you. Did you see that film called *Ordinary Fascism*? There you are now, that's real marching for you . . . So why can't you, my little pigeon, achieve the same excellence in marching as the men in the film? Now then, practise marking time.'

The man with the big ears goes to the centre of the yard and, marking time, lifts his knees as high as his chest. All the others marching round the yard redouble their own efforts. The fact of the matter is that the asphalt in the centre of the yard is slightly lower than that at the perimeter, a bizarre arrangement engineered on the personal initiative of Comrade Grechko, when he was still only Chief of the Kiev Military District. The idea is one of simple genius. During rain or melting snow, there is always a big puddle in the centre of the yard. Even during summer, when there is no rain, water is still pumped there under the pretext of watering the yard. So those who find themselves sent to the centre have to march round in the puddle. If there are about five men there at a time they will not only soak themselves up to the ears, but they will also drench the others marching round the yard by the splashes they produce. There is no way of drying oneself in the glasshouse, as it is heated only during the day when the inmates are out working and, towards the evening, when the inmates return to their wards, the stoves are already cold, and there are no radiators at all. I myself experienced 'Grechko's bowl' on my own skin in March when the snow melted by day and there was a biting frost at night.

Drill training takes place every single day, regardless of weather or temperature, as do all the other 'measures'. One and a half hours of drill at our standard speed of sixty steps per minute makes 5,400 steps in all, each with the maximum raising of the legs, and an intolerable downward stretching of the instep, because no one wants to be sent into the middle of the yard. This is why drill training is called 'individual practice' and is then followed by 'collective practice' or tactics.

Tactics, as distinct from drill training, are not based on the personal fear of each man, but on socialist competition among the collective as a whole, and this is why it is so much more exhausting than drill.

All tactics boil down to one tactical skill—crawling *Plastun**-fashion, with your head and whole body as close as possible to the ground, in our case to the asphalt. Hands and legs must move with the maximum agility and the body must twist and flex like that of a lizard. So now it's crawling. Every ward has now become an infantry section.

'Landmark—the birch tree! Section, towards the landmark, *Plastuny!* FORWARD!'

The stop-watch is turned off when the last man of the section reaches the birch tree and, if the time spent by the section as a whole proves unsatisfactory, then the last man home will be beaten in the ward during the night, because in the socialist world only beating ensures a conscientious approach.

'Well, your time wasn't bad'—and the filthy, wet with perspiration and suffocating members of the section sigh with relief—'but your speed will not be taken into consideration, as this handsome fellow here had his arse sticking up all the time and was trying to move forward on all fours instead of crawling.' So the handsome fellow is sure of a beating, as he has let down the whole collective in Socialist Competition.

---

*Plastuny were former Cossack infantry battalions, manned by poor Cossacks who could not afford the price of a horse. They were renowned for their skill in crawling on their stomachs like Red Indians. The word *plastun* is a derivative of *plast*, meaning 'layer'.

'Now then, let's try once more. Section to the departure point—at the double.'

'MARCH! Landmark the birch tree. Section towards the landmark, PLASTUNY—FORWARD!'

'Ah! . . . This time your speed was worse! Well, never mind, we will soon train you!'

At the end of the training session, the glasshouse Chief or his deputy sums up. First, the worst ward is told the name of the man whose fault it is that they are all going to have to undergo another trial, and then follows the order: 'Landmark—Oak tree.'

'Oak tree' means that they must crawl straight through the centre of the yard, straight through the icy water and straight over the water obstacle invented by that most ingenious and brilliant leader. He was a clever one for inventions, Comrade Grechko was, until the withering disease eventually caught up with him!

Food in the Soviet Army is worse than that for any other soldiers in the whole world. Nevertheless, on the first day in the glasshouse, after having spent all day hungry and cold, and after unthinkable burdens, a soldier, already accustomed to any privation, still cannot overcome disgust at what is called 'supper' in the glasshouse. The first evening he cannot touch what is called 'food' at all. He is still incapable of accepting the fact that he must eat, not from his own private dish, albeit a dog's dish, but from a communal pan, containing some kind of mess faintly smelling of soup or even of sour cabbage soup. And, while the senses of hunger and disgust are still fighting each other, the short sharp order is given: 'Stand up! Form up outside!' After that wretched episode called supper, comes the evening check.

Under the corridor ceiling, in the frosty haze, the yellowish lamps glimmer dimly. The inmates stand in formation, there is not the slightest movement. This is the evening check. All wait for the order. After a quick roll-call the order is given.

'Ten seconds . . . GET UNDRESSED!'

Hell! Where did that bloody burst of speed come from? It is simply astonishing. But ten seconds were quite enough for a hundred men to undress fully. To tell the truth, everyone was carefully and secretly getting themselves ready for this order. Even during supper, each man had secretly unbuttoned one button on each sleeve in order to have only one button on his sleeve to deal with when the order came. All the buttons of his tunic collar seemed to be buttoned up, but in fact a small part of each was already slightly pushed inside the buttonhole, and he had only to pull at his collar to have all five buttons open at once. Experience is a great thing and every soldier knows about ten such tricks.

'First rank, three steps forward, MARCH! Second rank, ABOUT TURN!'

Both ranks are now facing opposite corridor walls. Everyone is naked. The wind drives a few snowflakes along the concrete floor.

And, while those savage lance-corporals are on the floor rummaging among our tunics, our trousers and our dirty leggings, creating a scene like a Soviet customs post, Captain Martyanov, Chief of the glasshouse, or his deputy, First Lieutenant Kirichek, is performing that sacred ritual: the inspection of our anal passages. It is a very responsible job. Maybe somebody has found a nail while working outside and brought it in, in his anus, and will let his blood out at night as he lies on the plank-bed. In the daytime he is watched by the escort, but at night, although the wards are permanently illuminated by a blinding light, nevertheless trouble always lurks nearby; perhaps somebody had a cigarette hidden in his anus and will have a secret smoke during the night. This operation requires special skills and, as we have seen, mere lance-corporals are not capable of performing it. So, let them rummage in our dirty linen. But, with the other operation, only a Soviet Army officer is qualified to cope.

'Fifteen seconds . . . GET DRESSED.'

All the inmates go to their wards and 'jobs time' has arrived. The glasshouse is not like a jail. The *parasha** has no place in the glasshouse. There is a big difference between the glasshouse and a civilian jail. The jail authorities have plenty of time to influence a prisoner. The time available to the glasshouse authorities is limited and, naturally, they try to 'enrich the programme' to the maximum by exploiting any, or even all, of a man's physical needs to the full 'for educational purposes'. The exercise of one's physical needs is here elevated to the rank of their educational influence and is carried out under the vigilant eyes of the administration.

---

*Originally a girl's name, this has come to mean the communal bucket used as a latrine at night.

After the inmates are settled in their wards, the escort and the rest of the administration, sometimes including the Chief of the glasshouse himself, take up their posts and the procedure begins. Clanking the locks loudly, a lance-corporal and two members of the escort enter the ward. The prisoners are formed up, at attention, as if on parade. The lance-corporal then lazily pokes his dirty fingers at the chest of the first inmate:

'Off you go!'

The inmate rushes along the corridors and staircases. Another member of the escort is posted at every corner and shouts out:

'Faster!'

'Faster!'

'Faster!'

But the inmate needs no encouragement because he knows full well that at any moment, under the pretext of insufficient speed, he may be sent back, sometimes after having nearly reached the cherished door.

'It looks very much as if you, my little pigeon, did not really want very much "to go" at all. Now then—about turn. Back to your ward!'

But, coming towards you, there is already another inmate belting up and down the staircases, showing a clean pair of heels. Having finished with one ward, the lance-corporal and the escort lock the door and go on to another one. Often, the lance-corporal may 'forget' to send one or two of the inmates to the toilet at all, and sometimes he may even 'omit' a whole ward altogether. However, there is nobody to complain to in any case. Everything here is being done without any breach of Soviet laws.

I here affirm categorically that not a single letter of the law is being infringed in any Soviet glasshouse. Let us take, for instance, 'jobs time'. That most democratic constitution in the world—the Soviet Constitution—ensures, for all citizens, the right to work. Now where else, if not in the glasshouse, can you indulge this right to your heart's content? Or, let us take the right to education. Whether you want it, or whether you don't, you must give three hours a day to drill and tactical training, plus political training twice a week. Is that not education? Or, for instance, the right to rest. Every day they take you to and from work, so use this time for resting, or at night on that plank-bed take your rest, then right up to reveille, at 0530 hours—if, of course, you were not arrested during the night in accordance with the regulations concerning the right to work. But neither in

the Constitution nor in any other law is any mention made about
the exercise of one's physical needs. So don't go and demand
anything over and above what is stipulated in the constitution!
Or, are you setting yourself up in opposition to our Soviet rule of
law?

'Over here—Escort to me!'

At long last, after 'jobs time', follows what the inmates
have been dreaming of all day from the very moment of
awakening—retreat!

Once again the lock clanks, and once again the lance-corporal
with the escort appear in the ward. The inmates are all standing
to attention, and the senior prisoner in the ward reports to the
all-powerful one about general preparedness for retreat. A hardly
audible order is made with only a feeble movement of the lips
which can really be interpreted any way you wish. But the ward
does understand. Behind our backs, at a distance of approximately one metre, is the edge of our plank-bed. At this order,
which we have seen rather than heard, all ten of us, just as we
have been standing, backs to the communal plank-bed, we all
perform a most prodigious feat—a single jump backwards on to
the plank-bed. There is neither time nor room to plan or even to
move our hands: we have all been standing in one rank, tightly
pressed together and, from this position, we perform a jump
backwards into complete uncertainty. Who the hell really knows
what our heads will crack down on? Will it be the edge of the
plank-bed if I drop short, or will it be the brick wall if I
overshoot the target, or will it be the ribs, elbows and skull of
my nearest neighbour if the jump is right on target? In addition—
and the most unpleasant aspect of all—there is the complete
impossibility of swinging round and facing the bare planks, and
therefore the absolute impossibility of softening the blow, which
is always violently sudden.

There is the noise of crashing heads, a suppressed shriek, but
everyone freezes in the pose in which they hit the plank-bed.
One feels a terrible pain in the shoulder and a completely unbearable pain in the knee. One's head has at least not been split
open—that's one good thing. The dead silence is suddenly shattered in another ward, which means that the neighbouring ward
is being given some training. You see, the lance-corporal did not
much care for their first retreat. Will we be for it today or not?

'Get up.' The order is given in an extremely quiet voice and
the whole ward is immediately transformed from a horizontal to

a vertical position. In less time than it takes to say it, we all stand to attention, in ranks, ready to fulfil any party or government order. It looks as if it is all because of that fat soldier in Airforce uniform that they have dragged us up. He is one of the staff clerks, those dregs of humanity, but we'll show him when night-time comes. He'll soon learn how to fulfil orders!

'Retreat!'

Again, there is the sound of crashing bodies and suppressed groans. Again, the whole ward freezes as ten bodies hit the plank-bed. What a shame! The fat clerk has missed! He made a terrific jump, but his body was too fat for a soldier. He came a cropper sideways on the edge of the boards, and froze motionless, with his hands at his sides, his body on the planks but his legs hanging over the edge. His face is a picture of horror and suffering. 'You fat pig, you'll pay for that tonight. The worst is still in store for you.'

The legs of the fat clerk start slowly slipping lower and lower, getting nearer and nearer to the brick floor. He gathers every shred of his strength in order, without moving, to attempt to transfer the weight of his body on to the planks. The lance-corporal patiently awaits the result of his balancing act. All the blood rushes to the face of the fat fellow, he stretches his neck and the whole of his body, trying surreptitiously to raise his legs. It seems momentarily that his body, stretched out like a ruler, will succeed in overbalancing his slightly bent legs, but the very next moment his legs start slipping down again and, in the end, the sole of his foot gently touches the floor.

'Get up . . . What's up, brother? Don't you want to sleep? You get the order to retreat, everybody else lies down like normal people and you apparently don't feel like sleep. Everybody has to go into training because of you. Well, okay. Off we go! I'll soon find some entertainment for you . . . Retreat!'

The order is given quietly and suddenly, counting on our having stopped paying attention, but we have learned to expect such tricks. You can't catch us like that! Nine men make a terrific jump, there is a crash and all movement freezes.

The lock creaks and I fall asleep immediately with my cheek resting on the unplaned boards, polished by the thousands of bodies of my predecessors. In the glasshouse there are no dreams, only complete oblivion, as one's whole organism is switched off. There is a blinding light in the wards throughout the night. The boards are bare, the spaces between the planks are three fingers

wide, it is cold. There is only one's greatcoat for cover and it is
permitted to put it under one's head and side. The coat is wet,
one's legs too are wet. There is no feeling of hunger because,
you see, only the first day has elapsed.

The glasshouse is not a prison. In prison, there is a collective
of sorts, but it is still a collective for all that. Secondly, in
prison, one finds people who have revolted, if only once, against
laws, against society, against the regime. In the glasshouse, one
finds only frightened soldiers mixed in with officer cadets. And
cadets are people who voluntarily offer themselves as members
of that social grouping totally deprived of all rights: junior Soviet
Army officers. You can do what you like with them. Everyone
who has been there in the glasshouse, and with whom I had an
opportunity later to discuss all that I saw there, is unanimous that
conditions in any one of the thousands of Soviet glasshouses
could be made much more severe without the slightest risk of
any organised opposition on the part of the inmates, particularly
in large towns where officer cadets form the majority of all
glasshouse inmates.

I woke up in the middle of the night, not from cold and not
from the unendurable stench of nine dirty bodies compressed into
a single, small, unventilated ward. No, I woke up because of an
unbearable desire to visit the toilet. This happens when it is cold.
Half the ward was awake, jumping up and down and generally
dancing around. Through the peephole, the optimists, in the
lowest possible whisper, were begging the escort to have pity on
them, and take them to the lavatory. But there is no *parasha* in
the glasshouse. It's not a civilian jail but a military establish-
ment. Top brass visit this place and, in order to please them,
there is no *parasha*.

Theoretically, the escort (as the very name implies) should,
sometimes, at night, escort inmates, one at a time, to the lavatory. But this could completely undermine the educational im-
pact of such an important measure as 'jobs time'. That is why
the attempts of any liberal escorts (themselves officer-cadets,
who are changed every day) to acquiesce to the inmates' entreat-
ies are rigidly suppressed. It is quite a different matter with the
wards of those under investigation, or of the accused, or of the
condemned; they are escorted off there at their very first request.
And those in solitary confinement cells, where the position is
worse, even they are sometimes taken out during the night,
probably because they are usually psychopaths prepared to do

any kind of damage; but, in general, where normal men are concerned, it is very bad indeed. They are never taken to the toilet during the night, because the escort knows that the ward as a whole, fearful of common punishment, would never allow anybody to relieve himself inside the ward.

The heavy bolt suddenly clanked, signifying either an incomprehensible favour on the part of the escort, or his anger at persistent demands. All those who had been dancing about only a moment ago in the ward, promptly jumped as noiselessly as tom-cats on to the plank-bed and feigned sleep. But it was only the fat clerk being pushed into the ward, having cleaned out the lavatories during the night after 'jobs time', and the door slammed shut with a bang. The fat clerk was completely exhausted, and his eyes were red from lack of sleep, One could see his tears and his plump cheeks were trembling. Groaning, he crawled on to the plank-bed, and putting his dirty cheek on to the hard planks he was instantly out for the count.

Meanwhile, the ward had come to life again, and I, like all the others, had started to dance about in anticipation.

'Staff shit!' said the tall dark-haired CW soldier. 'He went and pissed in the lavatory and now he's sleeping soundly. He's just like any other fat cow, who's never really done its turn and yet's now set up better than anyone else.' All those who were already awake wanted sleep more than life itself, because only sleep can conserve any remaining strength. But he was the only one who was sleeping at that moment, and that is why hatred towards him particularly welled up in all the rest of us simultaneously. The tall CW soldier takes off his coat and covers the head of the sleeping man. We all rush towards him, I jump on to the plank-bed and kick his stomach as if it were a football. Quite unable to shout, he only whimpers softly. Because of the noise we all produce, the footsteps of the escort slowly approach the ward doors. His indifferent eye surveys what is going on, and his steps slowly move off again with the same indifference. The escort is a brother officer-cadet, most probably he himself has been under arrest on more than one occasion. He understands us and is completely on our side. He would not have minded coming into the ward and putting in the boot himself—but that is not allowed, the escort must not resort to violence. It is forbidden.

By this time it is probably already five o'clock in the morning. There are about thirty minutes left before reveille. This is the most difficult time of all. Oh, I can't stand it any more. Probably all those who performed badly during tactical training, or at work or during the evening check, or during retreat, are now being beaten in all the other wards.

I have never run so fast in all my life as at the first morning 'jobs time' in the glasshouse. Walls, floors, staircases and the faces of the escorts flashed past, and the only thought in my head was, 'I hope I arrive in time!' Nothing whatsoever could distract me from this thought, not even a familiar face, and those black tank corps shoulder-straps which rushed towards me. It was only later, after returning to my ward and getting my breath back, that I realised that I had seen a fellow cadet running from the lavatory just as I was. This officer cadet was a first-year cadet who had replaced us at the Check Point after we had been arrested, and this could mean only one thing: Colonel General Vladimir Filipovich Chizh, the Deputy District Commander, had arrested us upon entering our school and, in just one hour, upon leaving the school, he had arrested those who had replaced us. The Colonel General was a hard man indeed, and it is greatly to be regretted that he was only interested in one thing—the reception accorded him personally—and in nothing else whatsoever.

Kiev Garrison Detention Centre. 29 March, 1966.

Return from Communism

OF ALL THE billions of people who inhabit our sinful planet, I am one of the few who have lived under real communism and, thanks be to God, have returned from it, safe and sound to tell the tale. This is how it happened.

In the glasshouse, during the morning posting of inmates, Lance-Corporal Alekseyev made the following quick-fire announcement while poking our greasy tunics:

'You, you and you—project No. 8', which meant the tank factory, to load worn-out tank tracks, completely exhausting work with totally unattainable norms.

'You, you, and those ten there—project No. 27', which meant the railway station, unloading trucks of artillery shells, which was even worse.

The escort immediately collected together its detail of inmates and embarked them on a lorry.

'You, you, you and those over there—project No. 110.' That was the worst of all, it was the oil refinery, and meant cleaning out the insides of immense reservoirs. There, one absorbed such a stench of petrol, paraffin, and other foul substances that it was quite impossible to eat or sleep. There was no issue of special clothing, and one was not supposed to wash either. But, for today anyway, it looked as if we had escaped.

The lance-corporal approaches.

And where are we going today?

'You, you and those three there—project No. 12.'

Where is that?

The escort took us aside, wrote down our names and gave us the usual ten seconds to get ourselves on to the jeep. Light and agile as greyhounds, we leapt under the tarpaulin roof of the new GAZ jeep.

While the escort was signing for our souls, I nudged the puny officer cadet with the artillery flashes with my elbow. Apparently, he was the most experienced of our number, and upon hearing the figure 12 he had visibly quaked.

'Where is that?'

'To communism, to Saltychikha* herself,' he whispered and in the same breath swore foully and inventively.

I swore too, for everyone knows that there is nothing on earth worse than communism. I had already heard much about communism and Saltychikha, what I did not know was that it was called project No. 12. Our escort, with a clatter of his automatic rifle, jumped in over the side of the GAZ jeep, which sneezed a couple of times, jerked once for the sake of order and sped off along the smooth pre-revolutionary cobbled road straight on to communism.

Communism is located on the south-western outskirts of that ancient Slavonic capital—the mother of all Russian towns—the thousand-year-old city of Kiev.

And, though it occupies a large slice of Ukrainian soil, it is simply impossible for the uninitiated just to catch sight of it or even of its four-metre-high boundary walls. Communism is hidden in a dense pine forest, surrounded on all sides by military bases, depots and stores. And, in order just to glimpse the walls of communism, one has to penetrate a military base which is

---

*Saltychikha was a Tsarist landowner, notorious for cruelty to her serfs. The story goes that these same serfs later walled her up in one of the stone columns of her own mansion. This mansion eventually became a school for the daughters of the privileged, and the girls used to whisper to each other at night, in terror of the fate of the original owner.

defended by ever-wakeful guards armed with machine-guns and by fierce guard-dogs.

Our GAZ jeep was speeding on down the Brest-Litovsk highway and, after passing the last few houses, it dived smartly into an insignificant passage between two green fences, marked 'Entry Forbidden'. After about five minutes, the jeep stopped in front of grey, wooden, unpainted gates which in no way resembled the entrance to a shining bright tomorrow. The gates opened and, after having allowed us entry, instantly slammed tightly shut. We were in a mousetrap. On both sides there were walls about five metres high—behind us were some wooden, but clearly very solid gates, while those in front of us were metal and obviously more solid still.

From somewhere a lieutenant and two soldiers armed with submachine guns sprang forward to meet us; they quickly counted us, looked inside the jeep, into its engine and even beneath the jeep, and they checked the documents of both the driver and the escort. The green steel wall in front of us quivered momentarily, and then smoothly slid off to the left, opening out before our eyes the panoramic view of a pine forest, bisected by a broad and flat road resembling an airport runway. Beyond those steel gates, I had expected to see anything you like, but not a dense forest.

Meanwhile the jeep was still speeding on along the concrete road. On both right and left, among the pine trees, one could distinguish the huge concrete structures of depots and stores completely covered over by earth and overgrown with prickly bushes. After some minutes we stopped again in front of an unbelievably high concrete fence. The previous procedure was repeated: the first gates, then the concrete trap, the check on papers, the second gates and then beyond that a straight level road into the forest, although this time the depots and stores were missing.

Finally, we stopped at a striped control barrier, guarded by two sentries. On either side of this barrier, stretching out into the forest, were wire fences, attached to which were grey watchdogs straining at their leashes. I have seen all manner of dogs in my time but these particular ones immediately struck me as being somehow unusual. Only much later, I realised that every other chained dog barks furiously as it strains at the leash, while these enraged creatures were quite mute. They did not bark, but only growled, choking themselves with their own saliva and their furious rage. Being real watchdogs, they barked only in accordance with instructions.

Having overcome this last obstacle, the jeep stopped in front of a huge red placard, about six to seven metres high, on which prominent golden letters proclaimed: 'THE PARTY SOLEMNLY PROMISES THAT THE PRESENT GENERATION OF SOVIET PEOPLE WILL LIVE UNDER COMMUNISM!' And a bit lower in brackets was written: 'Extract from the Programme of the Communist Party of the Soviet Union, agreed at the XXII Congress of the CPSU.'

The escort yelled, 'Ten seconds!'—and, like little grey sparrows, we all flitted out from the jeep's interior and formed up at its rear side. Ten seconds—one could manage that, there were only five of us and to jump out of a jeep is easier than to clamber on to it over ice-covered sides; oh yes, and, in addition, we had grown much lighter these last few days.

A crude-faced lance-corporal with lordly manners appeared before us wearing officer's boots. He was one of the place's regular retinue. He explained something briefly to the escort, who then yelled, 'Hands behind backs! Follow the lance-corporal in single file!'

'Quick march!'

We moved singly along a paved path cleared of snow and, after rounding a beautiful plantation of young fir trees, we all suddenly stopped dead in our tracks without any order being given, we were so staggered by the unprecedented picture before us.

In a woodland clearing, surrounded by the young fir trees, buildings of amazing beauty were scattered about in picturesque disorder. Never before nor since, either in any fairy tale film, nor any exhibition of foreign architecture, have I ever met such a turbulent, passionate and rapturous fantasy of colours, such an amazing intermingling of nature, in light, colour, elegance, taste, simplicity and originality. I am no writer and it is beyond my powers to describe adequately the sheer beauty of that place to which fate saw fit to transport me, once upon a time.

Not only I, but our escort too, all of us, open-mouthed, admired the view. The lance-corporal, apparently accustomed to such a reaction among strangers, shouted at the escort to bring him to his senses; the latter, still spellbound, straightened the strap of his automatic, first cursed us and then our mothers, and we began to straggle our way along a footpath paved with grey granite, past frozen waterfalls and ponds, past Chinese bridges, arching their cat-like backs over canals, past marble summer-houses and pools covered with coloured glass.

Having passed through this delightful little town, we found ourselves once more in a young fir-tree plantation. The lance-corporal stopped in a small clearing surrounded by trees and ordered us to rake away the snow, under which was revealed a trap-door. Five of us lifted its cast-iron lid and threw it to one side. A monstrous stench issued from the bowels of the earth. Holding his nose, the lance-corporal jumped back into the snow. We did not follow him of course, as by doing so we could easily have got a short sharp burst between our shoulder-blades. We merely clamped our noses tightly shut as we drew back from the cesspool.

The lance-corporal took a gulp of clean forest air and gave the order: 'The pump and hand barrows are there, and the orchard is—way—over there. By 1800 hours, the cleaning of the cess-pool must be completed and the trees must be manured!' And then away he went.

This heavenly place where we had landed was called the 'Country-house of the High Command of the Warsaw Treaty Army', otherwise known as 'Project No. 12'. This country house was kept in case any member of the Warsaw Treaty High Command suddenly felt the urge to have a rest on the outskirts of ancient Kiev, Russia's former capital city. But the heads of the Warsaw Treaty organisation were more inclined to spend their rest periods on the Black Sea coast of the Caucasus. And so, the country house remained empty. If the Defence Minister or the Chief of the General Staff ever came to Kiev, there was yet another country house, officially named the 'Country House for Senior Officials of the Defence Ministry', or 'Project No. 23'. But, as the Minister of Defence and his First Deputies do not come to Kiev even once every ten years, this country house also remains empty. In the event of the arrival in Kiev of any Soviet Party or Government leaders, there were many other 'Projects' at the disposal of the Kiev Town Party or Executive Committees; yet others, more imposing still, at the disposal of the Kiev Regional Party Committee or the Regional Executive Committee; and, the most impressive of all, better by far than any of our military houses, which were of course entirely at the disposal of the Central Committee of the Ukrainian Communist Party, the Ukrainian Council of Ministers and the Ukrainian Supreme Soviet. Since there was really plenty of room to accommodate any cherished guests, Country House No. 12 was permanently empty. Neither the Commander of Kiev Military District nor his deputies ever used it for the simple reason that they were all entitled to have their own personal country houses. Therefore, No. 12 came to be occupied by the Military District Commander's wife. In country house No. 23 resided his only daughter, while the Commander himself lived with whores in his personal country house. (The organisation supplying leading personnel with prostitutes is officially named 'The Song and Dance Ensemble of Kiev Military District'. Such organisations are in existence for all military districts, fleets, groups of troops, as well as for all other organisations of high standing.)

The staff that waits upon the wife of Yakubovskiy is huge. And every day, to help the countless cooks, servants, maids, gardeners and others, five to eight or, sometimes, up to twenty glasshouse inmates are brought here to perform the dirtiest work. Today is no exception to the rule.

Among the inmates themselves, the Warsaw country house was known by that one very bad word, 'Communism'. It is difficult to say why it had been so christened—perhaps it was owing to the placard at the entrance, or maybe owing to the fairy-tale beauty and charm of the natural surroundings. Then again, perhaps it was because, here, mystery and fascination were so tightly interlaced with the daily humiliation of people, or else it was simply because, organically speaking, beauty and shit are so very closely related! And, when it came to shit, there was enough here for anyone.

'Is the cesspool deep?' asks an Uzbek military engineer.

'It reaches to the centre of the earth.'

'But it could easily be connected to the town sewerage system by a pipe!'

'You fool, do you really believe that an Army General would defecate in the same sewer as you! You are still not old enough to have that honour. This system has been devised for the sake of safety, otherwise some secret paper could fall in, and what then? The enemy is ever watchful and uses all possible channels open to him. That is why a closed circuit has been devised here, to avoid the drain of information!'

'So, according to you, this self-same drain of information occurs through the generals' arses?'

'You don't understand a bloody thing,' the puny fellow from

the artillery said, 'this system was invented simply in order to conserve generals' excrement, which, unlike ours, is full of calories. The quality of the shit is exactly proportionate to the quality of the food consumed, and if someone like Michurin had been given this much prime quality excrement, he would have glorified our motherland for centuries with the richness of the harvests he achieved!'

At this point our discussion was interrupted by our escort. It is of course an advantage if one's escort hails from the tank corps like oneself. Then, life is quite different, even though the escort knows full well that if he is too lenient towards prisoners, after his own stint of duty he, too, will find himself confined to the glasshouse, along with those same prisoners he was escorting only a little while earlier. But, all the same, a brother tank corps man is much to be preferred to a man from the infantry or the artillery. It is also not too bad when the escort, even if not one of the lads, is nevertheless an experienced third or fourth officer cadet. For, even though not from the same squad, they have probably been in the glasshouse at least once themselves: so they really do know what is what. The worst of all is when the escort consists of a bunch of young wet noses and strangers to boot. First year cadets are always the most stupid and the most strict. They go by the book. And it is one of these that we have been landed today.

He is tall with a big ugly face and, judging by his behaviour alone, he is obviously a first year man. Besides, everything he has on is new—coat, cap, boots—and such a thing would be quite impossible for an old-timer. The fellow's a rookie, and his badges are those of a signals unit, which in Kiev could only mean that he belongs to the Kiev Higher Engineering Radio Technical School or KVIRTU for short. In Kiev, these chaps are only referred to as 'Kvirtanutyy'. This particular Kvirtanutyy looks as if he is getting angry. So it must be time to start work.

And so our first working day under communism has begun. One fellow pumps up the shit, the remaining four carry the stinking sludge into the general's garden. My partner turned out to be that same puny artillery officer cadet who looked the most experienced of our number. The work was clearly beyond his powers. And, as we carried away our loaded hand barrows, he turned red in the face, groaned and generally looked as if he was going to collapse at any moment. I could not help him at all as I myself could hardly hold the handles on my own side. We could not sneak off with a lighter load either, as the other pair promptly started to protest: whereupon the escort threatened to report us to the powers-that-be.

But the poor fellow clearly had to have some support from somewhere, if not in deed then at least in word. With a loaded container, this was quite impossible, but on the return trip it was quite an easy matter as our journey took us about three hundred metres away from the stinking cesspool and from the escort so that we could get into conversation.

'Now then, artillery, how much longer are you in for?' I began when we had dumped our first load beneath a spreading apple tree.

'I have already served out my time,' he answered languidly, 'that is if we manage not to get "extra rations" today.'

'Lucky chap,' said I, sincerely envying him. 'Tell me, O God of War, how far are you off getting your golden shoulder-straps?'

'It's all been done already.'

'How so?' I just did not understand.

'Well, that's how it is. It's three days since the order reached Moscow. If the Minister signs it today—there you are—golden shoulder-straps, but he may only sign it tomorrow!'

I envied him once more. I had another year to wait. One more year at the Guards Tank School—a year is such a long time, unlike my comrades, I had not yet started counting in hours and minutes, but I counted only the days.

'You lucky bastard, artillery, you'll go straight from the glass-house for a bath and then on to a graduation party. Some people certainly have all the luck.'

'If we don't get "extra rations",' he interrupted gloomily.

'There is an amnesty in that case.'

He did not answer, maybe because we were getting near to the ugly-faced escort.

The second trip proved considerably more difficult than the first for the artillery man, and he hardly managed to drag himself to the first trees. While I was tipping up the barrow, he rested all his weight upon the gnarled trunk of a tree nearby. I had to support the poor chap. I had already wasted two trump cards as neither the thought of his imminent graduation from military school nor his early release from the glasshouse had cheered him up even a little bit. My only hope was to boost his morale to the required level. This approach simply could not fail. So I decided to toss him the idea of the bright future in store for us, of communism, so to speak.

'Do you hear what I say, God of War?'

'What's up with you now?'

'Listen, artillery, life is hard for us now, but the time will come when we too will live in a paradise, like this—under communism. That will be life! Eh?'

'How do you mean? With our hands full of shit?'

'Oh, no, I don't mean that', I said, grieved by such lack of vision. 'What I am saying is that the time will come when we too will live in such heavenly gardens, in the same beautiful little towns with lakes, surrounded by hundred-year-old pine trees, and apple orchards or, better still, cherry orchards. See how much poetry there is in it . . . Cherry orchards! Well?'

'You are a fool,' he answered wearily. 'A real fool, even if you are a tank corps man.'

'Why am I a fool?' I asked indignantly. 'Now wait a bit, you. Why am I a fool?'

'And who, in your view, will carry the shit under communism? And now shut up, we are getting near.'

The question was so simple and it was put in such a mocking tone, it was like being pole-axed. At the beginning, it did not seem to be insoluble, but it was the first time in my life that any question about communism had ever arisen to which I could not find an immediate answer. Before, everything had been absolutely clear: everyone works as he wants, as much as he wants, according to his ability, and receives whatever he wants and as much as he wants, i.e. according to his needs. It was absolutely clear that, say, supposing one man wants to be a steel founder; right then, work for the common good and for your own, of course, because you are an equal member of society. You want to be a teacher? Right then, every kind of work is honoured in our society. You want to be a wheat farmer? What work can be more honourable than to provide people with bread? You want to become a diplomat—the way is open! But who will be busy in the sewers? Is it possible that there will be anybody who will say, 'Yes, this is my vocation, this is my place, I am not fit for anything better?' On the island of Utopia, it was prisoners who did such work as we are doing now, but under communism there will be neither crime, nor prisons, nor glasshouses, and no prisoners, because there will be no necessity for crime—everything will be free of charge. Take what you like—it is not a crime, but a necessity, and everybody will take according to his needs, that is the basic principle of communism.

We tipped up the third barrow and I exclaimed triumphantly,

'Everyone will clean up after himself! And, in addition, there will be machines!'

He looked at me with pity.

'Did you read Marx?'

'Indeed I did,' I said passionately.

'Do you remember the example of the pins? If one man is producing them, there will be three per day, but if production is divided between three men, one cuts the wire, another sharpens the ends and the third attaches the heads, then there will be three hundred pins per day—one hundred per man. This is called division of labour. The higher the division of labour in a society, the higher is its productivity. But there has to be a master, a virtuoso, in every business, not just an amateur or dilettante. Now take Kiev, for instance, and see how each of its one and a half million inhabitants arranges his own sewerage system, in his free time, and cleans it and maintains it in good order. As for machines, Marx prophesied the victory of communism at the end of the nineteenth century, but at that time such machines did not exist, which means that at that time communism was impossible. Is that not so? These machines still do not exist, which means that communism is still impossible. Am I right or not? . . . And, so long as these machines are missing, somebody must rummage in somebody else's shit, and this, with your kind permission, is not communism. Let's assume that some day such machines will be invented, but even then somebody will still have to look after them and clean them, and that, too, will not be very pleasant work either. It's hard to believe that anybody will really ever want to do nothing but that throughout his whole life. Do you support Marxist theory about the division of labour, or aren't you a Marxist?'

'Of course I'm a Marxist,' I mumbled.

'The time is fast approaching and so there are additional questions which demand independent study. Who, under communism, will bury the corpses? Will it be self-service or will amateurs carry out the work in their spare time? Generally speaking, there is plenty of dirty work in society and everyone is not a diplomat or a general. Who will carve up the pig carcases? Have you ever been in a fish-filleting outfit? The fish arrives and must be dealt with immediately and there's no bloody mechanisation either. So, what then? And who will sweep the streets and cart off the rubbish? To cart off rubbish nowadays, one needs qualifications and not low ones either, and dilettantism is no bloody good either. And will there be any waiters under communism? For the time being it's certainly a profitable business, but when money is liquidated, what will it be like then? And finally, for someone who at present has not the slightest idea about how to set about shit-cleaning, like Comrade Yakubovskiy himself for instance, has he any personal interest at all in the arrival of that day, when he will have to clean up his own shit all by himself? So just think it over! And now, we are getting near to the escort again, so shut up!'

'You chatter too much, you should be working!'

'Look here, artillery, do you mean that in your opinion communism will never come at all?'

At this, he stopped dead in his tracks, thunderstruck by the very outrageousness of my question.

'Of course not!'

'But why not? You counter-revolutionary bastard, how have you managed to avoid the chop? You're a dirty anti-Soviet swine.' And, with all my might, I heaved that very heavy hand barrow down on to the ground and a stinking golden mass spilled out over the blindingly white snow and over the granite pathway.

'Damn your bloody balls,' the artillery man spat out in utter rage. 'Now we'll each get an extra five days—like nobody's business, you just see if we don't! But, no . . . it looks as if no one has noticed; let's cover it with snow.' And feverishly, we started to throw snow on to the dirty patch. But our escort was already running towards us.

'You idle bastards! What have you done now? You're chattering again, are you? But I'm answerable for you and I'll soon make you dance for it.'

'Wait! . . . Don't make a noise, we'll soon cover it with snow and no one will see anything. It's a very heavy carrier and it just fell out of our hands. It's good for the garden anyway. The snow will melt in a week and wash away all traces.'

However, the ugly-faced escort did not relent.

'You should work instead of chattering! But I'll make you dance for your pains.'

Then the artilleryman changed his tone.

'You complete fool! First serve for as long as we have and

then you'll have something to shout about. Report us and you'll be punished along with us for not noticing in time.' I supported these remarks.

'You are still young and silly and haven't experienced any real difficulties in your life. As for this man here, a report has already been sent and, in three days' time, he will be made an officer—but you are still a snotty boy . . .'

'Who are you calling a snotty boy? Right you are!'

He shouldered his automatic and shouted:

'Back—to—work! Step lively! I'll teach you to show your paces.'

The artilleryman looked indifferently in the escort's direction and calmly said to me: 'Let's go . . . It's no use trying to reason with a sheep . . . He's going to be arrested today . . . You can take my word for it.'

And off we strolled in the direction of the trap door.

'He'll report us for sure,' said the artilleryman confidently.

'No,' I said, 'he'll only play the fool a bit and then recover towards the evening.'

'Okay, but you'll see!'

'Don't be mournful, my friend, and don't sigh. Take life as a horse by its bridle.'

'Tell everyone to piss off, at the very least. So that they don't tell you first to fuck off!'

'That, artillery, is one of my firm convictions.'

'And mine too!'

Two kindred souls . . . in the General's sewer!

'Look here, you counter-revolutionary. Why do you claim that communism will never come?'

'Because . . . But don't throw down your shit-carrier again . . . Because neither our Party nor its Leninist Central Committee has the slightest need of communism.'

'You're nothing but a counter-revolutionary liar!'

'Blow your nose with both nostrils, you miserable idiot. Quieten down and stop yelling, it's impossible to talk here. Have patience and in a minute, when we have unloaded, I'll teach you all.' We unloaded.

'Okay. Just you imagine that communism arrives tomorrow morning.'

'No, that's impossible,' I interrupted. 'The material technical base has to be built first.'

'Just imagine that the year 1980 has arrived and that the Party, as it promised, has built this base. So, what exactly does our ordinary run-of-the-mill Secretary of a District Party Committee stand to gain from this communism? Eh? Plenty of caviare? But he's got so much caviare already that he can even eat it through his arse if he wishes. A car? But he has two personal Volga cars and one private one as well, in reserve. Medical care? Food, women, a country house? But he already has all of these things. So our dear Secretary of the most Godforsaken District Party Committee stands to gain bugger-all from communism! And what will he lose? He will lose everything. At the moment, he's warming his belly at the best health resort on the Black Sea coast, but under communism all men are equal as they are in a bath-house, and there won't be enough room for everybody on that beach. Or, let's assume that there's an abundance of products, just take whatever you like and as much as you like in any shop. Also let's assume that there's not even a queue. There will still be inconveniences, and you will still have to go and collect things. But what good is that to him, if the local yokels already bring him everything he needs? Why would he prefer tomorrow if today is even better? He will lose everything under communism—his country house, his personal physicians, his hirelings and his guards.

'So, even at District Committee Secretary level, nobody is interested in communism's arrival tomorrow, or the day after for that matter. And when it comes to the Yakubovskiys and Grechkos of this world, communism has long since ceased to be of any interest to them at all. Did you see how they jumped on China because of the so-called levelling process there, when everyone was wearing identical trousers, so to speak. And what about us, how will we live under communism? Will there be any fashions, or will we all be wearing prisoners' jackets? The Party says not—but if that is true, how can everybody be provided with fashionable clothes, if they are free and everyone takes as many as he wants? And where will you get all the fox and polar bear fur for all the women's coats? Yakubovskiy's wife wears a different ermine coat every day. If communism suddenly came tomorrow, would you be able to convince the milkmaid, Marusya, that her thighs are any less desirable than those of Yakubovskiy's wife or that her status in society is less honourable? Marusya is a young woman and she also wants ermine and gold, and diamonds. But do you believe that the old stoat, Yakubovskaya, will give up her furs and diamonds without a fight? Fuck off with you! This is why they don't want communism to come tomorrow, and that's all there is to it. And that is why an historical period is invented. Did you ever read Lenin? When did he promise us communism? In ten to fifteen years! Wasn't that so? And Stalin? Also in ten to fifteen years, though sometimes it was even twenty. And Nikita Sergeyevich*? In twenty years, and the whole Party swore to the people that this time there would be no deception. Do you really believe that in the year 1980 communism will finally come? Not bloody likely: and do you think anybody will ask the Party to explain this lie? No, there will not be a single questioning voice.

'And did you ever reflect, my dear tankman, on why all our rulers mention ten to fifteen years? It's to give them time for their own ''dolce vita'' and yet still not destroy other people's hopes. And, incidentally, also time for all those promises to be long forgotten. Who remembers now what Lenin promised, once upon a time? And when 1980 does arrive, precisely no one will recall that the promised year has, at last, arrived. It is certainly about time for an answer. The time is almost ripe for the Party to give an account of itself.'

'Are you really a communist at all?'

'I am not a communist, but I am a Party member and it's about time you saw the difference!'

He became silent, and we did not speak any more until the evening.

Towards evening, we had finally succeeded in cleaning out the pit to its very bottom. We had scooped out everything when there suddenly appeared on the path a skinny, wrinkled woman, wearing an ermine fur coat and accompanied by the lance-corporal, whose face had by now lost its lordly expression and was wearing that of a country yokel instead.

'Now look,' warned the artilleryman, 'if Saltychikha sentences us to extra days in the glasshouse—don't you go kicking up a fuss. She's only a mere woman but she'll have you up in front of the tribunal, quick as look at you, if you don't watch out.'

The lance-corporal inspected the cesspool and the garden, and

---

*Nikita Sergeyevich Khrushchev, the Soviet Party leader subsequently deposed by Brezhnev.

reported in oily tones, 'They have done it all. I kept them at it all day.'

She smiled faintly, approached the cesspool and looked down into its depths.

'They did not work badly, all day I . . .' the lance-corporal continued unctuously.

'But they dirtied the path and covered up the dirt with snow,' observed our escort.

The lance-corporal cast a stealthy look of utter hatred at the escort.

'Which path was that?' enquired the skinny woman almost tenderly.

'Well, just let's go over here, let's go and I'll show you,' and he began to stride off along the path with the skinny woman tripping along behind him.

Night was falling and it was getting frosty and the escort had some difficulty in kicking away the lump of frozen snow which covered the dirty spot.

'Here it is, they covered it with snow and thought I wouldn't notice it. But I see everything!'

'Who is responsible?' shrieked the old hag.

'Those two there . . . they thought they would get away with it and pass unnoticed . . . But we notice everything . . .'

'Five days . . . each,' hissed the old hag. 'As for you, Fedor . . . as for you . . .' and, her face distorted by rage and without even finishing the sentence, she wrapped her fur coat more tightly around her and swept off in the direction of the fairy-tale small town. The lance-corporal's face twisted in a grimace and he turned towards our escort who, apparently, had not yet realised that he had accidentally dropped the all-powerful Fedor right in it.

'Take your rabble away then! I won't let you forget this, you bastard!'

The puzzled escort looked at the lance-corporal:

'I was only doing my best . . .'

'Get out of here, you scum. I'll get even with you one day!'

We stamped off past the wonderful little town, which in the darkness managed to become still more entrancing. Children splashed about in a pool, separated from the frost only by a greenish, transparent wall. A tall woman, in a severe blue frock and white apron, busied herself with them.

● ● ●

First Lieutenant Kirichek, the Deputy Chief of the Kiev Garrison glasshouse, had already been informed of the 'extra rations' handed out to us as he awaited our return from communism. The first lieutenant opened a thick ledger.

'Five days each. So . . . we write down . . . Five . . . days . . . arrest . . . From the Commander of the Military District . . . for . . . bre . . . ach of military discipline . . . —Oh, hell,' he exclaimed suddenly, 'the Commander has flown to Moscow for a Party congress. How can I . . . ?' He looked at the book, and then, on second thoughts, inserted the word 'Deputy' before the word 'Commander.' Now everything was in order. 'So, Suvorov, your first five days were given to you by the Deputy Commander and so were the second five days. Now, let's see who'll give you the third lot.' Amused by his own joke, he gave a sort of neighing laugh.

'Escort!'

'Yes, comrade First Lieutenant!'

'Put these two pigeons in 26. Let them sit there for one or two hours to learn that extra rations is not just extra time to serve, but something with rather more bite.'

Ward 26 in the Kiev glasshouse is known by the title of 'Revolutionary', because once, before the Revolution, a famous petty criminal called Grigoriy Kotovskiy, on trial for rape, had escaped from it. Later, in 1918, Kotovskiy and his gang joined the Bolsheviks and, for invaluable services of a criminal nature, were later officially renamed revolutionaries instead of pickpockets on the personal instructions of Lenin himself. But the experience gained from this famous revolutionary's escape was exploited to the full, and there were no further departures from the notorious ward.

There is neither plank-bed nor bench in this ward, only a spittoon in one corner. And it is not just standing there by chance, it is filled to the very brim with chlorine. The window through which that hero of the Revolution escaped has long ago been bricked up, and the ward itself is so small, and there is so much chlorine, that to remain there longer than five minutes seems a complete impossibility. Tears stream from one's eyes, one chokes for breath, saliva fills one's mouth and one's chest feels like bursting from the pain of it.

As soon as we were pushed into the ward, the experienced artilleryman, though himself already coughing and choking, still managed to push me away from the door which I was going to kick. Bowing to his experience, I gave up the attempt. Much later, I discovered that, as usual, he was quite right. It emerged that, just opposite our ward 26, there was ward 25, expressly intended for those who could not stand being in ward 26. After a sojourn in ward 25, anyone and everyone calmed down and returned meekly to ward 26.

Meanwhile, a third person had been pushed into our ward. I couldn't have cared less who he was and did not even try to discern his features through my tears, but the artilleryman had been awaiting his arrival. Nudging me (it was absolutely impossible to speak), he gestured with his hand towards the third man. And, after I had rubbed my eyes, I recognised our very own escort.

Usually, a period under arrest does not start with wards 21, 25 or 26. Only those given 'extra rations' pass through one of these wards and, sometimes, even through all three of them. Our first-year 'Kvirtanutyy' had started his particular epic in ward 26. Was this because the all-powerful lance-corporal had complained to the ADC or to the deputy commander, or was it because our escort had protested when, after surrendering his automatic and cartridges, he had suddenly learnt that his platoon was actually returning home but that he, for some unknown reason, was to remain here, on a charge, for ten days. Or maybe the first lieutenant had decided to put him with us just for the fun of it, knowing in advance what our reaction was bound to be.

In the whitish haze of chlorine fumes, the new inmate choked in his first fit of coughing. His eyes filled with tears. Helplessly, he groped in the void, trying to find a wall. We were no three musketeers, and the two of us had not the slightest inclination to forgive. It might be said that it is wrong to beat a helpless and temporarily blind man, especially at the moment when he least expects any assault. This may very well be true for anyone who has never seen the inside of this ward. But we construed the appearance of our escort as a gift of fate, for the one and only time when we could beat him up was when he was quite helpless. At any other time, he would have made us scatter like cats, he was much too powerful. I write all this exactly as it happened. I, personally, showed no finer feeling at all, and have not the least intention of falsely attributing to myself any high ideals. But those who have been there will understand, and those who have not can never be my judges.

The artilleryman made a sign and, as the tall escort straightened himself between fits of coughing, I kicked him hard in the crotch. He let out an inhuman scream and bent over double in agony. At this same moment, the artilleryman kicked him as hard as he could on the left knee-cap. And, as the escort writhed on the floor, the artilleryman kicked him again, twice, in the stomach. As a result of all this exertion, we had swallowed a lot of chlorine. I vomited, the artilleryman choked. Meanwhile, the escort was lying prostrate on the floor, and we could not have cared less. I vomited again and felt quite certain that I was not long for this world. I had no wish for anything, not even for fresh air. The walls shook and started to rotate around me. From afar, I heard the clank of the door being opened but I was totally indifferent.

Apparently, I regained consciousness quite soon. The escort, still unconscious, was carried past me along the corridor. And, suddenly, I felt unbearably sorry that, when he regained consciousness on the plank-bed, he would still not understand what had happened to him in ward 26. Immediately, I decided to put matters right and to finish him off while there was still time. I strained with all my strength to get up from the concrete floor but all the effort dissolved into a pitiful attempt to move my head.

'He's come to,' said somebody from somewhere above my head.

'Let him have another whiff.'

The artilleryman was still on his feet and now he was vomiting. Somebody quite close to me said, 'On the orders of the Defence Minister, he's already an officer!'

'The Minister's order came today, but it was signed yesterday,' objected another voice. 'That means the amnesty covered only the time served yesterday. But, today, after becoming an officer, he was put on another charge by the Deputy Commander of the District and therefore this period is not covered by the ministerial amnesty.'

'Bugger it, can't we approach the Deputy Commander personally in connection with this case since it's so exceptional?'

'But the Deputy Commander has never set eyes upon your newly-fledged lieutenant. It was done on the orders of Himself's wife. Himself has gone to the Party conference. You do not propose to ask Herself, do you?'

'Too right!' agreed the second voice.

'And we can't set him free under the amnesty either! Otherwise, what will happen if she comes tomorrow to check up? Then all our heads will roll!'

'Quite right!'

And so it happened that, while our artilleryman was cleaning the sewers, the Minister of Defence had signed the orders, promoting him and, with him, another two hundred fortunate officer cadets to the rank of lieutenant. In such cases, the ministerial order is normally an absolution. But, while this order was on its way from Moscow, our artilleryman had been put on a further charge purporting to emanate from the Deputy Commander of the Kiev Military District. And no one could do anything about it.

But, even so, he had officially become an officer, and his place was in the officers' quarters which were separated from those of the common herd by a high wall. So, we embraced like brothers, like two men who are very close and yet who are destined to part from each other for ever. He smiled wanly at me and, just as he was, filthy from the excrement of the wife of the future Commander-in-Chief of the Combined Armed Forces of the Warsaw Treaty Powers, Marshal of the Soviet Union Yakubovskiy, but now at long last without any escort, he went towards the iron gates leading to the officers' quarters.

On that very day, in the capital of our Motherland, in that most heroic city of Moscow, to the accompaniment of the thunderous applause of thousands of delegates and of our numerous brothers, assembled from all the corners of the earth, in the Kremlin Palace of Congresses, the work of the XXIII Congress of the Communist Party of the Soviet Union began. It was an historic occasion. From that day forward, the Party promised the present generation of Soviet people . . . nothing at all!

Kiev Garrison Detention Centre. 31 March, 1966.

Risk

IT MAY BE argued that political training in the glasshouse is the very best time of all. Just sit there on a stool for an hour and a half, just nod off and do absolutely nothing. It would seem hard to invent any better form of relaxation. Any such thought is pure imagination and could only enter the head of one who has never seen the inside of a glasshouse or of someone who has not been warned in advance how to behave during a spell of training there. For the inexperienced inmate, the seeming simplicity of it all can turn out to be a load of trouble. The inmate is pleased beyond bounds by his first attendance at a political training session but he has only to let himself be distracted for a single moment, to forget for a single second where he is and what he is there for, and misfortune will instantly strike.

Exhausted by lack of sleep and the terrible cold, by damp and hunger, by punishing work, by constant humiliations and insults and, what is worse, by the expectation of still more terrible things to come, after one has calmed down a little and got warm, one's organism does finally relax for a moment or two.

And if one slackens, even momentarily, this steel spring, taut from the very first moment of being in the glasshouse, gets instantly out of hand and unwinds spontaneously in a flash . . . and one loses all control.

Exactly that is happening nearby to a little soldier who, most probably, has never been in the glasshouse before—his eyes are glazed, his eyelids stick together, he is going to fall asleep . . . any moment now he will bury his head in the dirty, hunched-up back of that weedy sailor who came to Kiev on leave and was picked up by a patrol at the railway station. It looks as if the sailor will also drop off to sleep at any moment. I am sorry for the soldier, for the sailor, and for myself too . . . but my feet are getting warm . . . and my head feels intoxicated. I can hear the ringing of little bells . . . they sound so sweet . . . my head droops on to my chest . . . but my neck seems to be made of cotton wool, it will never bear the weight of my head . . . it will surely break . . . I must relax my neck.

And there you are, my little one, you are done for and, instead of a nice warm plank-bed, a stinking lavatory awaits you at night, and the kitchen awaits you too, which is still worse. And, when you have served your time, you will be given an extra three days, just to teach you not to dream of a nice little slice of black bread, or of dry socks, but, instead, of the policies of our beloved Party, which open before us such bright new horizons. And that is how it goes.

It was not the first time for me—not in the Kiev glasshouse, it is true, but in Kharkov. And there is no real way of distinguishing which of the two is better. Of course, 'communism' in Kharkov is not the same, but a rather more modest affair. But the tank factory is a good deal bigger than that in Kiev and every day half of all the glasshouse inmates are raked in there and it's no picnic. But, when it comes to political training, I have known the ropes for a long time and you won't ever catch me on that score.

At first, I did not think about sleep because I was much too hungry, but I also tried not to think about food either as such dreams made my stomach ache. And there was another thing which had been bothering me from the very start of political training and that was how to change my socks. Those I was wearing had been wet through for six whole days and it made no difference how you put them on. Outside, frost and slush alternate. It's cold to the feet, it's wet . . . I wish I could change my socks . . . Stop! That's a very dangerous thought. One must not think about dry socks! Such thought is pure provocation! It must be promptly driven out, otherwise, one is in very deep water indeed. Now, it seems to me that my feet are completely dry . . . that I had put them on the radiator during the night, although there are no radiators in the glasshouse . . . and that they have dried out during the night. They are so dry now that they won't even bend . . . and now my feet are so warm . . . STOP IT! I'm not asleep! Two hefty lance-corporals, charging through the room, are bearing down on me. Fuck your mother, you bastards, I wasn't asleep! . . . The lance-corporal angrily heaves me aside and continues to carve his way through those seated behind me. Involuntarily, I turn my head to watch him and, the very next moment, realising the danger, I turn it back again. But one moment is enough to take in the faces of those seated behind. All, without exception, were the faces of men crushed by fear. Sheer animal terror and supplication registered in about fifty pairs of eyes. Only one thought registered on all their faces. 'Oh, please don't let it be me!' Probably the same expression had been on my own face a moment before, when I thought the lance-corporals were homing in on me. God, how easy it is to frighten us! How pitiful is a frightened man! To what depths will he sink to save his skin!

Meanwhile, the lance-corporals have caught hold of a pilot officer cadet who sits slouched right in the very corner. This future ace, like a heavy wooden doll with strings instead of joints, wasn't sleeping, he had just switched off completely and was out for the count. And, while the lance-corporals carry this defender of the motherland out along the passage, his head hangs loose like some trinket on a chain. You are wrong, O Air Ace, you should not lose control of yourself! That will not do, little falcon! You weakened and, now, they will put you in number 26 revolutionary ward for a whiff of chlorine and you will soon come to and then you'll go into 25 and, only after all that, they will give you another five days, it's as easy as falling off a log! Hell! Just how long will the first lieutenant go droning on about our beloved Party? No bloody watch, no nothing! Seems like five hours we've been sitting here already and still he can't get it over with! If only I could change my socks, it would be easier to go on sitting here. I can't stand it any more. My head gets heavier by the minute, as if a pair of huge cast-iron dumb-bells had been placed inside it. Only . . . my feet are cold. If only new socks . . . Or even if the lance-corporals would carry away those who have passed out more often—it would make a change, it would relieve the monotony and I might manage to see it through. It would be good to get out into the frost now, or to the petrol refinery, or to the tank works. If only my feet were comfortable.

'ANY QUESTIONS?'

A resounding 'NO' explodes from a hundred throats. It's salvation! It's the end of political training! It's over . . .

Now comes the order! 'Form up for relief . . . you've got one minute and a half.' This means that I must rush, with all the combined might of my body and soul, with all my wish to live, straight for the exit, straight into a doorway choked with the stinking bodies of other dirty inmates like me and, then, heaving them all aside, break out into the corridor. It is very important not to stumble—one would be trampled underfoot since, naturally, everyone wants to live! Racing upstairs seven steps at a time, I must get to the second floor and grab my coat and cap. It is most important to find one's own coat quickly since if, later on, somebody gets yours, which is too small for him he will not be able to get it on and you will soon be caught and get five days for stealing, and the other big ninny will be put in the same ward as you for his sluggishness, and then both of you will have time to find out who is right and who is wrong and whose fists are stronger. Then, with coat and cap in hand, one must crash straight through the upward-rushing stream of inmates desperate to get their own coats and caps, and rush back down. There's already a pile-up at the exit and the lance-corporals are on the look-out for the stragglers. So just launch yourself into the crowd like an ice-breaker—smash, break and crunch. One and a half minutes have nearly expired but you still haven't formed up, you are still not properly dressed, your red star is not yet lined up with your nose, and your cap is still not sitting precisely two fingers above your eyebrows . . . it's no good . . .

The order 'Form up to receive orders' will be given at any moment. Everybody stands tense, ready for a superhuman effort, ready to rush and crash headlong into others, to carry out the order . . . but the first lieutenant hangs back on purpose . . . to test our readiness to be standing to attention in one and a half minutes . . . Is everyone imbued with the importance of the moment? Has everyone screwed himself up into a tight ball? Is everyone so strained that he is ready to gnaw at his neighbours with his teeth? But the first lieutenant's gaze strays off somewhere into a corner, and no one dares to turn his head to find out

what could possibly have attracted the attention of the Deputy
Commander of the Kiev Garrison glasshouse at such a moment
as this. It is a hand which has attracted the first lieutenant's
attention, a dirty hand which has been cleaning lavatories for the
last two weeks and which has not been washed once in all that
time. And at that very moment when the first lieutenant asked
the traditional question 'Any questions?'—the answer to which is
always, as loudly as possible, 'NO QUESTIONS'—this hand
was raised in a distant corner. Now, no one ever asks any
questions in the glasshouse; so much is clear from the very first
moment. And here you are! Just fancy, somebody now wants to
ask a question!

The first lieutenant knows absolutely all the answers to all
possible questions. In addition, he is so mighty and all-powerful
that he can destroy anyone who presumes to disturb his peace
with such impertinence. Even after the report of some First
Secretary of a District Party Committee, no one dares to ask any
questions. And here we have a member of the lower orders
trying to disturb the peace of the Deputy Chief of the Kiev
Garrison glasshouse himself!

The first lieutenant is clearly very interested by this phenomenon, the more so since he sees that it is not the inmate's first day
in the glasshouse and that he must fully realise the degree of risk
to which he is exposing himself and all those who, like himself,
are under arrest.

The first lieutenant is a psychologist and he certainly realises
full well why this officer-cadet with the hollow eyes, an expert
in electronics, is taking such a risk: clearly he has only one or
two days left to serve in the glasshouse but, if he is then sent to
the tank factory, of course he will not be able to fulfil his norms
and will surely be given another five days, which could trans-
form him permanently into an oppressed, humiliated, intimidated
semi-idiot. It is conceivable that his service and his career will
even be furthered by such an ineluctable process, but this is not
what the officer-cadet wants nor what he is ready to take any risk
to avoid. He has obviously decided to ask his question simply in
order to flatter the first lieutenant and thus to secure for himself a
timely discharge. But it is not an easy matter to flatter the
omnipotent! And if that flattery is taken exception to as being
crude flattery . . . ? So then, the flattery, in the form of a
question, must clearly combine within itself something very

original and must even verge upon the permissive . . . And well
we all knew it!

'What do you want?' the first lieutenant enquired politely,
thus emphasising his respect for the bravery on display.

'Officer-cadet Antonov, arrested for fifteen days and thirteen
of them already served,' he reported efficiently. 'Comrade First
Lieutenant, I have a question!' A sinister silence descended upon
the room. We had all been waiting for this moment, but the
unusual impertinence of it struck us all very forcefully. It was as
if a fly, after having warmed itself on the hot stove, were to dive
down on us from the ceiling with the thunderous boom of a
strategic bomber. We shuddered and hid our heads in our shoulders, as if trying to soften the blow, if sheer unadulterated rage
descended upon any head in that room.

'Put your question . . .'—and then, as an afterthought, the
first lieutenant added, 'Please.'

'Comrade First Lieutenant, tell me, please . . . will there be
any glasshouses under communism?'

My shoulders cringed, and my head sank down even lower. I
was not the only one who expected a pole-axe in the neck. Only
the man who had asked the question stood there, proud and
straight, his sunken breast thrust forward and looking, with those
intelligent grey eyes of his, straight into the eyes of the omnipotent one. The latter was thoughtful for a while, then his thick lips
parted in an almost childlike smile. He obviously enjoyed the
question. Mischievous lights caught fire in his eyes and he
pronounced the words with complete conviction and faith! 'There
will always be a glasshouse!' Whereupon, he burst out laughing.
The omnipotent one looked once more at the electronics expert
and then added heartily, 'Good lad! And now . . . and now . . .
at the double . . . to the lavatories, and see to it that before
evening comes they shine like a cat's testicles!' Hundreds of
throats sighed with envy at the very thought. 'Right you are,
Comrade,' he responded joyfully.

And can anything better than that ever be invented. It is true
that, after morning high-speed 'jobs time', the lavatory is a
pretty filthy place but, in two or three hours, it can easily be
licked clean enough to be proud of it. And then . . . and then,
throughout the whole day, just pretend that you are improving on
what has already been done. After all, it is not that bottomless,
stinking pit of communism itself! Oh, no! Not that! This is only
a lavatory when all is said and done. It's only at night that it's

not very pleasant to clean it, because that's instead of sleeping, but during the day, in the warmth and in comfort . . .

'Form up for duty detail, you've got one minute and a half!'

With the weight of my whole body I lurched forward.

That was a wonderful day, and I was lucky for, as one of a small group of inmates, I found myself in the regional Military Hospital lugging about bales of dirty linen. Our escort was a fourth-year artilleryman who had obviously been in the glass-house himself more than once. And when, late in the evening, he gave us a ten-minute break and we sat about on ice-covered logs of wood leaning our weary backs up against the warm walls of the furnace, and a tender-hearted, sprightly nurse from the skin-venereal department brought us a whole box of chewed scraps of wonderful white bread, we ate them with delight. I am quite incapable of describing the ecstasy of that unforgettable day. But I, for one, am sure that each of us, in that moment, thought only of that brave officer-cadet, about the risk he had taken upon himself, about the exactness of the psychological calculation he had made and, in general, about the limitless possibilities of the human mind.

April 1967. The final days before graduation from the Kharkov Guards Tank Commanders' School.

Ever Ready!

THE BOOTS SHONE so that you could have used them as shaving mirrors and the trousers were so well pressed that, if a fly had brushed against the crease, it would have been sliced in two. We were to take over as town patrol and our outward appearance was checked personally by Colonel Yeremeyev, the Military Commandant of Kharkov. And he didn't like jokes! The smallest fault in one's uniform meant ten days under arrest. Everyone had long been acquainted with this as being the accepted norm. And now the Colonel was giving his briefing. 'In conclusion, the productivity norms: railway station—150 convictions; town part—120; airport—80; the remainder—60 each.' The Colonel here omitted to mention the main point, but there was no need, as everybody knew that those guilty of under-fulfilment were not relieved at 2400 hours, as prescribed, but were sent out on the 'bigger round', that is to say on all-night duty; and if, towards morning, the patrol did not get another thirty convictions, then it was the glasshouse for them all and yesterday's patrol would find itself in the same wards where the earlier victims of this very same patrol were already sitting. All this was well known and there was no need to remind anyone of the facts. Norms are scientifically based, and are verified in practice over many years' experience. Well then, our objectives were clear! Our tasks had been clearly defined! So now, get to work, Comrades!

Our patrol consisted of three men: Captain Sadirov and two officer-cadets in their last year. Our tour of duty would last a total of 480 minutes. We would be relieved at 2400 hours. Our quota was sixty offenders, or one arrest every eight minutes. In other words, any military man we met must be guilty of something. So if, during these eight hours, we only manage to find fifty-nine soldiers, seamen, sergeants, warrant-officers and officers, then a 'bigger round' was guaranteed and, at night, where on earth are you supposed to catch another thirty men?

The success of patrol work depends to a large extent on the character of the patrol chief himself. If he is strict enough and resourceful enough then the quota can be fulfilled.

'Comrade Sergeant, you are breaking regulations on the correct form of dress.'

'No, comrade Captain.' Everything the sergeant has on is shining, and there is obviously nothing to quibble at.

'In the first place, you are arguing with the head of the patrol and, secondly, the top button of your tunic shows the symbol of Soviet power facing the wrong way. Show me your papers!'

And it was a fact that the shining button, with its hammer and sickle, within a five-pointed star, was sewn on rather unevenly, or possibly it was not sewn quite firmly enough and had got loose and, as a result, the hammer was not facing upwards as it should but slightly sideways. You could catch anyone on this pretext, even the Minister of Defence himself. How can one possibly ensure that all buttons have their hammers unfailingly straight up? The captain then scrawled on the sergeant's pass in bold letters: 'Leave cancelled at 1604 hours, owing to crude violation of the rules of dress and for arguing with a patrol.' I wrote down the sergeant's name and unit number, and the offender saluted the captain and set off for his unit. Now the sergeant was completely defenceless since his pass was no longer valid and if he was stopped by another patrol on his way back to his unit he might be clobbered with 'absence without leave'.

We caught the first one in four minutes, so during the remaining 476 minutes we had to catch another fifty-nine.

'Comrade Private, you are breaking regulations on dress.'

'No, Comrade Captain, I am not.'

'Comrade Private, you are arguing with a patrol chief!'

'No, Comrade Captain, I am not arguing, I only wanted to say that I am not breaking regulations on form of dress.'

'Guards Officer-Cadet Suvorov!'

'Here!'

'Call the duty car—this is a serious offender!'

While my fellow cadet wrote down the name of the serious offender and the captain was catching yet another, I ran to the nearest telephone box. Yes, the sergeant was more experienced, he shut his mouth before uttering the second sentence, but the little soldier was still a bit green. And that is why you, my little darling, will be taken away with honour in a car any moment now. I ran back from the telephone and saw that, beside the serious offender, there already stood a pilot officer-cadet guilty of 'sloppy saluting'. Sixteen minutes of our tour of duty gone and three offenders already in the bag, I hoped it continued that way.

'Comrade Warrant-Officer, your peak is not two fingers from your eyebrows!'

'No, Comrade Captain, it's exactly two fingers.'

'You are arguing! Your papers!'

There was no time for boredom with our captain. He was a fine fellow and no mistake. But what was that there in the bushes? Surely it was a dead-drunk defender of the Motherland? It was indeed! There were some stunted shrubs between the street and the pavement, and in their midst had fallen an inebriated warrior. Tunic unbuttoned, right shoulder-strap torn off and chest, trousers and boots all covered in vomit, there he was, completely filthy, his cap long since vanished. We turned him over on to his back. Oh, what bad luck! He was an officer-cadet of our own beloved tank school, a guardsman like myself. We never lay a finger on one of our own. There is intense socialist competition between all units of the garrison! One cannot ever let down one's own school. Air force, artillery and all the others—be on your guard—but not one of our boys! He had just drunk a bit too much. Who doesn't do the same sometimes? A car, summoned from our school, took the drunken tankman away. He was not included in the statistics, of course, he did not count, and anyway he was taken home merely to prevent him from freezing to death or catching cold. You see, the ground was cold because it wasn't summertime.

'Comrade Lieutenant, you are breaking regulations on dress.' The lieutenant obediently kept silent. He was literate, this one.

'Your gloves, Comrade Lieutenant, are black, they should be brown!'

'Yes, you are right, I am guilty, Comrade Captain.'

'Papers!'

Our own captain's gloves were also black. Where can one possibly find brown gloves? Gloves are not issued to officers, because the industry does not in any case produce brown ones. Officers are given money to buy their own gloves. Buy them yourselves, but unfortunately there is nowhere to buy them. I repeat, Soviet industry does not produce any brown gloves. Anyone who has served in Germany would have bought at least twenty pairs, a life-time's supply. And anyone who has never served in Germany is prey to the patrols. Before going on duty, all officers are issued personally by Colonel Yeremeyev with a pair of brown leather gloves for which they sign, to wear, temporarily, while on duty. But these gloves are so well worn, tattered and out of shape, that it would be indecent for an officer to wear them. This is why our captain immediately took them off and folded them tidily and put them in his pocket. God forbid that he should lose them!

'And why are you breaking the regulations, Comrade Lieutenant. Does an order of the Minister of Defence not concern you?'

'I am sorry.'

'You may go!'

'Right!'

This lieutenant's name also graced our book of statistics. When the time comes for the lieutenant to enter the academy, the top brass will look at his personal file. Oh, heavens, he has been stopped by patrols a hundred times in one year and on each occasion for the same violation! He is incorrigible! He should be locked up! And you recommend him for the academy! Use your brains, man!

'Comrade Senior Lieutenant, you are breaking regulations on dress . . . Your gloves are black. Or maybe you did not read the order of the Minister of Defence? Well then, why do you break it? Is it deliberate? Does it spring from a love of violating rules?' The captain took off one of his own black gloves and wrote down in his black book the name of the senior lieutenant.

There were two hours and seventeen minutes left before we were to be relieved. There were sixty-one offenders in the black book. In the darkness, obviously quite oblivious to us and humming something under his breath, a dead-drunk artilleryman was staggering all over the place and our captain somehow managed not to notice him.

'Request permission, Comrade Captain, to arrest this God of War.'

'Oh no, let him be, he's in the 62nd and always remember this, Suvorov, the target must be passed, but only minimally. This is the law of our life. It's time you understood that norms are scientifically based and verified many times over by life itself. In a couple of months, we will be on patrol again, and then they'd make it not 60 but 65 or even as many as 70 offenders. And you just go and try making it 70. The existing norms are the direct result of the work of the ninnies like you who tried too hard to overreach the target, and now these same ninnies are themselves being caught by patrols, that's what.'

The lucky artilleryman, quite without noticing us, staggered off. If all the patrols in his path had already slightly overshot their targets, he might quietly drift along right through town along all the main streets, drunk, unbuttoned and dirty with that fixed insolent, intoxicated expression on his face. Meanwhile, the number of drunken and half-drunk soldiers, officer-cadets and sergeants continued to grow. The vast majority had long since cottoned on to the advantages of the planned system and hid their faces until evening. The feeling was that control weakened simultaneously in all districts of the town. All patrols tried to fulfil their plans as soon as possible in order to insure themselves against the 'bigger round', and that was why everything had changed. The most experienced villains and alcoholics used this 'release of tension' for their own, far from noble, purposes. From 2400 hours onwards, all of them, even those who were paralytically drunk, put their tails between their legs precisely because they knew that the stupidest, most inept patrols, for whom a whole day was not even long enough to catch anybody, were now out on the prowl.

In spite of the growing flood of real offenders, drunks and hooligans, we had absolutely nothing to do and here we were sitting on a bench under the bare leafless willows. The captain instructed us on the tactics of the German tank forces. After all, the passing-out examinations were not very far off.

'Tactics, brothers, are the most complicated subject on earth. But just tell our generals that tactics are more complicated than chess and they laugh their heads off, they simply don't believe it. But it's really no laughing matter. Chess is the crudest form, the most superficial model of a battle between two armies and the most primitive of armies at that. In all other respects, it's exactly like war. A king is helpless and lacks mobility but his loss signifies complete defeat. A king is the exact personification of headquarters staff, cumbersome and lacking in mobility—so just destroy them and it's checkmate. The queen is the intelligence service, in the fullest sense of the word—an all-powerful and invincible intelligence service, capable of acting independently with lightning speed, and thwarting the enemy's plans. Knight, bishop and castle require no commentary. The likeness is very great, especially when it comes to the cavalry. Think of the battle of Borodino and the cavalry raid carried out by Uvarov and Platov on Bonaparte's rear. That was 'knight's gambit' for you in both meaning and form. Just you look at the map! The Russian cavalry neither fought nor charged, but simply appeared in the rear and that was that, but their appearance stopped Bonaparte from sending his guard into battle. And in many respects this one move decided both the battle and the whole destiny of Russia. And that was knight's gambit for you.

'A contemporary battle,' continued the captain 'is a thousand times more complicated than chess. If you want to model a small contemporary army on a chess-board, the number of chess-men, with all kinds of different capabilities will have to be sharply increased. Somehow, you will need to designate tanks, anti-tank rockets, anti-tank artillery and artillery, pure and simple, an air force including fighters, low-flying attack planes, strategic bombers, air transport and helicopters—you just can't list them all . . . and all demand a united plan, a united strategy and the closest possible co-ordination. Our misfortune, and the main difference between us and the Germans, consists in our habit of counting our bishops and pawns, with total disregard for their competent deployment. And, you know, the Germans started the war against us with a paltry three thousand tanks against our eighteen thousand. Now, we propound many different versions, but we refuse to accept the main conclusion, which is that German tactics were much more flexible than ours. Mark my words—if something happens in the Near East, we will be smashed to smithereens; they won't give a damn for quantitative and qualitative superiority. What's the good of having three queens, if you don't know how to play chess? And our advisers simply cannot play, and that's a fact. Look at the Head of Faculty, Colonel Soloukhin, just back from Syria . . .'

'But how so?' I could not refrain from asking.

The captain looked at me and then slowly said: 'It's the system itself that's at fault.'

The answer obviously did not fully satisfy us and so he added, 'Firstly, our chiefs are appointed on the basis of their political qualifications, they don't know how the game is played or even wish to learn how to play it but they're ideologically well-groomed. Secondly, our system demands the rendering of accounts, reports, and achievements. Upon this we stand! The reports which announced the destruction of thousands of German tanks and aircraft during the first days of the war were so phoney that the political leadership of the country changed to quoting territorial indices instead, as being more convincing. This gave birth to reports of the capture of towns and mountain tops and such like. But you just try playing chess without annihilating the enemy's army, but by capturing his territory, regardless of your own losses! What will happen? The same as happened to us during the war. We won only because we showed no pity for millions of our own pawns. If our General Staff and military advisers take it into their heads to seize Israeli territory instead of first annihilating their army, it will cost us very dear indeed. Of course, the Jews won't achieve checkmate, but the annihilation of Israel by our tactics will still cost us dear. And it will be worst of all if, God forbid, we ever come up against China. In that case, our pawns won't help us at all because they have many more pawns at their own disposal.'

Here the captain spat angrily and kicked an empty tin can with the toe of his varnished boot. The can rolled along the dark pathway under the feet of a well-oiled sapper who was making advances to a young girl. The silent struggle in the darkness apparently reminded the captain that we were still on patrol. He yawned and abruptly changed the subject.

'Guards Officer-Cadet Suvorov, your conclusions please about today's patrol duty. Quickly!'

I was slightly taken aback.

'A tank commander must instantly evaluate the situation. Well? Your conclusions?'

'Uh-h, we arrested many offenders . . . Uh-h, we have improved discipline . . . thanks to you . . .' I tried, awkwardly, to interlace the flattery.

'You haven't a clue, Viktor, and you a future lieutenant, or don't you want to understand . . . or else you are just plain cunning. Listen—but it's only between the two of us. In a fully planned economy, terror also can only be a planned affair, i.e. absolutely idiotic and ineffective, this is the first point. Secondly, we have been working today according to the methods of the second five-year-plan, that is to say the methods of 1937 and 1938, the only difference being that we didn't actually arrest or shoot the offenders. Thirdly, if today the order were given to repeat the second five-year-plan, then not only the organs of State Security, but every armed man, even every ordinary Soviet citizen, would rush headlong to carry out this order: that is how we have been trained and we are ever ready. And fourthly . . . you and I too, Viktor, for that matter, are not insured against these bloody five-year-plans . . . we have absolutely no insurance . . . If the order were given tomorrow, everything would start all over again—the Berias, the Yezhovs, the NKVD, etc . . . It's just that, for the present, we have a completely spineless General Secretary in charge . . . but only for the moment! But supposing he's replaced tomorrow? . . . What then? Okay, don't get upset, let's go . . . our tour of duty is over for today.'

'Comrade Captain, maybe after all we should drive off that sapper, otherwise he'll rape her, sure as eggs is eggs!'

'Tomorrow she'll complain, that it was a soldier, and on our patrol route too,' added my other comrade, hoping to give weight to my remark.

'But this is still no concern of ours,' he smiled, and pointed to the luminous dial of his watch. We smiled too—the watch showed 0004 hours.

Kharkov 1967.

Theatre

BEFORE THE ARRIVAL in Severodvinsk of Marshal of the Soviet Union Grechko, the high command of the Northern Fleet decided to paint the shore-line cliffs grey. In all, over twenty kilometres of coastline were painted. The sailors of two whole divisions and the men of a marines regiment laboured over this titanic work for several weeks and, in the process, used up the whole allocation of anti-corrosion paint supplied to the entire fleet for a whole year. The Minister liked the colour of the rocks, and from that time forth the painting of rocks before the arrival of a high-ranking commander became one of the more remarkable traditions of our Fleet.

Before the arrival of Marshal of the Soviet Union Chuikov at the Moscow Higher Combined Arms School, the School Commander decided to level up all the pine-trees along the 'Golden Kilometre'—the woodland road leading towards the school—using caterpillar tank tractors.

Before the visit of Marshal of the Soviet Union Sokolov to the Fifth Army of the Far Eastern Military District, more than 500 portraits of the Marshal were hung about the walls of the barracks of that Army's mobile rocket-technical base.

The history of our glorious army records tens of thousands of such examples, here I quote but a few of those seen with my own eyes. The system itself is to blame. That is how our army is organised. And don't think that it's only marshals who are greeted with such joy. Any major from a neighbouring division, who comes to make some check-up or other, is given the same hospitable reception. We are all trained to expect it and we cannot live otherwise. All is boiling energy, turbulent fantasy, and the rare qualities and abilities of the majority of all Soviet officers and generals are squandered on outdoing their competitors in the hospitality stakes. Rarely does one come across a general who is not keen on such displays. But our army is a huge one and exceptions do occur. I knew one such general, a freethinker who considered the painting of grass with green paint, if not idiotic, then at least as not being his paramount task. The Head of the Tank Training School, Major-General Slukin never once appeared either at the tank training ground, the armoured troop carrier training ground, or at the artillery range. Underwater tank manoeuvres, firing practice, the battle training of tank platoons and companies he considered as being work for dumb soldiers and an unnecessary waste of time. Our general was sold on culture and considered it his duty to implant in future officers something rather higher than mere military science.

At the same time it must also be said that, as a general rule, in Soviet military schools and academies, culture is neither cultivated, taught, nor implanted in any form. And it was this very gap that our chief tried to fill. The trouble was that his notions about culture were rather peculiar. He considered, for example, that a cultured man is only one who regularly goes to the theatre and that the number of such visits defines the degree of one's culture. Literature, painting, sculpture, architecture and so on were totally beyond the general's sphere of vision. The Theatre and nothing but the Theatre! It does not matter which, as long as it is a theatre. The general's only care was a register of personal attendances.

The life of an officer-cadet at tank school is exceptionally arduous. Anyone who has experienced, if only once, what it means to load forty-three projectiles into a tank, to change a tank-track (which weighs one and a half tons), or just to sit for three hours behind the controls of a T-55, will understand to the full what it is really like to spend four years at a tank training school. But, when all is said and done, the hardest ordeal of all for us was still the theatre. And we were obliged to attend it at least once a month. The whole school had to attend, to the joy of all those theatres which were going bankrupt and were usually never patronised by anybody. And, for this very reason, the Political Directorate of our Military District loved our general very much and always quoted him as an example; and it was no joke either as our school alone provided the district with 12,000 'man-attendances' per year. This was really something to be proud of, even if there was complete failure in all other areas.

Attendance was carried out herd-fashion, in formation, with colours flying and music playing. In front of the theatre, the general assembled the whole school (a thousand officer-cadets) at attention and yelled his instructions into a megaphone so loudly that they could be heard three blocks away. 'Inside the theatre . . . No spitting on the floor! No spitting in the corners! This is a theatre! Don't blow your noses on your sleeves! Use your handkerchieves! . . . And most important . . . No swearing! I expressly forbid it! If I hear any at all, I will put you on a charge! This is a theatre!'

When we marched to the theatre for the first time, thousands of people came running out to feast their eyes upon the spectacle of these dashing defenders of the Motherland—these future officers. But after they had heard the loudly-shouted instructions, they did not know where to look for the shame of it. We meanwhile were all standing to attention, not daring to move a single muscle. The rumours about us soon spread throughout the town. Formerly, no tank officer-cadet was known in the town otherwise than as 'Guderian' after the German tank commander, but now we earned for ourselves a new honorary title—'Snotty' —and the name stuck. No sooner did any officer-cadet appear anywhere, than there were shouts of 'Don't blow your nose on your sleeve'. Attendances at the theatre continued, accompanied by the obligatory instructions. But now, when people heard the roll of the drums and the measured tread of our boots, they fled instantly, expressly in order not to witness this disgraceful spectacle.

One night, after the usual theatre visit, I was awakened by my friend Genka Bulakov. It was probably two o'clock in the morning but the lad simply could not get to sleep, in spite of the accumulated tiredness of the previous week.

'Viktor! Please explain to me . . .'

'What do you want?'

'There is one thing I simply can't understand, I mean . . . our general . . . Of course, he is a cultured fellow, far better than other generals . . . But I cannot understand one thing . . . Why, every time, in front of the theatre, does he have to shout like that into his bloody megaphone? He could give us those instructions back at the school. What the hell does he have to shout at the top of his voice for? We know his instructions by heart and so do all the locals.'

'In the old days it would have been considered an insult.'

'Pull the other one!'

'No. In the old days, he most certainly would have been challenged to a duel . . .'

'Go on! Do you think I never read Kuprin?* I did, you know. But I still never came across any cases of cadets challenging generals to duels. Of course, it would not be a bad idea, at that, to challenge him to a duel and to shoot at him with armour-piercing shells. General he may be, and a cultured chap at that, but I bet he would fuck up shooting, on the move, with a low-energy release shell with double stabilisations. I would be the first to challenge him to a duel myself . . . But what you say is all tripe and never happened . . . and never could happen either.'

To tell the truth, I did not know for sure myself whom, and under what circumstances, one could challenge to a duel, and I had not come across any examples of such incidents in literature. So, then, I just expressed my own feelings.

'Of course, one could not challenge generals to duels over things of that kind, and I personally think it was because cultured generals did not exist in those days. None of the generals then was ever interested in the theatre, and that is why nobody

---

*The descendant of a Tartar Khan, called Kuprya, Kuprin served as an infantry officer in the Tsarist army. He wrote several novels highlighting the negative sides of the private life of the officer corps. The most well-known and biased was his novel entitled *Duel*. After the Revolution, Kuprin lived as an émigré in France.

challenged them to duels . . . The army only became cultured after the victory of Soviet power . . . It's a pity, though, that duels were forbidden then.'

'Yes, it's a pity,' mumbled Genka, falling asleep.

PART TWO

Summer 1967. The Ukraine.

Operation 'Dnieper'

ON THE DAY after our passing-out evening celebration, all two hundred of us young lieutenants, the latest graduates of the Kharkov Guards Tank Commander School, were formed up on the parade ground and an order from the Minister of Defence concerning our re-training for our new battle techniques was read out to us. Usually, after passing-out celebrations, young officers are given a month's leave, after which time, in accordance with the Minister's order, they go to join their division or regiment and are thus scattered throughout the whole world, from Havana to South Sakhalinsk, wherever the Minister orders. And now this tradition of many years' standing had been broken, owing to the simple fact that a new tank, the T-64, had been introduced into service in the Soviet Army some few months before our graduation. Before our graduation, there had not been enough time for detailed study. As it was, our curriculum was already overloaded with other subjects. And so it was decided to re-train all young officers, but from one tank school only, rather than from all five; and not to distribute the re-trained officers over the whole vast expanse of our territory, but to confine them to those divisions and districts which are habitually re-armed first.

It should here be mentioned that the very newest battle technology is always introduced first to the troops of the second line of defence, that is to those of the Baltic, Byelorussian and Carpathian Military Districts, and most certainly not to the Group of Soviet Forces in Germany or to any other troops stationed abroad. New technology is only introduced in such places after five to eight, and sometimes more, years after its adoption in frontier districts. Our T-64 first appeared in Germany exactly ten years after it began to be mass produced. And at the time of the first mention in the West of this tank, as a new Soviet experimental tank, its mass production had in fact long since ceased altogether—it was being replaced by the new T-72s.

This system has several aims. First, it greatly increases secrecy and, in case of war, it puts the enemy at a great disadvantage. Secondly, it facilitates the sale of obsolete technology to our allies, from Poland to the Arabs. In this way, the technology available to the Group of Soviet Troops in Germany can be made out to be of the very latest design.

Never before, at the introduction of a new tank into service, had young officers been kept back for re-training, which was formerly done at divisional level as a part of everyday service. This is understandable: all previous tanks, from the T-44 to the T-62, represent the continuation of one line of development, in that each successive model retained, in its construction, many elements possessed by the previous model, and, therefore, re-training was a comparatively uncomplicated process. Now, this line of development had been exploited to the full and the new T-64 was based on entirely new principles. Everything in it, from its general lay-out, to stabilizers, optics, signals and drive, was unusual and completely new, and, as it turned out later, also totally unreliable.

The study of the new techniques, equipment, electronics and tank's armament took four and a half months—from 1 June to 15 October, 1967. At the end of September, we had to take part in large-scale manoeuvres and to put into practice our newly-acquired skills and abilities. We had to postpone our leave until October.

The process of introducing new battle techniques into an army is always a secret. Dracoian measures are taken to stop any details connected with this process from being leaked. Simultaneously, all official channels disseminate false information. For instance, at a parade, or during special show exercises, something which is absolutely contrary to actual practice may be demonstrated.

That same day, in the evening, as we stood to attention, an order was read out to us prohibiting young officers from wearing officers' uniform during re-training: only tank-crew overalls were to be worn. Tank-crew overalls in our army are standard issue and carry no badge or rank, with the result that a soldier is indistinguishable from an officer. This is an old tradition of ours, born of war. The order seemed merely to indicate a means of camouflage and there was nothing strange about that. The odd part emerged a bit later. It turned out that over a hundred re-engaged men, all instructor-drivers, were going with us. For a mere two hundred pupils, a hundred instructors were out of all proportion. Seventy would have been enough for the whole school, for all thousand officer-cadets. And yet they had assembled the school's entire complement of instructors, thus, for all practical purposes, arresting completely the whole training programme throughout the school; in addition to which, many more instructors had been sent directly from the Kharkov Malyshev Works, which officially produced railway locomotives and, unofficially, also tanks. The fact that instructors had been brought straight from the works was absolutely inexplicable. Clearly, they must be desperately needed there, if mass production of a new tank had started.

A second inexplicable factor was that our own supervisors were not going with us. The teaching process normally proceeds as follows: a lieutenant colonel, the supervisor, explains the theory, after which instructor-sergeants, under his control, give practical instruction. But there were too many instructors and not a single supervisor!

A third surprise awaited us in the train itself. After our departure, a secret order was read out in all carriages, announcing the formation of the 100th Guards Tank Training Regiment. The Deputy Commander of the School, who read us this order, introduced to us the young Colonel of the newly-formed regiment. It was also announced that the regiment would have ninety-two battle tanks and nineteen battle-training tanks.

It was dead of night as the train wended its way along the track, making a lulling knocking noise on the rails. But no one was sleeping. And there was good reason for this: as a new regiment has been formed, then, a colour must be presented to it,

the more so since it was a Guards regiment, all of which made
the ceremony of the presentation of the colour all the more
momentous. According to regulations, a new Guards colour must
be received by the whole regiment on its knees, but, in this
instance, nothing of the kind was happening. And, secondly,
why so many tanks for a training regiment? Thirty to forty
training tanks would have been quite enough, and battle tanks
were not even needed in the first place.

On the sly, every kind of hypothesis, on what all this meant,
was being advanced. Some suggested that we might be sent to
the Arabs, where the situation was daily worsening with lightning speed.

'It would be great, brothers, to go abroad at least once in our
lifetime. To Poland or even to the Egypt place.'

'A hen is not a bird and Poland is not abroad! But to visit the
GDR or Egypt, that, of course, would be interesting. Only now,
with this new T-64, we will not be going abroad for five years at
the very least.'

'Perhaps we really are going to help the Arabs?'

'They don't need any help! Did you read how many tanks they
have? Well! . . . And which type . . . know what I mean? . . .
Of course, they're not T-62s, but neither are they Shermans like
those used by the Jews.'

'And they also have thousands of our advisers and all the war
plans are worked out by our own General Staff.'

'Oh! They'll knock hell out of the Jews. I even feel sorry for
them.'

'Better pity their poor balls! Pity, my foot!'

'How long will the war last?'

'Three to four days—no more than that. It shouldn't take long
to overrun the whole of Israel with tanks. The Jews are surrounded on all sides and, if the war does drag on for a week,
they'll have to surrender. As they'll be surrounded on all sides
and blockaded by sea, they'll soon run out of food!'

'But I heard, lads, that the Arabs are bloody awful soldiers!'

'Do you think the Jews are any better? They'll scatter at the
first shots.'

'And that's a fact!'

'In America, they're already singing requiems for the Jews.'

'Don't be in too much of a hurry to celebrate victory. Unless
the UN troops are recalled from their positions and stop separat-
ing Jews from Arabs, there won't be any victory at all.'

'Never mind, our people will cook up something in that case.'

'I hope the UN troops will be removed as soon as possible, and then the comedy can really start!'

'And the golden rain of orders and medals will pour down on the heads of our advisers! There won't really be a war. We will just overrun this Israel place with our tanks and there you are, we'll be heroes overnight.'

'What is there to overrun anyway, the whole of Israel is smaller than one of our larger firing grounds!'

At this, everybody burst out laughing, although it was really no joke. In the Soviet Union, there are indeed many army firing ranges which exceed in size not only Israel but also some of her warlike neighbours into the bargain.

'And now go to sleep, lads!'

'Oh, we graduated too late. At least half those who graduated from our school last year were sent to the Arabs as advisers. Even at this minute, they're probably making holes in their tunics for the medals they're bound to receive. That's the only real preparation needed for a war like this!'

Next night, in the pouring rain, we disembarked at a small country station somewhere in the Chernigov Province. A column of lorries covered in with tarpaulins was waiting for us. After another three hours, in the haze which precedes dawn and in the midst of the warm mist, we disembarked once again close to our tents, in the forest.

What we saw before us at daybreak both surprised and puzzled us. The sight recreated visions of Batyy's* hordes at the time of his last stand before the gates of Kiev. As far as the eye could see, along the length of the forest clearings, stood the serried ranks of green tents. Here and there, small glades could be seen, and beyond them there were endless rows of marquees hidden under camouflage netting. Canvas, canvas, canvas stretching to the horizon and beyond in all directions. There were tens and maybe even hundreds of thousands of people: artillerymen, rocket men, anti-aircraft gunners, combat engineers, infantry men and commandos. Where the hell were we? What was this army all around us and what was its purpose?

Just behind us were the regular canvas rows belonging to some motorised infantry regiment—probably a show regiment, or so-

---

*A famous Tartar Khan.

called 'court regiment', where all the soldiers speak only Russian. All infantrymen invariably possess insolent faces as well as insolent tongues.

'Did you hear, brothers, about the new decree, that new coins are to be minted to celebrate the Anniversary of Soviet Power?'

'Yes, we heard!'

'We must lay in a stock of these coins—after the new revolution, these coins will be very valuable.'

Whereupon, unanimous laughter exploded from the infantry's smoking quarters.

In our life, we hear anti-Soviet remarks every day and at every turn. But, never before had we ever heard conversation of this type carried on so blatantly and in front of such a large assembly of strangers. During breakfast, we decided to send a small delegation to the infantry to explain to them, cautiously, that we were not simple soldiers but were in fact officers, only without our insignia of rank. In this way, we could suppress, at the very start, all attempts at familiarity.

I was on that delegation. The infantry greeted us with enthusiastic cries of welcome.

'The armour is strong and our tanks are fast, and our men—ah, our men, there is no need to speak of them!'*

'The infantry salute the tank men!'

'Give the tank men something to drink!' ordered a tall, slender soldier. Whereupon about thirty soldiers' flasks stretched out from all sides in our direction. But we were in a serious mood and turned down their invitation. Have you ever seen any officer drinking with soldiers and lance-corporals?

'Comrades,' Lieutenant Okhrimenko, the head of our delegation began severely, 'although we have no badges of rank, we are none the less officers!'

This remark was greeted by a friendly roar of laughter.

'And who do you think we are?'

'We also are officers!'

'Only wearing soldiers' shoulder-straps!'

'May we introduce ourselves, the Kiev Higher All-Arms Commanders School. Two hundred freshly baked lieutenants!'

'On your right are graduates of the Poltava Higher Anti-Aircraft Artillery School—one hundred and eighty lieutenants in all.'

---

*A quotation from a soldiers' song.

'And further down there is the Ryazan Higher Airborne Troops School.'

'So let's have a drink! After all!'

So we did.

'But, little falcons, what are you doing here?' we asked.

'It's known officially as re-training for new battle techniques but unofficially as a "big show" in honour of the glorious jubilee of our beloved Soviet Power.'

We drank some more. It doesn't go down too well in the morning but, nevertheless, we knocked it back.

So that was it! A grandiose spectacle was being organised in honour of the fiftieth anniversary, and we were taking part in it. We were to provide the crowd scenes for the film.

'It's going to be ballet like no one's seen before. And there'll be more troops than ever before.'

'Every kind of secret technology'll be on display.'

'The front-line troops will be two divisions made up entirely of young officers and instructors. The back-up divisions will be manned by officer-cadets in their last year, all men within five minutes of becoming officers.'

'There'll be specially selected soldiers, just to raise a cloud of dust on the horizon and create the illusion of vast numbers.'

'And we were told that it was a re-training exercise!'

'So were we! And we've been given a wonder-machine, the Infantry Battle Machine, the BMP-1, you may have heard about it?'

Our spirits fell abruptly, in spite of the amount of vodka we had drunk. For we knew only too well what a show turn-out is like, and what the training involves, especially for one designed to fête such a great jubilee.

That same night, the first sub-units of the 120th Guards Rogachev Motorised Infantry Division, the 'court' division of the Commander of the Byelorussian Military District, started to arrive in camp. Every district has something similar: in the Moscow district it is the 2nd Guards Taman' Motorised Infantry Division and the Kantemirov Tank Division, in the Carpathian District the 24th Iron Samaro-Ul'yanovsk Motorised Infantry Division, in Kiev the 41st Guards Tank Division. All these divisions exist solely for show. They only know parades, demonstrations, solemn visits by foreign guests, guards of honour, and they have no battle training whatsoever. All these 'court' divisions— and there are nine of them in the Soviet Army—are absolutely incapable of fighting. But they are kept always at full strength, with 12,000 men in each, which represents 108,000 of the very best soldiers and officers in all the Soviet land forces. And on this occasion, for this unparalleled peep-show, it was found necessary to reinforce even the 'court' divisions with newly-fledged officers as well.

Next day, the reforming of troops intended for the main action was carried out. Somewhere, near at hand, was located the field headquarters of the 38th Army. For Operation 'Dnieper', the composition of this army was strengthened by the addition of the 41st Guards Tank, the 79th, 120th, 128th Guards Motorised Infantry and the 24th Iron Motorised Division, the N-rocket brigade, the N-Guards artillery brigade, the N-anti-aircraft rocket brigade, the N-tank destroyer artillery regiment and the many other support sub-units including an army mobile rocket-technical base, an army mobile anti-aircraft rocket base, two liaison regiments, a pontoon-bridge regiment, as well as some sapper and CW battalions. In addition, several motorised infantry battalions representing penal battalions were included. The use of these battalions either in war or during training requires neither knowledge nor practice: the Army Commander merely hurls them into the very thick of battle, where artillery is useless, or into those areas which have not been reconnoitred. As a general rule, such battalions are deployed for one battle only. For the next battle there are other battalions, composed of other *shtrafniki*.* On this particular occasion, separate motorised infantry battalions were recruited not from *shtrafniki* but from young officers, wearing soldiers' uniform.

Alongside our 38th Army, a further three armies were being raised. Taken together, the four armies represented the 1st Ukrainian front, itself a part of the 'Eastern' forces.

On the right bank, the 'Western' forces were forming up. Troops and battle armaments continued to pour in. Every day, every night, every hour. During preparations for Operation 'Dnieper', the Soviet Army, to all intents, completely lost its combat preparedness. Judge for yourself. To build up only one show division, over 10,000 officers were required—because offi-

---

*Members of penal battalions, virtually condemned to certain death by the impossible nature of the task allotted to them.

cers were cast in the role of ordinary soldiers. And where can such a multitude be gathered? Even every graduate from every military school and academy would not have been sufficient. And, for this reason, it was decided in addition to call upon the majority of the officers of the Baltic, Byelorussian, Kiev and Carpathian military districts. I repeat: each of these districts forms an army group. Now, just imagine four of the largest groups of armies, utterly devoid of officers. What does one do with all those soldiers? But don't panic. Four army groups represent twelve to fifteen armies. That's not really so many, after all. Five Soviet armies in Germany, that's certainly a vast number of troops, but fifteen armies spread over the entire territory of the Soviet Union is not a lot, because these armies are all *'Kadrirovannye'** or, as we prefer to call them amongst ourselves, *'Kastrirovannye':*† many officers, lots of armament, but basically held in reserve as they have so few soldiers. As the saying goes, when the war starts, we will soon round up the peasants and throw them straight into battle. It doesn't matter that they've never even seen such weapons. They'll soon learn! Provided they're not all killed off first!

One army at full strength means 60,000 to 65,000 men. So fifteen armies mean 900,000 to 975,000 men. And, even if these armies have only ten per cent of their complement of personnel during peacetime, that represents nearly 100,000 men. What do you do with them? Tell them to get busy digging up potatoes? The inherent danger of such a state of affairs is that the frontier districts possess the biggest adjunct of battle technology, more powerful and more up-to-date than what is available to Soviet occupation forces. In peacetime, frontier districts are very considerably under strength and are not, in essence, on a war footing. But, after mobilisation, according to Soviet practice, troops of these same districts must be superior to troops of the first echelon in both strength and in the quality of their armament.

On the eve of the great jubilee, mobilisation in these, and indeed some other, districts proved impossible owing to the absence of a basic nucleus around which the mobilisation process could be carried out. In the event of a sudden attack by the enemy, the Soviet Army would lose a colossal amount of its

---

*When only officers and technical cadres are at full strength.

†'Castrated' rather than 'skeleton'.

first-class armament and would be unable to call upon its basic striking force. Such short-sighted treatment of second-echelon troops bears witness once more to the fact that no one on the General Staff believes in the possibility of a sudden attack from NATO forces.

1967, the year of the great fiftieth anniversary, was also the year of a record harvest. Few people ever bother to ask themselves why these good harvests happen at all. But the key is quite simple. We have record harvests every year, only there is nobody to gather them in. But, if there is a chance of throwing into the business of collecting the harvest the army, students, schoolboys and girls, intellectuals, etc., there you are, the harvest is a record. The army plays a major role at harvest time, not because soldiers want to work more than students, but because the army brings its own machines. So, in the year of the endless peep-show, it was possible to deploy not hundreds of thousands, but millions, of soldiers in gathering the harvest. They were used also in building work and in industry in general, and, of course, to ensure our own little piece of theatre—that is to say, our famous training exercise.

Have you ever seen tanks moving under water? It is a phenomenon easily described. Through a pipe installed on the tank turret, the air passes into the battle section, and then on into the engine. Exhaust gases are expelled by the engine straight into the water. Before going into the water, the driver fixes a setting by means of a special device known as a hydro-compass on some marker on the opposite bank. Under water, the needle of this device points permanently towards the marker. In addition, a command post is mounted on the bank, which watches the movement of every pipe above water level and, in case of emergency, can give directions: '212th, keep left, still more left, fuck you . . . !' If the engine stops, divers will hook cables on to the tank and the tractors which are waiting on the bank will haul the tank out of the water. That is all there is to it, the entire science! The trouble is that a tank, regardless even of its great weight, is nevertheless a reservoir for air. And its grip on the bottom, under water, is considerably less than on dry land, and a river bed is not an evenly rolled and flat surface. That is why driving under water requires great practice. If the steering lever is pressed only a fraction too much, the tank can turn through ninety degrees, exactly as would happen on a concrete road.

Indeed, this can happen to a tank even on a concrete surface. Remember, in Czechoslovakia, how many of them were lying about in the gutters. It is quite pointless trying to explain to any soldier that, under water, it is better not to touch a single lever, if the tank is not moving straight, just to spit on it, and if you must touch any levers, then turn them as little as possible. Later on, I came across one fairly sensible soldier, who could even understand Russian quite tolerably, and he drove a tank around underwater for an hour and ten minutes, while crossing a little river about thirty metres wide. At the beginning, he turned the tank to face down-stream and, when he was ordered to turn it just a little to the right, he moved it through 180 degrees to face up-river.

Having done this over and over again for some eighteen turns, eventually he emerged from the river on the same bank from which he had started his epic journey. During the 'Dnieper' exercises such epics were of course taboo and, for this reason, all sensible soldier-drivers were replaced by instructors and officers.

But the Dnieper is a great Ukrainian river, it is not the Vorskla or the Klyaz'ma, and the Dnieper had to be crossed not by mere tank battalions but by four whole armies, one of which was a tank army. (At that time, every all-arms army possessed 1,285 tanks, and a tank army 1,332 tanks, without counting any of the floating reconnaissance tanks.) The entire armada of 5,187 tanks had to cross to the other bank of the Dnieper in a strictly limited time. And the whole performance before the very eyes of the Politburo itself, to say nothing of the distinguished foreign guests!

Tanks belonging to the other advancing fronts simply crossed by bridges. Such things are permissible while there are no foreign observers actually to see what is going on. But in full view of the government observers the tanks had not only to travel under water, but they had also to tow artillery pieces in their wake. And if something were to go wrong? What if one of the tanks suddenly started dancing about under water? In that case, the simple use of instructors and officers would not be enough, even more essential precautions would be necessary. And in the end a solution was found. While the officers were undergoing training, thousands of soldiers were literally paving the bed of the Dnieper. Thousands of tons of steel armature and steel mesh were laid on the river bed at the crossing points. At the same time, concrete panels were placed along the sides of the steel mesh to form barriers, like crash barriers on a motorway. The

steel mesh on the river bottom provided the tanks with a more
reliable grip, and the concrete barriers prevented them from
straying from the path. The tanks trundled across as if they were
in a furrow. And no less than a hundred such furrows were
constructed. Only God knows how much steel, concrete and
human labour was wasted in the process. The structure took
many months to complete and the work was first class. The
furrows were completely invisible from above. First of all, the
tank simply went down under water, only then manoeuvred itself
into the prepared corridor, and at the other bank emerged on the
surface as if nothing had happened. Such tricks are, of course,
absolutely impossible in wartime as the enemy would hardly
allow you to spend four months splashing about in a river paving
its bed. It would also be somewhat difficult to supply so many
thousands of tons of building materials while under fire! But, in
Operation 'Dnieper' it must be said, all the thousands of tanks
crossed the river without incident, to the great astonishment of
any uniformed observer.

But this is to anticipate. While I was engaged on the construction of these 'Potemkin' crossing points, I met my friend Yura
Solov'yev, who had graduated from school one year before
me.

'Yurka, damn your bloody eyes, it is really you?'

'Viktor! How are you, you old bastard?'

'How are you? Where the hell have you been?'

'I'm all right. And it's the devil who's brought me to
Byelorussia!'

'What dizzy height did you manage to reach?'

'Battalion commander! Do you remember Sashka Starkov?'

'Of course!'

'He's with me, as chief of staff. Private Abdukhmaev!'

'Yes, comrade Lieutenant!'

'Ask the battalion's chief of staff to come here!'

'Of course!'

'And you, Viktor, what's your rank?'

'Tank-crew gunner!' I reported, loud and clear.

We both burst out laughing. It was pure Chekhov, only one of
us was not fat and the other thin, we were both young and
slender.

Then Sashka Starkov came running towards us, and we embraced warmly.

'Well, Commander, shall we invite the gunner to have a drink?'

'Of course!'

We drank. And we drank. We were together again.

'Where are the rest of our lads? What news of everybody?'

'They're all with the Arabs. Our lads are getting the holes in their tunics ready for their new medals. Things'll start moving there any day now. And the others like you and me are getting ready for the glorious Operation "Dnieper"! They've rounded up all the officers from our regiment, every company, platoon and battalion—some of them as gunners and the others as loaders. There are only two officers left in the whole battalion. I'm the commander and Sashka is chief of the battalion staff! That's a fact. And it's the same thing in the regiment. A captain commands the regiment, and he has a couple of old men as his deputies. Ten officers in the whole regiment! All the rest are taking part here in your comedy!'

I sympathised with my friends. We were all lieutenants and we all got the same salary. But I had no responsibility at all, while they, being one year senior to me were battalion commanders and to make matters worse, commanders with no subordinate officers.

'How do you manage, brother, to keep that mob under control? Even when all the officers are at their posts there can't be any bloody discipline at all!'

They looked at each other.

'But we don't even try to keep up discipline. The triumvirate does it for us.'

'Really?'

Yes, indeed! In all divisions of the four districts, where the officers had been seconded for the peep-show, field tribunals consisting of a commander, his political deputy and the divisional prosecutor had been created. And indeed the soldiers worked away diligently and conscientiously while their commanders were knocking back vodka in the bushes.

'You, Viktor, just pay us a call anytime. We've always got something put by for you!'

'And don't get too full of your own importance either, you may also be given command of a company after the peep-show, or even of a battalion. And then you'll know what it's like at the sharp end of being the commander! And we have nothing but this bloody peep-show the whole time!'

• • •

Nobody had a radio. Rumours were rampant, but in the main they spoke of victory.

'Our lot certainly showed them how! Thousands of Jewish tanks destroyed in a single day!'

Tales of thousands of Israeli tanks were heard at all levels— even the commander of a division gaily repeated them. It made me prick up my ears. I had been attentively reading the limited circulation magazine called *Military Matters Abroad* which was intended for officers' eyes only, and I knew perfectly well that Israel did not possess many thousands of tanks. Egypt—yes, but Israel—no! How then could our people possibly destroy a thousand, if a thousand never existed in the first place. Of course, we had destroyed all the Jewish tanks, but not thousands of them.

In the evening, a small spluttering radio receiver was unearthed at the infantry officers' quarters and we all rushed there to listen to it. As usual in infantry quarters, there was great animation. After a day spent in strenuous training, under the burning sun, they had recovered already and were slightly tipsy. A spirited song was issuing from their smoking area:

> 'This is a hammer and this is a sickle
> This is our Soviet emblem
> Reap if you like or forge if you will
> Whatever you do, you'll get fucked!'

Never before had I or any of my comrades come across such a centre of anti-Soviet feeling as in the Kiev Higher All-arms Commanders School which is named after Frunze. One does, however, encounter anti-Soviet feeling in the Soviet army at every step. Political anecdotes, songs and stories spread quickly and don't die down for a long time. But I had never seen it so open before. Either they were not afraid of political informers, or the informers were also inclined towards freethinking. I just do not know. The fact is that graduates from this particular school hold the record in the Soviet army for the largest number of flights to the West. Regardless of the difference between our shoulder-straps, we maintained the closest contact with them. I personally retain the pleasantest memories of them, and I am sure that if they had been in Novocherkassk at the time of those bloody events* they would not have lifted a finger against their own people. Unfortunately I cannot say the same about my own comrades, the tank men.

'Quiet, you bastards, it's working.'

After some preliminary hissing the radio started: 'Comrade Brezhnev met today in the Kremlin . . . News from the fields . . .'

'You mark my words . . . there's been a cock-up there. Our advisers gave too much bloody advice!'

'Shut up, you bloody prophets.'

But the radio was in no hurry to report our victory in the Near East and the capture of Tel Aviv.

'. . . Towards the glorious jubilee . . .'

'I tell you, brothers, that it's all a lot of bullshit.'

'. . . The oilmen of the Tartar ASSR, after long hours . . .'

'Is it really true . . . ?'

'. . . News from abroad . . .'

'SILENCE!'

'. . . Today Comrade Fidel Castro . . .'

Nobody could stand it any longer and a flow of the most obscene abuse was hurled in the direction of that bearded hero.

'. . . Events in the Near East . . . Fierce battles . . . Heroic resistance by Arab troops . . . Gaza . . . El Arish . . . Solidarity . . .'

The information was short and absolutely incomprehensible. Neither figures nor facts were given. The main problem was who knew where El Arish was situated, on whose territory, and how far from the frontier.

'Who's got a map?'

'Shall we take an armoured personnel carrier into the village? There's a globe in the school.'

'Go on then! Let's get it!'

'Arish is a Jewish name and El is Arab.'

'I'm telling you that if they said the word "solidarity", that's the end! The bloody end!'

'What bloody end? Do you really believe that they can possibly destroy all our tanks?'

'Of course not! But the fact that our people didn't capture the capital which is close to the frontier on the very first day means that it won't be captured tomorrow either.'

---

*The 'bloody events' mentioned here refer to the ruthless suppression by tanks and machine-guns of the local population in 1962.

'Belt up! I'll bet ten bottles of vodka that our people will capture Tel Aviv tomorrow! Don't you know how many tanks the Arabs have? How much artillery? And aircraft? And the quality of the armament? Don't you know that every Soviet internal district is totally without tanks and artillery because it was all sent to the Arabs? There's not a single officer in the frontier areas at present because they're all at the peep-show. And the internal areas haven't got officers or armament, because it's all with the Arabs as well! Can you imagine how many thousands of our officers and generals are there? There's no space left to spit without hitting an adviser!'

'You can piss off with all this talk about advisers. They're exactly like you and me, or like our battalion and division commanders. They're useless, they can't even conduct a training exercise properly. It's all show! God help us from getting entangled with China, then the shit would really hit the fan thanks to our peep-show.'

Eventually, the globe arrived and very small indeed it was. Neither El Arish nor Gaza was shown on it, and even Israel itself could only be located with great difficulty. Only the UAR and Syria were visible, threateningly covering a good slice of territory.

Our doubts and fears appeared so unfounded and unimportant that we all burst out laughing and promptly forgot the latest news and the war in the Near East. Clearly the superiority of the Arabs was undeniable, even on the globe.

Next day, however, once again there was no news about the annihilation of Israel and the capture of Tel Aviv. As usual it was confused and totally incomprehensible: 'Stubborn battles . . . heroic resistance . . .' and the names of some inhabited areas without any indication of where they were situated. In addition, there was a warning note about the Israeli air force bombing peaceful towns and villages as well as schools and hospitals. It made us all start thinking again. When peaceful people are being shot in Budapest or Novocherkassk, the radio never calls for 'solidarity', and suddenly here they were starting to mention peaceful Arabs. What did that signify?

'I told you that Tel Aviv wouldn't be captured by our advisers, even on the second day. I'm prepared to bet it won't happen. Nor tomorrow either. If our people were on the outskirts, that would have been announced immediately. But, for now, it's a very far cry indeed from Tel Aviv. Of course, in a week or so it'll be captured anyway, but our Chief of the General Staff ought to be put on trial for such bad planning.'

'He's a fornicating old fool, Comrade Zakharov.' And it was certainly very difficult not to share such an opinion.

'Maybe our people have thought up some trick? Maybe they'll try to decoy the Jews on to our territory and then cut them down with lasers!'

'Why the hell bother to cut them down with lasers if we already possess thousands of tanks, and what tanks!'

'T-54s and T-55s. Not those prehistoric Jewish Shermans.'

'We've got overall superiority in both quality and quantity, so why not destroy them with tanks and be done with it?'

'I tell you, lasers would be better!'

'Why are you so keen on lasers? There's no such thing!'

Just take a look around you! All kinds of fireworks have been gathered together here in our camp for the big show—T-64s and BMPs and BRDM-2s and Shilkas and Luna-Ms—but there aren't any lasers to be seen. And if our General Staff can't deal with two divisions of antediluvian Shermans, what on earth will we do with the Bundeswehr? And with the British Chieftains? Shall we put all our trust in lasers? Then why the hell are we as happy as billy-goats about the T-64? And what the bloody hell are we all doing here anyway?

'I must tell you one thing, brothers, it's a pissy tank!'

'I quite agree.'

Our first introduction to the T-64 tank had taken place before we graduated from our military school, when the first machine, all wrapped in tarpaulin, was brought in at night and hidden away in a hangar. It was a very fleeting acquaintance but, from the very first look, we all liked the 125 mm gun. It was the most powerful gun in the world and no tank had ever had anything like it before. Because of its amazing initial velocity, its shells could tear away the turrets of tank-targets and hurl them a distance of about ten metres (tank turrets weigh eight or even twelve tons).

But now, upon closer acquaintance, our delight with the T-64s had begun gradually to fade. The gun was certainly all-powerful but, in their endeavour to increase the initial velocity of the shell, the designer had made it not rifled, but smooth-bored, as in the T-62, and this immediately adversely affected its accuracy. In fact, it was an all-powerful gun which always missed the target.

The tank's tracks were also based on entirely new principles. Before, tracks had to be changed after every 2,000 kilometres and now they could stand 10,000. The only trouble was that they constantly fell off. Imagine a boxer whose trunks fall down when the moment comes for a decisive punch. And, finally, the engine itself was not only bad, it was disgusting. Several teams of workers and engineers, and a gang of designers, were sent along simply to maintain our one tank regiment. But they could not hope to solve problems arising from the engine's design, try as they might.

The latest news bulletin next day put an end to all doubts. In a cheerful voice, the announcer informed us of a decisive defeat suffered by the Israeli aggressors in the area of El Kantara and the Mitla Heights.

At last everything became clear. If the Jews were being called the aggressors that meant that they had already taken a solid slice of territory from the Arabs. There could be no other interpretation. The announcer had somehow completely forgotten that, between the Israeli and Arab armies, stood the UN troops, and that Israel alone could not have jumped over them or demanded that they be removed. So how, then, had she become the aggressor?

Mention of Mitla Heights and El Kantara raised the curtain on everything that had been passed over in silence on the radio. From our course in the history of the art of war, we all knew the whereabouts of Mitla and El Kantara. It was clear to us, but not to our divisional commander. Major-General Moskalev had studied the history of the art of war a long time ago and he didn't know where the places were; he believed that our people were destroying the Jews wholesale and that, if not by tomorrow, then at least by the day after tomorrow, the final victorious communiqué would be issued.

In such situations neither officers nor generals unless they are directly involved in events receive any additional information. I do not even bother to mention common soldiers, sergeants and mere civilians. Everybody else listens to the radio and reads *Pravda* and has to make do with that. During my long service in the Soviet army I never had any connection with the war in Vietnam and, therefore, all my knowledge of events there was based on *Pravda* leaders and rumours. Officers who were not involved in events in Czechoslovakia did not have the slightest idea about the scandalous breaches of the law and the crude mistakes committed during the preparations for and execution of that disgraceful operation. I was in Czechoslovakia but my knowledge of events there and my battle experience spring only from what I myself saw. There is never any examination, let alone revelation, of mistakes, after such measures have been carried out. It is not surprising, therefore, that the same mistakes in strategy, tactics, organisation and management and guidance of troops are being repeated over and over again year after year. It is hardly astonishing either that the majority of officers have very confused notions about what we are likely to face in any future war and what we must really prepare ourselves for. It is still less astonishing that the majority of Soviet tank corps, who, of course, have never been in Sinai, are convinced that a Soviet tank is invincible, just as the majority of Soviet pilots, except those who served in Vietnam, are convinced that it was the Americans, and not ourselves, who suffered colossal casualties in the air battles there (as publicised in *Pravda's* daily reports).

Although the news over the following days was cheerful and almost victorious in tone, it no longer held out the hope of a speedy destruction of Israel. 'The peoples of the World demand an end to aggression . . . Workmen of the Likhachev works call it a disgrace . . . Conference of the Security Council . . . Speech by the Soviet representative . . . Peoples of the World must strengthen their solidarity . . . Liberate occupied territories . . .' And so on and so forth.

Then a sealed letter from the Central Committee of the Party was sent to all communists, and read out at closed Party meetings. Its fundamental leitmotiv was: 'The Arabs are poor fighters: they were busy saying their prayers when they should have been repelling attacks.'

But there was no secret letter for officers. There was a war on, mistakes were made, but, as is well known, one learns from one's own mistakes. But what exactly was the cause of defeat, and which exactly were the mistakes made, all this remained an impenetrable secret to us. The explanation to the effect that Arabs are poor soldiers was highly popular with generals, officers, soldiers and civilians. All interest in the campaign immediately subsided. Incidentally, the overwhelming majority of Soviet military advisers, from generals down to lieutenants, also shared the same point of view: 'Poor fighters'—full stop! And somehow the thought never entered anyone's head that we had known beforehand that they were poor fighters. And that, if we did know, why the devil did we demand the removal of the UN troops, who were protecting these poor fighters? If we knew to begin with that they were not fighters, then why did we spend billions of roubles, and lose thousands of tanks and aircraft, for nothing? If we knew beforehand that Arabs are inclined to pray at certain hours of the day when they should be fighting, then why were measures not taken? There should have been much foaming at the mouth in the Central Committee, to prove that there must not be a war and that the problem must be solved peacefully and that the UN troops must not be removed. But maybe the Soviet General Staff did not know what the Arab army was really like. In that case, such a General Staff and its Chief Intelligence Administration are not worth a kopek of anyone's money. How many years had thousands of colonels been kept in Egypt and Syria and still it had not dawned on us that the Arabs were not ready for war, in spite of the billions spent on first-class equipment and on Soviet advisers? We were too busy counting the numbers of tanks and aircraft. On paper it all looked infallible.

After another whole week a top secret order came addressed to officers: 'About the lessons learned in military action in the Near East.' To this day I remember that order with mixed feelings of shame and indignation. The order of the Minister of Defence repeated, almost word for word, the text of the closed letter of the Party Central Committee. 'Disgrace to the aggressors . . . Arabs prayed, but did not fight . . .' And that was all, not another word. No reference to the casualties on both sides, to innovations in Israeli tactics and armament, not one word about our mistakes. So why this order was top secret in the first place no one knows to this very day. It could safely have been printed in *Red Star* instead of the editorial. In fact foreign broadcasts went into far greater detail. In the evening, we tank crew members, with a good few drinks under our belts, were discussing this order with the other young infantry officers.

'One should not blame the mirror if one has an ugly mug.'

'Were the Arabs not taught in our military academies?'

'In the Arab armies absolutely everything was the same as in ours: organisation, armament, tactics and even peep-shows were identical.'

'Some day it will all cost us very dear!'

'If only we had given them the T-64 and the BMP-1!'

'You're a fool, but don't be offended just because I tell you that they had overwhelming superiority in both quantity and quality!'

'Now all the advisers will probably be turfed out of the army, their shoulder-straps will be torn off, and some of them will even be put on trial . . .'

'Don't be offended, Viktor, but you're an idiot. Didn't you read the letter? The Arabs are not good fighters, didn't you understand that? Consequently, our advisers *are* good fighters! Before the week is over they'll all be getting medals and promotion. If our advisers were to be put on trial, so would the Chief of our General Staff. And the Minister of Defence must be kicked out too, as well as the Minister for Foreign Affairs, because of their policies, and perhaps somebody even higher up because of waste, stupidity and short-sightedness, and for his inability to direct the army, the country and its foreign policy.'

And, indeed, before that week was over, secret decrees from the Praesidium were signed awarding decorations to the Soviet military advisers. The decrees themselves were kept secret so as not to reveal the number of advisers or the number of posts occupied by them. But, in reality, secrecy was also maintained just to protect the new heroes from being jeered at by the West. There were thousands of names on the rolls, colonel-generals, major-generals, lieutenant-generals, majors, colonels, lieutenant-colonels. It was a wearying business listening to thousands of names in the heat of a June day.

On that same day, another order was read out in our regiment concerning the replacement of the T-64 by the T-55; by our dear old 'Fifty-fives', which we knew by heart, which we loved and which we dreamt about; the 'Fifty-fives', whose tracks never fell off and which possessed, if not that extraordinary fire-power, at least reliability and precision: those same 'Fifty-fives' which constitute the very foundation of tank troops in the Soviet Army and in the armies of its allied powers.

It is difficult to say why this decision was taken. Was it in order to hide the T-64 from the defeated Arabs, who might have complained that they had not been provided with them, or was it from fear that, during some training exercises, the engines and tracks might cause trouble. Probably both these factors played their part. In any case, the T-64s were taken away from us. They reappeared only after training, at a closed parade with no foreign guests present. They managed to cross the flat concrete without incident . . .

Meanwhile, the intensity of training increased. Each day, without rest days or leave periods, an unprecedented performance was being prepared, covering a huge territory. I do not know how many billion roubles it cost, but judge for yourself when the potential capacity of the T-55 is only 500 driving hours. After 500 hours, it must go in for a complete overhaul, and literally every part has to be changed, leaving only the hulk in which a new engine and new transmission must be installed, its whole running gear completely changed, all other apparatus, and so on . . . Then, the tank has another 250 hours of life, after which it is written off for good. A tank is not a tractor, it is too heavy and wears out very quickly. This is why the overwhelming majority of tanks spend all their life in moth-balls, waiting for war, and only the oldest of them, which have spent ten to fifteen years being preserved, are used for training. This is also why tanks are always transported in echelons or on trailers. Every hour in motion costs too much. Tanks are very rarely taken out of moth-balls and used for training. In the Soviet army there is a standard for battle tanks—200 kilometres per year—and the General Staff, suspicious even of district commanders, watches the observance of this standard very closely. 200 kilometres per year means that if, in one year, a tank has done 400 kilometres, the whole of the previous year must have been spent in moth-balls. (If a divisional commander has used up the allocation in advance, he can be brought before the military tribunal.) And, all this does not even take into account the cost of technical maintenance as well as ammunition and fuel.

Now try to visualise the following picture: thousands of tanks, day and night, taking part in training exercises without any notice being paid to motor resources, just as if it was a state of war. In wartime, this would have been entirely justified—that is why tanks are created, but what is the valid reason for throwing away billions of roubles in peacetime? During training, over a period of four months, our 38th Army completely ruined every one of its 1,285 tanks, and the same happened in all the other armies. One general replacement occurred before the main exercises started: all tanks, tracked armoured personnel carriers and gun-tractors were removed, and nearly new ones were distributed instead, so as to avoid breakdowns.

Twelve hours a day were dedicated to training: every movement at each stage of the coming exercises was worked out in the most minute detail. Only now did we understand how Suvorov's* principle, that 'each soldier must know his manoeuvre', is still applied in the Soviet army.

Preparations for the exercises were going on in one huge field set out with marker pegs. Every soldier (or disguised officer) studied his own task: jump down from the tracked armoured personnel carrier at this bush, move nine steps forward, give one burst of automatic gun-fire, thirteen steps forward and there's my target, another burst of fire, and there's the target of my right-hand neighbour, if he didn't hit it, I'll help him to do so, here the tank will fire armour-piercing shells—and again, and again.

These exercises seemed to have taken more than a whole year to work out, and when we arrived for our training everyone had been given a file with his role plainly indicated, not only every step but even every breath: seven steps forward, there will be a flash; hold breath: close eyes, put on gas mask, breathe out; short burst of automatic gun-fire. It was the same for the infantry, for us, for the artillery corps, landing forces and everyone else: tank emerges from water, puncture the water-proofing on the gun barrel with an armour-piercing shot, throw off the pipe, remove the stopper from gun and turret, lower gun, now four hostile tanks will appear from behind that birch tree; concentrated fire by the whole company; my target is the far left tank, after having knocked it out, I shift my fire to the next target to the right and, if that one is also knocked out, I shift my fire still more to the right . . .

A week after our arrival in the camp everyone was obliged to pass an oral examination on each individual role: all the hours, minutes and seconds, when, where and what kind of target will emerge, distance towards it, its speed and angle of motion. Every one of the tens of thousands of people involved knew precisely in advance each action of the enemy, the composition of his forces and resources, and all his likely moves.

After this theoretical examination, practical training started. To begin with, each man, alone, went over the whole field, tidying up the smallest detail in his mind. At this juncture, anyone in the tank corps was on foot. After that, sections and crews started to be formed. There were four of us: the driver-instructor and three officers (the commander, gunner and loader).

---

*A famous commander in the Tsarist army who, throughout his long career, never suffered a single defeat. The present writer is no relation.

Once more we strode out across the field, a distance of ten to twelve kilometres.

Commander: 'Here I'll give the order Landmark—2. 100 to the left, tank, destroy.'

Gunner: 'I'll shout armour piercing.'

Loader: 'I'll throw a shell on the rammer.'

Driver: 'I'll shout "make way", and brake slightly.'

On the left, on the right and behind us, thousands of people were walking in groups, each following its own route. Everyone was muttering the details of his own task and quietly exchanging words with his mates. For the time being, he was still permitted to do so. Behind us were the infantry, in front were reconnaissance, and sometimes aircraft 'flew past'—but even pilots were training on foot.

The following day, everything started all over again, but this time with the formation of platoons, and now only tank crews could exchange remarks inside the individual 'tanks', though one 'tank' was allowed to communicate with another. The day after, everything was repeated once again; with companies being formed. After that came the general inspection, for everybody. And, only after that, did training in battle technique actually start. One day was taken up with company exercises—every company separately and without firing. The next day, battalion exercises, the next regimental, then divisional, army, and finally the whole front. Every field was carefully covered with metal netting and armature, to prevent tanks from ploughing it all up with their tracks. Only before the final exercises was this grating removed, and within two weeks the grass had grown up.

Once every task in one region had been mastered, a new region replaced it. Thus, from the Chernigov region in the Ukraine we gradually moved over to Byelorussia, to Bobruysk, after which we returned to where we had started and repeated everything all over again, and so on ad nauseam. By this time, not only had our front rehearsed its tasks, but all the others had done the same. Then the exercises were conducted as prescribed, at full speed, with the participation of several fronts. It was still not yet Operation 'Dnieper' itself, but just the preparations for it—'the dress rehearsal'. And only then were we returned once more to our camps, where the replacement of battle equipment took place. Meanwhile, tens of thousands of soldiers were following in our footsteps, eradicating every sign of our training and gathering up metal, filling in shell holes, removing shell cases and searching for blind shells.

. . . And then, only then . . .

A column of a motor-rifle battalion was moving forward towards the water boundary. Meanwhile the artillery and the air force were 'preparing the way' for the advance of this first of many battalions. Its task was simple: a forced crossing of the Dnieper to take possession of a bridge-head on the right side of the river and so secure a crossing place for our tank regiment with its artillery: after which the crossing of three armies would at once start, with a simultaneous tactical helicopter assault on the enemy's rear. That would be followed by the building of railway bridges and the crossing of the army's second echelon, and the landing of two airborne divisions in the enemy's deep rear. Then would come the crossing of two other fronts and engaging of the 'Westerners'. But, for the present, just one motor-rifle battalion was advancing . . .

This was an unprecedented honour for the battalion, although it had already been completely written off and would take no further active part. Two artillery brigades plus eight artillery regiments cleared the battalion's way, which meant 612 guns to support one battalion. In addition to this, a tank regiment was put forward just at the riverside cut and destroyed targets on the other bank—600 guns and 100 tanks to support 300 men! Such a thing could only happen in honour of a great jubilee! Armoured personnel carriers plunged into the water, lifting up columns of fine spray, and swarmed towards the enemy bank which was wrapped in the smoke of exploding shells. Stumps and trunks of trees were being lifted high up into the sky. Fragments of shells rained down endlessly, sometimes reaching the middle of the river. According to plan, at the moment when the armoured personnel carriers reached their half-way mark across the river, the artillery should have switched to firing in depth, thus letting the battalion reach the bank and disembark its landing force. But the artillery showed no sign of conforming to plan. On the contrary, the rate of firing was increasing. This was either because the artillery observers had missed the right moment, or because the battalion had started its crossing two to three minutes early, but in any case it was impossible for the armoured personnel carriers to continue and they started to circle on the spot, crashing into one another as they fought against the strong current of the Dnieper.

All this happened bang in front of the government observers. The Secretary General looked in bewilderment at the Defence Minister who shouted something quite unprintable into the microphone and the gun-fire immediately stopped. About thirty guns still maintained their fire, but the main chorus had ceased. Gradually the remainder also stopped, in a somewhat bashful fashion. Armoured personnel carriers meanwhile were continuing their pirouettes on the water. Apparently the battalion commander did not dare give the order to advance, because he could not guess what the bloody artillery would get up to next. In any case, he was under instructions not to pass the middle of the river until the artillery had switched to fire in depth. But any piece of artillery needs two to three minutes to alter its gun sights, and so the battalion foundered in the water. During training it had all been so good—and now just look at that bloody mess . . .

At last the artillery, slowly and with great reluctance, started to fire in depth, and the battalion moved towards the bank . . . but not one of the armoured personnel carriers succeeded in getting out of the water. During training, the artillery had always been very well organised, but now either the gunners were nervous or something else was wrong, but the whole riverside cut, which should have been left untouched, had been ploughed up and dotted with shell-holes. So, it was time for improvisation. The battalion commander ordered his men to jump into the water and swim to the bank. The river was shallow in some places but by no means everywhere. Everything got into a tangle. Instead of an accurate deployment, there was an unruly mob.

The situation was saved by the commander of the battalion, Colonel Rubanov: 'Forget it's a manoeuvre, it's a real battle.' Later, the military correspondents praised the gallant commander to the skies. His order was especially liked by the Head of the Chief Political Directorate, General Epishev. But the battalion commander was not seeking for effect. By this command, he was simply ordering disguised officers to forget about the big show, to forget the roles they had learned by heart, to forget all this 'ballet' and to act in the way prompted by their own common sense and by the experience obtained during their years as officer-cadets. The young officers understood their battalion commander, their lines straightened, company and platoon commanders evaluated the situation and, after a couple of minutes, the battalion commander flung his men into the attack from the very brink of the water, totally abandoning the armoured personnel carriers. After this, everything went almost according to the book, but there was just one more hitch. The armoured personnel carriers could not get out of the water and we tankmen were seriously afraid that one of them might land in one of the secret underwater channels. Then the leading tank would come up against the armoured personnel carrier, all the following tanks would stop also, and there would be an almighty scandal.

But the valiant battalion commander saved the situation once again. He had already progressed a good distance with his infantry, when suddenly he remembered the tanks and radioed for his armoured personnel carriers to go off down river, thus clearing the way for the tanks. So, every armoured personnel carrier was to be captured by the enemy, or to come under enemy fire, but at least the way was open for all the advancing troops. This decision saved the whole of our peep-show but it ruined the colonel. After the exercises, Comrade Grechko assessed the colonel's decision as 'unjustified', and ordered his dismissal from the army.

Our tanks crossed the river without incident, pulling after them, under water, the artillery of the whole division. Ammunition and crews were transported on sapper carriers. After this, the whole ballet got into its swing once again. The 'Westerners', as expected, stampeded away in panic the moment they saw us on the horizon. Targets fell all over the place, the shells did not touch them, and, most important of all, the roar was quite deafening. The high command of the 'Easterners' had 'guessed' all the perfidious plans of the 'Westerners' and delivered suitably crushing blows. In short, everything worked out disgustingly to plan.

Three days later, we were brought to Kiev. Later, of course, the parade was shown on television and in the cinema, but only after substantial work had been put in by the censor. The parade was to take place on the military aerodrome.

The very sight of the aerodrome staggered us. Countless numbers of tanks, stretching, it seemed, from one horizon to another, were standing in the field alongside the runway. Later, photographs of this field crammed with tanks were to be published in all the newspapers of the world. At the time, some Western commentators expressed the opinion that perhaps these were only dummy tanks made of rubber standing there. Certainly, there were far too many tanks, indeed it was the biggest assembly of tanks in the history of humanity, but even though they were not made of rubber, they were quite lifeless. They were tanks used for training exercises and had definitely exhausted their resources. They were not tanks any more, but former tanks, and now they represented only raw material for the steel industry. After the parade, a few went to the Kiev tank-repairing works for a total overhaul, many thousands went to the Chinese frontier to be used as immovable firing-posts, but the major part were sent to be melted down. This jubilee year turned out to be a record year for melted steel.

It is impossible to say how much this peep-show cost our peace-loving people. Even without taking into consideration ammunition, fuel, wear on artillery barrels and the thousands of tons of steel armature and concrete, and only counting worn-out tanks, the figure would approximate to billions of roubles.

On the world market, the British Chieftain, which was the contemporary of our T-62, could easily fetch 210,000 dollars a piece. During exercises, our 1st Ukrainian front completely wore out over 5,000 tanks and considerably shortened the motor resources of another 5,000—and there were at least five fronts taking part in Operation 'Dnieper'. Out of fairness, it should be noted that, although other fronts' training exercises were similar to ours, they were still not as intensive. But, even so, we can take the amount of worn-out tanks as at least 10,000. Multiply this number by the price of one tank, and it will immediately be clear why the Soviet Union cannot overtake Spain in the production of motor cars.

The parade passed off without a ripple, as the saying goes, though there was just one jarring note. . . . The troops drawn up on the aerodrome awaited the arrival of the important guests. Those on the dais also waited. The parade, as usual, was to begin at 1000 hours, but Brezhnev, Podgornyy, Kosygin and Shelest were late, or, as we put it, they were delayed. (Bosses are never late.) The beginning of the parade was delayed, and this caused nervousness. In addition, in contrast to Moscow parades, a fly-past had been planned. The airforce was to fly from Borispol, and the flights were calculated down to the last second . . . but the big chiefs were delayed. Marshal Grechko, as he stood on the dais softly cursed our Beloved Party and

Government and all the members of the Political Bureau with superbly refined abuse. Naturally he cursed them in a whisper but the microphones on the dais had been switched on at 1000 hours exactly, and his *sotto voce* was transmitted over a distance of ten kilometres—indeed over the whole of the parade. That is why the Kiev parade was eventually conducted somehow especially dashingly, I would even say gaily. Half an hour later, when the troops solemnly marched past the big chiefs' dais, there was not the usual expression of stern resolution on the officers' and soldiers' faces. Instead all the faces blossomed out into smiles. And the big chiefs smiled back and waved with their fat little hands.

1967. Moscow—The Ukraine.

Operation 'Bridge'

'COMRADES,' BEGAN THE Defence Minister, 'in this new year of 1967 the Soviet Army will have to undertake a number of extremely complicated and responsible tasks, and thereby celebrate the fiftieth anniversary of the Great October Socialist Revolution.

'The first and the most complicated of these tasks is to achieve a final solution to the problem in the Near East. This task lies completely upon the shoulders of the Soviet Army. The fiftieth year of the existence of the Soviet Union will thus become the last year of the existence of the Jewish State. We are ready to accomplish this honourable task, but we are held back only by the presence of the UN troops between the Jewish and the Arab forces.

'After the solution of the Near East problem, all efforts will be thrown into regulating the European problem. This task is not only for diplomats. Here again, the Soviet Army will have to solve a number of problems. In accordance with the decision of the Politburo, the Soviet Army will "bare its teeth". Under this heading, we include a number of separate measures and an unprecedented air display at Domodedovo. Immediately after

ictory in the Near East, grand naval manoeuvres will follow in
ie Black Sea, the Mediterranean, the Barents, the North and the
3altic seas. After all this, we will carry out the colossal "Dnieper"
xercises and we will complete our demonstrations on 7 Novem-
er with an elaborate parade in Red Square. Then, against the
ackground of these demonstrations of force and of our victories
1 the Near East, we will urge the Arab countries to stop all oil
upplies to Europe and America over a period of one or two
veeks. I think'—and here the Minister smiled—'Europe will
1en be more amenable to signing all those documents which we
hall propose to them.'

'Will there be any developments in the space programme?'
nquired the First Deputy of the Commander-in-Chief Land Forces.

The Defence Minister frowned.

'Unfortunately not. During the period of "voluntarism", fla-
rant errors were tolerated in this sphere. Now we have to pay
or them. In the next ten or fifteen years we will not be able to
o anything basically new in space, we shall only be repeating
ld successes with slight improvements.'

'What will be done concerning Vietnam?' asked the Com-
nander of troops in the Far East Military District.

'We will be able to solve successfully all European problems
nly when the Americans have become tied up in Vietnam. I
1ink we should not hurry to defeat Vietnam.'

The assembly became extremely animated, demonstrating its
bvious approval.

'To finish with general matters,' continued Marshal Grechko.
I would like everybody to give some thought to the following.
imultaneously with all our demonstrations of might, and quite
part from the number of individual troops involved and their
-aining, it would be no bad idea to organise something which
as never been seen before, something stunning and completely
ew. So if anybody among you, Comrade Generals, comes up
vith an interesting idea, do not hesitate to apply to me or to the
:hief of the General Staff. I ask you in advance, however, not to
ncrease the number of tanks, guns and aircraft. You have no
dea how many of them there will be—we shall gather every-
1ing we have to put on display. New technology, of course,
hould not be suggested. We will show everything which it is
ermissible to show, the BMP and the T-64, the MIG-23 and
AIG-25, and possibly all the experimental machines. This, of
ourse, is dangerous, but we must show them.'

Everyone present took the final words of the Defence Minist as a promise of high rewards for any original idea. So be it. Ar all the military minds started to work on the idea. Only, wh could they suggest besides quantity and quality?

Nevertheless, an original idea was found. It emanated fro Colonel-General Ogarkov, a former sapper officer.

Ogarkov proposed demonstrating not only the might of t army, but also that this might rested on the rock-solid base military industry. Of course, he had no intention of revealing th whole system of supply, and there was no need to do so. T convince his guests of his wealth, the master of the house do not need to show all his treasures. One genuine painting Rembrandt will be quite enough.

Ogarkov wanted to show just one element, but a sufficientl convincing one. What he proposed was to build a railway bridg over the Dnieper in record time, in say one hour, and then to l the railway echelons loaded with battle equipment and colum of tanks cross the river by means of this same bridge. A bridg of this kind would not only symbolize a strong back-up, b would also demonstrate to Europe that the Rhine was no protectio

Ogarkov's idea was met with delight by the Defence Ministr and by the General Staff alike. This was exactly what w required. Of course, the Soviet Army did not possess any suc bridge and there was not much time left before the beginning the exercises. This fact, however, worried nobody, the ma thing was that the desired idea had been found.

Colonel-General Ogarkov was endowed with absolute powe no less than that of the general designer before the launching the first cosmonaut. Ogarkov himself was not only a brillian erudite and experienced engineer bridge-builder, but also a unusually exigent and wilful commander, as only Zhukov ha been before him. That, of course, made the fulfilment of the tas all the easier. All the scientific research establishments an railway troops, as well as all the industrial enterprises producin the army's engineering technology, were switched to his dire leadership. The entire production of these enterprises was stoppe pending the order to begin the production of something s unprecedented.

At the same time, while the designers were busy making th first sketches and outlines for the future bridge, which was to b used only once, the selection of the youngest, healthiest an strongest officers, as well as the cleverest and most experience engineers, started. In addition, competitions were arranged in the Soviet Army railway and engineering schools, open to officer-cadets who were graduating from these schools and were therefore already officers. As a result, thousands of the best officers and officer-cadets put on soldiers' uniform and came to Kiev from every corner of the Soviet Union. And in Kiev the 1st Guards Railway Bridge-Building Division was raised.

While it was not yet clear what kind of bridge was to be built, the division was launched into a training programme of unprecedented severity, since whatever kind of bridge was to be built, it was clear that everybody engaged in assembling it would have to work like acrobats under the circus big top.

While the original idea of the ultra-high-speed erection of a railway bridge continued to be developed and deepened, it was proposed that, as soon as the erection was complete, a track-laying machine and contingents equipped with rails should go across and, just as speedily, build a section of railway on the right bank, so that troops and battle equipment could be sent over. This idea was similarly accepted and approved.

Meanwhile all the design bureaux, each engaged independently on the development of the bridge, declared unanimously that to build even a floating bridge, with a load capacity of only 1,500 tons, was impossible in such a short period of time. Ogarkov saw red. Both his reputation and future were at stake. He reacted swiftly and accurately. First, he applied to the Central Committee and obtained their positive approval that the designer who succeeded in building such a bridge would be awarded a Lenin Prize. Secondly, he invited all the designers to a conference and, having let them know the Central Committee's decision, proposed discussing all the details over again. At this conference, the plan to pass track-laying machines and echelons with rails over the bridge was rejected, as was the idea of columns of tanks crossing simultaneously with railway echelons. It was also decided that all wagons making the crossing must be empty, and that a column of empty lorries would move across alongside the train. Only one problem still remained. How to get across a locomotive weighing 300 tons? Naturally, someone suggested reducing the locomotive's weight by as much as possible. Two locomotives, a basic one and a duplicate, were urgently modernised and as many steel components as possible were replaced by aluminium ones. The steam boilers and fire-chambers were also changed. The locomotive's tenders were completely

empty, they carried no coal and no water but only one very small
barrel containing some kind of high-octane fuel, maybe aviation
benzine or paraffin.

Time was racing past. The plan for the bridge had already
been finished at the works, and the majority of the 1st Guards
Railway Division's officers were sent there to acquaint themselves with its construction during the actual process of manufac-
ture. Factories, which had not been operating for several months
while the project was being planned, were now switched to a
military regime. They worked twenty-four hours a day. All the
workers were paid enormous wages and promised that, if they
finished the work on time, they would receive unprecedented
rewards from the Defence Minister personally.

The first elements of the bridge were meanwhile duly delivered to the division, and the training programme started. New
elements were delivered every week, and during each training
period, the bridge got longer and longer. Theoretical calculations
proved that it should hold the weight of an empty echelon; but
how it would work in practice no one, of course, knew. The
most dangerous consideration was that, if the bridge sagged too
much under the weight of the locomotive, the train's wagons
could overturn into the water. Locomotive crews and drivers
from motorised troops, all disguised officers, who would be
moving over the bridge simultaneously with the echelon, started
urgently to study the use of life-saving techniques, intended for
the use of tank crews while under water. They could not, however, be given any practical training in crossing the bridge,
because some sections destined to connect the two banks were
still missing.

On the very day when the last two pontoons were delivered to
the division, the mightiest military manoeuvres in the history of
mankind began. They were code-named 'Dnieper'.

The floating railway bridge across the Dnieper was built in
record time and, when the last piles were hammered in on the
right bank, a locomotive smoothly glided on to the bridge from
the left bank, slowly pulling behind it a long train. Simultaneously, a column of military vehicles glided on to the bridge.
The leaders of Party and Government and numerous foreign
guests watching the construction of this gigantic bridge never
guessed that it was being built for railway communications. So,
when the locomotive arrived on the bridge, all those on the
Government dais applauded enthusiastically.

As the locomotive moved further and further from the bank,
e sagging of the bridge beneath its weight became threaten-
gly more noticeable. Heavy, sluggish waves fanned out from
e bridge and spread towards both banks of the river, then,
flecting back, returned to hit the bridge, rolling it from side to
de. Immediately, the three small figures of the frightened
gine-drivers appeared on top of the locomotive. Until now,
ne of the foreign guests had paid any attention to the strange
ct that there was no smoke issuing from the locomotive's
noke-stack, but the appearance of the engine-driver on top of
e locomotive was noticed by everybody and provoked condes-
nding smiles.

Later on, these frightened engine-drivers were skilfully re-
oved from all photographs and films recording this famous
ossing, but at that particular moment the situation was in need
' saving, because the whole enterprise on which so much
oney and energy had been expended, could so easily have
rned into a farce.

The slowly-swaying locomotive with its three engine-drivers
top lumbered nervously onwards.

'What is that there on the top?' asked Marshal Grechko slowly
rough clenched teeth.

All the other Soviet generals and marshals lapsed into com-
ete silence.

Colonel-General Ogarkov stepped forward and reported smartly:
Comrade Marshal of the Soviet Union! We have thoroughly
corporated the experiences learnt during the recent Arab-Israeli
ar, where aviation played such an exclusively important role.
'e therefore took measures to protect all rear communications
gainst an enemy's air attack. Thus, in the event of war, we
ovide in addition to three engine-drivers, who are inside the
comotive, another three men with automatic grenade-launchers,
rela-2s. These grenade-launchers have not yet been delivered
the troops, but we have already started training their crews,
hich is what you are seeing at the present moment.'

All the foreign guests were staggered by such efficiency dis-
ayed by the General Staff and by such a lightning reaction to
anges in the practice of waging war.

The Defence Minister was also staggered by this ability to lie
ith such speed, aplomb and aptitude, without batting an eyelid
d at the psychological moment. 'Fine fellow that,' thought the
efence Minister, 'he will go far with such capabilities as those.'

After the exercises, when the bridge was taken apart and se:
for melting down, and the Guards Bridge-Building Division wa
disbanded, as being of no further use, and after all the designe
and builders had been generously rewarded, it was unanimous!
decided to entrust to Ogarkov the organising of all future oper
tions of this kind. And this is how the Chief Directorate (
Strategic Camouflage, the first head of which was Colone
General Ogarkov, was born. Shortly afterwards, Ogarkov wa
promoted to the rank of Army General.

Ogarkov's Chief Directorate started by taking over all milita
and later all state censorship, and later still also the majority (
all the organisations dealing with misinformation, snatching man
titbits even from the very jaws of the KGB. After this, the Chi
Directorate's tentacles stretched out towards the armed forces:
future training exercises undertaken by the army, air force (
navy could only take place after the approval of Ogarkov. A■
military building, from space centres, launching silos and n▪
clear submarine bases, to the barracks of the KGB's fronti.
troops—everything must have the approval of Ogarkov. The ne
step was the subordination of all industry and building in th
Soviet Union to him since, in our country, all objects have
military significance. And when the post of Chief of the Gener
Staff became vacant, no one who knew about the existence (
GUSM* and its real might had the slightest doubt as to wh
would land it.

Having attained the rank of Marshal of the Soviet Union ar
the position of Chief of the General Staff, the former enginee
bridge-builder did not, of course, rest on his laurels. The futu:
belongs to him . . . unless his rivals devour him first.

_____

*The abbreviation for Chief Directorate of Strategic Camouflage.

The 287th Novograd-Volynsk Motor Rifle Training Division. Oster, the Ukraine, October 1967.

Training

'PUKE! AND THAT'S an order!'

The young short-haired little soldier looked round pathetically for support. A platoon of equally young and equally short-haired soldiers, in front of whom he was standing, obviously did not sympathise with him a bit. In the first week of their service they had fully assimilated the iron rule of training: if one person does not obey the order, the whole section will suffer; if one section does not obey the order, the whole platoon will suffer; and if one platoon does not obey the order, then the sergeants will pick one of the platoon's soldiers and train him until he loses conscious-ness, or 'until he lies down'—and if he can no longer obey the orders efficiently, his section will suffer, and then the whole platoon and so on, ad infinitum. And there are too many kinds of training. For instance, you can order a section to dig trenches on an old ferro-concrete surface, and make sure that 120 centimetre-deep trenches are dug in thirty minutes, and those who do not obey the order will have to train again as a punishment.

The short-haired little soldier stood in front of the formation, but the formation was beginning to get angry—because it knew what lay in store for it if the order was not at once carried out.

I stood some way off, watching my second-in-command's actions. On the third day of my service as a platoon commander, I clearly understood one more law of the training division: do not interfere with the sergeant's work, otherwise you will have to do the work yourself.

Guards Staff Sergeant Kokhar', having waited ten seconds for effect, gave a clear order:

'Second section! Ten steps forward! Quick march! Platoon, listen to the order! Private Ravdulin was thirteen seconds late for parade, because he was in the canteen.'

Every day, every soldier in a training division has twenty minutes' free time after lunch and ten in the evening. Once he has broken away from lunch, a hungry soldier dashes off to the buffet, which is managed by only one sales-girl. There are 1,500 soldiers in a regiment of whom a good half, the hungriest ones, or the most optimistic, try to get through to the counter. The majority, having got as far as the buffet are unable either to reach the counter, or to force their way out. For being even a second late on parade they will be severely punished, but the number of those trying to break through to the buffet never decreases. One wonders where they get the money if they are paid monthly three roubles and eighty kopeks, out of which they must also buy all their toilet articles. The answer lies in the fact that every day for two or three months they try to reach the buffet and always fail—there is the economy.

At that moment, all the regiment's forty platoons were formed up in the garrison backyard ready to start cleaning their weapons. No officers were to be seen and the sergeants, each in his own way, were correcting any infringements. Some were endlessly performing 'get-up-lie-down'; one platoon was crawling *plastun*-fashion over the courtyard, which was thickly covered in a layer of pig-shit.

My deputy had decided to limit himself to forcing the buffet culprit to vomit publicly what he had eaten, or rather what he had wanted to eat. But the culprit did not carry out the order well enough, so the whole section was going to have to put this mistake right. The first and the third sections, with a mixture of hatred and hope in their eyes, were waiting for their fate to be decided. 'One for all, all for one' is, after all, the basic principle of education.

'Second section! Bend forward!'

Ten backs smartly bent forward.

'Put two fingers . . . of the left hand, IN THE MOUTH!'
The section smartly obeyed the order.

'From the right! . . . One after another! . . . PUKE!' Wriggling convulsively, the section carried out its commander's order and emptied its stomach in perfectly acceptable time.

'Section, ten steps forward! Quick march! Private Ravdulin, take your place in the formation! Stand easy!' The sergeant turned away, ostensibly to find a suitable place for the platoon to clean its weapons. At that precise moment, Ravdulin received two heavy blows in the stomach from his nearest short-haired comrades. Trying to choke back a broken, long-drawn-out moan, he crashed down on his knees, and then slowly fell into his own vomit.

During training, sergeants and officers never beat soldiers—that is an iron law in any training division.

Oster, the Ukraine. March 1968.

The Artists and the Craftsmen

THE RECENTLY ARRESTED man was brought to the regiment and locked up in the guardroom cell. He sat in the corner, looking sullenly at the floor. This sergeant had been arrested in Omsk, 4,000 kilometres from his native training regiment.

The military investigator arrived; the investigation began. How? Why? The matter is serious! and everything depends on a higher authority to look at what has happened, and interpret the present offence. If you class it as absence without leave, the sergeant will be given fifteen days under arrest, as a maximum. If you class it as desertion, it will be fifteen years at the very minimum.

If the sergeant had been caught within his own military district, the matter would have been hushed up of course, because there is good socialist competition between the districts as to which has fewer offences and violations. But since he had been caught in another district altogether, and Moscow therefore knew all about it, the commanders would do their best to show their determination to eradicate fully all such violations regardless of the consequences. But here again a contradiction creeps in—if this is indeed a desertion, then why was it not reported to Moscow six days ago, when the sergeant first disappeared?

A very unpleasant day had dawned for all the sergeant's direct superiors from platoon commander to military district chief.

The sergeant's name was Zumarov, and I was his platoon commander. That is why I was the first to see the investigator.

'Your sergeant?'

'Mine, Comrade Lieutenant-Colonel.'

'How long have you served together?'

'Fifteen months, Comrade Lieutenant-Colonel.'

He had been a cadet in the training platoon under my command, and later, after being promoted, had been left in the platoon, in command of the second section.

'What can you say about him?'

'Comrade Lieutenant-Colonel, I have never seen him before in my life!'

Apparently, the investigator had long since penetrated so deeply into the stern realities of the army that my statement produced no impression at all upon him.

'Was he a craftsman?' was his only question.

'Yes, a craftsman,' I confirmed.

This ended the investigation.

After me various other witnesses were called, the company commander, the political deputy of the battalion commander, and finally the battalion commander himself. Interviews with them also took no more than a minute. None of them had ever seen the sergeant in their lives before.

If all property is nationalized in a country, in other words subordinated to the state, then the natural aspiration of each person to rise, to distinguish himself and to improve his status can be achieved only within the limits of the state apparatus, which incidentally requires many (far too many) professional officials, or executives with higher education.

Any degree certifying graduation from a higher educational institution opens the way into any number of spheres: the Party, the Trade Unions, the Young Communist League, the KGB, Sport, Literature and Art, Industry, Agriculture, Transport, anywhere you like. This is why in any socialist society the following paradox can be observed: nobody seeks a profession, only a degree, and it does not matter what kind. Of course, it is better if the degree has a slight inclination towards the social sciences, rather than to the exact sciences. This is simpler, and more useful in life, because the most important thing in one's career is 'to learn to talk smoothly'.

And, owing to the fact that everyone rushes into learning Marxist-Leninist philosophy and Party history, people who can do something with their hands, and not their tongues, are few and far between. Hence, such persons are worth their weight in gold. You only have to look at how they live now—the car-mechanics, the locksmiths, the sanitary technicians and the house-painters and floor-fillers (of course, I'm speaking about those who earn additional money in their free time, and who doesn't!).

People who can make something are especially honoured in the Soviet Army, because the system of control and evaluation of subunits, units and formations is constructed in such a way that it just cannot be managed without craftsmen.

Judge for yourself. Some kind of commission arrives in a regiment, so where will it start its check-up, what is it interested in? Before everything else comes the ideological state of the troops—are they true believers, or has the decay already set in? How are you to check whether the bourgeois, or the maoist, or the revanchist, the nationalist or the zionist or any other band of propaganda exerts any influence upon the Soviet warrior? It is very simple. First, the commission must inspect the whole camp. Are there enough portraits of the Party and Government leaders, are there enough placards and slogans, is there enough visual agitation in general? What shape is the club in? The room devoted to the glorification of battle? How is the Lenin room in each company, in what shape are each company's paper and satirical news-sheet? And what about each platoon's daily 'battle leaflet'?

After all this, one must discover what a soldier does in his free time. What is he doing? What is he thinking? And that is quite simple too: a concert and sports competition are laid on for the commission. Everything is in order! There is more evidence—cups, pennants, banners. This one is for sport, that one for amateur activities in the arts. Well, things are clearly all right there, but how do they stand with internal order, and with the observance of military regulations? Here again, there are no problems. Feast your eyes: fences are painted, paths are swept, windows are washed, beds are made and perfectly ranged in line, it would be quite impossible to arrange them any better.

Believe me, if any regimental commander succeeds in giving a better account concerning all these points than his colleagues, and in addition manages to hide all crimes and disciplinary offences, which are happening every day, his promotion is assured. The most important consideration is to be able to hide all the unattractive aspects, but exercises and manoeuvres will not be taken into consideration.

In order to win a victory in this interminable competition, every commander, from company commander upwards, must have painters, artists and sportsmen, preferably of a semi-professional level. A special term has been invented in the army for these craftsmen, they are called 'dead souls', because although they are registered as gun-layers, loaders, radio-men, etcetera, they are nevertheless occupied with quite other matters. Some are concocting newspapers day and night. Some are strumming guitars, some are defending their company's honour in sport. According to their particular qualifications, the craftsmen are divided into categories—at company, battalion, regimental or divisional level. For example, in every district there are special sports battalions, sub-divided into light athletics companies, basket-ball platoons, or even high jump platoons.

The struggle to acquire craftsmen goes on permanently between commanders at all levels. All lower-ranking officers hide their best painters and artists from the higher-ranking officers who, in their turn, haunt the various clubs and sports rooms hoping to grab the best craftsmen for themselves. It is open war, with all the rules and methods, the appropriate unwritten laws and traditions. There's enough of it to fill a novel. Direct exchanges also exist, although these take place more often between independent commanders: 'Give me a weight-lifter and a guitarist, and I'll give you a house-painter and a painter,' or, 'Comrade Colonel, don't give me a bad mark for that exercise' (this kind of bargain would be struck via a middleman from another division) 'and I'll give you a sculptor! He'll make a model of anyone you like for the officers' mess in your division. Lenin or Andropov, anyone you wish!'

All craftsmen work on the piece rate system. The principle of material self-interest is sacred. Payment alters depending on the category. Sometimes it happens this way: 'If you become an Olympic champion—we'll give you the rank of senior lieutenant!' And anyway what does it cost the Defence Minister to give away one or two additional little stars? One footballer even attained the rank of major-general without serving a single day in the army, although it must be admitted that the footballer's name in that instance was Yuriy Brezhnev.

In the Kiev military district, at the tank works, the repairing of thousands of private cars was organised. The district chiefs were filling their pockets with millions of roubles, and the craftsmen who were repairing these cars were given leave every evening, and everybody was happy, generals, craftsmen and consumers. The quality of the work was excellent and it is a pity that the shutters were eventually put up. Now there is nowhere in the whole of Kiev to have a Zhiguli car repaired.

Even if the craftsmen had not been paid at all, their work would still have been highly efficient, because to swill all day or to hit a tennis ball about is much more pleasant than digging deep trenches in the heat and the dirt; similarly, drawing a satirical paper in a warm store-room is much more pleasant than changing tank-tracks in the frost. That at least is established fact. In addition, all craftsmen receive endless periods of leave and holidays, all at the expense of others, of course. It is from this that the decay of an army springs (it is not the only cause, and certainly not the most important, but it is one of the basic ones). Let us say for the sake of argument that a drunk, dirty, scruffy soldier is walking along the street. Notice how all the patrols stand aside: it turns out that he is the personal cabinet-maker to the divisional commander. And that one over there, who is also drunk, turns out to be the personal workman of the divisional staff chief, for whom he is engaged in digging a private swimming pool. It is far better not to touch these fellows, or to have anything to do with them.

But let us return to our sergeant with whom we started this story. By profession he was a jeweller, and the son of a jeweller to boot. He joined the army complete with the tools of his trade—little saws, little vices and little tweezers. It is an everyday occurrence for young chaps to join the army with their guitars and balalaikas, with their brushes and canvas. The Soviet people have long understood our fine army customs and they exhort their sons to reveal their particular talent from their very first day in the army.

Zumarov demonstrated his talent immediately after joining our training regiment. He was promptly ordered to fashion a small silver tank which could be presented to the head of some visiting commission. He was reckoned to belong to my training platoon, and I was given six months to make a perfect sergeant out of him, a future commander of a T-62, but I never once saw him throughout his entire service. Out of a total of thirty men in my platoon I had six others like him. True, the six others—a painter, a violinist, a pianist, and three sportsmen—were non-residents; so that sometimes, perhaps once or twice a week, they did turn up in the platoon, and I managed to teach them something.

Officer-cadet Zumarov was not even present at the passing-out inspection. How could he be? He had seen nothing except minia-ture tanks which he was carving from bronze and glass. The regimental commander took the test for him and whispered to the inspecting commission. As a result, Zumarov became an excel-lent soldier, was awarded the rank of sergeant and then left behind in our regiment as a section commander in order to train a new generation of tank commanders. He was posted as a section commander to my platoon and, from that day to this, I never clapped eyes on him.

Do not imagine that I was the only one who had problems with the 'dead souls'—every other platoon commander had six or seven corpses on his register. Here at least distribution is just and no one is offended. This is how we train cadres for our beloved army. When such a tank commander/ignoramus arrives from training to join his battle regiment, he honestly reports at the very outset, 'I am not a tank commander, I am a singer.' Of course, they are pleased in the regiment. 'You are just the thing we've been waiting for!' As a result, the tank is commanded by the gunner, and the baritone just sings his way through operatic arias, and everybody is pleased. The best craftsmen, such as our jeweller, would never under any circumstances be surrendered by a training regiment to a battle regiment, but would be held on to, under any pretext, most frequently as nominal instructors.

But Sergeant Zumarov had come to the notice of the divisional commander, and then of the army commander, and had conse-quently moved first to divisional, then to army, level. He could have risen even higher, but unfortunately he was arrested by a patrol and, what is even worse, in another district.

After the first interview with the military investigator, I promptly decided that there would not be a second one, as I knew abso-lutely nothing about the sergeant—at what level he was now, who his real commander was, or how many times a week he was given leave. But the second interview nevertheless did take place.

'Where is his oath of allegiance?'

'I do not know.'

I really could not know that.

The fact is that every Soviet soldier after a month of primary training eventually takes the oath of allegiance. This can be done only after the soldier has fired his weapon for the first time. The oath of allegiance is printed for each soldier on a separate piece of paper and is signed by him personally. This is done so that this separate sheet can be put on his criminal file, if the need arises.

But, at that moment when the whole training platoon was on the shooting-range prior to signing the oath, Zumarov was making his first tank.

'Never mind,' the regimental commander had said. 'You can go with the next platoon.'

But then the regimental commander apparently forgot to see to it—poor chap, he had so many problems! I, too, as his immediate commander, was unable to see to it. I was told not to interfere in matters which did not concern me. So I didn't. I simply had no means of doing so.

Now it became clear that Zumarov was neither a sergeant nor even a soldier. Nor was he under military jurisdiction as he had never signed the oath of allegiance—so he could not even be judged under military law, and under civilian law he had not committed any offence as he had just gone from one town to another. And of course he lost the whole year and a half which he had spent in the army. This period could not be counted because time in military service is calculated from the day of signing the oath. Now, Zumarov could have started a commotion. 'I don't know anything about it. I joined the army and served conscientiously. It is not my fault but yours! Why didn't you put me under oath?'

And indeed a scandal flared up and had to be nipped in the bud, because not only pawns like regimental commanders might have suffered in the process but some people much higher up. The scandal was hushed up at the level of the Kiev Military District. A compromise was found. According to the law, Zumarov had another six months to serve but he was offered immediate demobilisation on grounds of health. Zumarov accepted the compromise. It was reported to Moscow that Sergeant Zumarov of the Kiev district had indeed been arrested in Omsk but that he was no longer on active service, but had been prematurely demobilised. The sergeant was said to be suffering from mental derangement, as a result of which he did not produce the relevant documents when requested to do so by the patrol.

The Zumarovs of this world are the lucky ones, but there are a lot of them in our indestructible army—more's the pity.

Headquarters, Leningrad Military District. Early 1969.

Misha

'THE LITTLE KEY?'

'Comrade Private, first button up your tunic, you are addressing a Lieutenant-Colonel, the duty officer of the military district staff.'

The private simply did not react at all to the lieutenant-colonel's words.

'The little key!' quietly repeated the young soldier with the broad peasant face which showed such superiority and contempt that the duty officer simply did not dare exercise the power of his nearly limitless authority.

The duty officer of the district staff is a very superior being altogether. So much so, that having caught sight of him from afar, any officer absentmindedly assumes a dignified air and straightens his belt and the peak of his cap. Whereas now, a young soldier, who should tremble in front of any lance-corporal, stood in front of him and simply did not react at all to his reprimand.

'The little key' repeated the soldier, evidently savouring the situation to the full. Deliberately, he did not say which key he wanted, and the key itself, in defiance of regulations, he called

115

'little key', which theoretically is quite inadmissible between a soldier and an officer.

At this moment, a major with a red stripe on his left arm—the duty officer's deputy—entered the room. Having appraised the situation in a trice, the major suddenly gave a radiant smile, and jumping up he went to a huge safe and jerked open its massive doors. He snatched one of the hundreds of keys hanging there and, with an obsequious smile, stretched it out towards the arrogant soldier. The latter took the key between two fingers, measured the staff duty officer with a contemptuous gaze, unhurriedly turned his back and, after deliberately spitting on the floor beside a spittoon in the corner, he left the room, slamming the door behind him.

The duty officer was white with rage. Turning towards the major, and enunciating every syllable, he asked deliberately: 'Comrade Major, to whom did you dare give that key without my express permission?'

'But that's Misha, Comrade Lieutenant-Colonel,' said the major obsequiously.

'Which key did you give him?'

'The key to the study of the district commander's first deputy.'

'But you . . . but you . . . do you understand? Did you read the instructions? . . . There are state secrets in that study . .
Only a senior aide-de-camp or an officer on a special mission is entitled . . .'

'But that is Misha!'

'I don't want to hear anything about any Misha, you will be put under arrest together with your Misha! Only the senior aide-de-camp or an officer on a special mission can be given that key and then only after the deputy commander's order and only after the said officer has signed in duplicate for this key, in case anything should disappear. Surrender your pistol and cartridges . . .
Whereupon the lieutenant-colonel turned to me, the guards commander, and said, 'Arrest this Misha and the major!'

'Misha', declared the major suddenly, 'is the relief driver of the Commander of Leningrad Military District's First Deputy, Lieutenant-General Parshikov.'

'Ah!' The lieutenant-colonel stopped short. 'So, why did you not say so before?'

'And that's not all,' the major cruelly continued, 'that's only

officially, but unofficially . . . he . . . he drives Maria Mich-
aylovna, his wife . . . that's what!'

The duty officer slowly left the room.

'Now there you are, Lieutenant, you learn from that! They
keep sending all kinds of idiots here . . . They've got accustomed in the regiments to shouting at anyone, without knowing
the particulars . . . But here you've got military district staff!
Here, one must have a head on one's shoulders! Staff work is
subtle, not everyone can . . . It's a good thing that Misha is not
touchy . . . or we'd now be in a fine old mess!'

The whole night through I thought about Misha. The lieutenant-
colonel was old enough to be his father, but because of his status
he was not simply a lieutenant-colonel, battalion commander or
some kind of a regimental commander's deputy, no, this was a
lieutenant-colonel of a special kind, not a duty officer on the staff
of a division, corps or army, no, a duty officer on the staff of a
military district! One could clamber all one's life up the slippery
career ladder and still not reach such a dizzy height. And
suddenly Misha breezes in, just like Misha—no more and
no less—a chap who has served no more than six months
in the army, while the lieutenant-colonel has been through
the whole war . . . If fate had sent this same Misha to our
training division he would now be grovelling even in front of the
lance-corporals . . .

Where did he get his swaggering conceit from? Where did he
acquire that look on his face? It goes without saying that a relief
driver for Lieutenant-General Parshikov's spare car is not the
lowest figure on the military district staff. But, still, where did all
that contempt come from?

Maybe our leaders have some kind of special system for
selecting people who are marked with a stamp of churlishness?
The lad could only have driven the manure lorry on a farm,
nothing more, so where did he manage to acquire all this veneer?
Or maybe we are all like him and, when we reach the foot of the
pyramid of power, we forget everything except ourselves and,
blinded by our own authority, we show nothing but contempt for
all those lower than ourselves?

In that case what liberties must the cook and chamber-maid
permit themselves, they who are so much closer to Parshikov's
own person than Misha, and who have been in the job for years?
And supposing Comrade Parshikov suddenly becomes a colonel-
general and not only a deputy but the commander of the whole

military district? What liberties will Misha permit himself then?
The very thought made me feel giddy.

In my uneasy sleep, that swine-faced Misha pursued me along
the endless nightmarish corridors of absolute power with no one
to control him and nothing to stop him.

PART THREE

The Ukraine, 1967.

The Way towards Commander-in-Chief

EVERY COMMANDER OF a platoon or a battalion or a regiment must seek a way of distinguishing himself and showing himself off to his immediate superior, otherwise younger, more pushing officers will trample him underfoot.

The commander of our division was very clever at all kinds of tricks and probably owes to this his promotion to the rank of major-general. He looks like he's going higher still. In military matters, he rated an absolute zero, but this of course plays no role in the Soviet Army nor does it have the least effect upon one's military career. What one must possess is a talent for organisation and some 'savvy'! So it was that the divisional commander worked out that his career prospects would depend not on spotless parade grounds or neat rows of beds in the barracks, but on something more original.

His particular plan was as simple as it was original: to invite the Chief of the Kiev Military District, Army General Yakubovskiy, to a meeting with the officers of the division to say, 'Look, dear Comrade Chief, in our division, while all the others are busy with battle training and other assorted shit, if you will forgive the expression, our division is not. Our division can't

sleep or eat, we only long to see our beloved Chief and to hear
how he defended our beloved Motherland from her enemies and
why he was awarded his many orders and medals. And, in
general, please take good note of our love for you. Indeed, we
love you so much that we recognise no other authority. This is
the kind of division we are, and we have a remarkable divisional
commander.'

A top-secret conference of the district's military commanders
was in progress. Questions concerning mobilisation preparedness
were under discussion. The walls of the big hall were covered
with maps, graphs and diagrams. The discussion was serious and
businesslike. Worthwhile ideas about how to raise our battle
readiness and the improved training of troops were being put
forward.

There were strict time limits: three minutes for divisional
commanders and their chiefs of staff, five minutes for army
commanders and their deputies and chiefs of staff, ten minutes
for the district commander, his deputies and for the chief of the
district's staff. Everybody, without exception, must take part,
but only with specific criticism and specific suggestions, there
must be no waffle.

When our divisional commander's turn came, he rose and,
without even glancing at his notes, began:

'We lack battle experience, Comrades, we have lived so many
years without war that we have forgotten everything. Many
regimental commanders, let alone battalion and company commanders, have never even smelt gunpowder. And just look what
a chance we are missing! We are serving under the command of
such a glorious general as Comrade Ivan Ignat'evich Yakubovskiy,
who fought throughout the whole of the last war. This is where
we must accumulate our experience! In my division, I held a
meeting, and my young officers advised me . . . They said,
Comrade General, invite Comrade Yakubovskiy to visit our
division, let him tell us about war! Comrade Commander, I take
this opportunity of passing on to you the request of our division's
young officers!'

All the other generals present were disgusted by this blatant
flattery. The main thing was that our general had avoided making any specific criticism or any specific suggestions. And yet
his speech was accepted as making a specific suggestion and the
most valuable one to boot.

'Well, all right, I'll come then,' mumbled dear old Ivan Ignat'evich. 'Why not, after all?'

When the military chief had left the hall, the army commander's deputy, Lieutenant-General Gelenkov, turned towards our cunning divisional commander and, in a sugary voice, loud enough to be heard by all the others, he asked whether it was not perhaps his post that our efficient divisional commander was aiming at. Everybody laughed appreciatively. But the divisional commander was not offended: the deputy army commander was still his direct superior for the time being, and the divisional commander never took offence at his superiors. This was one of his basic principles which had never let him down.

After returning from the conference, the divisional commander got busy. All battle training was immediately stopped—tanks, armoured personnel carriers, guns, all were put into mothballs. Every soldier was thrown into 'sprucing up' work, cleaning and repainting cars and redecorating the barracks. More than half the division went off to do 'illegal' jobs: some to collective farms, others to unload railway wagons or to work in factories.

The director of any factory and the chairman of any collective farm are always asking military commanders to help them out with men. Nowhere are there enough people, in collective farms or in industry or transport. Such 'illegal' operations are mutually profitable. The military commander illegally receives cement, asphalt, bricks, steel, timber, nails and, what is even more important, paint, while the directors and chairmen are able to report increased productivity and an over-achieved budget. At present labour productivity is very much the fashionable criterion. Even Vladimir Ilich Lenin taught us, long ago, that in the end productivity is the most important single factor in the victory of new economic structure. Plan fulfilment is of paramount importance.

So, industry, agriculture and transport all welcome activity of this nature by the army. They are ready to accept any number of soldiers at any given moment and to pay for their labour generously in kind. The only problem the directors ever have is how to coax military commanders to let them have more soldiers on a more regular basis. The army is equally pleased with the practice. Indeed, the only person opposed to it is the Defence Minister. He carries on a merciless campaign against the system, but how can one person resist the will of the collective?

Suppose the Defence Minister gives a resounding order: only

he personally, and then only in exceptional circumstances, may order the troops to tear themselves away from battle training. The district commanders listen attentively, nodding their heads. Who could possibly impinge upon the monopoly of the Defence Minister? The Minister orders one of the divisions to work for three days in the fields or at the factory, and to pay all the proceeds into the Defence Ministry's fund. Very well, it shall be done!

For three days, the division works for the Defence Ministry, but on the fourth day it works for the military district commander. If a Moscow commission should arrive unexpectedly, it is always possible to justify oneself: 'We are working for you on your own orders.'

Every district commander issues a similar directive: only on his explicit orders may troops engage in collateral work instead of battle training, in all other instances their work will be considered illegal. The army commanders, of course, agree, but promptly issue similar orders in their own name to stop all unofficial work. In my own experience, our regiment nevertheless used to spend exactly half its time moonlighting. This state of affairs is quite common in the Soviet Army and exists everywhere, except among troops stationed abroad. Indeed, it seems that the Soviet Army could be halved without any damage to its fighting efficiency. This was exactly what Khrushchev attempted, but he failed to provide the army either with sufficient rations or with the necessary supplies. Khrushchev's reforms were not a success, and the army, though cut by nearly half, still continued its moonlighting operations just as intensively as before.

But let us return to our brave divisional commander, who so resolutely directed 4,000 soldiers to carry out unofficial work.

He was a bold man, but he took a calculated risk. Neither the district staff nor the army staff could reproach him for anything, because Army General Yakubovskiy had consented to make his unofficial visit, thus allowing the divisional commander to prepare an appropriate welcome for him.

Having allotted jobs to every soldier in his division, he ordered the chief of staff to take charge of building materials, and his deputy to organise the complete renovation of the whole barracks. He, together with the chief of the Political Department, busied himself with the most important task of all—the planning of the reception itself.

There was not much time left, only two months at the most,

during which it was necessary to learn by heart the life history of our beloved general, to select from it the most striking and memorable details, and to prepare suitable questions; seemingly innocent questions, but ones which would stimulate the general to go into detail about his most heroic and amazing feats. It was also necessary to organise a competition among the young officers, to choose those who would ask questions from the floor, as well as supplementary questions, and then to carry out lengthy training for both these groups. Another competition was arranged to discover the best painters and craftsmen, who were then ordered to draw a gigantic map pinpointing events in the commander's war career and to prepare souvenirs to be presented by the personnel of our division. And, of course, there would be a big concert and banquet, to be laid on by the Political Department and the chief of the divisional rear services.

In the competition among young officers, I happened to be one of those selected and, at the distribution of roles, became the third relief for the officer who had to ask: 'Comrade Commander, please tell us how you shoed Churchill.'

All my friends and I too had heard this story a thousand times, and now we had to stimulate Yakubovskiy into telling it yet again. During the war, Great Britain provided the Soviet Union with Churchill tanks. But they were not ideally suited to the conditions of a Russian winter, and their tracks skidded on the snow. Then, one of the soldiers in Lieutenant-Colonel Yakubovskiy's tank brigade proposed putting spikes on the caterpillar tracks, as a result of which the practicability of using the tanks in the snow increased greatly. That very day, it was reported to the front commander that Yakubovskiy's brigade had 'shoed' Churchill. At a suitable moment, the front commander reported to Stalin that Lieutenant-Colonel Yakubovskiy had shoed Churchill. The joke pleased Stalin and the Lieutenant-Colonel after many months at the rear in the front line reserve, became a Hero of the Soviet Union and a personal favourite of Stalin. Gradually, with the rise of Yakubovskiy, this story began to change in detail and became encrusted with new heroic overtones.

These two months' preparation for our important guest in a small Ukrainian town called Oster were for me the very best time in the whole of my service in the training division. My soldiers were working away somewhere, I did not know exactly where. Every morning after breakfast, all those who had been selected to put questions to our guest gathered in the officers' mess and the rehearsal started: first question, first question understudy, second question, second understudy, etcetera. After a week of intensive training, a theatre director was invited down from Kiev and the whole thing started to go with a swing.

There is no doubt that our commander was a genius, but even if he had been an absolute idiot we could have turned him, in the space of two months, into a veritable Napoleon Bonaparte. That, at least, was the considered opinion of all the division's officers, of everyone who took part in the preparations for the reception of our beloved general.

After marinading for a month in this extraordinary ragout I fully understood the whole process of the cult of the personality for the rest of my life. It became quite obvious to me why we loved Lenin and Brezhnev so much, and why we loved Khrushchev and Stalin so much. All of us who were preparing for the reception of Yakubovskiy were mere amateurs, we were about to glorify one of the sixteen district commanders, not even the Commander-in-Chief, Land Forces; we had a mere two months at our disposal. Give me a couple of years, a staff of professional speakers and all the State's resources at my disposal, with the right to annihilate if necessary millions of dissatisfied people, and I will create for you from a bald, stuttering, impotent, mad Herod, a genius for all times and for all peoples!

The great general mounted the platform, took a sip of water, put his papers in front of him, cleaned his spectacles with his handkerchief, checked them against the light, cleaned them again, coughed slightly, put his spectacles on his nose, drank some more water and started to read.

'Comrades! The whole Soviet people in-spi-red by the his-tor-ical de-ci-sions of the Party Congress . . . etc . . . with seven-league boots . . . astronauts ploughing the furrows of space . . . milking and wool-shearing . . . millions of tons and billions of cubic metres . . .'

Then smoothly, as if through habit, he switched to the Imperialists, the Maoists and the Zionists, the enemy intelligence services and other disruptive elements; and then, equally smoothly, to the glorious Soviet Army, vigilantly watching over . . .

After two and a half hours, he neared his conclusion: 'And the gallant soldiers of our Red Banner District, and the gallant soldiers of the whole of our army, will spare no pain . . . or effort . . .'

Two and a half hours without once deviating from his prepared text, two and a half hours reading at dictation speed about things which we are all obliged to read every day in the editorials of *Red Star*. And that was all! Nothing else. No questions, no answers, not a personal word. Not a single word.

He collected up his papers, finished off the bottle of water, took off his spectacles, and departed to the accompaniment of thunderous applause.

Hundreds of officers, ready for anything, but not for this lunacy, were wildly clapping while trying not to catch one another's eyes, for the shame of it. Everybody was struck by the dullness, callousness, colourlessness, absolutely inhuman heartlessness of a stupid, corrupt, overfed official who was as fat as a bull.

'Where did such an idiot spring from?' I asked rhetorically after the first glass. Of course, I didn't expect an answer, knowing Yakubovskiy's background maybe better than he himself knew it. However, I was deeply mistaken, as we clearly knew only the visible part of the story.

'He distinguished himself at the battle for Moscow.'

This answer, totally unexpected, revolted me.

'At the battle for Moscow there was certainly no trace there of Yakubovskiy.'

'I'm not talking of 1941—I mean 1953.'

'Get on with it then. Your audience is waiting for you!'

'Being one of Stalin's favourites, our old friend Yabukovskiy* had become commander of the Kantemirov court tank division. When the trouble started the commander of the Taman' Division was reluctant to raise his hand against the State Security people, and he was eventually put up against the same wall alongside them. But Yakubovskiy did not hesitate. He's always ready to carry out any order from Party or Government, but it all depends whose order comes first: if Beriya had given the order first, Yakubovskiy would happily have hanged the whole Politburo, but Beriya didn't give the first order . . . After that, his star rose even further as all the leaders were so grateful to him.'

'He may become a marshal, or Chief of the General Staff.'

---

*By means of this simple juggling with the letters, his surname becomes a thing of ridicule and approximates in meaning to 'Fuckerskiy'.

'No, never. Men like him are given more delicate posts, governing peoples' democracies for instance.'

These prophetic words came true exactly three months later, when Army General Yakubovskiy was promoted to the rank of Marshal of the Soviet Union and given the post of Commander-in-Chief of the Combined Armed Forces of the Warsaw Treaty Powers. On the other hand, maybe the lieutenant who predicted this was not a prophet at all, but just had a contact somewhere at the base of the power pyramid, where everything is known already—the past and the future of all 250 million souls.

About two days after these changes in the upper echelons of the Soviet Army, our battalion was ordered to go urgently to Kiev 'to carry out the work of transferring equipment from the command points'.

We were taken to Yakubovskiy's country house (not the one where his wife lived, but his own personal house). A young aide-de-camp and about ten soldier-gardeners were directing the work there. There is, believe it or not, a famous horticultural training school in Moldavia, whose graduates are drafted into the army and appointed not as machine-gunners or snipers, but as gardeners at numerous military 'establishments'. That is actually how it is put on their military cards. Gardeners serve two years in the army, three years in the navy, and they acquire extremely high standards in their art.

Our work at Yakubovskiy's villa was somewhat unusual. We dug up the best trees according to the gardeners' instructions, wrapped their roots in sacking and then carried them to the airfield, where heavy aircraft of Military Transport Aviation, especially allotted for this operation, awaited us.

It is difficult to say what the point of all this was. Maybe Yakubovskiy or his wife did not want to be separated from familiar trees or perhaps, by removing them, he wanted to demonstrate his contempt for his successor, Lieutenant-General Kulikov, who was then a complete nonentity, and only later received the rank of colonel-general.

My deputy, Sergeant Kokhar', was more puzzled than the others by this air transportation of trees.

'Why the hell by air? Look what a long way it is from here to the airfield—the roots will get damaged. It would have been much simpler to give us a railway detachment since the branch line runs just beside the house, and it would have taken them only one night to reach Moscow. What a crazy idea—aircraft! A train would have been much more economical!'

The all-army conference of young officers, the Kremlin,
Moscow. 26 November, 1969.

New Ideas

THE RUMOUR THAT the Head of the Chief Political Directorate of
the Soviet Army, Army General Epishev, suffers from the sever-
est form of sclerosis has been persistently repeated. Sharp tongues
maintain that, when he turns over a page, he promptly forgets
completely what he has just read.

I don't usually believe rumours, simply because I know only
too well where so many of them originate. But, subsequently, I
had an opportunity to prove that, in this instance, the rumours
were very accurate indeed.

Epishev mounted the platform, cleared his throat, drank some
water and, in a dreary monotone, started to read about the
historic decisions of the Party Congress (decisions which, incidentally, for some funny reason, never seem to bear fruit),
concerning the care of our beloved peasant workers and the
further development of agriculture, and the strengthening of our
defences.

At the speaker's first words, the many-thousand-strong audience lowered their heads over their notebooks and started com-
pulsively to summarise the words of this man who occupied such
a high position in the Party, the Army and the State. I too

owered my head and pretended to write. Personally, I have a deep antipathy to writing summaries and, in the present case, it was anyway completely absurd—first, because his speech would be published in all the military newspapers, and secondly because Epishev would certainly not tell us any more than is printed every day in *Red Star*.

Everything was going just as usual when suddenly the audience flinched. Epishev's vivid and memorable harangue had suddenly stopped in the middle of a word. Then he began to read it all over again from the very beginning. 'In the name of and at the request of . . .' he welcomed all those present, who answered him with a storm of applause. And everyone started to write down precisely what they had already noted down only a moment before.

After about five minutes, Epishev again stopped and began to read a new sentence, absolutely unconnected with the previous one. The audience sensed, rather than understood, that the speaker was repeating himself, that he was giving the same examples which he had already given, and that he was shouting out the same slogans which he had shouted just a short while ago.

Suddenly, everybody guessed, everybody understood, what the matter was. Owing to the negligence of the researchers (why must they consume so much caviar?), Epishev had been given a speech written by somebody else, but *in duplicate:* beginning with the two first pages, followed by the second ones, and so on. In our army, no one reads his speech before he delivers it in public, and Epishev was simply following this unwritten regulation. The audience was somewhat perplexed. But the speaker, who was obviously not accustomed to noticing public reaction of any sort, continued his monotonous reading. In this way, he read forty pages instead of twenty.

After finishing his historic speech, the Head of the Chief Political Directorate returned in triumph to his place on the platform where the Minister of Defence, Marshal of the Soviet Union Comrade Grechko, was sitting with the other sclerotics and decrepit senile old bodies. None of them even so much as noticed what had just happened.

A cynical critic may not believe this story, but I have more than 2,000 witnesses; indeed, more than that, since many of them summarised this speech in their notebooks with two introductions, two conclusions and twenty repetitions, starting and ending in the middle of a word.

The most astonishing thing is that all this happened in 1969 at the time of the USSR young army officers' congress. A good ten years have passed since then and the young officers have become mature ones, but Comrade Epishev is still at his post. Untiringly he fights on. Boldly he instils the most advanced and effective methods throughout the broad masses of the army. He resolutely reflects, through the prism of the class struggle, the newest development of world history and brings to the army the unfading light of Leninist ideas.

The Group of Soviet Troops in Germany. Spring 1970. As one of a group of observers, I took part in 3rd Shock Army manoeuvres.

Determination

THE COMMANDER-IN-CHIEF of the Group of Soviet Forces in Germany, Army General Kulikov, liked to control everything himself. Sometimes, he flew over the roads in a helicopter, watching Soviet military vehicles exceeding the speed limit. Sometimes, he lay in the bushes, eavesdropping on what his officers were talking about in their smoking room. But most of all he enjoyed putting on sports clothes and bicycling through Vünsdorf, especially in the evenings.

It was a Saturday evening and officers' pay day. All the beer houses were packed with staff officers, as everyone was taking the opportunity to drink as much of that lovely beer as he could, because when you returned to the Soviet Union where would you find such good beer?

The Commander-in-Chief flitted like a ghost past the brilliantly-lit windows of restaurants and beer houses, and anger welled up inside him. He could not understand the passion of Soviet officers for German beer. The sated can never comprehend those who are hungry, and he was always supplied with the best wines and had eight cooks, who are always in the Commander-in-Chief's baggage train ready to prepare the most recherché dishes for him. Like any true communist, Kulikov roundly condemned drunkenness and crusaded against it with great determination.

'Drinking, eh? Well, I'll soon show you, with your drinking!'

A sudden idea flashed across his mind, he smiled to himself, turned his bicycle round and rode back towards the Group of Soviet Troops Headquarters.

Without changing his clothes, he entered his study, thought for a moment and picked up a red telephone which had no selector dial. It was answered at once. The Commander-in-Chief blew into the receiver as was his wont and then imperiously ordered: 'The 215th independent sapper battalion—battle stations! Version 7, cypher 2323777.'

'Right, Comrade,' came the answer.

Half an hour later, the Commander-in-Chief was at the forest clearing where the sapper battalion was waiting for him. After a short consultation with the officers, the Commander-in-Chief finished with the words, 'Give no warning before destruction, just destroy and be done with it. Forty-five minutes to reach Vünsdorf, twenty-five minutes to perform the operation!'

Bellowing wildly and much the worse for drink, officers were jumping out of the windows, and wild shadows rushing about in the darkness. Tank engines were roaring into life. The noise of crashing was horrible. Everything was falling about. 'It must be war!' was the only thought which coursed simultaneously through a thousand heads.

'I always said that everything would happen exactly as it did in 1941,' shouted a lieutenant-colonel whose left shoulder-strap had been torn off.

Heavy army bulldozers quickly destroyed the fragile glass pavilions, and within a moment the clean little town was filled with dust and the spicy smell of good German beer. By morning, the soft green lawns were all that was left of the former restaurants and beer-houses. The warm summer rain settled the dust, and there was nothing to remind anybody of the night raid by a sapper battalion.

That is how drunkenness in Vünsdorf was eradicated for good. The Head of the Political Directorate delightedly reported to the Chief Political Directorate and to the Central Committee about the remarkable determination of the new Commander-in-Chief in his fight against drunkenness.

Exactly one month later, on the next pay-day, the Chief of the Finance Directorate for that group of troops timidly entered the

general's study and reported that there was no money in the till
to issue the officers with their salaries.

'Well,' said the Commander-in-Chief, 'write a report and we
shall bring the guilty ones to trial before the military tribunal!
But what, by the way, is the real reason? Is it because the
cashiers have been embezzling?'

'No,' the man from Finance explained shyly, 'we normally
receive only a very insignificant part of the necessary money
from Moscow. The bulk came from the military trade system—
from the beer-houses, is what I mean. The deutschmarks were
circulating, we gave them to the officers, they brought them to
the beer-houses, we took them back and gave them back to the
officers. But now there are no Soviet beer-houses in Vünsdorf,
so all the officers are using the German ones, which are fifteen
kilometres away. All the marks go there now instead. We have
asked Moscow, but Moscow doesn't give us any money.'

The Commander-in-Chief ground his teeth. Then he grabbed
the red telephone, the one without the selector dial.

This time the Commander-in-Chief did not himself go to the
spot where the sapper battalion was assembling, but sent one of
his aides-de-camp instead, with the order: 'Restore all the restaurants and beer-houses in Vünsdorf. You've got a maximum of a
fortnight!'

A training division, Oster. Early 1967.

Durov's Way

HE PUSHED THE remains of a herring backbone complete with tai
up his arse and shouted in tones of mock pathos: 'Comrade
officers, don't come near me. I'm a mermaid and I'm shy!'

It happened at a New Year party, during a competition for the
most original fancy dress. Senior Lieutenant Durov possesse
neither sharp reflexes nor a sense of humour, but when the
competition was announced, Durov responded in a flash, i
you'll forgive the pun. Apparently he had prepared his ac
beforehand. The Senior Lieutenant stripped off his guards uni
form, and simply donned the aforementioned herring.

Everyone was deeply shocked, regardless of their state o
intoxication and an age-old habit in the Soviet Army of neve
being astonished by anything. The chief of the regimental staf
stood up and left the room, banging the door behind him. The
other senior officers followed close on his heels.

At the first officers' meeting in the New Year, the commande
of the 3rd Battalion tabled a motion that Senior Lieutenant Duro
be brought before an officers' court of honour for insulting the
regimental staff. This proposal was supported by the chief o
staff, the technical deputy regimental commander, the head o

136

artillery and all the battalion commanders, except the 1st, and all the company and battery commanders, except the commander of 3rd Company. There is no prize for guessing that the senior lieutenant served in the 3rd Company, which is part of the 1st Battalion. If a platoon commander is found guilty, it puts a stain on the company's reputation, as well as on the battalion and, of course, on the regiment itself, or, more precisely, on the regimental commander and his political deputy, since it indicates a weak programme of education. This was exactly why the flushed political deputy jumped up and shouted:

'To condemn people, comrades, is the easiest thing in the world but to educate them is far more difficult. Too hasty a decision by us and we could spoil the career of an officer with a bright future before him.'

'His future belongs in a madhouse,' remarked the reconnaissance company commander.

Durov sat in the first row, unconcernedly staring at the dark window. It was all the same to him. The only thing he wanted in the whole world was to have another drink. January had only begun and there was still a long time to wait until pay-day, cherished date the 13th. And they had long since stopped giving him vodka on tick in the small garrison restaurant. Everybody could get vodka on tick but not him: it was a kind of discrimination. He did not care a damn about anything being said at this officers' meeting, only deep down it was all somehow distasteful.

It was not, however, a matter of indifference to the regimental commander. The decision to bring a young officer before an officers' court of honour was a matter for him alone. If he said yes, it would mean that the officers of the regiment would band together and remove one of the stars from the senior lieutenant's shoulder-straps, and they might even remove the shoulder-straps altogether—then you can go anywhere you like, former senior lieutenant, there'll be no pension for you because you are too young, and no future either as you are already too old to begin life anew. The divisional commander, the army commander and the district commander will automatically ratify the decision of the officers' court because, otherwise, the one who approves the decision takes upon himself all future responsibility for faux pas committed by dipsomaniac senior lieutenants. If the regimental commander says no, then the senior lieutenant will go on being educated until the next incident, after which the question of the commander's decision again arises.

A decision in the affirmative is always a painful one to make for every Soviet commander because, basically, his own personal career depends on the extent to which he manages to reduce the number of offences and breaches of discipline, as well as on how well the soldiers make their beds and on how well the fences of the cantonment are kept painted. The actual registration of offences is not governed by the quantity of offences but by the quantity of penalties meted out. Discipline in the Soviet Army is exceptionally low. In many areas, the army amounts almost to an undisciplined herd, precisely because every commander is busy struggling for his own survival. The victor in this endless struggle will be the one who, in general, never punishes his soldiers and officers, irrespective of the kind of offences they have committed. The only department which enforces some form of discipline is the Military Commandant's Office and that is only because its allotted task is to catch any soldiers and officers who might fall within its grasp. The Commandatura offices have another way of operating and a completely different system. Everything there is the other way round. They are anxious to detect as many infringements and breaches as possible. But, generally, the offices of the Commandatura operate outside military cantonments: in towns, at railway stations and at airports. It is their activities which create the illusion of discipline and order, but when all is said and done it is only an illusion.

The regimental commander had long been awaiting an opportunity to exercise his power, but this particular case was too risky. Discipline in the regiment had anyway already fallen to the lowest possible ebb and to start the new year with such a decision would have been ill-advised. Just suppose something really serious happened tomorrow which it would be impossible to whitewash or hush up. Then what? Then somebody would have to be punished and there would already be two infringements on the statistics. Meanwhile, in other regiments everything would be peace and light.

The commander stood up. To go against the almost unanimous decision of the other officers was not a good idea either, so he said grimly, 'Let's not be hasty: we must think it over.'

And they had to think it over for a very long time indeed.

A week later, the chief of staff telephoned the regimental commander and asked him immediately to forward the papers of his best platoon commander with a view to appointing the latter as a company commander in the neighbouring regiment. In ten minutes flat, the political deputy commander of the 1st Battalion and that of the 3rd Company were in the regimental commander's study.

'Comrade Officers, I have been commanded to send the best of our platoon commanders to the neighbouring regiment to be promoted. I think that Senior Lieutenant Durov will fill the bill. Of course, he does make slips from time to time, but who does not? I think he has fully realised his guilt and that this new responsibility will only help him. Is that not so? Trust does great things for people. With responsibility for a whole company, he will not have time to get drunk. One thing is clear, we must give the man a chance, otherwise he will be pecked to death. Just try telling a man every single day that he is a swine and he will soon start to grunt like a pig!'

The company commander wrote a brilliant character reference for Durov. The battalion commander added: 'I completely endorse these conclusions. Signed Commander of the First Tank Battalion, Guards Lieutenant-Colonel Nesnosnyy.' The regimental commander also agreed: 'Deserves to be nominated for the post of commander of a tank company. Signed Commander of the 210th Guards Tank Regiment, awarded the orders of Bogdan Khmel'nitskiy and Aleksandr Nevskiy, the Port-Arturskiy Regiment, Guards Colonel Zavalishin!'

The political deputy wrote a separate reference relating to Durov's moral and political qualities: 'Party activist, sportsman, social worker,' and everything else appropriate in such circumstances.

The papers went on their way to divisional staff where they were approved by the commander of the division.

'I've found a real winner to be the commander of the fifth company of the 299th regiment. He's not just an officer but pure gold. A falcon. He's an experienced activist, a sportsman and a social worker. You'll be grateful to me for the rest of your days.'

'And may I ask, Comrade General, who this man is?'

'Senior Lieutenant, what was his name . . . Yes . . . Durov . . .'
The Colonel turned pale.

'Are you joking, Comrade General?'

'Why? What's the matter?'

'But I know this Durov like the back of my hand, we live in

the same mess. And not only me, but the whole division knows him though they don't live in the same mess with him.'

'Wait, just a moment, it isn't the same Durov who got so drunk that he vomited his insides out at the 7th of November parade?'

'That's the one, Comrade General, and remember also how he once ruined a tank engine, this very same Durov?'

'Well! That's Zavalishin for you, the scoundrel. He must have decided to pull a fast one. But just you wait, I'll make you dance for your pains.'

'Well, Zavalishin, we've confirmed your little falcon as company commander.'

'Thank you, Comrade General.'

'Do you think he'll be able to cope?'

'He's proved his worth, he'll be okay.'

'But Zavalishin, all is not well with discipline at your place, is it? Eh? What?'

'We are doing our best, Comrade General. We didn't start this year too badly and we hope to continue in the same vein.'

'Do you know what occurred to us at Staff HQ? In order not to deprive you of one of your best officers, we decided in the circumstances to leave this excellent fellow, Durov, with your regiment, as commander of the 3rd Company. The neighbouring regiment is in need of a company commander, so we shall give them the present commander of your 3rd Company, and replace him by this same Durov. Let him remain in your regiment. Let him command a company and help to strengthen discipline there.'

And then, suddenly changing his good-humoured banter to those steely tones employed sometimes by all commanders, the divisional commander announced bluntly: 'The order relating to the switch-over of the said officers was signed today.'

And that is how Guards Senior Lieutenant Durov became commander of the 1st Battalion's 3rd Company of the 210th Guards Tank Regiment. There were practically no changes at all in his lifestyle. The only thing was that his income increased and so consequently did his drinking. Nothing could now be said about the court of honour—since his promotion in itself indicated confidence in him on the part of his superiors and forgiveness of all past sins. Neither the regimental commander, nor his political deputy, nor the battalion commander could possibly complain about Durov or take any steps towards his demotion, because each of them in turn had written such a brilliant character reference. Unquestionably, they must have expected their ruse to be discovered eventually, but they could never have thought that it would happen so soon. If the truth had come to light in, say, a week's time, after Durov's transfer, the commanders of the 210th could have put their hands on their hearts and sworn that to the best of their knowledge he was a good man and that surely something had suddenly gone wrong with him. Generally speaking, of course, subterfuges of this kind produce no complications when an officer is transferred to another town or even to another army or division. There is a cast-iron law: once the order is signed, it's done with! Of course Colonel Zavalishin was well acquainted with all these subtleties, he just did not have the time to wait for another opportunity to transfer Durov to another division. He had to move quickly and take a risk. As things turned out, he risked and lost.

With the appearance of its new commander, discipline in the 3rd Company broke down altogether. Battle-training and battle-preparedness also fell off sharply. The divisional commander, in no mind to forgive and forget what had happened, always hurried to inspect the 3rd Company whenever he visited the 210th Regiment, after which he invariably summoned the regimental and battalion commanders and had long talks with them. He had decided to teach them a lesson. In the end, of course, he would have to remove Durov from the company but for the time being he was in no hurry to do so, and any suggestions about Durov's replacement were invariably dismissed by the divisional commander.

The divisional commander was away on leave and his duties were being performed by his deputy, who had recently arrived from Egypt. The deputy commander had not yet had time to get to know the ropes.

Zavalishin and the battalion commander were both on the prowl, like caged tigers. The absence of the divisional commander must be quickly and resolutely exploited. Durov must be urgently disposed of. Where to was immaterial— Syria or Hungary, or the Transbaikal region or the far north; promotion or demotion—no matter.

After he had been presented with a dozen bottles of brandy, the chief of the divisional cadres department came up with a piece of advice: Send him to the Academy.

Brilliant character references were again concocted for this best of all company commanders in the 210th Guards Tank Regiment. They were approved by the divisional commander's deputy and urgently despatched to Moscow.

There were only six character references in Durov's personal file: two written at the time of his graduation from military school, two stating that he was the best platoon commander in the regiment, and two stating that he was now the best company commander in the same regiment. The references written at the military school were pale and inconsequential, neither fish, nor fowl nor good red meat (at school he simply had no opportunity to reveal himself as an alcoholic because an officer-cadet's pay is too low), but all the rest of the references were simply brilliant. Within a week, Durov was summoned to Moscow to sit an entrance examination for the Armoured Troops Academy.

'If he fails to get in,' said the regimental commander, biting his nails nervously, 'the divisional commander will have us for breakfast.'

'No, he won't get in, not that bloody alcoholic. How could he?'

'But why not? Maybe he will, idiots are invariably lucky. In any academy, idiots are given preference.'

'We've blundered . . . and how!'

'What do you mean?'

'It's time he was made a captain, and of course we did nothing about it. How can you make a captain out of a man like him? But in the Academy they're bound to harp on about it. Why, they will ask, when you have a company commander with such a distinguished service record, did you not promote him to captain long ago?'

The very next day, a recommendation to confer the rank of captain upon that excellent commander of a tank company, Senior Lieutenant Durov, was urgently despatched to Moscow.

Durov joined the Academy and a month later was promoted to Guards Captain. His unexpected rise could not leave even Durov unimpressed. The psychological shock produced by his elevation suddenly woke in him a superiority complex. He did not stop his drinking, but he did considerably reduce his activity in that direction. Now, he only drank alone, not so much out of any consideration for safety as out of contempt for his comrades.

His scant intellect never gave birth to a single original idea but he compensated for that by cramming and by learning the academic text books off by heart, thus staggering his professors by the exactness with which he reiterated the thoughts once expressed by these same professors, who had written the books in the first place.

He was held up as an example of a conscientious, competent and contemporary officer. After three years' study he graduated from the Academy with honours (it must here be stated that, to achieve this in the command faculty of the Armoured Troops Academy, one does not need to be very clever; a degree of application is called for and nothing more).

After graduation, Durov duly received the next military rank of major, by order of the Defence Minister himself. Having graduated with honours, he had the right to choose his posting and Durov chose his own regiment.

By order of the Minister of Defence, Guards Major Durov was appointed deputy commander of the 210th Guards Tank Regiment, that same regiment, in which only three and a half years previously, he had merely been the commander of the worst tank platoon. As well as all regimental majors, all nine lieutenant-colonels of the regiment were also subordinate to him, including the chief of staff, the chief of anti-aircraft defence, the chief of the rear column, the technical deputy commander, the commander's deputy and four battalion commanders.

The system of conferring ranks in the Soviet Army differs in many respects from that adopted in other armies. When a vacancy arises, it is not filled by an officer who is senior in rank, with prolonged good service, experience or official position, but by someone who, in the high command's opinion, is most suitable. One consequence of this policy is that high-ranking officers often find themselves directly subordinate to lower-ranking officers.

To quote one example, after the death of Marshal Grechko, Colonel-General Ustinov was appointed to the post of Minister of Defence. Simultaneously with his appointment, Ustinov received the next military rank, that of army general, and all other army generals, marshals and chief marshals of the other arms of the service, even Marshals of the Soviet Union Kulikov, Ogarkov, Sokolov, Batitskiy, Moskalenko and Admiral of the Soviet Fleet Gorshkov, all found themselves directly subordinate to Ustinov.

This system has one unquestionable advantage, which is that it allows 'our people' to be pushed forward without consideration for any laws or regulations. 'In our opinion, this captain is the most capable and he should be put in charge of all the majors.'

Position has an overwhelming advantage over rank. For instance, Major-General Salmanov, Commander of the Kiev Military District, enjoys incomparably greater authority than any colonel-general of a second-rate district like the Ural or Odessa Districts. And a major, who is also the regimental commander's deputy, has many more privileges than a lieutenant-colonel who is the commander of a battalion.

The conferring of ranks depends on the post occupied, on long service and on relations with the higher authority. Army General Ogarkov received the rank of Marshal of the Soviet Union on the same day that he became Chief of the General Staff, while his predecessor, Army General Kulikov, only managed to become a Marshal when he left this same post!

To revert to Durov, when the latter returned to his old regiment, the regimental commander, Colonel Zavalishin, had already retired and been replaced by a young lieutenant-colonel from the Chinese frontier. The majority of the officers, however, including the first battalion's commander, Lieutenant-Colonel Nesnosnyy, still remained in their posts.

Yet another entirely objective factor had influenced Durov's rise. During the second half of the 1960s, frontline officers who, after the war, could not make a way for themselves at the Academy reached the peak of their service career at battalion level. They could not be promoted any higher as they had not graduated from the Academy, and to send them to the Academy now would be inexpedient as they were too old. There was also no reason to lower their ranks as all of them were experienced, worthy and disciplined campaigners, while to retire them was also impossible because, after Khrushchev's reforms, the army was terribly short of officers.

The front-line officers had a tight hold at battalion level on the posts of battalion commander and battalion deputy chief of staff, and they thus created a blockage on the promotion ladder. On the one hand, it was absolutely impossible to promote young officers above company level, and on the other hand, there were no replacements for officers retiring at regimental level. That is why many young officers, who managed to join the Academy from company level, returned at regimental level, thus jumping two rungs on the promotion ladder, often those of deputy battalion commander and battalion commander. This was a general phenomenon.

Durov himself was extremely vindictive. He remembered all

those who had suggested censuring him before an officers' court of honour, though the one man who spoke out on his behalf also felt the sharp edge of his tongue. He found fault with the smallest, most insignificant detail and berated the guilty party with intolerable abuse. Durov entered without mercy any error committed by any officer in the officer's personal file, thus destroying that officer's career and deciding his fate for good.

Every officer changed his style, trying not to give Durov any cause to find fault. And it was in this way that the fame of Durov came to spread among higher-ranking officers as an exacting commander of principle. It was not surprising, therefore, that in a couple of years, while he was still only a major, he was given command of a regiment and that, only one year later, as the best of the regimental commanders of our division, he was sent to Syria in the capacity of military adviser to the commander of a Syrian tank division.

I knew Durov for many years and had to serve under his command. I met many officers who knew him at all stages of his career. Those small unwinking snake's eyes and that low threatening whisper still haunt me to this day in my worst dreams.

He had not the slightest idea about army problems or the possibilities of the army's development. However, those dogmas which he had learnt by heart were completely unshakable. The expression of any opinions differing from those expressed in text books written ten years before Durov entered the Academy of Armoured Troops was not only useless but even dangerous.

The way he behaved towards his subordinates could not be called uncultured, it was simply ill-mannered boorishness. We were astonished that he never read any books. We, his subordinates, saw in him only a combination of cruelty, intolerance and bestiality. I have never met anyone who served under his command who had a different opinion of him. But, to the powers-that-be, he was a model of how one's duty should be performed.

He was lucky: throughout the years of his stay in Syria he was never called upon to demonstrate his qualities as a commander in any battle with the enemy. After Syria, Durov's fortunes rocketed. I would not be surprised if, one fine day, I read in the newspaper that Colonel-General Durov has been appointed Commander of the Moscow Military District. That's just the place for the likes of him. They like his sort there, and then again perhaps I underestimate him? Maybe men of his ilk should be promoted higher still?

As a result of the unfortunate experience of the Middle Eastern adventure, the Soviet Army was hurled into the task of building aircraft shelters in the winter of 1967—68. These are my impressions of the Soviet combat airforce.

The Brick Bomber

GOOD LUCK FELL from the sky.

An American B-29 strategic bomber made a forced landing on Soviet soil. The bomber had been taking part in an air raid against our common enemy, Japan, and after getting shot up in battle somehow managed with great difficulty to reach the nearest airfield—Baranovskiy near Ussuriysk. The damage was superficial—its wings had been pierced in several places by machine-gun fire from a Japanese fighter, as a result of which the bomber had lost a lot of fuel. The commander had the choice of either bringing the bomber down in the ocean, thus dooming the crew to certain death, or trying to reach a faithful ally, repairing the holes, refuelling the bomber and, in a couple of days, resuming bombing Japan. The captain chose the second alternative. The bomber is worth a fortune, he reasoned, the damage is very slight. The crew is safe, and very experienced, and in war this is probably the most important thing. Why should I let such a crew be eaten by sharks while there is an ally right at hand? That is how the best strategic bomber in the world landed upon Soviet territory.

The news covered the distance from Ussuriysk to the Kremlin,

146

which is all of 10,000 kilometres, clearing all bureaucratic barriers in its path, in a matter of minutes. The event was reported to Josif Vissarionovich Stalin himself while he was in a meeting. Stalin thought for a moment then, having asked only the Politburo members to remain, he passed the news on to them and, with a cunning smile on his face, asked them to give their opinions.

The opinion was unanimous: to detain the bomber for a week under any pretext so as to enable specialists to acquaint themselves with the structure.

'And what if we do not return the bomber at all to our allies?' asked the Great Leader and Teacher, drawing on his pipe.

'The allies will be offended, Comrade Stalin,' Molotov objected cautiously.

'They may stop sending us supplies,' added Kaganovich. 'Then what shall we do without their Studebaker lorries?'

That splendid American army lorry was universally acknowledged as the best military vehicle by everybody from common soldier to marshal. The famous Russian Katyusha BM 13s were mounted exclusively on these American vehicles. The Soviet artillery was the mightiest in the world but its prime mover and ammunition transporter was that same American Studebaker. And, in addition to lorries, the allies supplied much else besides which was very important for the Soviet Army, including means of communication and jeeps, Aircobra fighters, armoured personnel carriers and tanks.

The supply could be stopped at any moment and, with that fact very much in mind, all the Politburo members fell to thinking. Very cautiously, everybody declared themselves against the proposition not to return the bomber. Only Beriya sat silent, trying to guess which way the Great Teacher's mind was inclining.

But the Teacher scoffed at the apprehensions of the Bureau and declared: 'As it is, we shall soon strangle Germany and what will be our next objective? How can we turn against England and America without a strategic bomber? The allies will put up with it,' he added, sucking his pipe. 'They will be a bit agitated for a while and then forget all about it. The bomber must be copied exactly, alike as two peas, and it must fly within the year.'

Beriya energetically supported Stalin while the other members of the Political Bureau readily agreed. They all knew only too well that the basic principle of their Leader and Teacher was that friends and allies should be treated like a woman—the more you beat her, the more she loves you. But every one of them doubted strongly in his heart that the allies would put up with it.

But the allies did put up with it. The American crew was returned, but not the best bomber in the world. The Soviet side did not even bother to invent any kind of explanation. We are not going to return it—full stop. Lease-lend supplies continued as usual because American diplomats were accustomed to discussing problems which arose without regard for questions of military supplies.

A. N. Tupolev, the best Soviet aircraft designer, was put in charge of the copying team and the new Soviet strategic bomber was named, after him, the later TU-4. A further sixty-four design bureaux and scientific research institutes joined in, copying the engines, the fuel and other materials used in the B-29's construction, as well as all its systems of navigation, sighting, internal and external communication network and much else besides. Co-ordination of all the work was entrusted to a member of the Political Bureau, Comrade Lavrentiy Pavlovich Beriya, and the aircraft designer, Yakovlev, was appointed technical consultant. The latter understood Stalin better than anyone else and he knew how to please him.

A huge new workshop was hurriedly built at the restored aircraft factory in Vorohekh where, incidentally, twenty-two years later, the unsuccessful attempt to copy the Concorde was made.

The B-29 was dismantled into thousands of the smallest possible parts, which were distributed among the various ministries, departments, design bureaux and scientific research institutes with the explicit command to copy each detail, aggregate or device and then to embark upon its mass-production within ten months.

The bomber probably received the unfortunate nickname, 'The Brick Bomber', owing to all these small parts and mechanisms being sent all over the Soviet Union. Many years later, in his book *The Aim of Life*, Yakovlev said that in 1945–46 we somehow missed out on the development of jet-propulsion. And, no doubt owing to his inborn modesty, Yakovlev completely forgot to explain why this happened. This was precisely the time when dear Comrades Yakovlev, Beriya and Tupolev were up to their necks creating the 'Brick'. Well might he have missed anything else. 'It must be ready to fly in a year's time'—this was all that Comrade Yakovlev remembered even while he slept.

Indeed, after the TU-4, all unsuccessful aircraft, especially those copied from foreign models, were unofficially nicknamed 'Bricks'. The most famous is, of course, the TU-144 Koncordskiy. But, on that occasion, there was no actual model to hand, only a few documents. Maybe also its failure was due to the absence of Lavrentiy Pavlovich's iron fist, without which all technical progress withered.

Difficulties arose from the very beginning of the copying process. To begin with, the use of the metric system of measuring was quite out of the question. If the weight of each rivet is only ten milligrammes less than it should be, it could lead to the whole structure's durability being diminished whereas, if the weight is just a bit greater, it could adversely influence the weight of the whole aircraft. Tupolev knew full well that if the aircraft was to be copied it must be copied in every detail, down to the last rivet, screw, nut and bolt.

Soviet trade representatives in Canada, England and the USA started to buy up measuring equipment in small quantities in order not to create any suspicion. And the retraining of thousands of engineers, technicians and workers, to switch over to calculating in inches, feet and pounds, began urgently.*

The training of thousands of crews and tens of thousands of ground staff, engineering and technical personnel for the hundreds of future new bombers began with the same urgency.

How many gallons of fuel would be needed at the normal rate of fuel consumption with no wind for a thousand-mile flight at a height of 30,000 feet? Elementary problems of this kind nonplussed not only the experienced aces, who had been through the whole war, but also the professors of the Aviation Academy.

Pressure in the piping is twelve pounds per square inch—is that a lot or a little?

It may not be so difficult for American and English specialists, accustomed as they are to operating with two different systems of measurement, but for the Soviet specialists it was problem number one. Thousands of mistakes were made and every one of them was mercilessly punished.

While the new system of measurement was becoming accepted in the Soviet aviation industry as a whole, another no less complicated problem emerged, that of keeping the secret, be-

---

*This system of measurement is still used in the Soviet Army.

cause in the eyes of the KGB anyone who displayed any knowledge of English measuring systems might easily be a potential carrier of State secrets to the enemy.

Everybody who saw Tupolev at that time remarked upon his gaiety and rather childlike, carefree attitude. Apparently, the old man was tormented by jealousy. He loved and yet he detested the B-29 and he tried to hide it from the others. The mechanical work of copying was sickening him and he concealed the fact under a mask of indifference. Tupolev had no problems then, solving with ease even the most complicated.

A little hole was found on the left wing of the aircraft. No aerodynamics or durability expert had the slightest idea what the hell it was for. There was no tube or wire attached to it and there was no equivalent hole in the right wing. The opinion of a commission of experts was that the little hole had been bored by a factory drill at the same time as the other holes for the rivets. So, what to do? Most probably, the hole had been drilled by mistake, and later no one had bothered to fill it in as it was much too small. The chief designer was asked his opinion.

'Do the Americans have it?'

'Yes.'

'So why the hell are you asking me? Weren't we ordered to make them absolutely identical! Alike as two peas?'

So, for that reason, a very small hole indeed, made with the thinnest possible drill, appeared on the left wing of all the TU-4 strategic bombers.

Here's a narrow pipe, through which one can crawl on all fours the whole length of the aircraft, and it has been painted light green (some design bureau or other struggled for a very long time in an attempt to copy it exactly) but, at its very end, several metres have been painted white. Maybe some soldier simply did not have enough paint. But the order was to copy it exactly, which is why all the Soviet bombers are the same colour as the American one. It was calculated exactly how much green paint there was and how much white paint. Later, this ratio was included in all instruction books on how to paint the interior of the bomber.

Meanwhile, another two B-29s made forced landings on Soviet territory. It was discovered that there was no hole in their wings, while the paint on one of them was light green and that on the other white. The chief designer was again asked what to do. But, once again, Tupolev had no problem. He had been ordered to copy the bomber which had landed first, and there were no orders concerning the others. So just go on copying!

It was later discovered, from the factory number, that the aircraft which had landed first had been built earlier than those which landed subsequently. It was therefore decided to follow the first model without a single deviation. Gradually, the number of problems started to decrease. Everybody got accustomed to the chief designer's standard answer, to do everything as it was on the first American aircraft. No one asked questions anymore. A little anecdote grew up. The question was, what kind of stars should be put on the mass-produced aircraft—white American stars or red Soviet ones? It was this question that completely foxed Tupolev. If you put white American stars, you risk being shot as an enemy of the people. And, if you put red Soviet ones, first it will not be a copy, and second maybe the Supreme Commander-in-Chief wishes to use the bombers against America, England or China and therefore keep the American markings. The question about the stars was the only one which Tupolev ever addressed to Beriya throughout the whole period of copying, pointing out to him that this was not a designer's business. Beriya was equally nonplussed. He was not accustomed to asking Stalin questions. He had risen to the very top precisely because, like any dog, he could anticipate the wishes of his master.

People say that Beriya told Stalin about the stars as if it was a funny story and that by the way in which Stalin laughed at the joke Beriya knew unerringly which stars should be used. This last problem was solved and mass-production started.

A 'golden rain' fell upon all those who had taken part in the creation of the 'Brick Bomber'. Ninety-seven prizes were distributed over a short period of time 'for the development of new battle technology'. In addition to which Beriya, Tupolev and Yakovlev all received the Order of Lenin.

PART FOUR

Tension was building up in Czechoslovakia. Because of this, our training division held an extra pre-term graduation of students. They were replaced by other cadets in a pre-call-up age group. The word 'training' disappeared from the division's title and henceforth it was designated only as the Novograd-Volynsk Motor-Rifle Division. The Ukraine. Beginning of summer 1968.

Preparation

THE DEVIL ONLY knew what was going on with the armoured troop carriers. The standard allocations for every motor-rifle regiment should be 31 tanks, 6 howitzers, 18 mortars and 103 armoured personnel carriers. Tanks, howitzers and mortars were all in order, but there was only a total of 40 armoured personnel carriers. Trouble was obviously in the air. Something similar had happened in brotherly Hungary in 1956 and was obviously about to happen in brotherly Czechoslovakia. It was obvious that we would have to help. But how could we with such a shortage of basic armament such as armoured personnel carriers in our motor-rifle regiment?

After our third glass together, I put this question to a captain whom I had known at military school and who now occupied the post of Assistant Chief of Staff for Mobilisation. The captain regarded me attentively and, it seemed to me at the time, a trifle foxily, and then said vaguely, 'Hm . . . m,' filled up our glasses, ate a piece of cucumber and suddenly asked:

'But do you know why we've got any at all in our regiment?'

'What an odd question. We've got them because they're prescribed under our allocation, the only thing is that there aren't enough of them to go round.'

'We've got them in our regiment because once a year they take part in a parade at Kiev. Thirty-six of them are needed in the parade and that's why our regiment has them. The other four are just in reserve.'

Apparently the captain rightly felt that he had not satisfactorily dealt with my question, so he asked me another leading question.

'Do you know how many motor-rifle regiments there are in our district?'

'Of course not!'

'But approximately. Just try to guess without being too exact.'

'Well, if only approximately . . . First there's a tank army and two all-arms armies. That makes . . . ah . . . ah . . . six tank divisions and eight to ten motor-rifle divisions.'

'Right!'

'That makes twenty-six to twenty-eight tank regiments and thirty to thirty-six motor-rifle regiments.'

'Right again. So then, of all the district's motor-rifle regiments, out of all thirty to thirty-six, only our regiment has forty armoured personnel carriers, and all the others haven't got a single one.'

'Go on, that's a lie,' I blurted out.

'I'm not lying.'

I was certain that the captain knew his job, and I knew he wasn't lying. I also knew for certain that two other regiments in our division had no armoured personnel carriers. But I did not want to believe that our regiment was the only one in the whole district which had any at all.

'Then where are they?' I finally asked. 'In Egypt? Or, to be more exact, in Israel?'

'Yes, there are some there but not very many. Israel captured a lot of tanks and artillery but no armoured personnel carriers.'

'But where are they then? Were they given to the Warsaw Treaty Powers?'

'Yes, but very few. Czechoslovakia, which receives nearly all its armament from us, still produces her own armoured personnel carriers, to her own standard specifications, and supplies them to the Germans and the Poles, while the Rumanians, because they're so poverty-stricken, usually transport their motor-infantry in ordinary lorries.'

'But when all's said and done, where are ours then?'

'Nowhere!' He looked at me searchingly and repeated 'No-where. They don't exist!'

'But how so?'

'Just like that. How many of them did we produce before or during the war? Not one—not a single one. Isn't that so? All the armoured personnel carriers were American.'

'That's right,' I agreed. 'M-3s they were called, half-tracked, and there were some others with wheels and they were American too.'

'And now let me ask you another question. How many types of armoured personnel carriers have we produced throughout the whole of our history?'

'Lots! Let me see. There were the BTR-40 and BRDM.'

'No, we can't count those, they were only reconnaissance machines and not infantry ones.'

'Of course,' I agreed. 'We won't count them.'

'We don't count the BTR-50 either.'

No, that armoured personnel carrier could not be included in our calculation. It is a splendid machine, but apparently much too good for us. There is only one of them in each regiment and then only for the use of the regimental commander himself. The chief of the regimental staff and the commander of the artillery and regimental reconnaissance are considered as part of the hierarchy, but even in battle they have to travel on ordinary lorries. The BTR-50 is solely for the regimental commander, so it cannot be considered as an infantry armoured personnel carrier. In fact, one regiment of the Taman division was fully supplied with the BTR-50P, but they were only for parades. The whole army knows that this regiment has never taken part in any real manoeuvres but only in peep-shows, like all other 'court' divisions.

'We can't count the BMP either,' continued the captain. 'For a start, it has only recently appeared and second the BMP is not the BTR and its existence does not solve the problems of transporting infantry during battle. The BMPs were supplied only to some selected, privileged infantry units. What about the others, the majority of the ones who'll actually decide the outcome of any war? What will we transport them on during the war? . . . So then, how many types of armoured personnel carriers have we actually created throughout our whole history?' he repeated his question.

'Two,' I answered, and blushed. 'The BTR-152 and BTR-60P.'

'You do know, of course, what kind of armoured personnel carriers they are?'

Unfortunately, I did know that the BTR-152 was the very first Soviet armoured personnel carrier. It was a simple lorry, a ZIS-152 with armoured plating fixed on top. The BTR-152 was a copy of that splendid American lorry, the Studebaker. The copy, as distinct from the original, was not a success and, after another five tons of armour had been added, it looked like anything on earth but a battle machine. It was impracticable, it lacked manoeuvreability and speed, and had no armoured protection. In addition it was produced by the same factory which produced the ZIS-151. And this factory has many problems. Either brotherly China needs machines, or brotherly Indonesia, or brotherly Korea, or brotherly Albania, and we need machines ourselves either for the undeveloped areas or for the Bratsk Hydro Electric Station.

The second Soviet armoured personnel carrier, the BTR-60P, was developed to replace the first one, though there was really nothing to replace as the overwhelming majority of the Soviet divisions only possessed them in theory anyway. This new armoured personnel carrier had the shape of a coffin and it was never known by any other name except the 'coffin on wheels'.

Owing to the shortage of diesel fuel in the country the BTR-60P, like its predecessor, was powered by petrol and as a result burned in battle with an especially bright flame. But diesel fuel was not the only problem—when it was built the country did not possess a single really strong and reliable petrol engine, so two weak engines from the normal collective farm lorry, the GAZ-51, were installed in the BTR-60P. So, it began life with two engines, two clutches, two transmissions, two distributors, four transmission boxes, two starters and two distributor and contact-breaker units. Of course, all these mechanisms were neither reliable nor synchronised, and when the synchronisation of the two engines broke down, which happened every day, one of the engines started to throttle the other. So, one of the engines had to be urgently disconnected, and then the 'coffin on wheels', weighing twelve tons, was hardly able to move on the one 90 horsepower engine.

The letter P in the BTR-60P stands for amphibious. And, although the coffin's shape gives it some buoyancy, even so it floats only in theory. The armoured personnel carrier goes bravely into the water and doesn't swim too badly, but it can hardly ever get out of the water under its own steam since its weak engines can only turn either the wheels or the screw propeller, but not both simultaneously. As it leaves the water, the propeller screw is no longer effective in the shallows, and the wheels don't have sufficient grip on the ground. If the engines did operate simultaneously, it might somehow be able to clamber out but, as it is, when faced with even a small river the whole of the infantry remains without means of transport and reserve supplies.

The BTR-60P is produced by the Gorkiy car factory, which, as well as its own army, must also supply the whole of the national economy and all the Soviet bureaucrats with personal cars. In addition, all Soviet taxi-cabs without exception are produced exclusively by the same works, plus supplies for brotherly Egypt, brotherly Chile, brotherly Sudan, brotherly Somalia and many more besides. And there is still only one Gorkiy works!

'So we should build more car works!'

At this remark he smiled, but not without a certain malice.

'We would if we could but, as it is, we are compelled to buy from Italy! Up to now, we have not built one single automobile factory ourselves.'

I was forced to agree with him. True, I had only visited a Soviet car works once in my life but it had produced a very bad impression on me. Its equipment had been built in America in 1927 and sold to Germany, where throughout the whole pre-war period as well as during the war it had been used mercilessly, to the point of exhaustion. In 1945, this completely worn out and damaged equipment was transported to the Soviet Union where construction of Moskvich cars started. This Moskvich factory does not anticipate replacing its equipment before the year 2000. And what will really happen then remains to be seen! But it is highly probable that yet one more record will be established in the Soviet Union.

'But how, Captain, shall we be able to save Czechoslovakia?'

'By pure cheek, as usual! Of course we've got armoured personnel carriers in the front-line troops, in the GDR, in Poland and in the frontier districts. But here, in the rear, in the second and third echelons, we must just make a lot of noise and generally demonstrate our readiness.'

'But what if the war does really start? What if the Americans really do intervene?'

'Don't worry! Nobody will ever intervene. They'll put up with anything. The more impudent we get, the more patient they will be. Of course they'll hurl stones at our embassies but later they'll repair everything at their own expense, down to the very last penny, and then the usual improvement in international relations will start and in a week's time everything will be forgotten. It is in their government's interest to allow things to be forgotten as soon as possible. Well, let's have one last drink and that's that. Mobilisation will start soon.'

The 1968 mobilisation went on openly without any attempt at camouflage. First, the press announced large-scale exercises, then the call-up of the reservists followed and, when the exercises were over, the reservists remained in the army.

Large-scale exercises involving the strategic rocket troops were carried out over some months, then there were naval exercises, and exercises for anti-aircraft defence and of the military air force, as well as countless exercises for the armies and divisions of the land forces. Then followed training of liaison forces, during which all elements connected with the direction of a gigantic army were checked; and there was training of rear forces, during which thousands of tons of ammunition and tens of thousands of tons of fuel were moved to the western frontiers; and finally command-staff training took place on Czech territory, and all commanders down to battalion and, in some cases, company level studied their tasks actually in situ, in the event of an invasion. All this looked very impressive from the outside. But from the inside it looked rather different.

The process of complete mobilisation of any army consists firstly in bringing the existing units, sub-units and formations up to strength, secondly in forming new ones, and thirdly in their training and knitting together into overall battle preparedness.

The process of bringing our division up to strength proceeded generally without any special difficulties. In peacetime, most Soviet divisions have a reduced personnel, for instance each artillery crew, instead of seven men, has only two—the commander and the gun-layer—and on mobilisation the vacancies are filled by reservists. Even in those cases where they have not even served in the army for ten years and have forgotten absolutely everything—after a short training period, they are fully prepared for war. The same thing happens with the infantry, tank-men, sappers, etc. In a far worse position, at times of mobilisation, are the units of liaison, air defence missiles, anti-tank rockets, reconnaissance and chemical warfare. After a full four months of training, all these units were still not ready for battle.

In official terminology, as we have seen, divisions with reduced personnel are called *Kadrirovannye*. And this really is a fact, especially for units where the percentage of reservists is very high. For instance, in our tank battalion there were three men to every tank instead of four—the loader was missing. When he was added to the crew, the tank promptly became ready for battle. In all remaining tank battalions—and there are seven of them in every motor-rifle division—there was only one man in each tank—the driver. There were only twelve men in a company: the commander of the company, a captain and ten drivers. At mobilisation all the missing members, gunners, loaders, tank commanders, even the company sergeant-major and the platoon commanders, came from the reservists. All except the platoon commanders had served in tank units five or ten years previously, sometimes in other types of tanks. But the platoon commanders had never served anywhere before and knew nothing, not only about tanks and contemporary techniques and tactics, but about the army in general. The platoon commanders are all former students, who once upon a time in some civilian institution attended a course of lectures on military questions and on graduating received the rank of reserve junior lieutenant.

After four months of intensive training, only one tank battalion in seven, the one which had reservists only as loaders, was accepted as being ready for battle. If war had started then, the division would not, of course, have had four months for training, but only one to two weeks maximum. It would have been thrown into battle and would have been destroyed. And no wonder, since only one out of every seven battalions would be fighting fit. Now just imagine a division without reconnaissance, without liaison, without a communications network and without anti-aircraft and anti-tank rockets!

But the biggest problems lay with the infantry—not only because in peacetime its cadres are reduced by an even greater extent, nor because the infantry is recruited from among the worst soldiers, who very often do not understand either their commanders or one another. The worst fact of all is that the infantry has no support technology. A motor-rifle division should have 410 armoured personnel carriers and we had only forty—and that was in our special parade regiment. In the other regiments of the division, in other divisions of the army and in the other armies of the district, there were none whatsoever. Many regiments had three to four armoured personnel carriers for battle training but even these immediately became the personal machines of the battalion commanders, thus leaving nothing at all for the battalion.

Of course, in case of necessity, the infantry can be transported by lorries. But there were no lorries either. The lorries which were in moth-balls in our division were only sufficient for two battalions. The third battalion was issued with armoured personnel carriers, and the remaining six battalions had to make do with vehicles received only on mobilisation.

All Soviet civilian cars are military-registered. If you buy a Volga car, you are warned that at any moment it may be requisitioned for military purposes. This includes dump-trucks, taxis and petrol-tankers. Each and every one of them is specially registered and, at mobilisation, goes straight into the army. At mobilisation, the whole country's national economy comes to a standstill because all the cars, tractors, bulldozers, cranes and excavators—all go into the army. It is difficult to say who created such folly. The system has existed for a long time but it could pass muster in the 1930s and 40s when the country was still able to feed itself, when even at times of general famine some food reserves still existed, when the basic means of transportation in a village was the horse. But now, when the country is unable to feed itself, when it has no food reserves (as was demonstrated to the whole world in October 1964), and when the national economy has no more horses, it is complete madness to take away all the men, all the tractors and all the cars simultaneously. Those who plan any future war must, in these conditions, count on a sudden, short, lightning war, using nuclear force within the first few minutes, or anticipate defeat if the war lasts longer than one month.

Meanwhile, the division began to receive these mobilised machines. What we actually got was a sheer mockery. These were machines which had entered the army long ago directly from the works. The majority of machines absorbed by the army are put into long-term moth-balling. Ten years later, they become normal working army machines whereupon new machines replace them in the moth-balls. After three, four and sometimes five years of vicious use, in adverse conditions and on appalling surfaces, the machines are deemed to be totally useless for further exploitation. Only then do they go to agriculture, though every one of them remains on the military register and has to be returned to the army in case of mobilisation.

In 1968, before Czechoslovakia, we were issued with machines built in 1950 and 1951. During their lifetime, Malenkov had replaced Stalin, Khrushchev had replaced Malenkov, and Brezhnev had replaced Khrushchev. During their lifetime, the Soviet Union had performed a titanic leap into space with the Sputnik and Gagarin (but then, having used all the advantages of surprise as well as of captured German technology, had refused to participate further in the space race). But these superannuated vehicles remained, like old spinsters still waiting for their day to dawn. And now indeed their hour had at last come!

After receiving its 'battle technology', the infantry was forbidden to leave the cover of the forests. On the roads and fields, only tank crews, the artillery and one parade battalion of armoured personnel carriers were training. All the remainder were standing along forest cuttings and in forest clearings. Viewed from outer space, it must have looked menacing, but not from the ground. The military hierarchy was afraid of frightening the locals by the look of our army: fat, untrained and undisciplined soldiers, who had forgotten all they ever knew, in old worn-out vehicles of all possible types and painted all the colours of the rainbow.

The Soviet military leaders must be given their due. None of these 'wild divisions' ever appeared in Europe, or even moved in daytime over Soviet territory. But their very existence gave the Soviet Union a considerable advantage. From outer space, the Americans saw new divisions increasing like fungi. Their reconnaissance noted mighty tank columns on the roads and calculated that innumerable infantrymen lay hidden in the forests. And so it was, in fact, but this infantry was neither organised nor controlled and, what is most important of all, was incapable of fighting.

After the first stage of mobilisation—the bringing up to strength of the existing units—the second stage started: the development of the new units, sub-units and formations.

The reservists continued to arrive, and 'battle vehicles' as well. The units were becoming swollen and, one beautiful night, the order was received to divide into two. The deputy divisional commander became the commander of the new division, while the deputy chief of staff became the chief of staff. Battalion commanders became commanders of regiments, and company commanders became commanders of battalions. The only pity was that platoon commanders, former students, who had never seen a real army, also became company commanders. And reservists were pushed up to become platoon commanders.

After this splitting into two, every division and every regiment started once more the process of bringing itself up to strength, though this time with even older reservists and vehicles. The number of reservists became a real threat, and the army totally lost its professional face. Of course all this did not happen within the divisions intended for the seizure of Czechoslovakia, or if it did happen, it did so to a much smaller degree. But it did not make our position any easier. Those divisions, too, had to be brought up to strength somehow, and suddenly we saw with horror that, from what had already become our two divisions, they were starting to take away, little by little, both men and machines; and of course they were the best men and the best machines which were taken. From the tank crews created with such difficulty, they started to take away combat soldiers, replacing them with simple reservists.

In a couple of days, this wave reached us. We were ordered to get ready to send twenty of our forty armoured personnel carriers to the Carpathian Military District. The next day, twelve of our regular young officers received orders transferring them to the same district. And after that the process really snowballed. There was more news every day: all the tank drivers were taken away, the regular liaison men and the regimental chief of staff went too. It was our second month in the forest. Reservists were still joining us; discipline was lapsing. In early June, an order was received for the creation of field tribunals in each division. It was about this time that the number of 'wild divisions' had so increased and each of them was so drained by the constant departure of regular officers, sergeants and soldiers, that it had become impossible to govern this horde other than through field tribunals.

In a short while, the tribunals restored order, but not troop training. Every day, training sessions were going on. New difficulties arose in our regiment. After sending away half our armoured personnel carriers, we only had twenty left. The commanders of the 2nd and 3rd Battalions were given two each, so that left only sixteen in the 1st Battalion: and they were divided, as between brothers, one to the battalion commander and five to each company. A company consists of seventy-six men. Each armoured personnel carrier accommodates fifteen men apart from the driver, so everybody had his place, in theory at least. In practice the first armoured personnel carrier goes to the company commander, and with him travel his political deputy, the medical instructor, the company's machine-gun section with a very large provision of cartridges, and the sergeant-major with all the company's belongings. The commander's armoured personnel carrier is not only absolutely full on the inside, outside it is hung about with all manner of cases, casks and canisters.

For the three remaining platoons, consisting of twenty-two men each, there were four carriers: one for each platoon, and one to be shared between them. The fact that, in battle, the platoons and sections would all be torn to pieces, perturbed no one at all because, for the moment, one must not think about the battle, but how to accommodate men in armoured personnel carriers. Nobody would give us any additional machines, even if they were broken down and worn out. Where were they to come from? And, even so, our regiment was the luckiest in the three armies of the district. This had to be appreciated. No one else had such privileges.

So, in each armoured personnel carrier accommodating fifteen men, we had to put sixteen—that wasn't really too bad. During training, we used to transport far more than that. We managed about thirty men and even that wasn't too bad! But training and pre-battle conditions are two different things. In pre-battle conditions, every armoured personnel carrier, in addition to all infantry armament, also has one grenade-launcher RPG-7 with ten grenades, and ten grenades constitute two big cases. In addition there are twenty hand grenades, F-1s, which means another case, and one machine-gun, the SGMB, with 2,000 cartridges, which means another two cases. An armoured personnel carrier must also have two additional fuel tanks, which are suspended on top of the spare wheel, and can only be accommodated on the armoured roof, after which one of the hatches will not open. Then, in addition, every soldier carries on his person an automatic rifle or machine-gun or a grenade-launcher, 300 cartridges for every automatic rifle and 1,000 cartridges for every hand machine-gun. Every soldier also has two grenades, a bayonet, a gas-mask, protective rubber overalls, anti-nuclear rubber boots and gloves, greatcoat, rain cape and ground sheet, a change of underwear, rations for five days, a water bottle, a spade, and individual medicine and anti-nuclear pack. When all this is put into an armoured personnel carrier, there is no room left for one person, let alone sixteen. It was much better before, when armoured personnel carriers had no armoured roof and one could put everybody one on top of the other like peasant wenches on a hay-cart. After Hungary, the production of such armoured personnel carriers was stopped. Now we have to push all sixteen in through the hatches under the carrier's roof.

This is not an easy task, especially if you take into consideration the reservists' corpulence. The sergeants just have to hammer them in under the roof. Sometimes, this operation takes about forty minutes. If something happens, if the machine overturns or catches fire, no one, except the driver and the commander whose positions are separated from the others, will get out alive. We are not even talking about the battle itself. How do they breathe there, squashed together worse than sardines in a tin? The soldier's good sense, however, soon finds a way out of that situation. Everyone puts on his gas-mask after disconnecting the filter container from the pipe; then the pipes are fed out through the open hatches and embrasures. During the summer it is not very pleasant in a rubber mask, pressed from all sides by backs, bottoms, boots, barrels and butts, but at least there is air to breathe.

During training exercises, especially when overseas attachés are present, things happen quite differently. Exercises are one thing, especially peep-shows, while harsh army reality is another matter altogether.

Late one evening, after the usual training practice of loading soldiers into armoured personnel carriers, which left no time for any other type of training, I received an order to go immediately to the staff of the Carpathian Military District. My post was to be taken by the 1st platoon commander, a junior lieutenant-reservist. When he heard about his appointment as a company commander, he looked sadly at our armoured personnel carriers, at the reservists, whom the sergeants were extricating with great difficulty from the hatches, then he gave a long-drawn-out whistle and swore loud and long.

The hurricane of transfer, re-groupings, re-formations and bringing up to strength caught me too up in its wake and hurled me into the 2nd Battalion of the 274th Regiment of the 24th Samaro-Ulyanovsk, Berdychev, Iron, three times holder of the Red Banner and holder of the Order of Suvorov and Bogdan Khmelnitskiy, Motor-Rifle Division of the 38th Army, which forms part of the Carpathian Military District.

Liberators

WHAT A THRILLING sight the changing of the guard at the Mausoleum is! I've been to Red Square hundreds of times and I'm still lost in admiration at their accuracy and military bearing. I am simply drawn there and could stand for hours feasting my eyes.

And how could it be otherwise? The very cream of the cream, trained to the point of artistry, trained better than Soviet gymnasts for the Olympic games. Handsome fellows.

Their regiment is stationed within the Kremlin Walls, a whole regiment of the KGB! Just go round from the side of the Alexsandrovskiy garden and count the storeys in their barracks. It looks like two, but if you look more closely there are really four. The windows are too vast and there are two storeys to each window. Look carefully and you will see that there are indeed four. They extend above the Kremlin wall. And how many storeys are covered by this wall? Now go inside the Kremlin itself and look at the barracks from the side of the Tzar Bell and you will see that it is not just an ordinary house but a huge rectangular construction with an inner courtyard. Now go out again through the Troitskie gates into the Alexsandrovskiy garden and try to calculate the length of this building by pacing it out. So, there you are—not just a regiment but something far bigger can be accommodated in there, without tanks and artillery, of course.

And now, any Sunday, go towards the Kremlin and see how many of these lads are just strolling around aimlessly. But the regimental commander can only give leave to five per cent at any one time: that goes for the commander of an ordinary regiment, but the one in the Kremlin is no ordinary regiment. And, even if the commander allows only five per cent of his eagles to go in to town to enjoy themselves, there must still be plenty left in the Kremlin. And if it's not five, but only two to three per cent we're seeing, then how many of them have been left inside?

The lads strut up and down importantly and they look very proud. And why shouldn't they be proud? Their uniform is most imposing: greatcoats, caps, boots—all officers' issue. They have blue shoulder-straps with the letters 'GB' shining like gold. But why not 'KGB', why only 'GB'? It needs to be explained. 'K' stands for Committee. That's certainly not solid enough. 'MGB' would be better ('M' could mean Ministry), but 'GB' is best. It stands for State Security—plain and simple! How weighty it sounds, how imposing! It takes precedence over all ministries and committees, including even the Central Committee of the Party. 'GB' is a crystal-clear dream. But not only a dream of course.

So they are the cream of the cream. A whole regiment, lacking only tanks and artillery. But the tanks would not really be necessary—the Kremlin's walls are still strong.

But suppose something happens, some kind of revolution breaks out, especially one by the army with tanks against the Leninist Central Committee? What then?

Don't worry on that score, brother: there is a whole Dzerzhinskiy Division created for just such an eventuality, with tanks and artillery and everything else which may be required. Of course it is true that the division is called a Division of Internal Troops, which means that it is part of the Ministry of Internal Affairs. But don't you believe in such a masquerade. The KGB has used plenty of disguises in its time! So, don't give a glance at the Dzerzhinskiy Division's uniform. It's indeed a masquerade! Since when did the protection of our beloved leaders fall into the hands of the MVD? It has always been the KGB's prerogative: that's why this division was created. This is what is written in all the reference books raised on Lenin's personal instructions and for

Lenin's personal protection. But then you have Comrade Roy Medvedev writing about the protection of our beloved Lenin, and the existence of the Dzerzhinskiy Division is somehow forgotten. In contrast, the division itself is very proud indeed of its role: 18,000 men guarding one man, Lenin. The Latvian riflemen pride themselves on their role just as much as the Moscow Military School named after the Supreme Soviet, and the Kremlin machine-gun detachments—just see how many of them there are.

In addition to the Dzerzhinskiy, the KGB possesses other regiments and divisions. All are made up of the very best soldiers, and there are a great many of them. Some liaise with all ministries and departments, with all republics, territories and regions, with all test-firing grounds, space centres, prisons and camps, with works, factories, mines and pits, with all military districts, armies, corps and divisions and, of course, with the brotherly socialist parties. And there is liaison within liaison: cables, switchboards, cypher machines, eavesdropping posts. And all such things have to be built, maintained and guarded; and all this needs troops, troops and more troops. The very best ones, of course. Because every day one is forced to hear secrets and tell no one. And, even though the secrets are far from comforting, one is not allowed either to hang oneself, or to run away to America. And so many soldiers are needed for this job! But it is still not the Soviet Army nor is it the Defence Ministry. These same troops eavesdrop and report even on what is said within the Defence Ministry. And that is not the end of it, that is not even the main arm of strength of the KGB. The frontier troops—there lies their strength, and they control nine districts! All the rest of the Soviet Army has only sixteen military districts. There are nine frontier districts controlled by KGB troops, with tanks, helicopters, artillery and warships.

Each one is, of course, made up of the best crack troops, since a frontier guard was invented specifically to prevent anyone from running away from this splendid society of ours. But he is not guarded by anyone. He stands on the very frontier itself: one step sideways and he is over the border. So, to prevent that, the very best soldiers are chosen for all nine KGB districts.

All those who have not eventually landed up in this gigantic organisation go into the Internal Troops. This too does not come under the Defence Ministry but under the Ministry of Internal

Affairs. It is still not the army although it has regiments, divisions, tanks and guns.

'What are you doing, brothers?'

'Guarding a camp!'

'Well, it's a necessary job, responsible too. How many people are there there?'

'Oh, there are a lot of people. Under just one law, the one about the intensification of the struggle against hooliganism, over the last ten years, eight million people have been imprisoned. But there are many other decrees and laws leading to imprisonment. We have to guard all those people.'

'And I suppose they take on only the very best for this job.'

'Of course. They need people who have never themselves been convicted, nor anyone in their families. And also those, who, after being in contact with the prisoners, don't pick up any wrong ideas, and if they do happen to pick up any ideas they should not absorb them, and if they do happen to absorb them, they must not disseminate what they've picked up from the prisoners, or in any case not disseminate it too widely.'

'But where can you find such people?'

'Well, we do our best.'

So then, those who have landed up neither in the GB nor the Internal Troops—they are the ones who join the invincible and legendary Soviet Army.

Every self-respecting army consists of three types of armed forces, each of which is split into different kinds of troops. The Soviet Army has more respect for itself than all the others and, therefore, does not consist of three but of five arms. In addition to the land forces, the air force and the navy, there are two other branches of equal importance, the anti-aircraft defence troops and the strategic rocket troops. And, in addition to all these, there are also the VDV or airborne forces, which are not separate but are answerable solely to the Defence Minister and commanded by an army general. And the VDV consists of eight divisions, no less, whereas the whole of the British Army, for instance, consists of four divisions: three divisions in Germany, and one actually in the United Kingdom. When one compares these simple statistics, one's ideas about the aggressiveness of NATO tend somewhat to fade.

So the VDV are selected also from the best soldiers, the most courageous, the most convinced, developed and physically strong. They would have to be: jumping in all weathers, often at night, operating in the enemy's rear against its most important targets; completely isolated from their own troops, without any supplies of ammunition, fuel, food, and without their wounded being evacuated. Paratroopers must kill their own wounded, so they are never taken prisoner and give away the operation's plans and intentions. The air descent must always be a surprise attack.

Those who have not been taken into the VDV join the strategic rocket troops or RVSN. Again, they need the very best. The real question is: how many of these crack soldiers are really required for the RVSN? The RVSN has three armies altogether: every army consists of a number of corps, and every corps of several divisions. So, it would be futile to make any comparison with the British Army.

After the RVSN, it is the turn of the country's anti-aircraft defence. That requires enormous numbers of soldiers and, again, all of them must be the best. They are intended to deal with sputniks, intercontinental ballistic and other missiles, and strategic bombers. The country's anti-aircraft defence consists of three types of troops: air force, air-rocket and radio-technical troops. The anti-aircraft air force possesses the fastest aircraft-interceptors. The radio-technical troops operate thousands of locators which guard the sky day and night. Finally, there are the air-rocket troops. All three arms are concentrated in two districts, Moscow and Baku, and each district forms a group of armies for anti-aircraft defence. But, apart from these two districts, there are also several separate anti-aircraft defence armies, which are directly subordinate to the Anti-Aircraft Defence Commander-in-Chief.

Next comes the air force, which is not to be confused with the anti-aircraft defence air force. In general the air force, or to be more exact the VVS, or military air force, has nothing in common with the anti-aircraft defence air force. The VVS has many air armies, ranging from a front-line force through the strategic air corps known in Soviet terminology as the long-range air force, to the divisions of military transport aviation. Each front-line army consists of six divisions, and the corps of long-range aviation have two to three divisions each. Without doubt, the air force must have the best soldiers.

The navy comes next. It, too, is huge. It has a colossal number of strategic rockets, and the demands made on the sailors operating them are extremely high, because the launching of a rocket from a submarine underwater is so complicated. The navy also has its own anti-aircraft defence and a mighty air force separate from the VVS and the country's anti-aircraft defence. And, of course, the cleverest, the most literate, the boldest and most resolute, the strongest and the sturdiest, are essential. And everything that's left goes into the land forces!

The best are sent abroad: let the liberated admire their liberators! The best are needed there so that our reputation in Europe is not spoiled. That is perfectly understandable. But how many soldiers are needed to be sent into liberated Europe? Let us take, for instance, West Germany and its fierce Bundeswehr, with which, in the Soviet Union, they frighten everybody from pioneers to pensioners. Well, that Bundeswehr has twelve divisions. Against these twelve divisions, we maintain five armies in the field and one air army from the VVS. These six armies are called the GSVG—The Group of Soviet Troops in Germany. But, apart from the GSVG, there is the Northern Group of Troops, which are the Soviet forces in Poland, the Central Group in Czechoslovakia, and the Southern Group in Hungary. And these four groups must be made up of the very best soldiers. It was not for nothing that the poet Yevtushenko composed a song:

> It's not only for their Country
> The soldiers perished in that war
> But to provide quiet sleep
> At night over the whole World.

So, Europe can rest in peace—our armies and their crack soldiers will never leave it. We like Europe!

Those young soldiers, who for some reason have not joined the hundreds of thousands of picked troops in liberated Europe, go into the land forces at home actually on Soviet territory. It must be said that the remaining soldiers are very good, though perhaps not as perfect as for instance those in State Security, the Frontier Troops of the KGB, the Internal Troops of the MVD, the Airborne Forces, the Strategic Rocket Troops, the Anti-Aircraft Defence, the Navy, the Group of Soviet Troops in Germany, the Central Group of Troops, the Northern Group of Troops or the Southern Group of Troops. They are, of course, first class, but not of quite the same calibre.

The Soviet Army Land Forces, representing sixteen districts, is a gigantic organism. Neither China, nor America, nor anyone else, not even all of them put together, can match it in size. But how can this army be brought up to strength? The biggest one in the world? And what happens if there is no one left to harvest the crops?

I inspected my guards company, bit my lip and said nothing. I did not call the officers in for a talk. I did not speak to the sergeants. Nor did I go and meet the commanders of the neighbouring companies. I just looked at my company and that was enough.

After he has met his men, the done thing is for the commander to examine the battle vehicles and armament of the company and later its equipment and ammunition. But I didn't do that. No . . . I went straight to the officers' bar which rejoices in the lyrical name 'Little Star'—which particular star is not specified, the one in the sky, the one on the shoulder-straps, or the red one on the chest.

I placed an extra crumpled rouble in the hands of a big-bosomed barmaid, and bribed her to bring me a bottle, because an officer officially should not drink. I put this small bottle under the table and gradually emptied it, in proud solitude. But it did not make me feel any happier, in fact it only increased my depression. Why the hell, I wondered, did they invent this bloody system? Who invented it? However you interpret things, it is the tanks and the infantry who will fight on the battlefield, not the rocket men or the KGB people. You have to fight your enemy not with numbers alone but by your skill. And my guardsmen didn't even understand the Russian language! The language of their commander! Nor did they understand one another because all the nationalities had been mixed up. Those who did under-stand at least something had all been sent to the artillery or liaison a long time ago. What was the good of having this pack? Why hadn't they all been sent off to building units, that would have been much more useful! Have a smaller army if you must, but at least let them all understand one another a little better! If war were to break out, it would be a hundred times worse than the Arab troops, who could at least understand one another. What on earth was I to do with them?

Well, I thought, leaving war aside, it is peacetime and they all have to be drilled into some sort of shape. Tactics, for instance. If the pupil doesn't understand his teacher, you can't even teach him to play chess. And at least, in a game of chess, the whole situation is like the palm of your hand, any threat is clearly visible. The situation in battle is far from clear, and a threat can appear suddenly from anywhere. The enemy does not wait for you to work out your counter move, he acts and goes on acting. And payment for losses on the field of battle is not a chess title, not even a couple of million dollars, but the lives of millions of people. And everyone wants to win. The enemy is not an idiot! Each one of his moves on the battlefield he has previously worked out a hundred times over on his electronic calculator. So how shall we manage to fight? In 1941, there were no rocket troops but at least our best infantry divisions were made up of first-class soldiers. Maybe, that is why we were able to hold out. And there were also national divisions in those days—Latvian, Georgian where the divisional commanders understood Russian and that was enough. But what now?

I ordered another little bottle and, having drunk half of it, I felt so sorry for myself and my unfortunate Motherland that it was quite unbearable.

Just before the bar was due to close, two infantry captains sat down at my table. Perhaps they wanted to get to know me or perhaps they were just looking for a third drinker. I didn't answer their greeting very politely.

'New officer, eh? . . .'

'Crying, of course . . .'

'All the new ones cry in this corner . . .'

'Never mind, he'll recover . . . he'll get acclimatised. All of us start this way.'

Those were the last words I heard. Probably these two captains, having understood perfectly the state I was in, somehow dragged me off at the dead of night to the officers' mess.

The same night, dead drunk, I was dragged again from the officers' mess to my own company. I was put into the commander's car, and the column moved off.

That very night, our regiment was put on alert. Our brothers in Czechoslovakia had asked for our help and protection.

The Carpathian District is transformed into the Carpathian Front. The Western Ukraine. August 1968.

On the Border Line

'THE GRAIN WILL soon start to fall from the wheat as it stands in the fields.'

'What are the people at the top thinking of?'

'Do you think things are easy for them? The Czechs are not giving us real grounds for going to protect them. Communists still haven't been killed there and no ''Chekists'' have been hanged from the lamp-posts. There is no one to protect them from. So, how can we move our troops in?'

'They must consider themselves and their own country first, and not bother about some Czechs or about public opinion. It's the right time to go in and that's all there is to it.'

'Those people up there understand whether it's the right time or not.'

'They bloody well don't understand anything. If our troops are not in Czechoslovakia within a week, it'll be the end for all of us.'

'Why?'

'Because the wheat will start to fall, because there's no one to harvest it, because all the peasants and all the machines have been taken away from the *Kolkhozes*. And if we don't harvest our wheat everything will start all over again just like 1964.'

'The Americans will help us!' said the assistant chief of staff confidently.

'And if they don't?'

'They will, what else could they do?'

'In any case, they wouldn't be able to feed all of us. Did you see how many people were being mobilised! In 1964 at least some of the harvest was gathered in, but now there'll be nothing. The Americans wouldn't be able to feed all of us.'

'Don't you worry about the Americans. They're rich. They've got plenty of food. There's enough for everybody.'

Doubts about what would happen if the Americans failed to support us did not evaporate, however, and conversation to the effect that it was about time we finished these long drawn-out proceedings and let the peasants get on with the harvest kept on cropping up.

'What about letting the peasants and the whole army get on with the harvest now without delay and then liberating Czecho-slovakia afterwards, in October or November?'

'That would be disastrous. It would be the end of us and the end of all Soviet power and all Socialist achievements. We have to go in now, otherwise everything will collapse, and there will be nothing left to protect.'

'They say they are building a different socialism, with a human face.'

'That's enemy propaganda,' interrupted the political deputy, 'all socialism has the same face. The bourgeoisie, Comrades, have invented this theory of compromise. This theory contradicts Marxist teaching and does not contain a single drop of common sense. You cannot sit on two chairs with one bottom, it's just not comfortable. Judge for yourselves: what compromise can there possibly be if not a single advantage can be torn from socialist achievement. You surely remember how one anti-Soviet, during the era of Voluntarism, penned an infamous slander against our regime. It was called *One Day in the Life of Ivan Ivanovich* or *Ivan Trofimovich* or something like that. What came of that? All the politically immature elements got on the move and started disseminating the slander. There was even some distrust of Party policies, and so on. It was nipped in the bud at the right time; otherwise who knows how it might all have ended?'

One could not disagree with that. I myself had never read about this Ivan, the book just did not come my way, but I distinctly remember that the effect it had was deafening.

'So, what did they think up, these Czech communists?' continued the political deputy. 'They completely abolished censorship. They opened the sluices to the full force of bourgeois propaganda! Let everyone print whatever they like! And where will that lead? To compromise? Not at all! To capitalism! It's enough for the bourgeois influence to make a small hole in the dam and then the flood will destroy the whole system! We've already had one small hole like that but, thanks to the Party, it was closed in time. But in Czechoslovakia it's not just a little hole, it's already a full flood of water! It must be urgently quelled. What kind of compromise is it if everyone is allowed to say just what he likes? It's not a compromise, it's sheer bourgeois anarchy!'

One could not disagree with this either. If, owing to one little story, the whole system had nearly collapsed before, what would happen if censorship were completely abolished? There is no third way—either you have censorship or you don't, either you have the necessary organisation or you don't, either with a Central Committee or without it. Really, what talk can there be of any compromise? If there is a Central Committee, that implies that there is a Party policy. The necessary organisations protect the Central Committee and censorship protects the Party's political line. This is what socialism is all about. And, if you take away any one of these elements, the whole orderly system will collapse and anarchy will ensue with all its inherent vices, like unemployment, crises, slumps, inflation and all the rest. This is what this obscenity Capitalism is all about. Indeed, however you look at it, there is no room for any compromise or for any so-called human face . . .

'Please continue, Comrade Lieutenant-Colonel,' they shouted from the rear ranks. 'We fully support you.' The new political deputy was different from the previous one, the new one spoke persuasive good sense.

'Yes, I will continue, Comrades. There was somebody here who suggested sending the army in to do the harvesting and waiting to liberate our brothers until October. I consider this proposal disastrous for the whole socialist system. Let's say for the sake of argument that we don't liberate Czechoslovakia in the immediate future: by October there'll be nothing left there, neither socialism nor any human face. Socialism is an orderly system like a diamond and as strong as a diamond, but if the diamond-cutter makes one false move all the stability of the crystal may be shattered. In Czechoslovakia, it has already happened. The diamond is falling to pieces. But it represents one organic component of the whole socialistic camp. The diamond formed by World Socialism can also fall to pieces and very rapidly too. Bad examples are highly infectious! If the bourgeoisie triumphs in Czechoslovakia, do you really believe that Hungary will not follow her example? We've already had one example of this kind. There, too, everything started from this business of a human face. Of course Rumania is already moving further and further from Marxism. If there is the smallest change in Czechoslovakia, then the same will happen in Poland and in the GDR. We've already had this experience once. You know yourselves what kind of situation already exists in Poland! And in the GDR—I won't even speak about that! The bourgeoisie is already calling for compromise. That means removing the Berlin Wall. Isn't that so? If that's done, the immature elements of the population will all rush off into West Germany! Comrades, our revolutionary vigilance must not be slackened. The frontiers must be kept under lock and key. We must neither remove the wall, nor abolish censorship. Otherwise, you know yourselves what will happen.'

The political deputy took a sip of water from somebody's flask and then continued:

'Let's say for the sake of argument that some socialist countries break away from the socialist partnership—the infection could quickly reach our own Baltic Republics like Estonia, Latvia and Lithuania, where bourgeois nationalism is still strong, as well as the Ukraine and Byelorussia, especially their western parts, which are precisely those adjoining Poland and Czechoslovakia. I won't elaborate further. You yourselves understand perfectly well what might happen there.'

We answered him with cries of indignation. The chief of staff of the 3rd Battalion smiled foxily and then calmly asked, 'But when will it happen, Comrade Lieutenant-Colonel? For a long time now we've been ready to carry out our international duty.'

The political deputy was not confused by this new question, although he himself, of course, had not the slightest idea of the answer.

'We must be ready for the moment!'

We all applauded the gallant political deputy for organising such a successful improvised meeting.

Events were coming to a head. Everybody could plainly see that we should be going in soon, but no one knew exactly when. Two days previously there had been a secret order, for officers' eyes only, concerning the formation of the Carpathian Front on the basis of one tank, one air and two all-arms armies. Colonel-General Bisyarin was appointed commander-in-chief.

The same day we learned of the movement of the 8th Guards Tank Army from our front on to Polish territory. Our 38th Army, with which I had taken part at the Dnieper exercises, was still in the Ukraine and would probably enter Czechoslovakia from Soviet territory.

That day, we learned of the formation of the Central Front under the command of Colonel-General Mayorov. The Central Front was developing in the GDR and Poland to the west of Krakow. It consisted of two armies taken from the Baltic District and the 20th Guards Army of the Group of Soviet Troops in Germany, in addition to which it had some Polish and German divisions. Some of the Polish divisions were included in our Carpathian Front. Apparently one further front had been developed in Hungary, which was to consist of Soviet armies and Hungarian corps, plus some Bulgarian units. But, at that time, we had no definite information, we just guessed. Later I learned that a Southern Front had indeed been developed on Hungarian territory, plus an operative group called 'Balaton'. The Southern Front did not go into Czechoslovakia. It only covered and protected the active group of troops. Only the 'Balaton' group, which was more than an army and less than a front, actually entered Czechoslovakia. As part of the Soviet forces, there were also Bulgarian and Hungarian units in this group, as we used to say, in order 'to make up the furniture'.

And now the grains of wheat were really falling on to the ground.

We had already been standing in the forests for several months. There had been training, check-ups, command-staff training and general training followed yet again by further checking of equipment. After more time had elapsed, an order was issued concerning the creation of the Danube High Command, to consist of the Central and Carpathian Fronts, the 'Balaton' group and, as a fourth separate element, two airborne divisions. For the first day of the operation, in order to ensure the success of an airborne landing, five divisions of military transport aircraft were put at the disposal of the Danube High Command.

Army General Pavlovskiy was appointed commander-in-chief, and his command post was established somewhere in Poland.

Everything was ready, but the liberation still didn't start: somebody at the top still had doubts about something, though there was really nothing to have doubts about. If we invaded Czechoslovakia it might lead to catastrophe for everybody including our own system, or on the other hand maybe not . . . If we did not invade Czechoslovakia, it would lead to catastrophe for our system. There was no choice for the Soviet leadership. The first alternative was obviously the better. To drag out the liberation process was also impossible. The harvest could not wait.

Our regiment was ordered to stand to at 2300 hours. The order 'Now is our time' was passed by secret channels to all fronts, armies, divisions, brigades, regiments and battalions. Commanders were instructed to open one of the five packets in their possession and, in the presence of their chiefs of staff, to burn the other four without opening them. The operation had been worked out on the basis of five different alternatives. Now that one of them had been approved, the others lost all significance.

The directive signed by the Defence Minister ordered Operation Danube to be put into effect. Military action would be necessary, continued in accordance with the two plans 'Danube-Channel' and 'Danube-Channel-World'.

The liberation had begun.

The final stop before the state frontier. Outskirts of Uzhgorod.

White Stripes

THE BATTALION CHIEF of staff looked at me with leaden eyes and imperiously commanded: 'Repeat!'

I straightened myself and, clicking my heels, repeated parrot-fashion the words known to us all for so long—'Instructions for mutual support during Operation Danube'. 'A white stripe is the distinguishing mark of our own and allied forces. All battle equipment of Soviet and allied origin without white stripes is to be neutralised, if possible without a shot being fired. Tanks and other battle equipment without stripes are to be destroyed immediately in case of resistance without prior notice of orders from above. In the event of contact with NATO troops, immediately stop and do not shoot without first being ordered to do so.'

The chief of staff moved away down the line, ordering first one then another officer to repeat aloud these instructions which had been dinned into us all. At last he finished his round, came to the middle of the formation and ended his briefing with the words:

'Comrade officers! Not shooting at NATO troops does not necessarily mean any hesitation in showing firmness and resolution! Where our first tank meets their first tank, a platoon or a

company must immediately deploy into formation. If possible
without firing, try to push them back from the territory they have
occupied. Our task is to seize as much territory as possible. Let
the diplomats decide later where the frontier between Eastern and
Western Czechoslovakia is to be drawn. It is a matter of honour
that we should make Eastern Socialist Czechoslovakia larger
than Western Czechoslovakia. If shooting does start, do not lose
your heads. It is better to retreat one or two kilometres. Do not
spoil for a fight, as they too have no wish to start it. But, if the
affair does come to a fight, be prepared for the worst.'

The chief of staff struck his dusty boot with a willow branch
and added in a low but distinct voice:

'Any scoundrel who takes it into his head to desert to the
stripeless or Western side will be immediately shot. Any attempt
to eradicate our white stripes and desert to the camp of the
stripeless can be dealt with with the utmost severity. This right is
given to every one of you. Unfortunately, one must remember
that the elimination of white stripes is possible, not only among
Hungarian and Polish units, but among our own units too. Let's
hope for the best.' And, changing his tone, he roared, 'STAND
TO!'

We all rushed to our vehicles, where sergeants and soldiers
were bustling about carrying out a last inspection before departure. Suddenly, from the other side of the column, a sizeable
group of soldiers and sergeants who had just received their
instructions from the officer of the special department of the
KGB, came running towards us. *Stukachi*, as KGB informers are
nicknamed, are always given their instructions secretly. But
here, at the very frontier, the special department had apparently
received new instructions, which had to be passed urgently to its
executives. All around them was nothing but open fields, and no
time to spare. How could they hide? The only way was to give
them their instructions in sight of the whole battalion. What they
were talking about was not difficult to guess: they were being
given the power to kill us, the officers, if we started to wipe the
white stripes off our vehicles or tanks.

I started to run as fast as I could, and saw that all my brother
officers were also running. Each one of us wanted to reach the
column before the *Stukachi* and to see them all together in a
group before they dissolved into the grey-green mass of the other
soldiers.

Here we come! A single tight group of like-minded individuals. We were starting to divide into smaller groups, each running towards its own company. Familiar faces—oh hell, that dark fellow! I would never have thought he was an informer. As far as I remembered, he couldn't even speak Russian. How had the KGB found a common language? And now they had melted completely into the dense mass of soldiers. Their comrades did not seem to have the least idea of the reason for their absence: they were still young soldiers and even spoke different languages. They did not understand too much of what was going on. But the KGB was not quite as silly as all that. As they were out in the open, the KGB had not gathered together the whole lot of them, only some. I would have staked my head on it that my own signals operator was a KGB informer. But he had not been called out for instructions. Maybe he had been given his instructions earlier, or maybe one of those who had attended the meeting would inform him secretly later what had been said.

Meanwhile, another dense group of soldiers and sergeants had detached itself from the armoured troop carrier belonging to the battalion commander's political deputy and run towards their machines. These, too, were *Stukachi*—but of a slightly different kind. They were the legal *Stukachi*, with their own line of responsibility. They were Party servants. In every platoon consisting of thirty soldiers and sergeants there is a Komsomol secretary and his two assistants, plus a platoon agitator, plus an editor of the *Boevoi Listok*. Indeed each detachment of seven soldiers has its own *Boevoi Listok* correspondent.

In the same platoon, some of the soldiers must belong to the company bureau, to the company board and company agitators' group. Provided they can say at least ten words in broken Russian, then one of these positions is open to them and they become the creatures of the political deputy, or indeed of the Party. They listen to what the Party says and the Party, through the ears of the political deputy, very attentively listens to what they say about me, my comrades, my commanders and my junior officers. Looking at the insolent faces of the legal and political *Stukachi*, it was only too easy to guess that, only a moment before, the Party had given them the right to shoot without warning any officer who dared to obliterate any white stripes.

Now, there was one last man running from the vehicle of the regimental propagandist. He ran fast, but not so fast as to disturb his special decorum. He was nineteen years old; he had a well-shaped face, a well-shaped nose, a well-built figure, well-shaped thoughts and a careful haircut. Such men's names generally figure on the board of honour and they are elected to the Praesidium at solemn gatherings. He was a Candidate Member of Our Great Party. There was only one like him in my company. He was quite another matter. He represented a particular thread of information with direct access to our regimental political God. He was yet another man authorised to shoot me in the back, if the KGB *Stukachi* just happened to hesitate. And he would shoot at both the obvious and the hidden KGB *Stukachi*, if they faltered, and if, of course, I happened to be a second late in killing them.

The Candidate Member of our Great Party climbed into my vehicle and took his seat at my left side. On my right was a signals operator (a hidden KGB *Stukachi*), behind me sat the machine-gunner (an obvious KGB *Stukachi*), in front was the company's agitator, the Party right-hand man. The huge fuel supply vehicles pulled away with a roar from the armoured column, and we started smoothly on our way.

Invasion

THROUGHOUT THE ENTIRE night, in an endless stream, the troops were marching past our armoured personnel carriers and tanks. Towards morning, in spite of the dew, our machines were covered with such a thick layer of dust that neither identification signs nor numbers could be seen; and the troops were still marching on and on.

The only command was to close up, and this was broadcast repeatedly over the air. We all knew our battle standards only too well. On the march, the distance between battle vehicles should be 100 metres and, between auxiliaries, 50 metres. So the length of one division on the march is 150 kilometres. But now, through the narrow roads of the Soviet-Czechoslovak frontier, two armies were on the move, consisting of twelve divisions in all, plus replacement and supporting units and the reserves of the Carpathian Front.

All established standards went by the board and were forgotten, for, if it had been decided to observe them, troops would not have entered Czechoslovakia in less than a week. 'Close up!' This categorical demand was accompanied by highly select abuse and threats by all commanders to their subordinates. At 0820 hours came the order from the Carpathian Front commander to push off the road any broken-down vehicles, regardless of type or responsibility. Hundreds of tanks, artillery tractors and vehicles containing top-secret cypher equipment rolled down the slope. In the 79th Motor-Rifle Division, a rocket-launcher whose engine had failed was also pushed off the road.

At 0930 hours the 38th Army commander ordered all repair vehicles to be moved out of the column so that they could be left behind on Soviet territory. Ten minutes later a similar order, covering all three armies, was issued by the Front commander.

Meanwhile, we were still standing at the roadside allowing the first echelon to pass. The call to 'Close up' still echoed. The commanders' helicopters hung in the air over the dense clouds of dust. Divisional and army commanders, generals and officers of the front line staff urged on their hapless regimental and battalion commanders from immediately above their heads.

At noon, we were joined by the helicopters carrying the generals from the commander-in-chief of the Danube Staff. Orders to remove regimental and divisional commanders who could not sustain the speed of marching and did not 'Close up' were issued on the spot. Battle vehicles were scattered in the gutters. Units of sappers, chemical and medical troops had already been removed from the composition of the column. But, still, thousands of tanks awaited their turn on Soviet territory to enter the narrow mountain passage and to fulfil their noble mission. A mechanised Genghis Khan was rushing headlong into Europe.

At 1500 hours our division finally received the order to start moving in column formation. By then the roads were in such a bad state that to adhere to the prescribed speed of advance was absolutely impossible. The dust was so dense that all vehicles were moving forward with their lights switched on.

Towards evening our regiment reached the state frontier, but was then commanded to position their machines along the roadside to allow the Front commander's reserve to pass.

This enforced stop allowed us to have dinner. Some weeks earlier, during the training period, provision points had been established along all directions of troop movement. And it was here that the miracles started to happen. The provision points were equipped with a monstrous capacity, to serve thousands of people in only a few minutes.

The first surprise was an unprecedentedly luxurious table containing all kinds of foreign delicacies. It was announced that from now until the end of the operation all troops would be supplied only with foreign products, which were being provided by the governments of the USA, France, Canada, Australia and their other allies.

Towards daybreak on the liberation's second day our column finally left Soviet earth-roads and reached the extremely well-surfaced Slovak roads. The dusty haze which had pestered us for nearly two days was left behind on the Soviet side, but instead there came the frenzied crowds of people. Stones and rotten eggs, tomatoes and apples, were thrown at us. Insults and curses were hurled in our wake, but the thicker the crowd became, the more abundant became our food. This was a very precise psychological calculation and Bonaparte's words that the way to a soldier's heart was through his stomach were not forgotten. The food was of the very best quality. We had never seen such multicoloured labels printed in every language under the sun. The only Russian product among our rations was, of course, Vodka.

All officers were constantly reminded that they must keep their troops' battle spirits up to the mark. But there was no need for that, first because sergeants and soldiers alike hardly understood where they were and what was going on, and secondly, owing to the abundant supplies of food, they were all ready for battle anyway.

Most of my company's sergeants could understand a little Russian. They were generally recruited from the distant-wooded districts and had encountered electricity for the first time in the army. There was no need to worry about them. Only, after five or six hours of moving through the infuriated crowds, one of them suddenly noticed the fact that the numbers of the machines were not quite standard ones, and he asked me a question about it. I answered his question with another question of my own. I asked him to name all the republics he knew. The sergeant was one of the cleverest and quickly named Byelorussia, the Ukraine, Lithuania, Poland, France and Uzbekistan. Then I told him that, in some republics, the numbers of vehicles are not standard; and that was that. The other sergeants did not even notice the cars' number plates.

It was even simpler with the soldiers. All of them came from beyond the clouds, from mountainous kishlaks and distant reindeer-breeding farms. They did not understand not only me but also one another: all the nationalities had been mixed up with the alleged purpose of developing friendship between the peoples. They knew only ten commands: Get up, Lie down, Right, Left, Forward, Back, Run, Turn round, Fire, Hurrah.

At our next halt in the forest, during supper, I decided to fulfil the order of the political deputy and to raise morale still higher. It was not difficult.

I climbed onto a box marked 'Made in the USA', lifted high above my head a tin containing stewed beef, smacked my lips in a sign of appreciation and shouted out 'Hurrah'. In response, a mighty and joyous 'Hurrah' rushed from hundreds of throats.

The tinned stewed beef was really excellent.

*The Reconnaissance Battalion of the 6th Guards Rovno,
Order of Lenin and of the Red Banner, Order of Suvorov,
Motor-Rifle Division of the 20th Guards Army, in the centre
of Prague.
August 1968.*

The Banker

OF COURSE LENIN was truly a genius, thought the battalion commander, Major Zhuravlev. Take possession of the banks, the post office and telegraph, the railway stations and bridges. That's all very well, but there's one thing that's still not quite clear. Is it possible that no one thought of such a simple thing before he did? The Major spat on a heap of cases packed full of money and angrily kicked one of them.

The day before yesterday, in the morning, the 508th Separate Reconnaissance Battalion of the 6th Guards Motor-Rifle Division of the 20th Army of the Central Front had been the first to set foot in the streets of a still sleepy Prague. The Reconnaissance Battalion was moving fast, having left behind its radio-reconnaissance company, and as a result had considerably outstripped the advanced detachment and the main forces of the division. The battalion's task was clear and categorical: take possession of all bridges and retain them until the arrival of the main force.

The commander of the Reconnaissance Battalion, Major Zhuravlev, knew all the town's roads off by heart. For four whole months, the battalion had worked at its task with maps and models. The battalion chief of staff had a complete set of photographs of all the crossroads along the route. Before Operation Danube, staff commander exercises had been held during which all twenty officers of the battalion had visited Prague and travelled by bus along all their future routes.

Zhuravlev was in the turret of the leading tank and gazed with renewed interest at the unusually colourful town. Suddenly on the façade of an old building he noticed the huge letters: BANK.

Zhuravlev knew perfectly well the distribution of responsibilities between the division's units, and he was absolutely sure that, at the time of the 'distribution of roles', the central bank had been completely missed. This entire area was to have been occupied by the 6th Guards Division and no other troops were supposed to be stationed here. Zhuravlev swore blind at the commanders' muddle-headedness and kicked the dozing radio operator, who had not slept for three nights.

'Closed channel to the divisional chief of staff!'

The radio operator answered after a few seconds.

'Closed channel to the divisional chief of staff, Bullfinch four, go ahead.'

Zhuravlev pressed the button on the speech control panel and, filling his lungs with air, he began:

'Bullfinch four, this is Kursk, Square 21341—bank. I have decided to take the bank myself with a reconnaissance company and the first tank reconnaissance platoon. My deputy will carry out allotted task together with armoured reconnaissance vehicle and the second reconnaissance platoon. This is Kursk. Over.'

'Kursk, this is Bullfinch four. Okay. This is Bullfinch four. Over and out,' came the short answer, and the transmitter fell silent.

When reporting his decision concerning the modification of the approved plan, Zhuravlev had secretly hoped that the chief of staff would not agree to his decision or that he would order somebody else, his deputy for instance, to deal with the bank and not him. Therefore, upon receiving the answer, he again cursed the stupid bungling of the leadership, meaning all those higher than himself.

'Kursk two, this is Kursk,' he addressed to his deputy over the open channel. 'Proceed with task, Kursk five and Kursk forty-two, Kursk three and Kursk forty-one to the left, into battle!'

Three amphibious tanks at once turned to the left without

reducing speed, while the long-range reconnaissance company left their machines and followed. The remaining column, filling the street with the roar of its engines and the clank of its tracks, quickly disappeared round the corner.

Major Zhuravlev pressed down the safety lock to point at 'automatic fire', and called out, 'Assistant to chief of staff.'

'Yes.'

'Blockade the entrances with tanks. Put one in the yard and two along the street!'

'Right!'

'Company commander!'

'Here.'

'Hand over the 5th Reconnaissance Group to the tankmen and, with the remainder, take possession of the objective. Don't touch any papers! I'll have you shot if you do! Go ahead!'

The long-range reconnaissance company rushed forward to the main entrance and knocked repeatedly at the metal grille covering the glass doors with the butts of their rifles. An old watchman in a grey uniform appeared behind the doors. He looked in terror at the fierce faces of the men knocking at the doors. Then he glanced uncertainly behind him. He looked again at the soldiers hammering at the doors and hurried forward and opened them. The company rushed into the echoing central hall and spread out along the staircase and corridors.

For some reason, it reminded the battalion commander of that famous painting *The Assault on the Winter Palace*.

Ten minutes later, all the bank's personnel—mostly night-watchmen—were gathered together in the big hall. Zhuravlev collected all the keys, ordered all the personnel to be searched and then locked up in the guard-room. The battalion commander went round all the rooms and sealed them with a notice reading 'Military Unit 66723'. The massive safes he secured with a secret seal: '508th Reconnaissance Battalion'. Then he personally checked the positions of the inner and outer guard, after which he returned to his command tank to report the completion of his task.

The closed channel was working normally. The divisional staff answered within a minute.

'Bullfinch four, this is Kursk. Bank taken. This is Kursk. Over.'

'Well done,' replied the divisional chief of staff, ignoring the call signs. 'Remain there until they relieve you. A tank regiment will arrive in a couple of hours.'

'Armoured reconnaissance vehicles alone, without our help, won't be able to hold the bridges,' implored Zhuravlev, breaking regulations. He did not want to sit there in the bank—if some kind of papers were lost, it would be his fault and he would be shot. So he tried every means to get somebody to replace him—for instance the battalion's chief of staff—so that he could go off to the bridges. He could not have pretended not to notice the bank as he moved along the street, things then might have turned out badly for him: the guilty party is always found out, and who else in this situation would have been guilty if not the reconnaissance battalion commander? And so there was only one possible decision: remain himself at the bank. The manual on reconnaissance treats such a situation very clearly. Simple and easy tasks must be given to the deputy; complicated and risky ones, do yourself. Furthermore the divisional chief of staff had just confirmed it: 'Kursk. To hell with the bridges. Hold the bank. Over and out.'

The battalion commander switched off the transmitter and swore loudly. Somewhere close by, there was a short burst of automatic fire followed by three long machine-gun bursts. The sound was rather muffled but the machine-guns the battalion commander could not fail to recognize unmistakably: SGMs. Somewhere on the bridges the Czechs had obviously fired their automatics, and then our people had replied with machine-guns. Then everything became quiet again.

At the sound of shooting, astonished, sleepy faces began to peer out here and there from their windows. Apparently the entry of several reconnaissance battalions into the town had remained virtually unnoticed, but the sound of shooting woke them up. An elderly woman stopped in front of the commander's tank, surveyed it and quietly went away. A yard-cleaner with a brush, instead of the usual home-made broom, stopped by another tank. The Czech army is equipped with the same tanks, and reconnaissance units wear camouflage overalls instead of field uniforms.

The camouflage overall had no insignia or badges and it was probably owing to this fact that it had not occurred to the inhabitants of the neighbouring houses that this was not the Czech army but something quite different. It is in any case only the 'court' divisions who wear badges, white piping and other adornments; tanks and armoured personnel carriers have no identification marks except the three-figure numbers on the armour, plus, in some cases, the identification marks of their division: a little rhombus, a deer, or oak leaves. On this particular occasion, in addition to these marks, the famous white stripes had been painted along and across the tanks. And it was precisely those stripes which had interested the elderly cleaner. He had a scar on his left cheek. For a long time he gazed, examining the tank, and then put a question to the reconnaissance troops sitting on top of the tank. The latter obviously did not understand the question, but, to be on the safe side, without answering they went down inside the tank and slammed the hatch shut. After standing beside the tank for a further few minutes, the elderly man moved away, shrugging his shoulders in puzzlement.

Zhuravlev, who had observed the scene from the bank window, ordered all the officers to gather in the central hall.

'Now the questions will begin . . . what is what, and why are we here . . . I tell you now to send them all to hell or even further. I've great experience in these matters after what happened in 1956—is that clear?'

'It is!' answered the officers cheerfully in unison, but Zhuravlev noticed that something was not clear to one of the youngest officers, the commander of the fourth long-range reconnaissance group.

'What's the matter with you?'

'Comrade Major, what about the political department's order: 'Every Soviet Soldier is a diplomat and agitator'?

'Let the political deputy do his agitating on the bridge, that is what he is paid for,' the battalion commander interrupted, 'and as long as he's not here, everybody can go to hell!'

And then, realising that his words might reach undesirable ears, he added in a more conciliatory tone, 'We are guarding an objective of special importance and, until we get reinforcements, there is no point in getting involved in discussions. The tank regiment will soon be here, then we shall start the agitation work.'

At this point, Sergeant Prokhorov, the deputy platoon commander, rushed into the hall.

'Comrade Major! Tanks. Without any identifying marks.'

'What type of tank?'

'Fifty-fives!'

'Battalion, prepare for battle!'

Broad white stripes had been painted on all the fighting machines taking part in Operation Danube, in order to distinguish them from the same types of machines in the Czechoslovak army. Any fighting machine—tank, assault gun, armoured personnel carrier or artillery tractor—without white stripes should be immediately destroyed.

There was at least an hour before the tank regiment was due to arrive and no help could be expected from any other source. Zhuravlev looked with anguish at the approaching leading tank, whose front armour plate bore not even a trace of white paint.

The long-range reconnaissance company took cover inside the bank and the three PT-76s* prepared to meet the Czechs with armour-piercing shells.

We are done for, the battalion commander thought sadly. Why the hell did I allow myself to get such a long distance from the main force?

The PT-76 barrel was smoothly lowered a little, and the turret slightly turned. It was ready to fire.

Convulsively, Zhuravlev pressed the button of the tone generator: Don't shoot!

Perhaps, he thought, the incident will pass peacefully. When the time comes to engage the Czechs perhaps our people will arrive, maybe the Czechs will not open fire first? And it did look as if the leading tank had no such intention because its gun was still pointing at the sky, and the tank commander himself was clearly visible on the turret. The tanks were approaching quite fast, knocking sparks out of the old blocks of the roadway with their tracks. The column seemed endless, as more and more tanks appeared from round the corner and engulfed the narrow street with the suffocating stench of their exhaust gases.

'Comrade Major, they look like ours.'

'Of course they're ours, look at their dirty overalls.'

'What the hell! They've arrived much too early.'

'Hello, lads!'

'Salute the liberators!' The head tank turned sideways and then stopped, leaving the way open for the column.

Zhuravlev and his escort hurried towards it.

A broad, impudent and utterly filthy face appeared from the turret. His overalls were soaked in oil—he was Russian. He was

---

*The PT-76 is an amphibious reconnaissance tank. For that reason, it possesses neither heavy armour nor an impressive armament. In comparison with the T-55, it is utterly defenceless.

about forty, which meant he was not an ordinary soldier, but who knew what kind of shoulder-straps he had under his over-alls? Perhaps he was an over-ripe junior lieutenant. On the other hand he might be a young colonel; one could only guess. If he was in the leading tank he might be the battalion or even the regimental commander. In overalls everybody looks the same.

'Why the hell are you roaming about over this brotherly country without any white stripes, like some counter-revolutionary?'

'We were in the reserve, they didn't want to bring us in but later they decided to do so, and by then there was no white paint left,' said the dirty-faced fellow, with a conciliatory grin.

'You bugger, I nearly hit you with our armour-piercing shells. Thank God your face is Russian and your overalls are dirty. You might at least have had a white stripe on the leading tank.'

The dirty-faced man looked contemptuously at the reconnaissance tanks: 'You and your advice can go and get stuffed.'

The passers-by listened with astonishment to all this foreign conversation, and the most intelligent among them clearly sensed that something was wrong. Meanwhile the head of the tank column had stopped and those behind were catching up and taking up positions straight across the tram-lines.

'Did you come to reinforce me?' Zhuravlev asked.

The dirty-faced tank commander raised his eyebrows in astonishment. Like most Soviet commanders he was pretty ill-bred and boorish, and he didn't bother to answer. Zhuravlev spat.

'Who are they?' the divisional chief of staff shouted into the receiver. 'Our first tanks are expected to enter Prague in about thirty minutes!'

The battalion commander switched off the transmitter, summoned his escort and went to find out who those tankmen were.

'Look here, lads, aren't you from the 6th Guards Division?'

'No, we're from the 35th.'

'Where's your commander? There's something wrong!'

'He's there,' said a young soldier, pointing at the dirty-faced fellow with whom Zhuravlev had just had such a nice chat.

'What's his rank and post?'

'He's Major Rogovoy, the regimental commander's deputy.'

Zhuravlev approached him again.

'Comrade Major'—this time Zhuravlev addressed him officially—'I am the commander of the 6th Guards Division's Reconnaissance Battalion. I have just been informed from HQ that your regiment is not in its proper position.'

The dirty-faced officer whistled. A commander can commit no worse error than to take his unit to the wrong place, and Zhuravlev's words produced the appropriate effect. Quickly, he produced his map and opened it out. Right in the centre of the map, there was a big red oval with an inscription in black: '35th Motor-Rifle Division.' Slightly higher up, in sprawling handwriting, there were the words: 'Confirmed by the Chief of Staff of the 20th Guards Army, Major-General Khomyakov.' There was no doubt about it, the tankmen were exactly where they should be.

'Right then, take over the bank,' said Zhuravlev. 'It's on your territory. It looks as if I am the one who made a mistake.'

'I don't know anything about a bank, there was nothing about capturing a bank in my assignment. Telegraph, yes—telephone also—but not a word about a bank!'

'Since it's on your territory, you've got it. I don't bloody well want it. My guardsmen will be off in a moment. I've been ordered to take possession of the bridges.'

'Seizing the bridges is the task of our division's reconnaissance battalion,' the tank man said confidently, 'and we came to reinforce them.' Once again, the tank man pointed at the map. The circle covered the bridges as well, there could be no doubt about it.

'Look here, does your reconnaissance battalion not have any white stripes on its armour as well?'

'I believe so, why?'

'I think that just now our two reconnaissance battalions were shooting at each other!'

'Oh, come off it!'

'I tell you!' Zhuravlev was hurriedly opening his map, trying to find his mistake. But on his map there was just the same red circle covering the town's central points together with the bridges. Exactly the same inscription was at the top: 'Confirmed by the Chief of Staff of the 20th Guards Army, Major-General Khomyakov.' The only difference was that on Zhuravlev's map was written the 6th Guards Motor-Rifle Division and not the 35th.

The commanders swore simultaneously. The army staff had given the same task to two divisions, and one of these divisions had no markings.

'Show me your photographs,' said the dirty tank man, laying out his own photographs on a board. The two sets of photographs were absolutely identical. They showed the same crossroads and in the very same order.

'But why didn't we see your reconnaissance battalion?' said Zhuravlev in surprise. 'It must have followed the same route.'

'Who the hell knows! Maybe there was something wrong with its route too!'

Both commanders ran to their machines to inform headquarters about the misunderstanding which had just come to light. But headquarters had already realised for itself that a great many serious mistakes had been worked out a whole eight months in advance. The columns of different divisions, armies and even fronts had been mixed up together, and control of the troops had in many cases been lost. All the call signs had got mixed up as well, there were hundreds of 'Cornflowers' and 'Cupids' and 'Nightingales' and 'Simfoeropols' all using the same frequency, obstructing one another and trying in vain to shout one another down. Central Front Headquarters had issued a directive not to shoot vehicles which did not carry white stripes. Apparently, headquarters had guessed that there had not been enough white paint to go round, or perhaps they had already received information about Soviet tanks shooting at one another.

It was half an hour later when Zhuravlev managed somehow to get in contact with divisional headquarters. He was ordered to remain where he was. He was also informed that he would not receive reinforcements that day, as the division's tank regiment had got lost and probably overshot Prague.

Zhuravlev again visited the dirty tankman from the 35th Division. The latter told Zhuravlev that he could not contact his headquarters. The lines were blocked. Zhuravlev described the general picture to him and invited him to the bank for a glass of 'tea'.

'To hell with your bloody bank! You'd better come and see me this evening. I've something to really entertain you with.'

Whereupon they parted.

Friendship between Soviet officers usually blossoms in such situations.

Meanwhile crowds were filling the streets. Young and old, men and women, they all rushed towards the Soviet tanks.

'Why did you come?'

'We didn't call for you!'

'We can solve our own problems without tanks!'

The soldiers really had no way of answering these questions, and they did not try to, except occasionally.

'We came to protect you.'

'The Americans and the Germans want to take you over. Have you really forgotten the war already?'

'Well, you come when they do start to take us over!'

The officers, especially the political activists, plunged into the crowds, but without any noticeable success.

'We were invited in by your own government.'

'You just name one member of the government who invited you to interfere in our affairs.'

'Comrades!'

'We're not your comrades!' And the political deputy was struck in the face. He reached for his pistol, but the soldiers pulled him back out of the crowd.

'Bloody fascists!'

'It's you who are the bloody fascists!'

'You brought your own country to a state of starvation and now you want all those around you to sit and starve!'

'Those are only temporary difficulties, later things will be much better in our country.'

'And without you it would have been better than ever!'

'Get the hell out of here, wherever you came from! And take your Marx and Lenin with you!'

'Citizens, keep calm!'

'Go to hell!'

'Citizens, by your unreasonable behaviour, you are putting all the victories of socialism on the verge of . . .'

'Your socialism should have been tested on dogs first, just as all normal scientists do. Your Lenin was stupid and no good at science.'

'Don't you dare speak in such a way about Lenin!' A rotten egg landed smack in the middle of the political deputy's red face.

'But if Pavlov had been given the task of introducing communism, he'd have quickly proved, by experimenting on dogs, that this way of life isn't suitable for a living soul!'

At the very back of the column, the discussion had taken on an even more agitated form. Youths were hurling stones at the last three tanks, forcing the crews to hide inside, and then with crowbars had broken open the spare fuel tanks which are fixed to the outsides of tanks during long advances. A minute later, the last but one tank began to smoke, and then another. Disorganised shooting could be heard. The crowd reeled back from the last tank, but only for a moment.

Two crews tried vainly to put out the flames while the third tank swivelled its turret sharply round, trying to throw off the youths who had climbed on to it. Two platoons of tankmen from the centre of the column fought their way through the crowd to help their comrades.

'Keep clear! The shells in the tanks will start exploding at any moment!'

'You bloody fascists!'

Zhuravlev, who had watched all this from the bank window, secretly rejoiced at the others' misfortune. Why the hell start a discussion? You've come here to liberate them, so get on with it. Don't start any political discussions!

The reconnaissance tanks of Zhuravlev's battalion were standing there too. But the crowd somehow didn't notice them. The soldiers were obediently carrying out their orders and swearing at everybody right, left and centre. The Czechs either understood the tones only too well, or else preferred not to carry on any discussions in such tones, or they were simply convinced that they would be unable to out-swear the Russians. In any case the people just did not linger near the reconnaissance tanks. All the swearing and scuffles took place in the tank column itself at those places where the political deputies were especially active, trying to convince the people of things that they did not even know for sure themselves.

'Stalinism and the personality cult in general were accidents in our history! Like hell, they were! For thirty years out of fifty, it was Stalinism. And how long during the last twenty years did you live without a cult? Without the cult of Lenin, Khrushchev and the others?'

'And why is there no personality cult in America? And never has been?'

'There is imperialism in America, Comrades, and that is much worse!'

'How do you know it's much worse? Have you ever been there?'

'Why is there a personality cult in every single socialist country from Cuba to Albania, from Korea to Rumania? All these countries are different: their communism is also different, but the personality cult is always the same. It all began with the cult of Lenin . . .'

'Don't you dare insult Lenin! Lenin was a genius for all mankind!'

'Lenin was a pederast.'

'Silence!'

An old man with a little wedge-shaped beard twisted one of the buttons on the regimental political deputy's tunic.

'Now don't go and get too excited. Have you read Lenin?'

'Of course I have!'

'And Stalin?'

'Ah . . . Ah . . . well . . .'

'Well, my old lad, you read them both and count how many times each of them uses the word 'shoot'. There are some very interesting statistics. Did you know that, in comparison with Lenin, Stalin was a pitiful amateur and ignoramus. Lenin was an out and out sadist, one of those degenerates who happens only once in a thousand years!'

'But Lenin didn't annihilate as many innocents as Stalin did!'

'History stopped him in time. It removed him from the scene at the right time. But remember that Stalin didn't let himself go completely from the very outset, but only after ten to fifteen years of unlimited power. Lenin's start had much more impetus. And, if he had lived longer, he would have done things which would have made Stalin's thirty million dead look like child's play in comparison. Stalin never, I repeat never, signed orders authorising the killing of children without trial. And Lenin did so in his very first year of power, isn't that so?'

'But, under Stalin, children were shot in their thousands.'

'That's right, Comrade Colonel, quite right, but you just try and name me at least one child who was shot without trial on Stalin's orders! There you are, you can't say anything! I repeat, Lenin was one of the most bloodthirsty degenerates who ever lived. Stalin at least tried to conceal his crimes, not so Lenin. Stalin never gave official orders for the murder of hostages. But Lenin killed children as well as hostages and never felt the least compunction about it. Lenin, Comrade Colonel, should be read attentively!'

'But now you're criticising not only Lenin and Stalin but Marx too!'

'What's the difference? Marx or Mao? Of course, neither of them called for the deaths of millions of innocents. But both Lenin, and even more so Stalin, didn't call for them either in their pre-revolutionary writing. In Lenin's works, the word 'shootings' appears only after the October revolution, and in Stalin's works it never appears at all. But you, my fine fellow, must agree that, where any form of communism appears, with a human face or without it, it always engenders a personality cult. Always! It is a rule with no exceptions. Of course, if it appears in France or Italy, the shooting of millions of people will not start at once, the conditions are different. For the time being! But if, as Marx taught us, communism eventually wins in the majority of all developed countries, such atrocities cannot be avoided, and there will be nobody left to be ashamed. There will always be a personality cult. There will always be a Mao or a Fidel or a Stalin or a Lenin. And the cult will always have to be defended by strength and by terror, a great wave of terror. The freer the country previously, the greater will be the terror. Your ideas are beautiful but only in theory: in practice, they can only be thrust upon people with tanks and brute force like yours, Comrade Colonel!'

'You . . . you . . . you're an Anti-Soviet! That's what you are!'

'And you . . . You are a Marxist–Leninist which, translated into human language, means a child murderer!'

A rotten tomato flashed through the air and landed on his peaked cap and splashed itself all over the colonel's face.

The crowd pressed close again. Somewhere, in one of the neighbouring streets, came the sound of renewed firing. And a light breeze from the river brought with it the smell of burning rubber.

At first glance, and before taking into consideration the huge responsibility involved, work in a bank may not seem too bad. There is a washroom with hot and cold running water, and it is a big house with railings. You are not taunted with stones or with rotten eggs: but, what is even more important, you can have a good kip after so many sleepless months. From his very first day in the army, Zhuravlev had understood that no one is ever compensated for lost sleep—if you do manage to snatch a couple of hours, it's yours; if not, no one will ever give it to you. Besides, this first night in Prague promised to be a very disturbed one. He checked the guard once more, looked through the window at the seething town, and then lay down on the sofa in the director's office.

But they did not let him sleep. About ten minutes later, in ran his personal driver, Junior Sergeant Malekhin, to report that two armed Czechs wanted to speak to him. Zhuravlev seized his automatic and carefully looked out into the street. At the entrance to the bank between two reconnaissance tanks stood a van with grilled windows, and two Czechs with pistols in their holsters were quarrelling with the sentries.

'But they've come to deliver money.'

The junior sergeant just shrugged his shoulders. He didn't understand.

Zhuravlev had an irresistible desire to yawn, but those two Czechs with pistols were trying hard to explain something to him. Then a third man appeared and, in front of the battalion commander, opened a carton crammed full of money. He indicated that his whole van was full of such cartons.

'The bank is not functioning,' explained the battalion commander, 'and will not be functioning. I arrested your people here but later let them go. Those were my orders. I can't accept your money.'

The three men with pistols held a long consultation between themselves and then threw a heap of cartons from the van straight on to the steps of the bank. One of them shouted something which sounded very offensive and the van vanished round the corner, clearing its path through the crowd with an unpleasantly shrill hooting.

Zhuravlev swore viciously. Then he ordered the sentries to bring all the cartons inside.

Fifteen minutes later the saga of the cartons was repeated. This time, the battalion commander understood that it was useless to argue and he just pointed in silence at the bank's door. The collectors threw their precious cargo straight on to the floor and then left without saying a word. Zhuravlev merely noted the van's number and the quantity of packages.

Then a whole flurry of black vans with grilled windows drove up. The mountains of cases, cartons and leather bags containing money grew menacingly. The collectors generally did not ask for receipts, but when they did Major Zhuravlev resolutely sent them to the devil and told them to take their packages with them. After some hesitation they threw everything on to the common heap.

It was difficult to understand where so much money had come from. On the first day of the liberation, the country was totally paralysed. Probably the money now flowing into the bank was from the previous day or even earlier. Long after midnight, when the last vehicle arrived, the mountain in the central hall recalled a picture of an Egyptian pyramid taken from a children's history textbook.

Sensing the inherent risk in the present situation, Zhuravlev dismissed all his sentries from the bank; the guard remained outside, while he alone was inside. It was safer that way.

There was no possibility of sleeping. Throughout the night Zhuravlev wandered about with a big bunch of keys among the depositories, opening armoured doors and steel grilles and locking them again and placing his seals on them. At his express wish the whole alarm system had been switched off by the nightwatchmen before he let them go.

It is an astonishing thing to wander alone about the vaults of a large bank. Zhuravlev came across gold bars marked with the Soviet hammer and sickle and with Czech lions, and gold plates with long serial numbers and the inscription 999.9, and thousands of the most varied coins. But most interesting of all was the foreign paper money.

He was absolutely indifferent towards money as such, but the intricate designs and the unequalled colour range attracted him. He spent hours on end studying notes which depicted kings and presidents, women and flowers, and thoughts of some unknown civilisation rose up in his imagination.

During all his thirty-two years he had seen quite a bit of the world. He had been in Siberia and the Far East, in Kazakhstan and in Polar regions. He had also studied at the academy in Moscow; he had taken part in parades in Red Square and in many of the largest training exercises. When he was twenty and still only a sergeant, he had found himself in Hungary, right in the centre of Budapest, in the very centre of that hell of fighting for the liberation of that brotherly people. Later still, he had served all over the Soviet Union. He served well: he went to Germany, and now finally he was in Czechoslovakia. During his lifetime, he had seen quite a number of those 245 million inhabitants. How often would you meet a man who had been in two foreign countries? And Zhuravlev had now visited his third country.

Once again he studied the designs on the crinkly notes and he felt a vague unease. These notes bore witness to some other completely unknown and unusual life. Every one of them had travelled a long way and lived a long life before landing in the vaults of a Prague bank and into the hands of a Soviet officer-liberator called Aleksandr Zhuravlev. Very soon all of them would be scattered abroad, and they would again return to their own mysterious world, while Major Zhuravlev would still be guarding all the honest people in his world. He would become a lieutenant-colonel and maybe even a colonel and then he would be retired from the army and tell colourful stories of his career to anyone who cared to listen.

Zhuravlev was awakened by a distant, regular and heavy knocking sound. Brought back to reality, he rubbed his eyes and ran down to open the heavy door. In came Lieutenant-Colonel Voronchuk, the chief of divisional reconnaissance. The sky was already clearing in the east and a pleasant coolness pervaded the air.

'Come in, come in.'

Quite recently, Voronchuk had been the reconnaissance battalion commander while Zhuravlev was his first deputy. Before this particular operation, during the shake-ups and rearrangements and replacements, both men had advanced one step higher on the service ladder. But this promotion did not interfere with their long-standing friendship.

'Well, banker, how's the battalion? It hasn't run away yet?'

'The ones with me haven't, but the ones with the political deputy, God knows what they're doing.'

'There's no political deputy any more. He's been taken to hospital. They smashed his head in with a brick this morning.'

'Was he busy agitating?'

'He was busy doing it himself and also urging all the other soldiers and officers to do the same, which is why quite a few of our people were beaten up on the bridges.'

'And who was shooting over there this morning? I'm cut off here and know absolutely nothing about what's happened to my companies.'

'The Czechs started the shooting and then two reconnaissance battalions were shooting at each other. The 35th Division hadn't got enough white paint, so some of your falcons had a go at

ıem. Fortunately, the tanks were not at the head of the column.
till, your fellows shot two of the reconnaissance scouts: one of
ıem slightly, but the other's seriously wounded.'

'Like to moisten your throat a little to keep me company?'

'No, Sasha, thanks. I have to see the divisional commander in
ın hour to put in my report.'

'When am I to be relieved?'

'Who knows? The tank regiment lost its way and we haven't
ıade contact with it. Two motor-rifle regiments are jammed on
ıe road. The artillery and rear column have dropped far behind.
Only one motor-rifle regiment in the whole of our division made
t into town properly. But you know yourself how chaotic it all
s. Generally speaking, too many units entered Prague by mis-
ake and there's nothing for them to do here. They came in by
ıistake and now they don't know what to do. They can't leave
ıe city for the time being either, since all contact's been lost.
t's like a fire in a brothel!'

'Well, let's have a drink. I've got some things to suck to kill
ıe smell.'

'Pour it out then, and let's drink to the devil!'

'After all that training, just look at the shambles. There you
re, you see!'

'If the Czechs had really started shooting, it would have been
vorse than Hungary.'

'But our people knew beforehand that the Czechs would never
ıhoot. They're ready to submit to anyone and they'll lie down
ınder anybody. They're not like the Hungarians. The Czechs
von't lift a finger for the sake of their own freedom. Did you
ıotice that, when the tanks just stand about not doing anything,
ıe Czechs consider it quite natural and even behave themselves.
Only when we embark on our propaganda and mind-bending, do
ıe disorders seem to break out.'

'Of course I noticed it. I told my men to get it into their heads
ıot to have any truck with that kind of talk. What the hell's it all
or anyway?'

'You'd better be careful, Sasha. If the political deputies find
ıut, you won't be able to lie your way out of it or to fight your
vay out of it.'

'I'm doing it while he's not around my neck. When the
ıattalion was split into two, I sent him off to the bridges.'

'In any case, be careful. Their ears are just as long as their

tongues. Sometime this morning have a few chats with th
Czechs just in case the soldiers sneak on you.'

'Okay, I'll do that.'

'The tankmen of the 35th Division are keeping an eye on you
They may do the dirty on you, and the political creeps aren'
asleep either.'

'Who do you mean?'

'Fomin, from the second long-range reconnaissance group
and Zhebrak who's with the tankmen.'

'I had my suspicions about them. I think Fomin's in contac
with the "specials", and Zhebrak's the political deputy's lapdog.

'Then there's Gareyev from radio reconnaissance.'

'Oh, him, I know about him.'

'Then there's Kurakin and Akhmadulin from the BRDM Com
pany. Kurakin for sure and Akhmadulin looks very like it.'

'I did think about them, but I wasn't sure.'

'And your personal driver, of course.'

'Oh, go on!'

'He's absolutely typical!'

'Have you got anything concrete to go on?'

'No, I just feel it in my bones. I've a special eye. I've neve
been mistaken yet. Do be careful, Sasha, the reconnaissanc
battalions are filled to overflowing with political spies. It's quit
normal of course: how could it be otherwise?'

'One more for the road?'

'Okay, but this'll be the last one.'

'Your health, Kolya.'

Next day, the flood of money cartons noticeably subsided an
the day after it stopped altogether. But the oppressive feeling o
heavy responsibility did not pass. Zhuravlev knew how difficul
it is sometimes to give an account of even one rouble, and her
were all the vaults filled with gold, currency and various kinds o
paper money. If some commission or other arrived, and all thi
had to be accounted for, a whole year would not be enough to d
the job. And suppose something was missing? How could h
account for all these cartons? Who knew how many million
there were? A lot of them were not even sealed. The futur
possibilities of all this deprived him of his sleep for nights
Zhuravlev lost his appetite, became pale, thin and pinched. The
town continued to seethe. All his friends were being assaulted b
volleys of stones and insults, the tanks were busy dispersing th

dissident elements and trying to locate underground radio stations. They were also continuing their agitation work and preaching and defending themselves against all comers. All those who knew where Zhuravlev was were extremely envious. The nickname 'Banker' stuck firmly. But, all the time, he was getting thinner, paler and more envious of those who were out on the streets.

Three times a day, a driver brought him food: unheard-of American tinned food, fragrant bread, delicious French butter.

'You'd better eat·something, Comrade Major.'

'Okay. Off you go.'

'Comrade Major, you just tell me what you'd like and I can provide you with anything you want! We've never seen anything like it.'

'Okay, okay. Off you go!'

'Comrade Major, may I just ask you one thing?'

'What's that?'

'Comrade Major, allow me to go just two blocks down the road in a tank.'

'What for?'

'There's a chemist's shop. But if I don't go in a tank our patrols will stop me or else the Czechs will bash my head in.'

'Why do you want a chemist's shop? Have you got a dose of the clap?'

'No, Comrade Major. I want some contraceptives. I'll get some for both of us.'

'I don't need them, and what the hell do you need them for?'

The driver smirked and motioned towards the bulging paper cartons.

'My right fuel tank is empty. No one has counted the money. We could invest a couple of million in contraceptives and put them into the fuel tank. Nobody would guess! Do you know how much money you can stuff into one contraceptive? It stretches . . .'

'You dirty scum!' Zhuravlev grabbed his pistol. 'Throw your automatic on the floor! Face the wall! Escort, come here!'

'I was only joking, comrade.'

'Shut your mouth, you scum!'

Late that same evening, the divisional chief of staff and three others dressed in civilian clothes, plus an escort, forced their way towards the bank in a tracked personnel carrier.

'What's going on here, Zhuravlev?' mumbled the chief of staff in dissatisfied tones.

'Comrade Lieutenant-Colonel, I have arrested driver Malekhin for attempted looting.'

'The comrades will investigate the matter. Where is he?'

Zhuravlev led them along a corridor towards the central hall. All three stopped dead in their tracks.

'We urgently need a radio station!'

'The driver is locked in that room.'

'We need a radio and not a driver!' the young shaven-headed 'comrade' interrupted rudely.

Zhuravlev was relieved of his duties quite suddenly and without any trouble whatsoever.

Half an hour after the 'comrades' had managed to contact their leadership, another two BTR-50Ps, packed full of officers and civilians, arrived at the bank. Zhuravlev spent the rest of the night on external guard duty at the bank. He was never allowed inside again not even to go to the lavatory.

Early the following morning, a tank battalion from the 14th Motor-Rifle Division, which was part of the army commander's reserve, approached the bank.

The tank battalion commander gave Zhuravlev an order personally signed by the 20th Guards Army commander, which instructed Zhuravlev to take his reconnaissance battalion out of the town immediately.

Zhuravlev sighed with relief. The order also mentioned that the part of his battalion at present guarding the bridges was also temporarily removed from his command, so he had nothing to worry about at all. And, merely to remove one long-range reconnaissance company and one tank platoon, was not a difficult task.

It took only ten minutes to get ready. Zhuravlev formed up his scouts and then checked their number, armament and ammunition. The tank engines began to roar . . . but at that very moment the tall crew-cut 'comrade' appeared on the bank's steep steps.

'Hey, Major! Wait!'

The insolence shown by the 'comrades', especially in the presence of soldiers and sergeants, always irritates the army officers, but of course they never show it.

'What's the matter?'

'Sign this, Major.' Whereupon, he handed over a sheet of paper covered in columns of figures. 'Don't be in any doubt, everything's in order. Our chaps were checking it all throughout the entire night.'

Zhuravlev signed without even reading or examining it. How on earth, anyway, could he have known how much of everything there was in the bank?

The young fellow smiled.

'Here you are, Major, keep it as a souvenir'—and he put his hand into his sagging pocket and held out to Zhuravlev a big gold coin with the profile of some elderly woman wearing a crown.

The Reconnaissance Battalion of the 6th Guards Motor-Rifle Division of the 20th Guards Army, to the north of Prague. First days of September 1968.

Counter-Revolution

THE MOTOR-CYCLE WAS burnt out during a drinking bout. While the platoon was cleaning its weapons, somebody brought a bottle of Czech plum-brandy, which was quickly dealt with. The cleaning session promptly became much more cheerful. After a long march, weapons were always cleaned by washing them in petrol. This method is forbidden but it is the most effective. After cleaning, there was a short break for a smoke which took place close to the bucket containing the petrol. The first section's gunner threw his cigarette-butt into the bucket and the petrol flared up gaily. The platoon commander's deputy, Sergeant Mel'nik, kicked the burning bucket, while the scouts happily laughed. But the bucket turned a somersault in the air and fell back on to the motor-cycle, whose tank was open, as the petrol used for cleaning had been taken from it. The rest happened in a single second. Only the black charred frame of the motor-cycle remained.

Their state of intoxication had been very superficial, and it evaporated at once. The whole affair started to smell not only of burning rubber and paint, but also of a military tribunal and even of a penal battalion for the culprits.

The platoon commander's deputy became very gloomy, then moved away and sat down under a birch tree, clenching his head in his hands.

The first section commander came to his senses before anyone else. Looking round, and making sure that there were no officers or soldiers about who did not belong to the platoon, he gave a firm order: 'Platoon, get into formation! In two lines! Level up! Attention. Now pay attention!'

The accident had frightened the platoon, and feeling a strong hand they formed up in quicker time than normal. Only the platoon commander's deputy stayed under his tree not paying attention to anything.

'Now pay attention!' repeated the sergeant. 'A Czech car, a Skoda, dark blue in colour with three Czechs inside it, was approaching us. They threw an incendiary bottle at us. We were cleaning our weapons and therefore couldn't shoot back. The platoon commander's deputy did not lose his head, and hit one of them over the head with part of his dismantled machine-gun. The attacker was a fair-haired fellow. They immediately made off. Is that clear? The deputy commander is one of us, we're not going to sell him up the river. He's going to be demobilised soon and he's only been carrying out his international duty.'

The platoon murmured approvingly.

'I repeat, a Skoda, dark blue in colour, three men inside, they threw the bottle. The deputy commander hit one with part of his machine-gun. One more thing! The car number-plate had been intentionally obscured with mud. And, one last thing, a commission will come to investigate; they'll try to catch us out on details. No one should invent anything; repeat only what I have said. As for the rest: I don't remember, I didn't see, I don't know, I didn't pay attention! Clear?'

'Yes!'

'Dismissed!'

'Kolya, Kolya, don't get depressed. Maybe everything will still be all right. Listen, Kolya—better send a scout to the company commander and let him report about the Czechs. There's a conference going on there now at the commander's place. Meanwhile, tell the platoon to get ready to defend itself, as if we are expecting a second attack.'

An hour later all the company officers, including the commander himself, arrived at the platoon. After examining the terrain, the company commander ordered all the soldiers to come and see him one at a time. He was standing about eighty metres away from the others and, as each soldier approached him, he asked him three or four questions. The conversation with every soldier was tête-à-tête and no one could hear either the questions or the answers.

Then the commander summoned the first section sergeant.

'Not very bad weather, Sergeant, is it?'

'No, Comrade Captain.'

'Only it'll probably rain towards evening.'

'Most probably, Comrade Captain'—the sergeant still could not understand what the captain was driving at. 'It's so boring, all this blasted rain.'

'Yes, it is boring,' agreed the captain. 'So you say they came in a Skoda?'

'Yes!'

'But where are the tyre marks? The earth is still wet.'

The captain was also a reconnaissance scout and to deceive him was not easy. But he did not want to have a blot on his company's record.

'Look here, Sergeant, where that bucket burned and where it flew into the motor-cycle, the earth must be dug over as if dirty oil rags had been buried there after cleaning. And all the ground round must be trampled down. In all other matters, stand your ground!'

'Yes! Stand our ground!'

'And tell the senior sergeant not to hang his head. If he did hit a counter-revolutionary on the head—why worry!'

Neither commission nor special investigator ever appeared at the platoon. Apparently they already had enough to do. Meanwhile the company commander wrote a report about battle losses during a clash with armed counter-revolutionaries in the pay of imperialistic intelligence services.

The battalion commander turned the report over in his hands and smiled.

'Well, I'll sign everything for you, but you must re-write all this, add that there was an anti-tank grenade-launcher, an RPG-7B, as well as the motor-cycle. You'll find its number in the 2nd Company. While we were still in Poland, those scoundrels sank it in a swamp and couldn't get it out.' The captain was prepared to object but, having caught the look in the eye of the battalion commander, he only growled sullenly.

'Yes, re-write it then!'

The report went on its way through the normal channels returning every now and then for another re-write.

When the report reached the rear commander of the Carpathian Front, who signed all reports concerning battle losses, he visualised a wonder machine which had been created on the base of a reconnaissance motor-cycle, the M-72. This miraculous machine was armed with a machine-gun and an anti-tank grenade-launcher; it had two active infra-red sights, a range-finder sight and an R-123 radio transmitter. The machine was also apparently intended for work in polar conditions as two bright new sheep-skin coats were on top of it at the time of the accident; and behind it, probably being towed, there was a 200-litre barrel of pure spirit. Unfortunately, it was all burned during the clash with the counter-revolutionaries.

The general turned the report over in his hands.

'Return the report, let them re-write it, add . . . Let's see.'

'In the 128th Division a BTR fell off the bridge.'

'As the result of an incident with counter-revolutionaries?'

'Yes.'

'That's better. Give me the report.'

And the platoon commander's deputy, Senior Sergeant Mel'nik, received a medal for his bold, decisive action while repelling an attack. There was even a newspaper report about him!

The outskirts of Koshitse. Early September 1968.

Flight

DURING THE VERY first days of liberation, when troops were almost constantly on the move, our battalion stopped one night near a small town where there was a small factory. We spent the night in a field close to the town, after first taking all precautionary measures and putting forward guard posts and mobile patrols.

Next morning a very unpleasant circumstance came to light. The small factory proved to be not just any old factory but an alcohol plant. The previous evening I had smelt that special aroma all round us in the air: the other officers also could not possibly have missed it. But, at the end of the day, everybody was so tired that we all fell fast asleep at the first opportunity.

But our little soldiers did not sleep, nor did they waste any time either. The spirit plant like all other Czechoslovak factories at the time was not operating. But at night, the town's inhabitants, not without evil intent of course, pointed out to our soldiers the way to the factory, hospitably opened the factory gates and showed them how to open the appropriate taps.

Towards morning every single soldier in the battalion was a bit drunk. But we must do them justice, no one was really stoned. Everyone understood full well that it was only one step to the field disciplinary tribunal, and that the field tribunal would operate on a war footing. So all the soldiers were not really drunk, only slightly inebriated, very merry—tipsy.

The battalion commander immediately removed the whole column from that damned place and informed the higher command about the spirit factory, which was promptly taken under special guard. At the very first halt a thorough search was undertaken. It was found that all containers, all objects capable of holding liquid, were filled to capacity with spirits: flasks, canisters, mess tins, even hot water bottles belonging to the battalion's first-aid equipment. Any alcohol thus discovered was religiously emptied out on to the road. All officers of the battalion became drivers and the column started on its way. Of course there were not enough officers to replace all the drivers, and as a result many of the armoured troop transport carriers moved over the liberated country in a slightly zig-zag manner.

Towards lunchtime, all the soldiers had sobered up. The battalion spent the next night in a field far removed from any habitation. By early morning, we began to feel that again something was wrong. The eyes of most of the soldiers were glistening like oil. None of them was drunk, but each was definitely tipsy. We carried out yet another careful search, but found nothing. There was nothing wrong in principle with the fact that the soldiers were drinking a little from time to time. You won't find any kind of prohibition in any Soviet Army manual. Under battle conditions, soldiers are entitled to have a little to drink to give them courage.

The real problem was the fact that the present situation approximated to battle conditions, but we were to fulfil a purely diplomatic function, that is to say we were to disperse people who did not wish to be liberated. And it was not really proper on our part to carry out this task smelling of drink. If the enemy propaganda machine were to find out that 400 Soviet soldiers were carrying out their noble mission under the strong influence of Bacchus, it could lead to a world scandal.

The next morning, the story was the same, and the next also. What happened was that the KGB and Party agencies found themselves drawn into the common scheme of things and did not give away the location of the miraculous alcoholic spring. In Czechoslovakia, incidentally, all these KGB and Party servants immediately put their tails between their legs and were not at all in a hurry to write reports. It was all quite understandable as everybody was armed and it would be so easy to get killed by accident, or to be run over, by mistake, by a tank at night. This kind of thing went on everywhere. The business of settling accounts was swift, regardless of the differences in language and interests.   .

Nor was the battalion commander in any great hurry to report what was going on as, by doing so, he would call down a mass of trouble on his head. He preferred to discover the alcohol himself, with the help of all the other officers of the battalion.

It was clear that the stocks of spirits in the battalion were huge: enough for at least one soldier's mug every day, for each of the 400 soldiers. The battalion was constantly on the move, which meant that the spirit was not in the forest and not buried underground, but was moving along with us. It was somewhere in our vehicles. But where? We examined everything millimetre by millimetre. We even checked whether the spirit was inside the armoured troop carriers' tyres. But it wasn't there.

If this regular drinking had been going on in my company alone, I might have been in very serious trouble, but it was going on in other companies as well, so I relaxed. The question of the alcohol disturbed me only theoretically: where the hell could it be hidden? I firmly decided to locate that alcohol, by all possible means, regardless of what sacrifice it might cost. But I had only one thing to offer as a sacrifice and that was my gold 'Flight' watch. It was the only thing I possessed. And what, except a watch and a comb, can any Soviet lieutenant be expected to possess?

The watch was a splendid one and I had noticed for a long time that one of the radio men from the signals platoon always looked at it with very considerable interest. I don't know why, but I always had the impression that this man was very greedy, although I really hardly knew him.

At lunchtime, when there was absolutely no one around the field signals office and when I knew that the radio man was on duty alone inside, I entered the office. A visit by a company commander to the battalion signals office is a most unusual event. Without saying a single word I took the watch off my wrist and held it out towards him. He looked at the watch without daring to take it and then waited to find out what I would demand in exchange. Being a signals man he did, of course, speak a little Russian.

'I need the alcohol.' Whereupon I threw back my head,

imitating someone drinking. 'Do you understand? Spirits.' Then I gulped, showing how it gurgles as it passes down the throat. He nodded. Even though he was a Moslem he still understood me. And apparently he also consumed his medicinal drink along with the others every day.

'Ten litres, understand?' I showed him ten fingers. 'Ten.'

He gripped the watch and said curtly, 'This evening.'

'No,' I said. 'I want it now.'

He turned the watch over and over in his hand and reluctantly returned it to me. 'Now is impossible.'

I put the watch in my pocket and slowly went towards the door, but just before I reached it I turned round sharply. The soldier was watching me leave with great sorrow in his eyes. Quickly, I took my watch and put it in his hand.

'I will take it myself.'

He nodded, seized it in a flash, wrapped it up in a handkerchief and put it in the top of his boot. At the same time he whispered a single word in my ear which I could not quite make out.

I hated the man; and yet, before coming to see him at the signals office I had sworn to tell nobody, not even the battalion commander, how I had discovered the alcohol. And so, in order not to give it all away, I did not run at once to the battalion staff, of course, but waited several hours. Only towards evening did I tap the commander's vehicle. The commander was sitting inside in complete dejection.

'Comrade Lieutenant-Colonel, would you like to take a mug of spirits with me?' It was the purest impertinence. But he, of course, forgave me.

'Where?' he roared, and, jumping up from his chair, knocked his head on the armoured roof. 'Where, you son of a bitch?'

I smiled: 'Inside the radiators.'

Every armoured troop carrier has two engines and, since they both operate in extremely arduous conditions, every one of them has a very well-developed water-cooling system with capacious radiators, which in summer are filled with clear water. The soldiers had poured out all the water and filled them up with spirits. They drank it every evening by getting under the engines, and pretending to carry out maintenance.

The commander immediately formed up the whole battalion and personally went along the column opening the drainage cock in each machine. The autumnal forest was soon filled with a wonderful aroma.

And, one day later, the signals man, who had given away the secret, was found beaten nearly to death in the bushes near the signals office. He was taken urgently to hospital, and the doctors there pronounced that he was suffering from a result of an encounter with counter-revolutionaries.

After a few more days, when the other events had overtaken the signal man's case, another signals man approached me and held out to me my gold 'Flight' watch.

'Isn't this yours, Comrade Lieutenant?'

'As a matter of fact it is mine,' I said. 'Thank you—but where did you find it?'

'Apparently one of the men stole it from you.'

'Is that why you beat him so brutally?'

He looked intently at me.

'For that, among other things!'

Koshitse—Prague. September 1968.

Farewell to the Liberators

THE ALARM SOUNDED at about five o'clock in the morning. It was beastly cold in the forest. Just the time to sleep and sleep, with your nose buried in the collar of your greatcoat. Slowly, I emerged from underneath my warm greatcoat—there were noises in my head after the previous day's jollifications. Not a single living soul paid the slightest attention to the alarm signal. During one short month, discipline had fallen catastrophically low.

From the depths of my memory I extracted a tirade especially prepared for just such an occasion as this, and in a low voice without any particular anger, I spoke it into the ear of the company sergeant-major, who was pretending to be asleep. The sergeant-major jumped up, not because he was frightened by my threats but only because the tirade was much too ingenious and interesting.

The sergeant-major went along the rows of sleeping men and sergeants kicking them with the tip of his boot and enveloping them in well-chosen abuse. Whenever I am awakened at dawn after a night spent in a cold forest, I always become very angry, I don't know why. The foulest curses accumulate in my throat, and now I was looking around choosing upon whose head I could pour them all out. But when I came eye to eye with the first of the soldiers, I controlled myself: there was probably even more anger in his eyes than in mine. He was dirty, unshaven, long-haired, and had not even seen hot water for many weeks. He had an automatic rifle over his shoulder and his cartridge pouches were full. You just go and provoke him now and he'll kill you without a moment's hesitation.

The officers were gathered together for a meeting. The chief of the regimental staff read out the battle orders, according to which our division was to be transferred urgently from the 38th Army of the Carpathian Front to the 20th Guards Army of the Central Front. We had to go many hundred kilometres across country and then towards evening form up to the north of Prague, in order to cover the troops of the 20th Guards Army. All tracked vehicles, tanks, tractors, and heavy armoured troop carriers were to be left behind and we were to move without baggage, using only wheeled vehicles.

The order was completely incomprehensible, even to our own chief of staff, who had received it from the top. But there was no time for discussion. The columns were quickly formed up and the signs of readiness—small white flags—started to emerge above the commanders' hatches (while troops were moving, radio signals are forbidden). In the end, white flags were displayed over every machine. The signals man of the first machine twirled his white flag above his head, clearly pointing to the west. Once more we set off into uncertainty.

There was enough food for anxious thought. If you take the power of one unit's tanks, then in comparison that of the motorised infantry is zero. Tanks in conjunction with motorised infantry can be indestructible. At the present moment we were rushing madly over the country in our 'wheeled coffins' having abandoned our tanks. Without them, we became a zero, though still a very big one. The question arose why, and for whom, all this was necessary. Particularly as we were moving without our tracked towing vehicles, in other words without our artillery. And, of course, all this tended to prove that we were not going to fight. So where were we going and what for? Were there really not enough troops in the Prague region already?

During the short halts, while the soldiers were checking the machines and topping them up, we officers gathered in little groups and shared our worst fears amongst ourselves. None of us could make up his mind to pronounce aloud the dreaded diagnosis, but the sinister words were nevertheless already hanging in the air. 'Demoralisation of the troops has begun.'

Oh, if only the Czechs would fire at us!

In our regiments, especially those from the Carpathians, at that time there were many officers who had been in Hungary in 1956. The Soviet Army paid with its blood for the liberation of Hungary. In Czechoslovakia the price was even higher. None of the Hungarian veterans ever witnessed the faintest hint of the demoralisation of the troops which was already starting here. The point is that, when you are shot at, the situation is simplified. There is no time to think: those who wait to think are shot first.

In the early days in Czechoslovakia everything went according to plan: they threw tomatoes at us, and we fired shots in the air. But very soon everything changed. I don't know whether it was a special tactic, or whether it was a spontaneous phenomenon, but the people changed their attitude towards us. They became kinder and this was exactly what our army, created in the hothouse of isolation from the world at large, was not prepared for. There was a mutual and extremely dangerous *rapprochement* between the local inhabitants and our soldiers. On the one hand the Czechs suddenly understood that the overwhelming majority of our soldiers had not the slightest idea where they were or why they were there. And, among the local inhabitants, especially the country folk, there arose an incomprehensible feeling of compassion and pity towards us. The absence of hostility towards the ordinary soldiers created in the soldiers' minds a distrust of our own official propaganda, because something did not fit. Theory contradicted practice. On the other hand, among the soldiers, there appeared and began to develop with unprecedented speed the idea that a counter-revolution is a positive event which raises the people's standard of living. The soldiers could not understand why such a beautiful country had to be driven by force into the same state of poverty in which we lived. This feeling was especially strong among the Soviet soldiers who came to Czechoslovakia from the GDR. The fact of the matter is that these select units are made up mostly of Russian soldiers. And the Russian population in the USSR fares at least twice as badly as my Ukrainian people, and many times worse than the Central Asian and Caucasian peoples, where nearly every third family possesses its own motor car.

In our second echelon divisions, consisting basically of soldiers from the Caucasian and Asian republics, demoralisation was just starting, while in the first echelon divisions, which had arrived from the Group of Soviet Troops in Germany, it had bitten catastrophically deep. Because for these Russians, particularly, the contrast between the Czechoslovak and USSR standards of living was especially striking, and it was particularly hard for them to understand why this state of affairs had to be destroyed. A certain part was, of course, played by the community of Czech and Russian languages, as well as by the fact that in the first echelon divisions all the soldiers were able to talk to one another and to compare notes, while in the second echelon divisions all nationalities and languages were purposely mixed up, thus preventing any discussion and comparing of notes.

We reached our destination at dead of night. Our very worst suppositions were totally justified. Our task consisted neither of stopping the Western tanks, nor of dispersing the violent counter-revolutionaries, but of neutralising the Russian soldiers who were being withdrawn from Czechoslovakia.

The 20th Guards Army is permanently based in the GDR in the region of Bernau, close to Berlin but completely isolated, of course. Many of my friends from the Kharkov Tank School served in its divisions. This army is the best of all the Group of the Soviet troops in Germany. It had entered Prague first and here it was now, the first to leave Czechoslovakia. It was a strange exit. The regimental colours, the staff and the major part of the senior officers returned to the GDR. Part of the battle equipment was sent there too. And, immediately, tens of thousands of fresh soldiers and officers were sent from the Baltic Military District to the 20th Guards Army. And everything fell into place. It was as if the army had never left at all. But the majority of the soldiers and young officers from this army were sent from Czechoslovakia direct to the Chinese frontier for re-education. And the liberators were sent *en masse*, in whole echelons, as if they were prisoners and we their guards.

Meanwhile, new echelons with young soldiers destined to serve in Czechoslovakia were already coming in from the Soviet Union. From the very first day these soldiers were protected by high fences. The sad lesson of liberation had been learned: and all of us realised that, for the next ten years, regardless of what happened in the world, nobody would dare send us to liberate any country with a higher standard of living than our own.

The Soviet Army after the liberation.

Form and Content

ANYONE WHO HAS studied at least the beginnings of Marxist–Leninist philosophy knows that a deep and indissoluble link exists between content and form. The Soviet Army more than any other army on earth is impregnated with Marxism–Leninism and, as a result, has had the opportunity of proving to itself every day that form is the very brightest and best expression of content.

Every new Defence Minister starts by changing the uniform of the whole army. During the sixty years of the army's existence there has been no exception to this rule. Every new minister has somehow to introduce himself to the army, to the Soviet people and to the whole world. Otherwise, how can he show his own dazzling individuality? For instance, when Stalin became Defence Minister, he introduced gold shoulder-straps for officers, which up to that time had been the symbol of White Guard counter-revolution. Marshal Zhukov preferred the Gestapo uniform, so he introduced it for all Defence Ministry personnel. Soviet officers in the Far East had just had time to receive the order notifying them of the new uniform and had just had their Gestapo uniforms made when the newly-appointed Defence Minister in Moscow, Comrade Malinovskiy, invented another new uniform, similar to that worn by the Americans.

Such a practice as this, especially on the scale of the world's largest army, works out extremely expensive. Tens of millions of sets of uniforms are needed for reservists in case of war. So, when uniforms are changed, not only the whole three million army uniforms have to be remade, but several millions of ready-made sets of uniform have to be thrown out from the stores and replaced by new ones. The wearing-out of old uniforms is expressly forbidden. If, in addition to a change in the cut of the uniform, the Minister also decides to alter its colour, this spells disaster for the whole sewing industry. Civilians go from shop to shop, swearing and cursing, and cannot understand why a good overcoat cannot be bought for love or money.

The situation was completely hopeless when the new Defence Minister, Marshal Grechko, came to power. This was no time for a change of uniform! It was simply a time for making both ends meet. The country had hardly recovered from the 1964 revolution, and now it had to destroy Israel. Nasser had been fed and armed to the teeth, and all to no avail. We had to start again from the beginning. Then just when things with Nasser had more or less been straightened out, along came the fiftieth anniversary of Soviet power. To honour this jubilee there were so many ruinously expensive demonstrations of might, and so many records were established, that the country was brought to the verge of economic disaster. For instance, the meat production record was beaten in 1967, and in 1968 there wasn't a cow or a pig left throughout the whole country. And these very same records are still an anathema to this very day. Then came Czechoslovakia: so what talk could there possibly be about a change of uniform?

But the new Minister was adamant and he had a very weighty argument to back him up. What did our Soviet forces look like when they entered Czechoslovakia? They were dirty and bedraggled, dressed in greasy tunics and wearing canvas-topped boots. A liberator must be resplendent not only in deed, but also in dress. What if tomorrow we dare to liberate Rumania or Yugoslavia or even West Germany?

With such arguments as these the Political Bureau could not possibly disagree; and the decision was sanctioned on one condition. If the uniform was to be changed in the first place, then let it be the most beautiful in the whole world. Let everybody feast their eyes and be impressed, indeed astonished by it.

And the uniform really wasn't bad. It was a beautiful uniform but, as everyone knows only too well, beauty requires sacrifices, beauty has to be paid for.

The first victims of all this beauty were the junior officers.

The new caps for the new uniforms have extended peaks, which is why they were immediately christened 'SS caps'. The regimental commander looks good in his new cap and so do the staff clerks in theirs, but young officers of the line have to demonstrate to the soldiers all kinds of rifle drill on the parade ground in the self-same 'SS cap'. There is one manoeuvre when with one sharp movement you have to throw your automatic behind your back in such a way that the automatic's strap lies straight across your chest. During this operation neither your head nor your body should move, and only the hands have to do the work as if one's a juggler. It's easy for the soldiers—they've only got little caps on the sides of their heads. But the poor officer! Every time he demonstrates how to do this movement, his high 'SS cap' flies off into the dust, or into the mud, or into a puddle. Or just suppose there's a physical training run, over a distance of five to ten kilometres; platoon and company commanders have to be out in front, that's the commander's place. All the sergeants and soldiers can run unimpeded but it is much worse for the officers. The aerodynamics of their caps are not good and, even in a slight breeze, all the officers' caps cartwheel away across the fields. And you just try and catch them! That's why all young officers began to appoint their personal armourbearers—if my cap rolls away, you run and catch it for me!

But the 'SS cap' is worst of all during exercises. If the command 'Gas' is given, all the soldiers put on their gasmasks, and their side-caps can fit into their pockets or in their tunics, or be tucked into their belts. But what can an officer do in such a situation? Where does he put his 'SS cap'? As it is, there are far more objects hanging off him than off any soldier. An infantry officer must have an automatic and 120 cartridges, a pistol, a two-way radio, a compass, a sack, a gasmask, anti-atomic boots, gloves and a cape and an extra cape, a supply of water and food, binoculars, a commander's bag with writing board, a steel helmet and a spade. So there is absolutely nowhere left to put his cap. During the cross-country run, it can be carried in the hand if the senior commander doesn't see it, but during exercises there is always an automatic in the officer's hand, or the radio, or the writing board. You have no time to turn round; but you are not allowed to be without a cap. The cap must always be on the officer's head or somewhere near by. That's an order! There have been many different suggestions for this cap, for instance to wear it only on parade and for everyday use, but to replace it in the field with something like a beret or a side-cap. But Comrade Grechko was inflexible: beauty comes first.

Meanwhile autumn came and our soldiers felt the effects of the changes which had been introduced into the army for the sake of beauty.

Formerly, a soldier's greatcoat was plain grey. With the new uniform, the greatcoat was preserved in its original form, as invented by Tzar Nicholas I 150 years previously. But the Soviet designers decided to freshen it up with some new details. Instead of the green shoulder-straps, they put red ones for the infantry, and on the left sleeve they put a beautiful golden emblem stitched on red cloth, while on the right sleeve they placed golden chevrons, to indicate how long the soldier had served in the army, and on the chest they put six gold buttons. Of course, these were quite useless as soldiers' greatcoats are anyway fastened with hooks, and the shining buttons were sewn on top just to make it look beautiful. To wear greatcoats like these in battle was, of course, impossible. With red shoulder-straps and shining buttons, a soldier would be visible even in the bushes a whole kilometre away. To crawl through a field was equally impossible. Before, the soldier's belly was as smooth as a serpent's and he could crawl wherever you like, but now the buttons caught on the ground. Therefore, in the end, it was decided to leave the field uniform as it was before: no buttons and plain green shoulder-straps and no red patches.

The only thing was that a soldier has only one greatcoat. In any case he serves during only two winters, and one greatcoat is quite enough for him. So what to do? The problem was reported to the Minister.

'What is the problem?' enquired the astonished Minister of Defence. 'If war comes we will cut off the buttons and change the shoulder-straps. It's quite simple.'

But the real problem is that a soldier would need to do this far too often. When during the night a division is put on alert, no one, including the divisional commander himself, knows how it will all end. Is it just a check-up on battle readiness to be followed by retreat five minutes later, or are there going to be major exercises, or is it the beginning of the liberation of Western Europe? Who knows?

Before, when the uniform was plain, only four minutes and thirty seconds were needed to waken, silently, all 300 soldiers of the battalion, to let them dress in darkness, to get their armament and to leave the barracks. No noise, great speed, and no light. It was never easy to achieve such harmony, but every battalion somehow managed to achieve it and there were even some who could do it still more quickly.

With the new uniform everything was changed. Now, at the sound of the alarm, the light had to be switched on in all barracks, which meant that when it was sounded a soldier had to run over to each window and black it out before the light could be switched on. Then, having dressed, everyone had to run to the wardrobe, find his greatcoat and return to his place, where he had to cut off all the buttons, shoulder-straps and chevrons with a razor and afterwards sew on new green shoulder-straps. Only after all that performance could he run to fetch his weapons.

Previously, after the alarm had been sounded, the commander looked round and saw that everything was normal, everybody had got up, dressed and silently taken their weapons. It was all okay. Not bad. Retreat! At this point there was no need to hurry him. The Soviet soldier values sleep more than anyone else. He knows that there will be no compensation for all these night alerts, and five minutes after retreat has sounded the whole battalion is sleeping soundly.

Things became much worse with the beautiful new uniforms. After retreat, every soldier must now sew six gold buttons on to his greatcoat, and in a special way, so that all of them have Soviet power facing in the right direction: the little hammer with the end of the sickle must be facing precisely upwards. Then he has to sew the stripes on the sleeves and then the shoulder-straps. But, in the morning at six o'clock, a new day starts and a soldier must be ready in his beautiful everyday uniform and not in his field uniform. So there he sits, a whole hour before reveille, changing his shoulder-straps. And if he lies down for half an hour before reveille there may suddenly be a new alert and this time it could be a real battle alert and everything starts anew. Cut off the buttons and stripes and change the shoulder-straps.

A rumour reached the ear of Comrade Grechko that this uniform did not allow enough time for the alert, even if it was the smartest uniform in the whole world. Maybe something could be changed.

'Well,' said Comrade Grechko 'it's a pity of course, but something will have to be changed!'

And what was changed was the time allowed for the alert from four minutes thirty seconds to twenty-four minutes. This, needless to say, lowers the battle preparedness of troops in time of war and raises the possibility of their being caught when still in their camps, as happened in 1941. All of which is not, of course, a very good thing, though it does mean that all that beauty can be preserved intact.

The Western Ukraine, near Mukachevo. 12 October, 1968.

Our Native Land

AS THEY LEFT Czechoslovakia, our divisions reminded one of the remnants of a defeated army, fleeing from the hot pursuit after a shattering defeat. What officer could look without pain at the endless columns of dirty tanks mutilated by barbarous treatment and deprived for many months of human care and attention? Our regiment had also been thinned out. While still in Czechoslovakia, many of the platoons and companies had been completely reformed into draft reinforcement battalions and sent straight to the Chinese frontier. Many of those whose term of service was shortly to expire were packed off home. Often there was only one driver left out of a whole tank crew and no one else at all.

Our native land greeted us with brass bands blaring and then promptly despatched us, whole regiments at a time, into field camps behind barbed wire. Some unknown engineer quickly examined the battle equipment, determining on the march then and there whether it needed a complete overhaul, dismantling or normal repair.

And we were examined by doctors with the same speed: fit—fit—fit. Others rummaged convulsively in our files and passed rapid resolutions: the Chinese frontier—the Chinese frontier—the Chinese frontier.

But, quite suddenly, the habitual rhythm was broken. Our sparse regiment was formed up along that broad forest clearing which represented the central road of our military prison camp. The chief of the regimental staff tediously read aloud various orders of the Defence Minister, the Military District Commander and the Army Commander.

Then, suddenly, an escort arrived and deposited a fellow out there in front of the formation. He looked about twenty years old. From the very beginning, I was astonished by the fact that, for some strange reason, he was barefoot. It was an unusually warm autumn in the Carpathians: but it was autumn all the same.

It was difficult to say by looking at him whether he was a soldier or not. He wore soldier's trousers, but instead of a soldier's field shirt he had on a peasant's shirt. He stood at right angles to the regimental line and peered myopically away somewhere far off at the blue summits of the Carpathians. He had a soldier's mess-tin in his left hand, and with his right hand he clasped to his breast some kind of parcel wrapped in cloth, which was apparently very dear to him.

Clearly and distinctly, the chief of regimental staff read aloud from a paper concerning the adventures of our hero. One year ago he had been called up for service. During preparations for the liberation he had decided to exploit the situation to escape to the West. But, during all those re-shuffles, he found himself in one of the 'wild' divisions, which did not go into Czechoslovakia. Then, brandishing his automatic, he went up into the mountains and several times tried to break out across the frontier. For three months he remained in the mountains, then hunger forced him to return to so-called civilisation, and he surrendered himself freely of his own accord. Now he must be punished. During peacetime, fellows like him are punished somewhere out of sight. But we were on a war footing and, since his 'wild' division had long since been dispersed, he was to be punished in front of our regiment.

While the chief of staff completed reading the sentence, the executioner—a shortish, very thick-set major of the KGB in soft boots, slowly approached the deserter from behind.

Never in my life had I witnessed with my own eyes the carrying out of the death penalty and imagined it somehow quite differently: a dark cellar, a layer of sawdust on the floor, gloomy archways, a small beam of light. In life, everything turns out differently; here was a forest clearing covered with a luxurious carpet of crimson leaves, golden spiders' webs, the crystal sound of a mountain waterfall and a boundless woodland space flooded with the farewell warmth of the autumn sun.

The action unfolded in front of us as if on a stage during a performance, with the whole audience biting their lips and digging their nails deep into the arms of their chairs, watching silently as death, stepping slowly, slowly approached a man from behind. Everybody saw it clearly except the one who was destined to die. Those who say that one always senses the approach of death are probably wrong. Our soldier did not sense anything. He stood there as silently as before and listened, or maybe he did not even listen to the words of the sentence. One thing was obvious, he did not even suspect that he was to be sentenced to death. And, of course, he could not possibly suspect that the sentence would be carried out the very instant it was pronounced.

Now, after many years, I could invent some noble feelings which I experienced then, but at the time I felt nothing. I stood and, like hundreds of others, I looked at the soldier and the stealthy executioner and I wondered if the soldier would turn round or not, and whether he would see the executioner with the pistol, and whether the executioner would shoot at once or not. The soldier was not tied up and, if he had seen the executioner behind him, he might have tried to run away, or shouted or knelt down.

The chief of staff filled his lungs with air and, clearly and solemnly, as if it was a government bulletin about the launching of the first cosmonaut, he uttered the final phrase.

'IN THE NAME OF THE UNION . . .'

The executioner smoothly cocked his pistol without a click.

'OF SOVIET . . .'

The executioner, moving as softly as a cat, took another two steps forward and placed his legs apart for steadiness. Now he stood one metre away from the hapless fellow, and one felt sure that the prisoner could hear the executioner's breathing. But he still seemed to sense nothing.

'SOCIALIST . . .'

The executioner stretched his right hand forward, holding the pistol so that its muzzle nearly touched the soldier's neck.

'REPUBLICS . . .'

With his left hand, the executioner squeezed the wrist of his right hand, so as to keep the pistol steady.

'SENTENCED . . .'

The sinister crack of a solitary shot whipped like a lash across my back. I hunched myself up and screwed up my eyes as if I was in unbearable pain, but I opened them immediately again.

The dead soldier hurled both hands over his head, and as he performed the last upwards jump of his short life, as if trying to seize hold of the clouds, he threw back his head in a way which would have been impossible for a live man. Probably at this very last moment, his eyes already dead met the executioner's calm, piercing blue gaze. And the echo of the shot rolled slowly away towards a distant wooded ridge and fell and subsided in an odd barking noise.

The soldier's body fell very very slowly, just like a maple leaf on a balmy autumn's day. Equally slowly, the executioner stepped aside to make room for the falling body.

'TO PAY THE SUPREME PENALTY.'

And so the chief of staff finished pronouncing sentence.

The executioner adroitly extracted the magazine from the pistol and, with a jerk, jettisoned from the chamber the unnecessary second cartridge.

A burial party consisting of five soldiers, carrying spades and a piece of tarpaulin, ran towards the dead soldier. And there he was, lying at our feet, gazing with his unwinking eyes into the endless depths of the sky.

Postscript

HAVE YOU EVER been acquainted with a man during that period of his life between the pronouncement of the death penalty upon him and its execution? If not, it is high time that you and I met, for I am such a man.

I am no longer a liberator. Not for me that role, nor for my country either. For it is my own firm conviction that only a country, to which people flock by the thousand from all corners of the world, has the right to advise others how to live. And the country, from which so many others break out, across its frontiers, in tanks, or fly away in homemade balloons or in the latest supersonic fighter, or escape across mine-fields and through machine-gun ambushes, or give the slip to packs of guard-dogs, that country certainly has no right to teach anyone anything—at least not for the time being.

First of all, put your own house in order. Try to create there such a society that people will not dig underground passages in order to escape. Only then shall we earn the right to teach others. And not with our tanks, but with good advice and our own personal example. Observe, admire, then go and imitate our example, if it pleases you.

These thoughts first came into my mind long ago. Perhaps they are silly or hackneyed—it does not matter, at least they are my own. The very first I have ever had.

I was most anxious that they should not perish with my life, and therefore I needed to share them with at least two other people.

But in my position that was totally impossible. We professional liberators are shot for such ideas—in the back of the head.

Of course, one can always share such an idea with one other liberator, but there would be no time left to share it with a second.

So that is why I left. I carried my ideas away with my brains intact. I prepared my escape for several years but I never really believed that the outcome would be successful. Under communist law, I am a turncoat and a traitor, a criminal guilty of the most serious crime.

I was sentenced to death in absentia by the Military Collegium of the Supreme Court of the USSR. In such cases, the method by which the sentence is to be carried out is never specified. The executioners are given a wide choice. They may execute the sentence by means of a car accident, a suicide, or a heart attack, etcetera, etcetera.

But first they have to find me! And, in the meantime, I am living out that last slice of my life. I am between the death sentence and its execution. It is the happiest time of my life.